PURSUIT
& PERSUASION

Also available in quality paperback by
Sally S. Wright

Publish and Perish
Pride and Predator

"*Pride and Predator* is a welcome retreat to the Golden Age of mystery. With a touch of Dorothy L. Sayers, this book is almost totally Ngaio Marsh in style and character. Definitely a must for those of you who relish classic mystery authors."

THE SNOOPER

"An evocative storyteller, Wright's descriptions of the ancient land of Scotland and the family relationships of its inhabitants are as compelling as the mystery itself."

MOSTLY MURDER

"*Publish and Perish* is put together with polish and precision. It echoes such classic writers as Dorothy L. Sayers and Ngaio Marsh without in any way imitating them."

THE WASHINGTON TIMES

"Archivist and amateur detective Ben Reese is a wonderful character, as far off the beaten path of fictional detectives as Brother Cadfael. It is delightful to get in on the ground floor with a mystery writer who, God willing, will be keeping us instructed, entertained, puzzled, and moved for many years to come."

LINDA BRIDGES, SENIOR EDITOR
NATIONAL REVIEW

"As she has before, Sally Wright shows us in *Pride and Predator* a good deal more about the mysteriousness of human existence than she tells. Beautifully written, compellingly told. A fine new writer has arrived."

RALPH MCINERNY, AUTHOR OF THE FATHER DOWLING MYSTERIES

PURSUIT & PERSUASION

BOOK THREE

SALLY S. WRIGHT

MYS
F
WRI

Multnomah®Publishers *Sisters, Oregon*

This book is a work of fiction. With the exception of Ben Reese (who is based on an actual person), James M. Shewan, and recognized historical figures, the characters in this novel are fictional. Any resemblance to actual persons, living or dead, is purely coincidental.

PURSUIT AND PERSUASION
© 2000 by Sally S. Wright
published by Multnomah Publishers, Inc.

International Standard Book Number: 1-57673-416-1

Cover photograph by Sally S. Wright
Cover design by Christopher Gilbert

Printed in the United States of America
Multnomah is a trademark of Multnomah Publishers, Inc.,
and is registered in the U.S. Patent and Trademark Office.
The colophon is a trademark of Multnomah Publishers, Inc.

FOR INFORMATION:
Multnomah Publishers, Inc., Post Office Box 1720, Sisters, Oregon 97759

Library of Congress Cataloging-in-Publication Data
Wright, Sally S.   Pursuit & persuasion/by Sally S. Wright.
    p.cm. – (Ben Reese mystery series; #3)   ISBN 1-57673-416-1
    1. Reese, Ben (Fictitious character)—Fiction. 2. Archivists—Fiction.
    I. Title: Pursuit and persuasion.   II. Title
PS3573.R5398 P87 2000   813'.54—dc21   99-050894
    00 01 02 03 04 05 06 — 10 9 8 7 6 5 4 3 2 1 0

Because of Marian and Clyde
who set the example
and helped the whole way.

List of Characters

Clive Baird: research chemist
Harriet Hamilton Barclay: owner of Druimneil House
Owen Barclay: husband of Harriet; chef
Judith Blair: student of Georgina Fletcher
Jennifer Burke: veterinarian; sister of Lady Jane Chisholm
Lord Alex Chisholm: writer; owner of Balnagard Castle
Lady Jane Chisholm: wife of Alex Chisholm
Jack Corelli: carpenter at Cairnwell house
Ian Cunningham: minister of church at Old Kinneff
Margaret Cunningham: wife of Ian
Andrew Eastland: Fellow of Magdalen College, Oxford
                                          University, professor of English literature
Capt. and Mrs. Ferguson: friends of Barclays
Gwen Fitzgerald: owner of Devon House
Georgina Fletcher: professor of English literature
                                          at Aberdeen University; teaching
                                          one term at Oxford University
Ross Fletcher: deceased husband of Georgina; former
                                          owner of Fletcher Tire and Rubber
Amanda Grace: student of Georgina Fletcher
Elsie Hamilton: Harriet Barclay's mother
Lady Isabelle Hay: neighbor of Georgina Fletcher
Sir John Hay: Isabelle's husband
Hazel: Tom Ogilvie's secretary
Peter Hume: husband of Alysoun Pryor Hume
Mary Hume: daughter of Peter and Alysoun
David Lindsay: poet; friend of Georgina
Graham Lindsay: deceased son of David

Kate Robertson Lindsay: writer; former wife of Graham

Penelope Long: owner of The Parsonage, Oxford

Emily MacAlpin: microbiology professor at Aberdeen University

Robbie MacAlpin: English professor at Aberdeen University

Alan MacLeish: fishing boat owner

Grace MacNicol: cleaning woman at Cairnwell House

Winifred MacNicol: housekeeper for Colin Ramsay

Robert Maxwell: assist. manager of The Parsonage

Sir Robert Morgan: Alex Chisholm's uncle

Anna Morrison: Georgina Fletcher's retired housekeeper

Donald Murray: owner of Cairnwell home farm and walled garden

Thomas Ogilvie: Ross Fletcher's nephew and a solicitor

Perkins: salesman staying at The Parsonage, Oxford

Alysoun Pryor (Hume): daughter of John Pryor

Elinor Pryor: widow of John Pryor

John Pryor: murder victim in Burford, England

Colin Ramsay: former Fletcher Tire employee, leases dower house at Cairnwell

Ben Reese: archivist at Alderton University

Dr. Mark Roberts: physician at Royal Infirmary, Aberdeen

Arthur Shaw: acting general manager at Fletcher Tire and Rubber

Michael Shaw: sculptor

Sarah Smith: waitress at The Parsonage, Oxford

Stephen Turner: Fellow of Balliol College, Oxford University, professor of microbiology

William Whitfield: bookshop owner, Oxford

Ellen Winter:	Ben Reese's apprentice at Alderton University; Georgina Fletcher's heir
Richard Witney:	trader in Burford, England
Robert Witney:	trader in Aberdeen

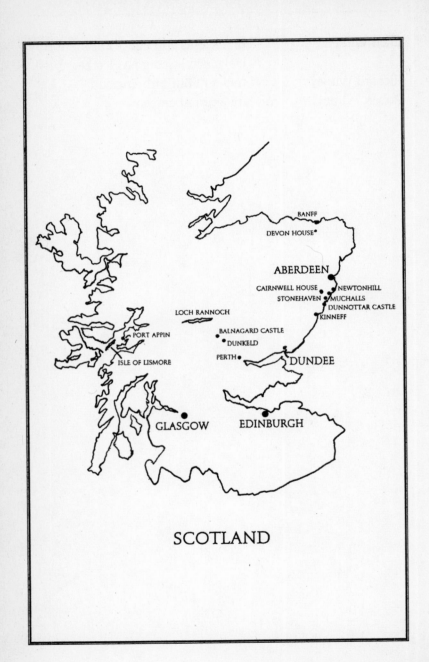

BANFF

DEVON HOUSE•

ABERDEEN

CAIRNWELL HOUSE• •NEWTONHILL
STONEHAVEN• •MUCHALLS
•DUNNOTTAR CASTLE
KINNEFF

LOCH RANNOCH

PORT APPIN

BALNAGARD CASTLE
•DUNKELD

ISLE OF LISMORE

PERTH•

DUNDEE

GLASGOW   EDINBURGH

SCOTLAND

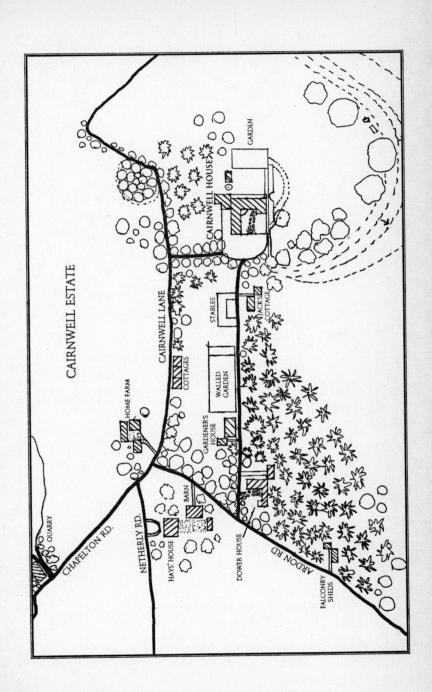

CAIRNWELL ESTATE

CAIRNWELL HOUSE

GARDEN

CAIRNWELL LANE

STABLES

BLACKS' COTTAGE

COTTAGES

WALLED GARDEN

HOME FARM

GARDENER'S HOUSE

BARN

DOWER HOUSE

ARDON RD

FALCONRY SHEDS

HAYS' HOUSE

NETHERLY RD.

CHAPELTON RD.

QUARRY

CHAPTER ONE

Wednesday, June 7th, 1961

THEY STOOD ON THE SIDEWALK in front of The Eagle and Child and stared past each other at the night. They both looked like they'd been slapped, as the door snapped shut behind them. Or as though they were reeling from some recent event that made them question their hold on reality.

The thin, tailored Scotswoman, who looked like she was in her early sixties, seemed more composed than the male American (who must have been a foot taller and was probably thirty years younger). And when he said, "You never get intimidated when you're teaching and I can't understand why you're running now," she just looked at him as though he were a spoiled child she was having to humor.

He was too young not to bristle, before he crushed his cigarette under a heavy boot and tugged on his black leather jacket. "You're letting other people make up your mind for you, and that's not the Professor Georgina Fletcher I've spent most of my life looking up to."

"I do see that it must be frustrating for you. Since you'd prefer to make up my mind yourself."

"I don't get it. I don't. Why won't you listen?" His face looked hot and red, even underneath his two-day stubble, and yet his stare was cold and controlled when he set his hands on his hips.

"It's a terribly complicated situation, and I can't explain fully at the moment. But if it's any consolation a-tall, if I *could* do as you ask, I would."

"Yeah, right!"

"Is it reasonable to be belligerent, do you think, when you, as I understand it, are the one seeking the favor?" She said it quietly in a soft English-educated Scottish voice, while looking him right in the eye.

"I'm trying to get your attention!" He glared down at her and shook his head, before he lunged at her and grabbed her purse. He shoved something into it he'd already pulled from his jacket pocket and tossed the bag back to her. Then he was gone without a word, loping south down St. Giles toward the Ashmolean Museum.

Georgina Fletcher had backed away from him before she had time to think, and she stood leaning against a narrow stuccoed strip of wall between the pub's door and the window on her left. She lowered the hand that had caught the purse and rested her head on the cool wall. Then she pulled her suit coat closer, while she stared at the very old hand-painted sign hanging above her head—the eagle snatching up a naked baby that hung by an arm from its claws.

She'd always thought it an odd choice for a quiet respectable family gathering place, frequented by civilized darts players and Oxford dons. But at that moment, she empathized with the dangling child even more than she had before.

She herself was unscathed, of course, only shaken and

slightly embarrassed. And it was that sense of exposure in far too private a moment that led her to glance up and down the street to see if anyone had noticed. There are always crowds coming and going in Oxford, certainly at ten o'clock at night, but no one appeared to have stopped in their tracks. And that was a relief for someone who likes to live tucked away far from the public eye.

She took time to feel through her purse, for whatever had been shoved inside it, and found three folded carefully typed sheets of paper, which she read while the creases in her forehead fought and her narrow mouth tightened. She slipped the pages in her purse, pushed a hairpin back in her French roll, smoothed her green wool skirt, and then turned to her left, walking north on St. Giles toward the Woodstock Road.

She crossed Little Clarendon Street, and drew up between a bakery and Grey's Restaurant. Then she waited for oncoming traffic before she crossed St. Giles and slipped into the narrow stone path between St. Giles Church and its cemetery.

It was cool and dark and slightly unnerving there at night, in the shadows of the cedars and the standing stones. And it irritated Georgina immensely that her first reaction should be so absurdly irrational. Which in turn made her refuse to pick her way out to Banbury Road any more quickly than usual.

She turned left on the uneven sidewalk, telling herself as she did many times each day to pull her shoulders back and stride briskly, in spite of all the creaks and crackles that had come with age and arthritis.

Then she was home, opening the wrought iron gate in the stone wall that wrapped around The Parsonage, the small stone inn next door to St. Giles church, where she always stayed in Oxford.

❧❧❧❧❧

She'd lit a fire in the fireplace of her large cream-colored room, and she sat staring at the flames from the desk between the two front windows. She'd addressed a letter and written the first sentence, but she couldn't think how to proceed.

There are moral decisions to be made. As always. And these are more critical than many. How much ought I to tell? How much should I imply? Should I draw attention to the person I suspect? And how much history should I dwell upon?

When I may be entirely wrong.

Pray God I am. For the pretense and the deceit, the sickness and the selfishness, hardly bear thinking upon.

Of course, even if I *am* right about the danger, and the outcome I fear from my own intervention, I may well be wrong as to the person responsible.

I don't *think* I am. There are too many threads pulled tight in that direction. And yet one must be fair and not prejudice the case.

For if one were wrong, one could mislead the investigation from its inception. Thereby endangering the innocent, and enabling the guilty to go free.

No, one must err on the side of mercy.

This time as always.

Even so, it has to be written. And written quickly, considering what I know now, and the danger it implies. Finished before Penelope Long settles down for the night.

Georgina groaned quietly, with her chin in her hand. And did write deliberately for a minute or two. Then she snapped the lid on her fountain pen and walked around the desk to one of the two front windows to study Banbury Road.

She didn't see anything alarming as she pulled the pins

from her French roll and shook out her dark hair. No one watching her windows, no one waiting in the shadows, no one in the courtyard below. Only tourists and students strolling past in one direction or the other.

She sighed and sat down again, gazing straight ahead, watching the firelight shiver on the peach-colored satin comforter at the end of the four-poster bed.

She finished one page, without much difficulty, then paced back and forth from the bed to the bureau, from the bureau to the bed, from the fireplace back to the front windows. Until she was ready to write a second page. And a third. And then read them all in the chair by the fire.

She changed three or four words, and added more at the end, then addressed an envelope on the arm of the chair.

She took a small key off the key ring lying on the desk and slipped it in a small envelope. She wrote an address on the outside of it, folded it inside the letter, and slid both into the larger envelope.

Then she locked her door behind her, climbed the twisting stairs, and knocked on Penelope's door. "It is I, Penelope. Georgina. May I speak to you for a moment?"

The door swung open, and a stout woman in a high-necked flannel gown stepped back from the doorway and smiled. "Of course you may. Come in, come in!"

"I hope you weren't asleep."

"No, I've only just seen to the downstairs doors. Would you care for a glass of hot milk?"

"Thank you, Penelope, but not just now. There's something—"

"It would settle you down nicely for the night. You work too hard, as you very well know, as Ross—"

"I must ask something of you, Pen, and I'm sorry to say it's rather important."

"Then sit down, my dear, of course. It will just take me a moment to close the windows." She threw a shawl round her shoulders and started toward the side windows of her long, crowded living room.

"Don't fuss, Penelope, please. Sit down with me for a moment and listen."

"Of course, G. dear. Whatever you say."

"I wish I could explain, Pen, but I can't. If I could, you know I would. We've known each other well enough, *and* long enough, that we—"

"Forty-two years and more."

"Yes, now I've written a letter I'd like you to post for me, without mentioning it to anyone, even the police, if I should die while I'm here in Oxford. Under *any* circumstances, you understand, even those that appear to be absolutely normal and natural."

"Georgina!" Penelope Long's plump unprepossessing face beneath the gray hair in pin curls had lost its easy smile by the time she pulled her shawl close across her throat.

"I know it sounds peculiar. Me, of all people, asking such a thing."

"You're not going to die, G.! You're much too young. Not now, surely." Penelope's scalp was pulled tight by the pin curls, but the folds of skin that hung from her neck wobbled as she stared at Georgina with something like the startled look of a newly plucked chicken.

"I hope not. There're too many circumstances I haven't had time to settle properly."

"I hardly know what to say." The voice was high and bewildered, but the gray eyes were concentrated and clearly quite intelligent.

"I know it sounds preposterous. I do see that, of course. But I have reason to ask in earnest. Please, Pen, mail the letter after I'm gone regardless of how normal the death appears. I hope I'm wrong, that goes without saying, and I very well may be. But if I'm not, I can't tell you how important it is that this letter be sent off without any discussion with anyone."

"I will, of course."

"Promise. Without telling the police."

"That's the sticky bit, isn't it?" Penelope Long was gazing at her lap, twisting the fringe of the pink wool shawl.

"It's nothing illegal. I would never ask you to do anything wrong."

"No."

"So promise me, please, and let us both get to bed."

"Of course, my dear. Yes, I promise."

"You're a great friend, Penelope. You always have been. You were the first person I could talk to, you know, after Ross died."

"Because of Albert, don't you think? And the years I've spent alone? Running the inn the way you've had to care for Ross's business."

"Yes, I'm sure you're right. Thank you, Pen. You're very good to me. I shall see you tomorrow at breakfast."

"Shall I send you tea in your room? Six, or a little after?"

"Only if Sarah isn't rushed off her feet."

Georgina lit three candles in her room and tossed four small logs on the fire. She turned out the lights, picked up the leather portfolio she'd laid on the bed, and sat down again in the over-stuffed chair by the fire.

She selected two large sheets of cream-colored paper from the left side of the portfolio, and read what she'd already written. She pulled out a blank piece, and wrote one short line, and then another, staring at the fire in between. She was staring more than she was writing, and she rubbed her nose where her glasses sat and laid down her silver pen.

She took her night things out of the armoire by the bathroom door and changed her clothes in front of the fire. Her lips moved from time to time, and she stopped ever so often, and stared at whatever was in front of her.

She sat down again, finally, in the same tan chair, in her pale silk gown and quilted robe, and wrote then, quickly, crossing off words and scratching out whole lines, writing them over, again and again, until she could finally reread the page without making a single change.

She threw the cast-off drafts into the fire, slid the finished sheet into the portfolio, and tied the brown ribbon that fastened it. Then she picked up the center of the right side of the mattress and slid the portfolio between it and the box springs, two feet or more from the edge.

She sighed slowly and stretched her arms over her head as though her back and neck hurt. Then she blew out the candles. And knelt beside the bed.

Thursday, June 8th

She was up again, underlining passages in a thick black book, before the sun had slipped through the front windows. She'd already taken her aspirin and her vitamins, and her brown wavy hair with the four narrow bands of silver (two at the temples, the others high on either side of her center part) was brushed and twisted again in a French roll. She was dressed too (in a long-skirted navy blue tweed suit, with a mandarin collared gray silk blouse and a string of freshwater pearls), and she'd long been considering the proper tack to take.

By the time sunlight was sliding across the floor toward the fireplace, Sarah had brought her tea. And Georgina had taken a cup to the windows to watch the morning rise across a forest of stone spires in a honey-colored city of colleges and churches, cut with glittering glass, blue and purple and gold, that seemed to shatter and melt in the sun.

She could hear singing from the window on the other side of the bed, and she almost went to look. Before she reminded herself that she still had pressing work, and the world wouldn't wait for her.

She pulled a thick file from her briefcase and sat at the desk making notes on a stack of typed pages, till it was time to lock the door behind her.

Georgina watched from the front terrace of the inn as a young dark-haired woman waved from the other side of the wall on her way south past St. Giles Church. Georgina smiled at her and said, "Thank you again," raising a small ribbon-wrapped box in salute.

She pulled off the silvery cardboard lid, picked up the single large beautifully molded coffee-and-cream filled chocolate, and popped it in her mouth—just as the salesman she'd seen at breakfast the day before stepped through the door behind her.

They mumbled good morning to each other, as a middle-aged

couple walked into the courtyard behind him. Both parties chose tables on the north side of the terrace, opposite the one where G. had laid her things, as Georgina settled herself in the sunny south corner closest to the inn.

Her back was to the sitting room window, and there was an orange tree in a stone tub on her right circled by pots of white lily of the Nile, and she inhaled the scent of orange blossoms as though she'd loved it all her life.

Bells were ringing all across Oxford, deep wavering heart-stopping b-o-n-g-s in amongst the carillon bells playing Bach and Handel. And Georgina sat with the sun on her face and listened, hands relaxed in her lap, sunlight scattering watery patterns across the insides of her eyelids.

Another sort of person couldn't have. Knowing what she knew. Fearing what she had reason to fear. But Georgina had learned, when Ross was dying of cancer, to let go of trouble she couldn't arrange. When she'd done what she knew to do, she took the free moments unto herself. For if what she hoped for, and prayed for devoutly, wasn't what should be, worry wouldn't help, and usually hurt.

"Excuse me, Mrs. Fletcher. Oh, I'm sorry. Were you asleep?" Sarah Smith's soft high voice broke through on Georgina's left.

"I wasn't, as a matter of fact. And thank you again for the tea this morning." Georgina smiled up at Sarah, shading her eyes with her hand.

"Mrs. Long has asked me to mention, knowing how much you enjoy them, that Mr. Morris has brought in a basket of lovely wild mushrooms, and if you'd like an omelet, cook will make you one. I know Mrs. Long was very pleased with hers, and the gentleman across the way has just ordered one as well."

"I would, Sarah, yes, thank you. A small omelet with brown toast and coffee."

Sarah nodded, her young pale freckled face looking willing, and pleasant, and shy at the same time as she said, "I'll bring you your coffee straightaway."

It was strong and wonderfully hot, and Georgina sipped it as the bells finished, their complicated melodies tangling together, then hanging for a minute, in the soft moist air.

She waited until every note had died. And then she opened a brown leather book.

She'd already laughed once, quietly to herself, as she read the description of Mr. Collins's proposal, when a man's voice, a low faintly Scottish voice, from the other side of the table, said, "I should've known, I suppose. Jane Austen, at seven in the morning."

Georgina looked up, and smiled carefully, as though it were the right thing to do. "Hello, Tommy. What are you doing in Oxford?"

"I've come to negotiate a contract between a client in Aberdeen and a manufacturing concern here, near Headington."

"Would you care for coffee?"

"Thank you, Aunt Georgina, I would, yes." He sat and crossed one pinstriped leg over another, having already balanced the handle of his black umbrella on the edge of the round teak table. "I didn't sleep a-tall well, and I could do with another cup."

"What brings you out so early?"

"I wanted to see how you were getting on."

"Thank you, Sarah, the omelet looks lovely. Thomas?" Georgina pointed to the omelet and the rack of whole-wheat toast. "There's much more here than I could possibly manage." Thomas shook his head, while Georgina ordered a second pot of coffee. "Are there strawberries today, Sarah? Ah, then a small bowl please, without cream. Thank you, Sarah, very much indeed." Georgina picked up her knife and fork and then looked at her late husband's nephew with the cool appraising eye of a practiced professor. "What can I do for you, Thomas?"

"Do? I was in Oxford on business and thought I'd stop by and say hello. You are my only living aunt, you know. One shouldn't assume that I wish you to do anything a-tall."

"No? No, of course not. Silly of me." Georgina smiled and laid her small tortoiseshell reading glasses beside her pot of coffee. "Any news from home? Ellen arrives today. She should probably be at Cairnwell by late afternoon."

"Ellen? Oh, I remember, yes, your former cook's granddaughter from America."

"I've *never* had a cook, Thomas."

"Haven't you?"

"She's my *grandmother's* former cook's granddaughter, to be precise, as well as my oldest friend's daughter. Which is much more to the point."

"I didn't intend to suggest—"

"She means a very great deal to me, Ellen Winter. The way she came to me and stayed after Ross died." Georgina watched Tom Ogilvie, his index finger following the rim of his cup, his long neutral unlined face, his light brown hair combed carefully to the side, his clean well-cut clothes worn till they were almost threadbare. Not out of need, as she very well knew, but out of a love of economy. "So what have you been up to, Tommy? Do you plan to take a holiday?"

"Not this summer, no. There're several rather pressing matters I need to oversee. It-tis difficult, in a small firm, to get away a-tall."

"It would also entail, in any case, some sort of outlay of

funds. Any new cases? Anything interesting in the wind?"

"Well, yes. In a way. The contract that brings me to Oxford is quite an ongoing adventure." He described the client, the particulars of the conflict, the products manufactured by the local firm, without naming any names. He chuckled at the attempts of an aged pensioner to patent a gadget (made largely from a funnel and well-worn spring) that was intended to fill a bird feeder when the level of birdseed became low. And then he touched upon the infringement of a noncompetition employment agreement. "There was something else I wanted to tell you too. What was it?"

Georgina encouraged him by raising an inquisitive eyebrow. Humoring him more than sometimes. Pretending to believe he'd actually forgotten the reason he'd come to see her.

"Oh, I know. Yes. I mentioned it last time we spoke, if you'll remember. That I've been approached by a gentleman I was at school with, who's been singled out by another party who's expressed an interest in purchasing Fletcher Tire and Rubber. Now, I know you say you don't wish to sell, and I certainly don't wish to interfere, but I thought perhaps—"

"How would it affect you, if I were to sell? A finder's fee perhaps?"

"Something, I suppose. Nothing to speak of, surely. I'm thinking of you and the company. You know Arthur Shaw can't manage it as it ought to be managed, not without Ross, and I hate to see Fletcher's wither away for lack of leadership. It isn't a-tall fair to those who've worked there all their lives."

"I agree, yes. And I'm approaching the situation the way Ross intended."

"Mrs. Fletcher, I'm sorry to interrupt, but a telephone call's come through for you."

"Thank you, Sarah. Excuse me, Tommy."

"Of course."

He watched Georgina's blue tweed back till it disappeared into the sitting room, and then he opened a small box he'd slipped out of his coat pocket. He took out a pinch of powder and dropped it in his coffee, and then moved Georgina's cup closer, away from the edge of the table. He'd spilled a trace of powder on her napkin, and he shook it off in the direction of her cup, then slipped the box in his pocket. He stirred his coffee with a silver-plated spoon, sniffed the jam in a covered pot, and poured more coffee in Georgina's cup.

She was back a second later, the thick-set heels of her black-laced shoes resolutely tapping the stone floor, as she returned to talk to Thomas. "A student, of course."

"At this hour?"

"I apologize for the interruption."

"Please, think nothing of it. As I was saying—"

"Before you do say any more, I think I ought to explain my position concerning the sale of Fletcher Tire. I shall give you a bit more detail than Ross gave you in the past, in order that we can put this behind us once and for all."

"I certainly don't wish you to feel pressured. I simply hoped—"

"I don't feel pressured in any way. But I shall be extremely clear and unequivocal so the matter can be put to rest. You deserve more of an explanation than you were given in the past, and I've been intending to have this chat for some time."

"You are keeping an open mind, I hope? One can't predict ahead of time the opportunities that may arise."

"First of all, I know where this offer for Fletcher Tire originates, no matter who the intermediary may be. Ross had no respect a-tall for the way British Tire does business, as you very well know. They could never be counted on to manufacture products of the highest possible quality, nor would they treat our people as Ross would wish, and neither of us would ever agree to sell to them, for that, and other reasons."

"But—"

"I know as well as you that Arthur Shaw is a man of…shall we say, 'limited scope'? He's a fine financial officer, and he was an excellent financial advisor when Ross was in command. But it was Ross's scientific and marketing mind that enabled Fletcher to become what it-tis, and without such vision any technically based firm suffers. When Ross became ill, he saw the need for finding a leader who understood the science involved, yet was also experienced in marketing. Someone who could think creatively, and plan well ahead, instead of reacting to whatever the competition does at any particular moment. Ross knew Arthur was ill-equipped to cope, and he hired an American to take over after he died."

"Ross never mentioned a word!"

"The gentleman didn't feel he could join us until the end of his contract in America, so there was to be a ten-month delay. Ross died, you see, during that time. And then, unfortunately, the American died tragically himself. On the Ile-de-France, as a matter of fact, on his voyage over. I then opened negotiations with Ross's second choice, but those negotiations failed. I am presently engaged in negotiations with Ross's final choice. Should I be unable to find a managing director whom I think capable of leading Fletcher, I shall then pursue plans for selling the company in a way that honors Ross's wishes. I would very much like to sell Fletcher to the employees, even though this seems to be an almost unheard of approach, and the way is not clear at this time."

"Fletcher's certainly must be wrenched away from Arthur."

"Arthur is quite cognizant of his own limitations, and he's well aware of the fact that I'm looking for someone who will provide him with proper direction. He's a kind and honorable man, though few would call him a man of vision. Fletcher Tire and Rubber needs, and is accustomed to being directed by, a man of both honor *and* vision."

"I agree, yes. Uncle Ross was a remarkable man."

"Are you sure you wouldn't care for a piece of toast?"

"If you're certain you won't finish it yourself. It would be a shame to let it go to waste."

They chewed for a moment in silence, Georgina leaving a third of the omelet to finish the last of the strawberries.

"Well…" Tom swallowed his coffee, and then looked over at his umbrella. "I suppose I must dash. I shall have to find a taxi to take me out past Headington."

"Try opposite The Eagle and Child. Cabs usually draw up there, in front of the war memorial."

"I shall see you next in Scotland, then. When do you finish here for the summer?"

"I shall be home the first week in August. You do understand now, don't you? I shall try to find a suitable leader. If I can't, I shall sell, hopefully to Fletcher employees. If I'm unable to manage that, I will handle the sale in my own way. I will *not* do business with BT under any circumstances whatever. I don't wish to dwell on the history of our relationship, but I shall not be moved. I'm speaking frankly because I have no wish to mislead you."

"I do understand, yes. Though I can't say I altogether agree. I shall see you in August, Aunt G. And I do hope the lectures go well."

Georgina watched Thomas Ogilvie walk through the wrought iron gate, and followed the bobbing of his head and shoulders above the five-foot wall as he hurried south toward the war memorial. She finished the rest of her coffee, once he was out of view. And then she pushed her chair away from the table as though she'd come to a decision.

Then she turned pale very suddenly.

She pulled a linen handkerchief out of one of her jacket sleeves and patted her forehead and her upper lip.

She rested a moment, before gathering her books and her purse. Then she stood up, swaying enough to be noticed, and rushed toward the lobby, stumbling twice, dropping her books and her purse inside the sitting room door.

"Sarah!" Penelope Long was in the women's room off the lobby with her arms around Georgina, trying to keep her on her feet. "ROBERT!"

Robert Maxwell, the assistant manager, ran in from the office behind the reception desk just as Sarah Smith appeared from the kitchen in the back.

"Help me get her to her room. She's been taken terribly ill. And bring a large bowl!"

Penelope Long called her doctor at a quarter after eight and spoke to him on the telephone at four minutes before nine.

The ambulance he ordered arrived at twenty-five past.

Mrs. Georgina Fletcher vomited once during the ride across town and was admitted to the Radcliff Infirmary at twelve minutes before ten.

The last four words she uttered in the hospital were "Lord" and "the poor dog," separated by a painful attack of sickness. It was unclear to hospital personnel whether the two were in any way connected.

Georgina Fletcher lost consciousness three or four minutes after saying those final words.

She died at twenty-two minutes past ten, choking on her own vomit, as an emergency room nurse was reentering the room to see if Mrs. Fletcher still lay on her left side.

CHAPTER TWO

Thursday, June 15th

"WHY IS HE TWISTING AROUND?" Jennifer Burke was hunched forward, wrapping her legs in a death grip around Alex's big chestnut thoroughbred.

Ben Reese slowed Malamaze, the even bigger bay he was riding, and looked over his shoulder at the tall thirtyish Englishwoman whose deep-seated fear of not being decisive had been making him smile since she got there the day before. "So you don't like sitting on a large quivering horse who's dancing from side to side?"

"No I don't, and don't be a tease!" Her black velvet hard hat had fallen forward, and her straight blond hair had slipped out of its clip, tangling around her shoulders.

"Matthew worries a lot, but he'll settle down."

"When, may I ask?"

"Soon." Ben was softening his hands on Malamaze's reins, squeezing and releasing his fingers very gently, asking him to relax his neck and stop clenching the bit. "Matthew's sensitive. You have to stay calm to calm him down."

"With a reasonable horse one could!" The small features in

the thin lined face were white and pinched.

And yet it looked to Ben as though the wide brown eyes were much more irritated than panicked. "Sit up straight and don't squeeze with your legs. Relax your seat so you're sitting way down in the saddle. And don't pull on the reins."

"It's my fault the idiot horse bolted?"

"No, fifteen pheasants took off behind him and startled him. We're almost home—"

"I *do* know where I am." She was trotting up too close to Malamaze, her legs squeezing Matthew's sides, her heels buried in his ribs, her reins pulling him back—telling him the exact opposite of what her legs kept ordering him to do.

Ben turned away, into the west wind, running down across the sheep ground from the high hill on their right. "Matthew knows he's close to home, so if he tries to rush, just hold him with your back without giving him a shot in the mouth."

"I *do* know horses like to rush to the barn! I *am* a veterinarian. I have amassed *some* equine knowledge in the last five years!"

"Yes, I'm sure you have."

Neither of them said anything else as they walked the horses down the last stretch of the old rutted track that snaked down from the high moors on Balnagard Estate. Jennifer kept her eyes on Matthew's head, but Ben watched the River Tay, when he could, sliding by below them on the other side of the B898 running north from Dunkeld, Scotland.

They crossed the one-lane road in silence, and then walked through the archway in the high stone wall straight toward Balnagard Castle, listening to the rhythm of metal-shod hooves crunching in deep gravel.

Seconds after they'd passed the drawbridge across the

grass-lined moat, the high iron gate at the castle end clanked open, and Lord Alexander Chisholm (the Eighth Earl, and the Thirteenth Thane of Balnagard) ran out from the castle's forecourt and shouted after Ben. "Oh, I'm so sorry, Jennifer, I didn't mean to startle Matthew. You've gotten an urgent call, Ben, from Ellen Winter. She's up near Stonehaven, and needs to speak to you straightaway. You do know where she's staying, I hope."

"No."

Alex's large square head half-listed to one side, and all six-feet-six of him managed to look mortified. "I thought I wrote her number on a page of notes on a very important Welsh battle in 573, but when I looked, it wasn't there!"

"I see." Ben grinned, his large gray eyes crinkling at the corners, as though this was not a surprise.

"I'm *terribly* sorry."

"Don't be. She'll call back if it's that important."

"Is she the young woman who was your apprentice this year, in the States, at your university?"

Ben nodded, as he raised his eyebrows and cocked his head almost imperceptibly toward Jennifer. "We better put the horses away. We've been out for quite a while."

"Has Matthew been difficult?"

"One might say that, yes!" Jennifer blew a stray clump of damp hair off her forehead, but it hit the visor of her helmet and fell back where it had been. "And don't look so superior! I can cope with horses on the ground, you know."

"Yes, I'm sure you can." Alex glanced at Ben.

And Ben looked back with a studiously neutral expression on his face.

"I've specialized in small animals for a reason, you know.

Equines are so terrifically stupid, one simply doesn't have the patience!"

"Yes. Well. Shall I help you feed them? And then join you for the walk to the farm?"

"I'm glad to see you Americans got this Shepard fellow back from space." Alex was leaning nearly horizontal in his wicker chair, staring at pale stars in a bright sky through the grape arbor at the back of BalMacneil (the old stone farmhouse north of Balnagard where they lived in the summer when the castle was open to visitors). He sat up suddenly and gazed round the table, first at his wife, Jane, then at Jennifer and Ben, and asked what they'd been discussing.

"*You* were talking about the children." Jane smiled at her husband.

And Jennifer laughed the short condescending snort exasperated parents use on children.

"Of course. Yes, I remember. It's their first experience, really, with even the thought of money to be spent, and we shall have to explain very carefully the obligations we must meet as a family. It was very thoughtless of you, Ben, to appraise the inherited oddments and tell us what to sell to save the estate!"

"I know. What could I have been thinking?" Ben popped a small chive-covered potato in his mouth, as Alex beamed.

"We must reroof the castle first, while sorting out all the housing repairs for families on the estate as well." Jane swept her chin-length champagne hair behind her ears, then leaned over and lit two hurricane lamps. "We haven't told the children how much the guns are worth, but when they come up at auction in a month's time, we shall have to explain then."

"They'll survive the horrors of having money. Anyone but you two would be celebrating." Jennifer pushed aside her salad plate, shaking her head at her sister.

"What's your opinion of the Bay of Pigs?" Alex was chewing a large piece of romaine lettuce with his eyebrows raised in Ben's direction.

"A disaster arranged by an amateur."

"It did seem to *me* to be ill-advised."

"And how many Cuban soldiers, because of the mistakes *he* made, are being tortured in Cuban prisons?"

"Kennedy *is* very attractive. He does bring a bit of panache to the office. And he expresses himself rather well, don't you think?" Jennifer was talking to Ben from across the table.

And Ben told himself to swallow the first word that had come to mind. "I guess I'd rather have wisdom, and ethics, and experience *any* day instead of style and delivery. If Ike had still been in office, he either would've planned it intelligently, or canceled the operation."

"If Kennedy's father had read history in the British Museum, instead of chasing women when he was your ambassador here, perhaps he could've advised Jack better." Alex laughed softly to himself.

And Jane looked at Jennifer and changed the subject. "Did you know that in the British Museum's earliest reading rooms the ventilation was so poor readers suffered from a malady called 'museum headache'? They were plagued by the 'museum flea' as well, a *very* nasty cousin of the household flea, more than twice its size."

"You don't have enough real work to do, or you wouldn't talk such arcane nonsense!" Jennifer Burke laughed, while rubbing her bare arms.

Jane didn't answer. She watched slivers of moonlight splinter across the water. "I love the summer light, at night, in Scotland. It's very ethereal, very luminous, like mother of pearl with the light behind it, and it makes me want to walk all night."

"It's often light enough that one could. May I?" Alex leaned over and speared the last potato on Jane's plate.

Jennifer shivered, and said, "Gloucestershire's *much* more civilized. It's far too cold in Scotland."

"I shall fetch you a wrap while I make coffee." Jane was already up, stacking dishes in the salad bowl she'd balanced on one hip.

"What time will the children be home?" Alex had pushed his chair back and was starting to stand up.

"You stay and talk. I can clear the table. They're to be back from *Exodus* by half-ten. Uncle Robert's driving."

Ben told Jane he'd do the dishes.

And Alex said, "I'll help," while fingering his thinning hair as though he were searching for something.

"That would be lovely, thank you. Your glasses are in your shirt pocket." Jane kissed the top of her husband's head and stepped through the French doors.

Jennifer cleared her throat, and straightened her spoon, and then looked purposefully at Ben. "Jane mentioned this morning that you're a widower. Did your wife work? Or was she a housewife?"

"She was a professor of English literature."

"I do think it's rather too bad about Jane." Jennifer said it conspiratorially.

And Alex and Ben both looked at her—the cool smile, the fine hair teased slightly around her face, the painted nails, the crossed leg swinging back and forth, the row of silver bracelets.

"Jane took a First at Oxford, and it's come to nothing. She's never held a job, not after she got her degree. And yet I remember how often she used to say she wanted to contribute to society in a very real way."

"When our children are older she'll take on something new. She is wonderful with all of them, and it-tisn't a-tall easy helping four very distinct individuals develop their characters and talents."

"So is the baker's wife wonderful with her children, and the hairdresser on every corner! Of course, if *you'd* learn to drive, Alex, it would make life a bit easier for her."

"I have tried. I can't seem to keep my mind on the road."

Ben was watching Jennifer, and the humor that usually hovered around his mouth was nowhere to be seen. "Jane's extremely well read, and she's interested in all kinds of things."

"She's a glorified housewife! Balnagard is beautiful, of course, and she cooks very well, but Jane was intended for a great deal more."

"And you're in a position to plan other people's lives?" Ben said it unemotionally, but ice had formed around the edges of his voice.

"You must admit she could do more. I know becoming a vet is unusual, one wouldn't expect—"

"How many employees do you have on the estate?" Ben was asking Alex, while fitting his fingers together on top of his head.

"Forty in summer when the castle's open. Somewhat fewer in winter when we live there alone. Many of them in estate housing, which has to be managed as well."

"And Jane oversees all of it, except the grouse moor. She

chooses the curriculum with the tutor, and neighbors' kids come here to study too, so it's a lot like running a school. She's planned, and designed, and is now managing the tea shop for tourists—"

"And if she didn't make substantive suggestions concerning my writing—"

"Why are you both so defensive? All I said was—"

"Ben…" Jane stopped by Alex's elbow, with Jake the boxer dancing around her, and handed a sweater to Jennifer. "A telephone call's come through for you. A woman named Ellen Winter. She says it's rather urgent."

"How would she have known to call me here at the farm? Ah. Of course. She talked to the local operator."

"Elsie would've told her 'the family *always* mooves to wee BalMacneil Farrm when the castle opens to tourrists.'" Jane's version of the soft purr of central Scotland made Ben laugh, as he followed her into the kitchen, with Jake trotting beside him, squeezing a tattered tennis ball gently between his teeth.

Ben was back five minutes later, stepping over Jeremiah, Alex's big black lab, carrying a tray of coffee. "I have to drive up near Stonehaven, so I'll need to rent a car. Where can I do that, Alex? Not Dunkeld. Perth?"

"Possibly. You may have to go as far as Edinburgh. You'd be very welcome to take one of ours, of course."

"I don't know how long I'll be gone."

"Is there an emergency?" Alex was watching him intently.

"The woman Ellen came to visit has died, and she's left Ellen her house, which has come as a big surprise to everybody. It's a complicated situation, and I have to go up there and help Ellen figure out what has to be done."

"The woman died of natural causes, did she?"

"The coroner's jury in Oxford thought so. She was teaching there when she died."

"What does it mean, that Ellen Winter is your apprentice?" Jennifer poured a second cup of coffee and handed it to Alex.

"University archivists often have apprentices. I try to teach mine a little about how to evaluate books and manuscripts, and date coins, and restore paintings. Anyway, she's here alone, she's in shock because of the death, and she needs some help from somebody."

"Will you leave tomorrow?" Jennifer didn't look at him, while she poured cream in her cup.

"As soon as I can in the morning."

"Do you know where Jane is?" Alex had dropped his napkin by his cup and was pushing his chair away from the table.

"I don't, no. She wasn't in the kitchen when I got off the phone."

"I think I'll trot along and see what's keeping her." Alex rushed off, the way he always did, as though he were afraid he'd forget what he was doing if he didn't run.

Ben and Jennifer sat in silence, watching candle flames shiver in hurricane lamps and avoiding each other's eyes.

Jennifer laughed a tight, dry, uncomfortable laugh and rubbed her neck as though it hurt. "Alex has told me about the murders you've solved. He seems to think you're quite the detective."

"I wouldn't say that."

"No, but then you hardly say anything a-tall."

"I suppose it depends on the situation." Ben Reese looked at her delicately made face and leaned his chair back against the cool stone wall. His eyes were hidden and unreadable, outside the circle of candlelight.

"I'm not always this difficult, you know. I've felt very much at a loss since I arrived, and when I feel awkward, I behave rather badly. Alex made it all too clear that they're trying on a bit of matchmaking, and I find it insulting."

"It's not something *I* look forward to."

"No, I can see that. No, of course."

"I hope Jane didn't hear herself being discussed."

"Jane wouldn't let it upset her. She's a very strong woman."

"Yes, as well as perceptive, and very kind. Anyway, I ought to start on the dishes. I want to get packed tonight."

"I'd be happy to help too, you know."

"Okay. Then would you rather wash or dry?"

Friday, June 16th

Ben turned west off the coast road, away from the small stone fishing village of Muchalls, and looked south across sloping land for the roof of Cairnwell House.

He was driving through smooth sunny fields under high blown clouds, past grain swaying in the wind, barley and oats in several shades of green, strung together by ditches and stone walls and strips of tall Scotch pine, thinned and pruned by the wind.

Five minutes later, when he was asking himself if he should turn around beside a field of black and white cows, he came to a lopsided T where small stone farm buildings leaned in various directions on both sides of the rutted track.

He turned left down the slope and at the next two intersections. And there, by a sign to CAIRNWELL HOUSE, he began climbing rising ground again toward a cultivated stand of trees.

A dry stone wall, six feet high and green with moss, started on his right, bordering those woods, then dropped down, half a mile later, to meet a four-foot pillar supporting a large stone griffin holding a carved shield guarding the drive to Cairnwell, with a second griffin twenty feet beyond.

It wasn't a long lane, two hundred yards or so. But it was lined with tall, willowy, delicately limbed pale-barked trees—sycamores, hundreds of years old—framing the first view of a small, tan, largely L-shaped Scottish castle with "harled" walls (stuccoed in sand and crushed stone).

Ben parked in the gravel by a high stone archway in the center of the front wall of a two-sided curtain wall (that connected the front end of the castle's long side on the left with the right end of the back wing, creating a rectangular courtyard). There were three shot holes on both sides of the gate in the front crenellated wall, below a Latin inscription.

Ben tried to read it as he stretched his arms over his head, but all he could make out at that distance was "Grip Fast" and "1541."

He walked through the gate's open wooden doors across the gravel courtyard on a flagstone path to the front door of the castle in the back right corner, where a short stairway section of the house came forward from the end of the back wing.

A heavy oak door with rivets around the outside edges was set at a diagonal across that corner, and Ben rapped on it twice with the long brass knocker, while he studied the crest above the frame. He thought about pulling the thick braided bell rope on his right, but the high bronze bell looked large enough to startle every farmer in the neighborhood. And he decided to look for Ellen on the grounds, when no one answered his knock.

He walked around the right side of the castle, down a short slope on a gravel path past a large weeping cherry tree, toward a wide expanse of nearly flat lawn where you could look down across fields to the sea. There were three huge beech trees at the far edge of the lawn—two on the right, one on the left—with a garden bench in between. On the left side of the bench was a large irregular stone that stood four or five feet tall and looked as though it might be carved.

Ben walked toward the bench, studying the stone, which *had* been carved, extremely well, so that a strong, calm, intelligent male face in deep concentration looked like it had pushed its way out of a natural rock.

But before he got five feet from it, he saw Ellen Winter leaning against the far side of the closer of the beeches on his right.

Her dark brown hair was pulled back in a braided ponytail and her straight black eyebrows were drawn together against what could have been sadness or worry—until she saw Ben, and looked disconcerted. "Dr. Reese! Thank you for coming. I know I shouldn't have bothered you, but—"

"No, I'm glad you called."

"You're the only person I know who's dealt with any kind of situation like this, and I decided I couldn't worry about you being my professor." She looked young and ill at ease, as she pulled a thick cream-colored envelope out of the pocket of her khaki pants. "You ought to read this first."

"What did the coroner say your friend died of?"

"The 'immediate cause' was asphyxiation. And the 'proximate cause' was aspiration because of vomiting. *If* I've gotten the terms right."

"So material was sucked into the airway while she was being sick?"

"Right."

"What caused the vomiting?"

"I don't think they have a clue. She ate a wild mushroom omelet for breakfast at the inn where she was staying, but all the omelets were made from the same batch of mushrooms, and the man who supplies the mushrooms has been doing it for forty years."

"I s'ppose she still could've gotten a poisonous one. The one mistake in the basket. Depending on when she ate the omelet."

"Two to two and a half hours before she died."

"There wouldn't have been any symptoms for eight to ten hours, so the timing's all wrong, even if she'd eaten a death cap. There was no sign of drug or chemical poisoning?"

"Nope."

"What did the coroner's report say about the vomiting?"

"The cause was of 'unknown origin.' She had dinner in a Chinese restaurant the night before she died and ate ordinary cultivated mushrooms. She also had curry with a student that day for lunch. She mentioned it to Penelope, where she'd gone and what she'd eaten. But the waiters in both restaurants made a point of saying that she didn't eat much of anything. And no one else died, or was admitted to a hospital. But the coroner did say that susceptibility to food poisoning varies a lot from person to person."

"Do you have the name of the student who had lunch with her?"

"No. Nobody does. Georgina ate with someone at the Chinese restaurant too. A young man they said, but no one knows who that was either. And whoever it was hasn't come forward."

"How did Georgina arrange it so you'd get the letter?"

Ellen explained about Penelope Long, and G. making her promise not to tell the police.

"When did you get it?"

"Day before yesterday. June 14. The day after the inquest in Oxford. Why Penelope waited two days to mail it I don't know. Maybe she forgot, with the shock of Georgina's death, and the confusion of the investigation. And then it took four days to get here."

Ben read it on the garden bench, the letter open on his knees, rubbing the scar on his left palm.

My dear Ellen,

I wish we could have met again. If you receive this letter, it wasn't possible, of course, for I shall be already dead.

This is not an easy missive to write, yet I shall plunge in and hope I manage to say everything that must be said.

First, I want you to know that I came to love you very much in the years you lived with me after Ross died. At the time of your brother's death, I felt such grief for you, you and Elizabeth and Carl, and yet was powerless to help in any way. I hope you and both your parents are much recovered, even though the loss will always be felt.

Now to business...

Cairnwell House belongs to you by all that's right and just. I don't have time to explain at the moment. You will find translations of two memoirs, Robert Witney's and Alysoun Pryor Hume's, in the locked compartment in my desk in my bedroom at Cairnwell which will explain only too well. I cannot right the wrong, or return to you what was taken, because of the changes wrought by the interven-

ing years. But having Cairnwell will, I hope, make some sort of restitution.

I have chosen to give it to you instead of your mother because her life is firmly settled now in America, and you, being younger and less fixed, might possibly wish to make your home at Cairnwell. Elizabeth is also placed in such a way that she does not need the financial advantages that Cairnwell may offer, while you are establishing yourself in life, and may find it a useful base. I do intend the house for Elizabeth, of course, as much as for you, in use and in pleasure, which I know you will see to on your own.

I am enclosing with this letter the key to my safety-deposit box at the Bank of Scotland in Aberdeen (address on the envelope that holds the key). Retrieve the deposit box (using this letter for additional authorization, should you need it, though I did add your name to the authorization list before I left for Oxford, and gave them as well a sample of your signature). There you will find the original documents, and see, as I have, the horror of what my family has done to yours.

I intended to give you Cairnwell House this summer, had I lived. I would not have taken no for an answer.

The matter will now be managed by my will, which is with Grant and Graham in Aberdeen. A copy is also deposited with Smith and Lloyd, Cornmarket Street, Oxford. The will clearly states that the house and lands are yours (as well they should be) along with money and various securities intended to enable you to care for it as it should be managed. Stock in Fletcher will also be discussed in some detail there. If you wish to sell the house, you must please yourself. You must feel no compunction on my account. Neither must you feel any obligation to create the summer haven for writers and researchers which I had intended to establish before I learned of my family's wrong-doing and realized such decisions were yours to make. You must use the house as you wish without considering my intentions in the matter. If, by chance, you should wish to continue with the writers retreat, there are funds set aside for such a purpose. But again, you must not seek to please me. Do what you wish to do yourself. There are certain refurbishments that may still be necessary at Cairnwell, regardless of whether you decide on the retreat. The scope of Jack Corelli's employment will, therefore, be for you to decide and arrange.

I do have one request, my dear, and it is decidedly no small matter. I ask that you undertake a "quest" on my behalf. I have reason to believe that my death was desired, planned, and perpetrated with great care and deliberation. Even if I am right, the circumstances of my death will appear to have been brought about by natural causes. The police will be satisfied, unless considerably more informa-tion is uncovered. I do not wish that they think otherwise until the person responsible has been found, and proof has been established. I do not wish to have the police trampling through the lives of my friends and colleagues. More impor-tantly still, I fear that if a police investigation were seen to be in progress, the murderer would either decamp alto-gether, or see reason to take more lives.

I have, therefore, established an account in your name at the Bank of Scotland on St. Giles Street in Oxford. This account will not be in any way subject to my will and estate, so the funds will be available to you immediately.

Use them to procure the services of a really competent private investigator who can examine the circumstances of my death and determine the identity of the murderer. I do not intend to reveal the name of the person I suspect, for my suspicions are merely that. I may be misconstruing all manner of information. My opinions may be the result of the most misleading subjectivity, and would then lead erroneously to the harassment of an innocent person. I have only the most tenuous and unsubstantiated data on which to assert any position. All I can safely say is that several apparently unrelated pieces of information have come my way over the last few months, which I have pieced together in such a way that I have been led to suspect a particular individual of committing several seemingly unrelated murders. The person implicated appears to be utterly removed from the circumstances and is known to be a respectable citizen.

If I am right, the deaths occurred when the murderer feared exposure. Therefore, any investigation must be accomplished with the utmost delicacy. If I am wrong, my tactics will mean that no one will be damaged and no pain will have been needlessly caused. If I am right, and the murderer can be identified and stopped, retribution will be possible, and further murders will be prevented.

I have laid a great burden upon your shoulders, my dear. One which you must not carry alone. Seek an advisor to help and guide you in this undertaking. (Either of your parents would be an excellent choice, should one, or both of them, be able to join you in Scotland.) The choice of the investigator is clearly crucial. It must be a person of character and perception, as well as of experience and ability.

You can rely on Ian Cunningham to help you face this responsibility, and search for the proper investigator. You may also rely on Gwen Fitzgerald for support, encouragement, and counsel.

May God bless you, my dear Ellen. May you marry as happily as Ross and I, and your parents. May you do work you were meant to do. May you raise children as well as your mother and father raised theirs.

Your fondest "Aunt,"
Georgina Leslie Witney Fletcher
(Oh, I also should have mentioned that you can trust D. L.)

"How long after she wrote this did she die?" Ben was staring at the side of the statue, holding the letter in one hand.

"We don't know. She gave it to Penelope late at night the night before she died, and Penelope had the impression that she'd just finished writing it, but she can't say that for sure."

"Who's D. L.? Do you know?"

"I don't know. I should, but I can't think who that is."

"Georgina's maiden name was Witney?"

"Yes."

"And what was she doing in Oxford?"

"Teaching an English literature course for a summer program."

"I thought the spring term at Oxford was just ending. Trinity Term, is that it? And that there isn't another till fall."

"This is a special program that's just started in the last two or three years. It began June 5, I think. Georgina went down to Oxford on the third."

"Too bad she didn't tell us who she suspected." Ben was standing at the side of the statue sliding his fingers along the chiseled throat.

"That's the way she was. She would've wanted an unprejudiced second opinion without her having colored the investigation."

"When did you live here before?"

"June of '58 to July of 1960. My brother had a motorcycle accident in the States then, and I went home."

"I'm sorry."

Ellen said, "Thanks," as she leaned over and pulled a small piece of loose bark off her side of the tree.

"So you're older than most people when they start their senior year in college?"

"I'm almost twenty-five. I worked for a year too, after I graduated from high school."

"Why didn't you tell me you'd lived in Scotland when we were talking about my sabbatical here and in England?"

"You don't make it easy to talk about anything personal." Ellen looked at him directly, then turned and gazed down across a field of cows, edged in brambles and yellow gorse.

"Maybe. There're certainly times when that's true. So tell me about the translations Georgina mentioned in the letter."

"The memoirs weren't there. Not in the locked compartment, and not anywhere else in the desk, or in her bedroom, or even in her downstairs office. At least not anywhere that I could find."

"May I look?"

"Sure."

"Who attacked the sculpture?" Ben had stepped in front of it so he could see the piece as a whole, and discovered that the entire left side of the man's face had been smashed.

"I wasn't here when it happened, but apparently it was Michael Shaw, the sculptor who made it to begin with."

"Who's it of? Georgina's husband?"

"Right. Ross Fletcher. He opened an abandoned quarry for Michael, up the road about a mile, and he let Michael use a shed there as a studio. Michael lives there too, for practically nothing. He's the son of someone who works at Ross's company, Fletcher Tire and Rubber. Anyway, I guess Georgina and Michael had some kind of disagreement right before she went to Oxford, and he destroyed the statue before Georgina could stop him."

"He's really a fine sculptor."

"He's an interesting person too. He loses his temper pretty easily, though. And then feels bad afterwards."

"So is this a good time to go look at the desk?"

It was a large mahogany knee-hole desk, sitting three feet to the right of Georgina's bedroom fireplace, perpendicular to the white-plastered wall, with the chair facing the hearth.

"The secret compartment—" Ellen stopped in mid-sentence, because Ben was already on his hands and knees between the pedestals looking at the locked compartment in the back panel of the knee hole with the magnifying glass from his key ring. "A lot of people could've known about it. G. used to talk about buying the desk in Wales."

"The door hasn't been forced." Ben had backed up but was still kneeling, this time in front of the center drawer, holding his head to one side, examining the top of the desk. "Have you got the key?"

"It'll take me a second. It's in a box of buttons in her bed-side table."

Ben opened the cabinet door less than a minute later and

studied the empty interior. Then he locked it again while he asked Ellen who'd been in the house since she'd arrived.

"I got here from the States the day G. died, and since then there've been a lot of people. Offering condolences, or coming for the funeral."

"The funeral was yesterday?"

"Yesterday morning. But there're several people who live on the estate. Jack Corelli, he's an American who's been doing carpentry and repairs and was supposed to fix up outbuildings for Georgina's writers retreat. He's the son of an American couple Georgina and Ross knew for years. Tom was here for a couple of days too. Tom Ogilvie. He's Ross's nephew, and a lawyer in Perth."

"Would he have inherited Cairnwell if you hadn't?"

"I don't know. Cairnwell was Georgina's family house, and Tom wasn't her relative, so I wouldn't say it was a sure thing. She might've donated it, to make her retreat, or for something else charitable. I know Tom used to tell her she ought to sell it and move into Aberdeen. And I don't know that Georgina would've wanted him to have it."

"Who else has been in the house?"

"Michael Shaw, the sculptor. He's been in and out. He…well…I think he's very upset by Georgina's death. Maybe because he's ashamed of ruining Ross's statue. Grace MacNicol cleans the house, so she's been here. Georgina's minister too, Ian Cunningham. And Lady Isabelle and Sir John Hay, her neighbors up the road. I have kept G.'s room locked since I got the letter. I went to the inquest in Oxford the day before and brought her things back, and I thought you might want to look at them without other people going through them first."

"Good, I'm glad you did. Is there time to get to the deposit box in Aberdeen before the bank closes?"

"Only if we leave this second."

They stood in a small room in the back of the bank looking at a long green metal box in the center of a counter-height table. Ellen turned the tiny key in the lock and raised the lid. And then picked up a very old vellum manuscript of loose sheets tied together with faded ribbon. Underneath it lay a brown calfskin book embossed with gold leaf, six inches by eight inches, darkened and stained, apparently by mold or mildew.

Ellen handed both to Ben and waited for him to say something. She watched the stillness, the concentration, the gray eyes growing darker, the skin stretched tight across the sharp bones of his face, as he studied the pages and the binding of the book with the magnifying lens on his key ring. His thick straight hair was almost the color of dried winter wheat, and it had fallen against the sides of his forehead as he leaned over. And Ellen found herself wondering why she noticed the way she did. And why he was always so cool and contained.

He handed her the leather-bound book without looking at her. And held the manuscript sheets to the light.

There were two slits through the vellum pages in the upper left-hand corner where a stiff brown ribbon that had once been red had been threaded through. It had been tied and then sealed with a large red wax seal, using a signet ring with a capital P wound through the antlers of a wild hart.

Ben tried to read the lines of faded brown ink, while Ellen waited silently and looked for one decipherable word in washed-out ink on the linen pages of the leather book.

Only the handwriting on the first of the vellum pages of

Alysoun Pryor Hume's manuscript was easily readable by either. Because there, right in the center, in beautifully precise Carolingian script, were the only words written in English:

> Here Lyeth the body of
> John Pryor Gent: who was
> murdered and found hidden
> in the priory Garden in this
> parifh the :3d: day of December
> Anno Domini 1546: and was
> Buried the :6th: day of the fame
> month in the :67th: yeare
> of his age

"What do you know about John Pryor?" Ben was watching her, seeing the strain as Ellen stared at the manuscript, her dark lashes hiding her wide blue eyes.

"Nothing. I've never heard of him. But I'm a Pryor. On my mother's side. My mother's mother was a Pryor."

"I see."

"It's a very strange feeling. Reading about the murder of someone in your family. Even if it was four hundred years ago."

"I've read this epitaph before. Word for word. In Burford."

"Have you? Where's Burford?"

"It's a country town in the Cotswolds, not far from Oxford, on the River Windrush. This is carved on a flat tombstone in the floor inside the church." Ben was examining the other vellum sheets. And he finished before he said, "The rest of the manuscript's written in Greek, and I can't read much at all. The Witney memoir is written in Medieval Church Latin and Medieval French, with the languages alternating from line to line. I can make out a few isolated words, but I'd never be able to translate it. It'll be tough for anyone, because of the way it switches back and forth."

"Who could do it for us?"

"And why'd they use the three languages?"

Ellen ran a finger down one smooth ivory calfskin sheet of Alysoun Pryor's manuscript. And then held it close to her face and inhaled the comforting musky scent of ancient vellum. "They didn't want anyone to be able to read what they'd written."

Ben turned the dry brown-spotted linen-rag pages of Robert Witney's memoir, very carefully and very slowly, humming quietly to himself, something low and faintly Wagnerian. And then he pulled out a tiny camera from inside the right side of his belt—a black Rolex (two and a half inches long, one and a half inches high, three quarters of an inch thick). "Could you hold the pages while I photograph them?"

"Sure."

"Until we know what we're up against, I think we ought to keep the originals in the deposit box. The humidity and light level are better too, than if we took them back to Cairnwell. Try not to touch the pages with any more skin than you have to. Oils aren't good for paper or vellum." Ben was leaning over Witney's memoir, shooting one page at a time.

And Ellen watched Ben as she turned pages, holding the leather boards as flat as she could without straining them. "Do you always carry the camera?"

"No. I stick it inside my belt when I go to libraries and museums."

"Are you allowed to take pictures in museums?"

"I can usually make arrangements. But I don't hurt anything when I can't, or use what I photograph for nefarious purposes. I don't have a lot of patience with red tape."

"Really?" Ellen didn't turn to the last page right away, she just stood and stared at Ben.

Ben laughed and said, "Did I detect a note of surprise and censure?"

"You seem so letter-of-the-law to me."

"I was trained *not* to be fairly efficiently. So maybe you can't always believe what you see. Now. The Pryor memoir." Ben was smiling to himself, while he loaded another roll of film. "The pages will be stiff when you turn them."

"What will we do when we finish here?"

"I'll call a friend in Edinburgh and get him to recommend an archivist in Aberdeen. Then I'll call the archivist and get the name of a film developer here who'll do a very good job fast."

"What do you think about the memoirs?" Ellen's right hand was on the wheel and she was looking across grain fields toward the headlands above a flat teal-gray sea, as they drove down the coast road just north of Newtonhill.

"They're late sixteenth or very early seventeenth-century manuscripts. And that means that aside from whatever family significance they have, they're valuable historical artifacts. Also, in answer to your earlier question, I do know someone who can translate them."

"All three languages?"

"Alex. I'll give him a call when we get back to Cairnwell. I don't know what kind of schedule he's on with the novel he's working on, but if he can help, he will."

"I know Georgina couldn't read Greek, but I think she

could've translated the Latin and French, even though they're medieval. She used to volunteer years ago at a museum somewhere helping the curator of medieval documents."

"Who do you think she would've taken the Greek to?"

"She must have had colleagues who were Greek scholars at Aberdeen. But if it were a personal memoir, if she suspected that it was compromising in some way, once she'd read part or all of Witney's, I think she would've taken it to Ian Cunningham. He's the minister at the church at Kinneff."

"That's right on the coast? South of Dunnottar?"

"Yes."

Ben didn't say anything for a minute. He laid his right arm across the back of the seat and stared at the North Sea. "So who took the translations out of Georgina's desk? Did you tell anyone else about Georgina's letter?"

"No."

"Or the transcripts?"

"No."

Ben was looking away from the water at a line of sitka pines casting long shadows in the low late-afternoon light. "We don't know that the thief knew about the transcripts ahead of time. Whoever it was might not have been looking for them at all. It could've been that the person knew that's where she kept important papers and was looking for something else."

"Maybe. Georgina didn't usually keep important papers in that desk. Most of her things are down in her office behind the kitchen. Of course, nothing there locks. She just used old file drawers from Ross's office that haven't had keys for years."

"It had to be someone who knew about the desk and had access to a key. Who either knew where she kept hers, or already had a copy."

"She told me about the one we used today when I lived here before. She was out of town, and wanted me to get her her copy of Ross's will. She kept it there for a few weeks right after he died. She could've asked someone else to do something like that another time. And there are quite a few people who know the house well enough to have seen the desk and know there's a locked door. Jack Corelli, the carpenter. Grace, the cleaning lady. Tom, the nephew. Michael, the sculptor. I forgot about Colin Ramsay. He just got out of the hospital the day before the funeral. He rents the dower house at the end of the back lane. He worked for Ross before he retired, and he's been a friend of the family for years. There are neighbors and estate farmers who go in and out, and the gardener who works here now. There were a lot of people here after the funeral. People from Muchalls and Newtonhill and Stonehaven. And Aberdeen too, from the university."

"The question I'd like to be able to answer first, so we don't waste a lot of time, is does the reason she's given you the house have anything to do with her death? Or is whatever the wrong is that her family committed an unrelated issue?"

"I couldn't tell from her letter."

"I know. I couldn't either. And I need you to tell me everything you know about your family *and* hers. After I go through her things."

They'd parked in the back, on the left beside Cairnwell's kitchen wing, and Ellen turned off the ignition. "I ought to start dinner anyway. Why don't we eat as soon as you've finished and then take a walk afterwards, so I can show you where everyone lives?"

CHAPTER THREE

THEY'D COME THROUGH THE COURTYARD, and were walking fast toward the griffin gate, when Ellen asked Ben if he'd found anything interesting in Georgina's things.

"Not really. She only did her social correspondence at the desk in her bedroom, and not a lot of that, so I've got to go through her downstairs office too. Is that where she did her household accounts?"

"Mostly. And wrote her books and articles, and read her students' papers. They've cleaned out her office at the university, and I had them put the boxes in her office here too. But there was nothing suspicious in her personal stuff?"

"Nothing that stood out. There're a lot of books in her room I'd like to look at, though."

"Would you rather stay there than in a guestroom?"

"It'd be easier to go through her books, and Ross's too, and get more of a feel for what they were like."

"Except most of his are in his office in front of the library. Did you see the 'laird's lug' in their bedroom?"

"In the tiny room? Through the low door past her bed?

"Yes, where there're newsletters from the Royal Scottish Geographical Society. Ross belonged to it for forty years."

"The laird's lug must be the hole near the floor that opens into a chimney."

"Right. The laird would slip in there and eavesdrop on his guests in the great hall downstairs. But there wasn't anything useful in Georgina's stuff from Oxford?"

"Not that I saw. There were clothes, books, toiletries. No prescriptions of any kind. Only vitamins and a big bottle of aspirin." They'd turned left into the gravel lane, and Ben looked at the rising field across from the griffin gate, at the distant line of high trees, while he slowly inhaled the scent of pine from the sitkas behind the wall on their left. "The vitamins were American, which is kind of interesting."

"My mom sent them to Georgina from the States. Most people in Britain don't take vitamins, but G. had for years. She took a lot of aspirin too for arthritis. Is it okay if we make a loop? Down the front lane, and around to the dower house, then up the back drive?"

"It's up to you." Ben had been considering telling Ellen about the typewritten pages he'd found in Georgina's purse. But as he looked sideways in the soft light, he saw the worry between her eyebrows, the sad eyes, and the set jaw. And he said, "It must be hard to assimilate. Georgina dying. Then inheriting a place like this. Not to mention finding out that her family did something horrible to yours, even if we don't know what."

"It *all* seems weird at the moment. It was wonderful of Georgina to give me the house, and I tell myself I ought to be thrilled, and I am, in a way. But then I think about her being murdered, and it makes me feel sick and sort of panicked."

"I don't know why it wouldn't."

"I thought the next few years of my life were already settled.

Finish college. Get a job on a newspaper, and learn to write books. Maybe it's being American too, and expecting to live there. But now I don't know. I used to work for an architect here as a secretary, and I look at the buildings in this country, and I start thinking about becoming an architect."

"Do you have to decide this second what you'll do for the rest of your life?"

"No. Except for the decisions about Cairnwell."

"You'll figure it out, and do it well. So what do we tell people that'll make it okay for me to ask questions without it looking like I'm investigating Georgina's death?"

"I don't know. I haven't thought about it."

"The truth is that you're my apprentice, and you asked me to help with some of the decisions because I was here in Scotland. Whether to do the writers retreat, for instance. Which we need to talk about in a lot more detail. I suppose we could say that I'm helping you evaluate the library here for writers too. What books are valuable enough that they'd need to be locked up if you did the retreat, and what you'd have to buy."

"That makes sense."

"But it won't make a lot of questions easy to ask. What can you tell me about your family history?"

"Not much. My grandmother was Georgina's grandparents' cook here at Cairnwell, and my grandfather managed the estate. Georgina and her father lived in the dower house then that Colin Ramsay leases now."

"What about Georgina's mother?"

"She died when G. was a baby. Her father thought his mother would help raise Georgina, but she didn't. She was a cold, formal, society type who left her husband alone here a lot while she lived in London or the south of France. So G.'s father hired a housekeeper who raised G. with a lot of help from my grandmother. Georgina was five years older than my mom, but they were pretty much raised together, and stayed best friends for years. Then my grandfather died in the influenza epidemic in 1918, when Mom was eleven. My grandmother's brother had already moved to America, so she took my mom and moved in with him.

"G. was just about to go to college, so it was a good time for her. She didn't get along with her grandmother, and after my mom was gone, G. didn't spend much time here."

"What was her grandmother like?"

"Picky. She made the gardener's kids drag a rake behind them when they played on the paths so there wouldn't be footprints in the gravel."

"I see." Ben shook his head and sighed quietly. "Did Georgina always know she'd inherit Cairnwell?"

"No, her father had an older brother who should've inherited, but he died of cancer a year or two before the war. He'd never married, so Aunt G.'s dad got Cairnwell. He was a patent attorney in Aberdeen."

"Your grandmother was the Pryor, not your grandfather?"

"Right. His name was Payne." Ellen didn't say anything else for a minute. She just walked fast, swinging her arms in her waxed canvas coat. "The Pryors came from England, but that's about all I know. Georgina's family was part English too. A male ancestor moved to Scotland and started a trading company early in the reign of Elizabeth. His name was Witney. That was G.'s maiden name. And I know he married a Leslie."

"Isn't the crest above the door the Leslie crest?"

"Yes, Cairnwell was the dowry the Witney guy got instead

of cash. The Leslies were Scotch aristocrats. The Witneys were merchants who made money. And they've stuck the Leslie name somewhere in every generation."

"What can you tell me about Georgina's friends?"

"Not much. I know Gwen Fitzgerald was her best friend, after my mom moved to the States. She lives up on the Deveron River near Banff. They met in boarding school and stayed close. Other than that, it was mostly just colleagues. Except for G.'s minister and his wife. Oh, and the poet too. I can't think of his name, but he taught with her at Aberdeen and retired several years ago. Colin Ramsay was a friend—the old guy in the dower house."

"Tell me about the people who live on the estate."

"I told you about Michael Shaw, the sculptor. He's up by the quarry on Chapelton Road. Ross opened the old quarry to help him out, and that was *not* a popular move with some of the neighbors."

"No?"

"No. Isabelle Hay—*Lady* Isabelle Hay as she prefers to be called—was absolutely irate. She and her husband live on the Netherly Road close to where Chapelton joins Netherly. You see, here," Ellen and Ben were coming to a lopsided T where a road from the left met the Cairnwell lane they were on, "that road coming in on the right is Chapelton. This Cairnwell lane runs straight into it, but Netherly joins Chapelton at a Y a quarter of a mile farther up. The road here on the left is Ardon Road. It's the only decent route south to the coast road, so the stone trucks come down from the quarry, drive almost past the Hays' house and turn down Ardon Road."

"How did Isabelle Hay react?"

"She organized a village meeting to try to force Ross to

stop. She said the blasting would be unbearable, and the trucks would be worse. But she didn't have the support to push anything through. Her only staunch supporter was the local poacher, which Ross thought was hilarious. But he still promised not to blast. He said they'd saw the rock face with diamond saws, which is a *lot* more expensive, and they'd only send out three trucks a week."

"Did that satisfy her?"

"No. Not Isabelle Hay."

They were standing at the intersection, Cairnwell behind them, Chapelton and Netherly coming together in front of them, angled slightly to their right, Ardon Road on the left, sloping almost due south. Ben pointed to the farmhouse back off the road on their right and asked if that was part of Cairnwell.

"It was. That's the home farm. I'll tell you about Donald Murray when we get to the walled garden."

They turned left onto Ardon and walked halfway to the dower house listening to the wind in the sycamores.

"So tell me about the guy who rents the dower house."

"Colin Ramsay. He's about seventy, and he's got some kind of bone marrow disorder that's sort of like leukemia. Aunt Georgina said it isn't life-threatening now, but it makes him very tired and weak and he has to go into the hospital every few weeks and get blood transfusions. I think he's also got a heart condition, but what kind, or how bad, I don't know."

"What'd he do at Ross's company?"

"Purchasing mostly. He and Ross were friends too. They both read a lot of history."

Ben and Ellen were standing in the back lane in front of the dower house—a harled L-shaped copy of Cairnwell House, a

third the size, with a turret stair too in the back left corner—
when the front door opened, in the center of the back wing,
and a tall, gray-headed, elderly man stepped out on the flagstone path.

"Ellen, my dear! I'm sorry I haven't been up to the house
since the funeral, but I thought I might drop over tomorrow to
see if I can help you settle in."

"Thank you, Mr. Ramsay. I appreciate it. This is Ben Reese.
He's an archivist at my university in the States. Dr. Reese, this is
Colin Ramsay."

Ben studied Colin's broad-boned face, with its dark eyebrows and white hair, and realized unexpectedly that it
reminded him of his father—though Colin was slightly jaun-
diced looking and very pale, even in fading light. "I wonder if I
could ask your help, Mr. Ramsay? I have a copy of a memoir
from the Campbell family of Cawdor which I need to translate
from the Greek before I do genealogical work in London. Is
there anyone nearby I could hire to do the translation?"

"Only one who comes to mind, and I very much doubt he'd
accept remuneration. You know him, Ellen. Ian Cunningham.
The minister over at Old Kinneff. He's a fine Greek scholar, and
I'm sure he'd be delighted to have a go."

"Good. Thank you. I appreciate the help."

"Please, think nothing of it."

"Good night, Mr. Ramsay." Ellen smiled as she started to
turn away.

"Good night, my dear. I shall hope to see you tomorrow."

"Why don't you come for dinner? About seven?"

"You're very kind. And I shall look forward to it."

The door closed as Ben and Ellen walked toward the back
drive, where Ellen watched Ben for a second, in the gathering

dusk, as they turned right into the lane. "I didn't know you had a memoir to translate."

"I don't. I wanted to find out if there was anyone around here besides Cunningham Georgina could've used to translate the Pryor manuscript. Though I have been doing genealogical work with the Campbells of Cawdor for American Campbells who've donated artifacts to Alderton. Does anyone stay with Colin?"

"He has a housekeeper, Winifred MacNicol, Grace's sister-in-law, who comes in for half a day and cooks him a hot meal. If he's really ill, or if he's just gotten out of the hospital, she'll sometimes spend the night."

"Ah. That reminds me. Should we get somebody, Grace or Winifred maybe, to come live in Cairnwell while I'm here? I don't want to start the neighbors talking."

"They've both got families, so neither of them could stay for long. And I don't think we need them to. You're on one floor. I'm on another. People come in and out all the time." Ellen looked embarrassed.

And Ben asked how long Colin had been retired.

"Five or six years. He was very good to Georgina after Ross died."

Their shoes scrabbled on a patch of gravel in the packed dirt lane while the firs rustled on their right and a dog whined somewhere in the distance on the left side of the drive.

"Where's the shed you told me about at dinner? The one Jack Corelli built for his hawks?"

"It's a quarter of a mile past the dower house on Ardon Road."

"What do you know about Jack?"

"Not a lot. He's been here since March doing refurbishing and repair on the castle."

"Why did Georgina hire an American?"

"Do you know anything about Fletcher Tire and Rubber?"

"No, and I need to."

"It was a fairly important company during the war, when Americans and British were trying to learn to mass produce synthetic rubber. The military needed a lot of rubber—"

"Because natural rubber from Malaya had been cut off by the Japanese."

"Right. So Ross was working with this hush-hush American group that was beginning to manufacture at several plants in the U.S., trying to set up production here at his own plant. Jack's father is one of the chemists Ross met in that group. I guess Jack is sort of the black-sheep son, and he was here traveling through the U.K., doing odd jobs, and Georgina hired him and then let him build the shed for his birds on her land. I know he also wants to start a falconry business on the estate. Rent the land and give hawking demonstrations, and take people out hunting so they can see how fascinating the birds are. Farmers shoot hawks and owls and probably eagles, if there are any left in Scotland, and he wants to do something to educate them so they'll stop. Georgina let him use her land, but she wouldn't let him start a business."

"What's the high stone wall on the left?"

"The walled garden. The gardener's cottage just this side of it is where my mother and grandparents lived."

"Tell me about the garden."

"It's kind of a long story."

"Good. Everything I can learn helps."

"Well, Georgina's grandparents—or maybe her great-grandparents, I'm not sure—bought a glass house from the Crystal Palace at the Great Exposition in the 1800s, and put it inside the walled garden for vegetables and tropical flowers, and then filled the rest of the walled garden with fruit trees and plants that need protection.

"Georgina's grandmother was an extravagant person, and after she died in the early thirties, her husband had to sell some of the land to pay her debts. He sold the walled garden very reasonably, along with the home farm, to Mr. Murray, the farmer who worked most of the land on the estate when G. was a little child. He was a wonderful man, but he died during the Second World War and his land was inherited by his son, Donald, who's a very odd person, to say the least."

"How? In what way?"

"It'll help if I give you an example. Georgina inherited this house when her father *and* her grandfather were killed together in the Blitz in London, but she and Ross didn't live here in the big house until 1950, and then only part time, until Ross got sick. Before that they'd used the dower house on weekends, and lived full time in the old part of Aberdeen.

"When they were starting to restore Cairnwell, they had to cut four or five trees that were too big and too close to the house, and Donald Murray tried to stop them. He instituted a legal restriction called a Tree Preservation Order. That meant that the cutting had to stop till some local council could decide if the tree ought to be allowed to be cut. He enforced the Order on each tree separately, which held up the work for weeks."

"Gee, what a helpful guy."

"Everybody could see the trees had to be cut, and the committee let them go ahead, but Donald would stand there the whole time as the trees came down, shaking his head like they were killing a human being. He also skulked around the house at all hours of the day and night, looking in the windows, watching Georgina and Ross and muttering to himself. He's let the walled garden go completely wild. And he's letting the greenhouse fall apart too. He told Georgina with great delight that 'the firrst pane fell in '55, and it will all go beforre I'm gone.' It used to drive her nuts."

"Is he violent in any way?"

"Not as far as I know. He's creepy, but he keeps to himself. With his unneutered cats and his miserable dog."

They'd stopped beside the garden door in the center of a dressed stone wall that must have been twelve feet tall.

Ellen scraped a flake of peeling paint and said, "Aren't the stone columns great? And look at the pediment above the arch. No one could afford to build it today."

"Not for a garden, anyway. Can we go in?"

"If Donald sees us, he'll be furious. He can drive up without us knowing, and this is the only way out."

"Oh, come on, be a sport." Ben opened the rotting gray-blue door. And they stepped into a wild garden. Weeds and grass three feet tall; fruit trees tangled (dead and alive together) in perfectly planted rows in the center of the garden; espaliered trees that should've been pruned flat against the walls, knotted into the snarled branches from the rows of trees in the center. "It's just like *The Secret Garden*."

"But he wouldn't sell to Georgina, no matter how many times she asked."

The rusting, white-painted metal-framed glass house was at the end on their right, beautifully built and proportioned, with hundreds of mullions and an elaborately scrolled iron peak, its panes shattering one at a time on a packed dirt floor punctured in patches by weeds and grass.

A rusted wheelbarrow stood two feet in front of them,

crumbling into orange dust. And they stared in silence. Caught by the strangeness. Stunned by the desire for deliberate ruin. Till the quiet was shattered by a revved engine.

Ellen jumped and started toward the door.

And Ben reached out and grabbed her arm. "It's a motor-cycle. A quarter of a mile away."

"Then it's Jack. Though whether that's better, I don't know. It depends on whether he's in one of his moods."

It was a big Triumph, a 650 Bonneville. And Jack Corelli slid it to a stop in front of them in a patch of gravel, a second after Ben and Ellen had stepped out of the walled garden.

Jack pulled off his helmet, fastened the strap behind the seat, and rubbed his scalp with both hands before he cut the engine. He glanced at Ben, and looked hard at Ellen, as he unsnapped the neck of his black leather jacket. "I thought we were going to go look at the stables."

"I'm sorry, Jack. I forgot."

"You still want me to start on them tomorrow?"

"Let me think about it for a second. Jack Corelli, this is Ben Reese. He's an archivist at Alderton University."

"Another professor, huh?" Jack was anything but impressed.

But they nodded to each other as Ben said, "Yes."

"So where do you want me to start tomorrow?"

"I don't know what I'm going to do yet about the writers retreat. So why don't you put up the shelves for Mr. MacNeil." She looked at Ben and added, "He's the gardener. It's his house here by the walled garden."

"Whatever you say." Jack shoved his gloves in his pockets, kicked the kick starter twice before the engine caught, then scattered gravel in a line up the lane toward Cairnwell.

Jack was wearing full leathers, and he was hard to see in the gathering dark. He was tall, obviously, and broad shouldered. And Ben watched his back with a speculative squint, his hands in the pockets of his corduroy pants. "I have a friend who collects motorcycles, and he loves the sound of a Bonneville. He calls it a 'sweet offbeat staccato clatter' and then looks distracted."

"I don't know why anybody rides motorcycles." Ellen threw a pebble up the drive and started after it. And then she didn't say anything for almost a minute. "Jack talks to women better than men. There's an edgy thing he does with men that sounds more hostile than it is."

Ben was listening to the rumble of the engine as they walked toward it. Till it stopped abruptly near the big house. "Tell me about the writers retreat."

"Well, I know Georgina started thinking about it after Ross died. They hadn't been able to have kids, and it seemed like a useful thing to do with the house. She was planning to fix up the stables and some old cottages and let impoverished writers and researchers come here, mostly in the summers, and work in peace and quiet. Those are the stables up ahead on the left. There haven't been horses here for years, so they're used for cars and storage. This is the original gardener's cottage here on the right."

"Where Jack lives." The big black Triumph was parked on the left of a small stone cottage, in front of a rear shed. "So what does he feed his birds?"

Ellen shook her head and said, "I don't ask."

"Ah."

"What will you do next?" She was climbing the steps toward Cairnwell's front gate, reaching for the iron railing.

"Call Alex and see how soon he can help with the translation of the manuscripts. Then arrange to see Ian Cunningham and Gwen Fitzgerald. Tomorrow, if I can, when I pick up the photos in Aberdeen. I've got to go through Georgina's office too, and I'd like to finish that tonight."

"I think I'll stay outside for a while. I like the back garden when it's getting dark."

"Maybe I'll see you later then." Ben went in through the gate in the curtain wall.

And Ellen took the path down to the cherry tree on her way to the back garden.

A retaining wall was on her left, and she was sliding her fingers across the plants that grew in the rocks, wondering why she could never tell what Ben thought of her. And why she cared as much as she did.

Because he's a man instead of a boy, that's why. Unlike every male your age at Alderton or anywhere else.

Ellen could almost touch the arched stone opening in the stone wall that led to the old crypt, and she was just asking herself what Georgina would have thought of Ben, when a man stepped out of the blackness behind the arch and blocked her way.

Ellen didn't scream, but she made a helpless sound in the back of her throat as she sucked her breath in against her teeth.

"I frightened ye, did I? I neverr meant to do that." It was a thin nasal high-pitched voice.

But it was hearing the insincerity that scared Ellen. "Then why'd you jump out in front of me?" Her own words sounded irritatingly tentative, and she told herself to lower her voice and talk more slowly.

"Nay, I didna jump. Why would I have jumped out at ye? I only want a prrivate worrd."

Ellen had never felt frightened of Donald Murray before, but he was moving closer, and she could feel the heat of his quick, wiry body. She could smell the sour sweat and the rancid clothes, the bad teeth and the whiff of whiskey. She could see the uneven stubble, even in the gathering dark, and what looked like grease smeared across his left cheek. "Why didn't you give me some warning?"

"Why would I want to frighten ye, a young lass like yerself?" His reedy voice slid higher, and it sounded as though he were toying with her, that there was mockery as well as malice behind the wheedling words. "Say ye forgive me, lass, for startlin' ye so."

"Why are you here, Mr. Murray?"

"I wish ye no harm. Even though ye don't belong here. Do ye lass? You, an American. And not Georgina either. She never should've come back."

"Why? It was her house."

"It wasna right a-tall." He seemed to be staring straight at her mouth.

And Ellen backed away from him. "Her family owned it for hundreds of years and she had every right."

"How'd they get it? Have ye asked yerself that? And what did they do with it, all those many yearrs? Aye, and who was here beforre?"

"The Leslies owned it, and a Witney married a—"

"Who had it beforre the Leslies? Answer me that! Small farrmers. Wee animals. The wilderness, as it was. Ye have no right to the wild garrden. You, and yourr 'friend,' the American. It's mine, as ye well know, and I expect ye to stay out!"

"I'm sorry. I just wanted him to see it. We didn't harm anything."

"It-tisn't yours! Ye don't understand a-tall, do ye, lass? Ye think it's daft. When I know this land betterr than the likes of you *everr* will. It's the way it was meant to be, with wee creatures making nests, living and dying in peace, in their own time, the way all the creatures on this land did once."

"But—"

"If ever I find you or yours in the garrden again, ye'll learn to think betterr of it, I promise ye."

"You're on my property now, Mr. Murray, and I don't like your tone of voice."

His hands weren't on her shoulders, but he'd held them up as though he were about to touch her. And Ellen had pressed herself against the wall, grinding her back into damp plants and sharp edges of rock, as Donald Murray stared into her eyes with undisguised loathing and contempt.

"I apologize, I'm sure. I wouldna want therre to be any ill feeling between us."

He left then. Crunching up the path and around toward the front lane. Leaving Ellen with her back crushed against the wall, shivering against her will. And her inclinations. And everything she'd once thought about Donald Murray.

Saturday, June 17th

"Have you remembered anything else Murray said or did last night?" Ben had his legs stretched out in front of him in a chair in the dining room watching Ellen eat breakfast.

"Not really. I knew him before, of course, when I was here, when he used to watch Georgina. But he never got this threatening. Of course we did go into his garden."

"That was my fault. Obviously. I should've listened to you."

"He didn't do anything that was any big deal, it was just creepy."

"He *won't* do anything either. Not now, or any other time."

Ellen watched the sharp cutting coldness that had taken over Ben's face, and told herself to think about it later. "I meant to tell you, by the way, that Grace MacNicol and I were talking when she came in this morning, and she said Ian Cunningham and his wife are out of town till later in the week. He had some kind of church conference to go to, so you can't see him today."

"I didn't know there were Franklin stoves in Britain." Ben was looking at the black metal woodstove standing in the big stone fireplace, twelve feet wide by eight feet high, opposite the French doors.

"Georgina imported two wood-burning stoves, one for here and one for the dower house. This was the original kitchen, and when she converted it, she wanted a stove to help heat it."

"Where do the steps lead?"

There was a rounded stone step on the right side of the hearth that led to others behind a white door that was propped halfway open by a wide flat stone.

"It's one of the old turret stairs that's closed off. We keep the door open so the cats can go in and out. They can get to the basement and the second floor, but it's walled off above that."

"It's interesting the way castles change."

"Yes. Georgina found a stoned-up archway at the top of the front stairs just this winter that she thought went to the keep, the original stone tower that was pulled down long before the L-shaped house was built."

"Can we go through all the rooms when I get back?" Ben stood up.

And Ellen nodded as she ate her last bite of toast. "Do you

want me to pack you a lunch?"

"No, don't bother. But I need you to find the answers to these." Ben handed her a folded piece of typing paper and waited while she read. "You may not be able to ask directly. You may have to be slightly devious."

"I know. I understand."

There was a knock on the French doors that opened to the back garden, and they turned to see Colin Ramsay wave and point toward the scullery door.

Ellen shouted for him to come in. But Ben pulled on his jacket and found his keys, before Colin made it in from the kitchen.

"Good morning all." He was pale and slightly breathless as he walked to the table and sat next to Ellen and set a small silver pitcher by her placemat. "Georgina brought this to me, full of peonies, shortly before I went into hospital, and I thought I should return it before I forgot."

"I better get going." Ben had pushed in his chair and was turning toward the dark oak door that led to the front hall.

"Please don't leave on my account." Colin looked embarrassed and slightly anxious, in that slow confused way elderly people sometimes have when they're afraid they've bungled, or been indiscreet.

"No, I was already on my way. I'll see you both at dinner." Ben smiled and closed the hall door behind him.

"So, my dear. A sad time for all, isn't it? How are you settling in?"

"I'm kind of overwhelmed at the moment. I never expected to inherit Cairnwell, and I don't know what to do with it. Would you like some tea?"

"Thank you. I would indeed."

"It's a good thing Dr. Reese was here on sabbatical. He can help with some of the decisions. Whether to do the retreat, and how to set up the library if I decide to."

"So he's an archivist, is he?"

"He knows about coins and paintings and antique guns, as well as a lot of other things. Did Georgina talk to you about the retreat?"

"I know she wished to use Cairnwell to benefit young or needy scholars. Including one particular young man in her department. She intended to select the scholars herself, with assistance from the poet, David Lindsay."

"*That's* it. I couldn't remember his name."

"She really was an exceptional woman, Georgina. Very much respected by one and all." Colin was wearing a long-sleeved cotton shirt under a wool sweater, but he was rubbing his hands as though they were cold.

And Ellen saw then that his hands were covered by bruises and splotches from all the IVs in the hospital. "Can I get you a jacket?"

"No, I'm fine. Thank you." He always spoke in a precise, educated English accent, but his voice sounded fainter and breathier than normal.

"You knew Ross for a long time, didn't you?"

"We attended the same preparatory school near Glasgow. I was six years older, so we had hardly more than a nodding acquaintance. Until we met at a history lecture years later in Edinburgh. He was running Fletcher Tire, and he found him-self in desperate need of someone who could sort out certain difficulties concerning his rubber suppliers. I'd grown up in Malaya, and I agreed to try my hand. Then stayed on for more than twenty years as chief purchasing agent. I wish I could've seen Georgina again. I was in hospital when she left for Oxford, and we had very little chance to chat. I had pneumonia as well this time, and they kept me for nearly a fortnight."

"But you're better now?"

"Oh, much better, thank you, yes."

"You probably shouldn't have come to the funeral."

"How could I not have paid my respects? Georgina and Ross were kinder to me than I can possibly express."

"So both houses were empty while she was gone. Of course, Jack would've been here. And Michael Shaw. In case there'd been an emergency."

"Neither of them was here. No, Winifred MacNicol, who keeps me up to the mark as you know, she mentioned that Jack was away when I was in hospital. Michael Shaw was somewhere in the south of England. And Lady Hay was off too at one of her antique shows. Sir John was so pleased to be home alone, he was seen walking the public footpaths day and night, throwing sticks for the dog and whistling military airs." Colin smiled and his eyes twinkled and the pale papery skin looked slightly pinker. "I apologize, my dear. It's very naughty of me to gossip behind our neighbors' backs."

"Yes, it is. You should be ashamed of yourself."

They both laughed, seconds before the huge bronze bell thundered by the front door.

"You go, my dear. I shall toddle off home through the scullery."

"Did you walk?"

"No, but I shall, I trust, very soon. I look forward to seeing you at dinner."

ℙℙℙℙ

"Lady Hay." Ellen was standing on the cocoa matting in the front hall holding the door with her left hand.

"Good morning, Miss Winterr. I hope I haven't called too early?" She was tall, hatted, sinewy, and thin, her pale lips set against each other and her eyes fierce.

"No, of course not. Won't you come in."

"Just for a moment. If it's quite convenient."

Ellen led her down the hall to the low studded dining room door, stooping slightly as she stepped through, before waiting by the long oak table. "If you'd like a cup of tea, I can make a fresh pot."

"No, thank you. I won't stay, and I don't wish to impose." She straightened the jacket of her gray suit, then pulled at the sleeves of her white cotton blouse.

"It won't take me a minute to—"

"I said no, my dearr. You needn't feel obligated. I wish to talk to you about the futurre of the county. May I sit?"

"Of course."

"As you know, your…benefactress…instituted cairtain changes on her property in the last few yearrs which affected the neighborhood as well. All too adversely, as any of your nearr neighbors will tell you. The public footpath has imposed on all of our good natures, as has the pony trekking."

"But—"

"The quarry is a loud, degrrading frivolity of Ross Fletcher's which was only underrtaken as a tax benefit, as I'm sure you vera well know."

"No, what he—"

"The excuse he gave was that he was using the stone for repairrs to the estate, while aiding an up-and-coming artist, but all of us have known from the beginning that it was nothing but a ruse to offset the ridiculous profits he made from Fletcher Tire."

"I know that's not true, because——"

"Don't be naive, my dearr. It doesn't suit ye. The new Fletcherr enthusiasms, the falconry centerr, of all things, and the writers retreat, will not be looked upon locally with a tolerant eye. The Fletchers had the funds to see litigation through. Whether you do or not, I don't know, but there will be local opposition, should you intend to carry out Georgina Fletcherr's plans."

A red tide was rising on Ellen's throat, and her eyes sparkled dangerously, as she clenched her hands in her lap. "Georgina was not starting a falconry center, as far as I know. Whether I will or not, I haven't decided. I'm considering the writers retreat. But in either case, I won't make a snap decision."

"I cairtainly hope we can count on you not to run roughshod over the wishes of your older neighbors. Those whose lives will cairtainly be altered for the worse by eitherr undertaking. There is much to be said for community feeling. Living in isolation can be vera unpleasant indeed."

Ellen stood, walked to the hall door and held it open, her ponytail swinging behind her, her straight black eyebrows pulled close together. "I understand you were a nurse before you married. You must have learned quite a bit about food poisoning, working as many years as you did. You weren't here when Georgina died, were you?"

Lady Isabelle Hay looked taken aback. She wore no makeup, and what color there had been seemed to have drained away. "I'm many things, Miss Winterr, but I'm not a hypocrite. I never pretended to admirre the Fletchers and their high-handed ways. Neither do I shrink from saying what I think. I came here today to lay my cards on the table, as you Americans say, hoping to appeal to your sense of fair play. If I have offended you, and clearly I have, I apologize. Still, I ask you to consider the rights of those who surround Cairnwell, not just the wishes of its…present owner. Good day."

"Thank you for stopping by."

Isabelle Hay heard the sarcasm, and she turned beside the stone well in the courtyard and looked at Ellen. She seemed to consider saying something more. But decided against it, finally, and walked away, the sturdy heels of her black oxfords sinking in the gravel between the flagstones.

CHAPTER FOUR

BEN DROVE NORTH THROUGH AS MANY SHADES of green as grew, in crops and grassland and strips of trees, along the boundaries of family roots—until an hour out of Aberdeen, he came to two stone columns in cut stone walls and read DEVON HOUSE etched in brass on the right.

He drove past into a tunnel of green—cool, shaded, sheltering, between tall slender moss-covered trunks, the leaves high overhead above hawthorn and rowan and wild redbud, thicketed underneath by shrubs Ben couldn't name.

It was a long drive in watery green light that ended in an arch of white where a quick left turn turned into the open in front of a white classical stucco house with a gray stone portico on five stone pillars.

A handwritten note was tacked to the black door:

On the river.
Walk round house on left.
Take path down hill.

"Be with you in a moment." Gwen Fitzgerald was fly-fishing in the middle of the Deveron River, ten or fifteen feet from the near bank, a basket creel hanging behind her in the water, a long loop of line in her left hand, her right whipping the pole like a gossamer wand, dropping the fly upstream with the delicacy of a ballet dancer flicking a silk scarf.

Her left hand twitched the line the way spiders play the threads of their webs, and the wet line glinted in the sun slinging beads of water, as the fly skipped the river.

Ben slung his jacket over his shoulder as he watched— knee high in coarse lush river grass, standing in bright sun, by a deep clear fast-moving brown river with a quicksilver skin reflecting the sky—admiring the precision, the concentration, the instinct and the understanding of the world of water and wind, the relaxed patient strength in the long thin arms and narrow shoulders.

She reeled in all her line the next time, and then started wading to shore. "Doesn't the sun feel grand?"

"It's my favorite kind of day." Ben was surprised when he saw her face. It was older than he'd expected, late fifties or early sixties, when the rest of her would've looked good on anybody thirty. "Did you catch anything?"

"Two middling brown trout. Enough for dinner. I've a couple arriving this afternoon to stay the weekend. You know I'm running Devon House as an inn?"

"Yes."

Gwen climbed out of her waders, refastened the wooden clip that held her caramel and gray hair at the nape of her neck, gathered her rod and creel and started off up the path. "So you're a friend of Ellen Winter's, are you?"

"Yes. May I carry something?"

"If I tried to rearrange the load, I'd fall on my nose." She smiled as she looked over her shoulder, until her eyebrows gathered over her sunglasses and her narrow mouth settled into a serious preoccupied line. "I've been brooding about Georgina ever since we spoke on the phone. I don't mean by that that I hadn't before. No, her death was a *very* painful shock. Losing the person who's been one's closest friend the length of one's entire life is no small matter."

"No, I'm sure it's not."

"But to hear that Georgina feared she'd be murdered, well...that's a terrible thought. You brought the letter, did you?"

"A photocopy."

"Good. Shall I read while you clean trout?" Gwen grinned back at Ben.

And he laughed and said, "I don't think it would be good for you to get away with it!"

"Well, one can't be blamed for trying it on." She was climbing a twisting path cut into the steep grassy hill toward a wood.

Ben was walking behind her, staring across the water at a wide green band of grain sweeping up to higher fields. "I could watch that for a while. The woods on your side of the river. The farms on the other."

"I know. I still look out my window in the morning and can't believe I'm here. I'm very, very grateful indeed."

"Do you own the bank on the other side?"

"No, and I have had the odd nightmare that the farmer's sold up and a housing estate's turned up overnight." She didn't say anything else for a minute, she just leaned into the hill and climbed. "So, you actually believe, do you, that Georgina was murdered?"

"I have no evidence except her letter. Though I do have a fairly strong conviction that Georgina was no fool."

"She was one of the most intelligent people I've ever met.

Though that hardly means one isn't a fool. As I'm sure you know, as an academic."

"Yes, only too well."

"They found no trace of poison, or any sort of drug? Georgina hated taking medication, and any would be suspicious."

"No. And she died of asphyxiation. Material was sucked into her lungs while she was being sick."

"I know. Dear Georgina."

"Yet they don't know what caused the vomiting. I suppose it could've been flu *or* food poisoning. Deliberately introduced or not. But if Georgina was right, and other deaths she knew of were undiscovered murders, *if* the same method was used, it's got to be tough to detect. And I've got nothing to go on."

"It's early days yet, after all." Gwen dropped her waders on the flagstone terrace by the kitchen door, and hung the bamboo rod horizontally on two hooks on the outside wall. She carried the creel to a wooden board bracketed to an oak on the edge of the woods, pulled a filleting knife off a hook at one end, and began filleting a speckled brown trout.

"Ellen says Georgina had a friend at Aberdeen who's retired now. A poet from her department."

"David Lindsay. He moved to central Scotland after he retired. Northwest of Dunkeld, I think. Possibly on Loch Rannoch."

"Would I find his number in her address book?"

"You should do, yes." Gwen worked for a minute in silence, then scraped scraps of fin and bone into a coffee can that hung from a nail on the tree.

"Did Georgina have any enemies you can think of?"

"That's an unbending word. Enemies. People with whom

she'd been in conflict? Those who were jealous of her abilities? Or her position? Or her possessions?"

"Those who didn't wish her well for any reason you can think of."

"One comes rapidly to mind, yes. Shall we pop these in the refrigerator and make a cup of tea?"

"Well?" Ben was sitting at a long pine table in a large rectangular bottle green kitchen, pouring boiling water into a brown ceramic pot, watching Gwen refold the photocopy of Georgina's letter.

"You mean 'the enemy' I suppose?"

"That, and your reaction to the letter."

"Well, first of all, it's important to remember that individuals of their sort, Ross and Georgina's, who start new ventures and develop businesses, who use their property in unusual ways, often put other people's backs up. They can't help having ideas of their own. They're easily bored with what's been done, and they can't seem to keep themselves from trying to make improvements. Ross ran his business efficiently and creatively, which must've offended those who don't like to be challenged. He reopened their quarry. Georgina established a footpath. She allowed pony trekking, and let Jack Corelli raise and hunt his hawks. She was very much taken up with this idea of opening a writers retreat. And there was bound to be opposition."

"Why do you think she opened her land to other people, when she must've known her neighbors might object? I don't mean she shouldn't have, but what went through her head?"

"Altruism, largely. A desire to use what fortune had bestowed on her for the benefit of others. It also may have come from not having had children when she'd wanted them rather badly. There was never the focus of energy that raising children demands. The organizing and planning and providing for the future of one's home and possessions with an eye to the welfare of the children. That was part of why being a professor suited her down to the ground. It provided an outlet. Took her from family to public considerations. To having many children over the years, instead of a few, in the students whose lives she touched."

"Who was especially irritated by the choices she made on the estate?"

"You must've heard of Isabelle Hay. And there were others too, on nearby farms, who thought she went too far, with the hawks, and the footpath in particular." Gwen stretched her arms overhead and rubbed her right shoulder before picking up the tea tray and leading Ben into the dining room. There was a long table in the middle of that large yellow and white room, but she set the tray on a smaller square table in the wide round bay that looked down across the terrace to the river. "Yet it's Robbie MacAlpin who comes to mind. He's a professor in the English department at Aberdeen."

"Ellen mentioned there was someone there who resented Georgina, but she didn't know much about him."

"How could she? Georgina refused to gossip. While I myself rather enjoy it." Gwen laughed, and handed Ben his tea. "I've seen a great deal of harm done in this world because someone won't call a spade a spade."

"I know what you mean, but isn't gossip an easy way out too? The attack behind the back. Isn't it as gutless as tiptoeing around what needs to be hit head on?"

"Perhaps. It-tis directness I admire. And Georgina herself

was very direct. Even though she wouldn't discuss her troubles coping with others except in the broadest terms. That's why all I know for certain about Robbie MacAlpin is that he's a gentleman of around forty who was very much of the opinion that the time had come for Georgina to get out of the department and make a bit of room. It's a matter of jealousy, as far as I'm concerned. And I think it started when the publisher who published her book on Trollope wasn't interested in his on Hardy. David Lindsay can tell you more. He observed the situation firsthand."

"Did Robbie resent other people in the department as much as he did Georgina?"

"I have no way of knowing. Though part of his trouble may be that his wife's a tenured professor, in bacteriology I think, at Aberdeen, while he has yet to be awarded tenure. Blaming Georgina came easier, I shouldn't wonder, than opening that particular can of worms, for G. was a woman of independent means who didn't need to teach. Whose staying on could be used to explain why promotion eluded him. I saw his reaction to G. myself at more than one departmental lecture." Gwen drank her tea, watching Ben over her white china cup, as he stared at the Deveron River, his eyes hard and his jaw set off to one side. "You look as though you've glimpsed a motive."

"No, not really. I was thinking about something else. Did Georgina talk about anything that struck you as unusual when you spoke to her in the last weeks?"

"I don't think so. Nothing occurs to me at the moment."

"Would you say Georgina was the kind of person who only talked about certain things with one person, and something else with another? We all divide our lives to some degree, but I have the feeling she was more like that than most. That she didn't just talk to her close friends about whatever was on her mind, the way a lot of people do."

"There was much she wouldn't discuss. It may have come from being isolated as a child. At Cairnwell. With no mother a-tall. An emotionally distant father. A grandmother who couldn't be satisfied. For you see, Georgina was very restrained when we met at the age of ten. Very polite and correct. Though there was steel in her backbone. When she knew what to do, she'd do it. But it took a very long time for her to talk about what she thought and felt."

"She talked to you, though?"

"I understood something of what she'd been through. My father died when I was quite young, and my mother took a job as housekeeper for a largish hotel in Dunkeld. I was raised there, virtually alone, the only English child amongst strangers, and I had to learn to shift for myself as well."

"Dunkeld House? Behind the cathedral on the Tay?"

"Yes, that's where I learned to fly-fish. I also learned to brazen it out, and take the upper hand when I could. Georgina watched the world very stoically, then quietly chose her own way." Gwen reached for the Moroccan box in the center of the square table, took out a filtered cigarette and lit it with a kitchen match she pulled from a Japanese cup. "We spent more than forty-five years questioning one another, and encouraging each other, and comforting one another too. I never could've bought this house without G. No, I worked in Edinburgh for many years, longing to find a house on a river I could run as a small inn catering to fly-fishing parties. But it was G. who found Devon House, and then loaned me the down payment seven years ago. When I was ready to pay back my first install-ment on the loan, she refused to take it. She said, 'Do the same sort of thing for someone else.'"

"That's the way it should be a lot more times than it is."

"I still feel uneasy about it. But it's been enough of a struggle here, managing all the repairs that had to be done straightaway that I wasn't able to insist as forcefully as I would've liked. The house had been open to the elements for twenty years before I bought it, which was why I could afford it a-tall."

"But she still irritated other people?"

"One or two." Gwen picked up two gold signet rings from a blue Chinese bowl on the table and slipped one on the little finger of her right hand, and the other on her wedding ring finger. "You must've heard about the batty farmer with the walled garden."

"Yes. But there was nothing that struck you as unusual about her conversation? Especially in the last month? No sense of worry, or a change in interest?"

"She did seem preoccupied the last few weeks, but I don't have the first idea what it could've been about."

"Is there family background I should know?"

"I can't think of anything." Gwen leaned forward then, in her chair, and crossed her arms on the table. "No, that's not true. During the war, in September of 1940—you'll see why I remember exactly when it happened in a moment—her grandfather wrote her father, who was working with the War Office then in London, to say that he'd found something in the attic that seriously affected the family. He'd been sorting it out to accommodate the belongings of the several children being sent to Cairnwell away from London and the blitz. And apparently a letter, or some sort of paper, fell out of the spine of an old family Bible.

"He was journeying down to London to discuss what

ought to be done, because of it. And G.'s father wrote to her, telling her what the grandfather had written, and saying he'd let her know what the old gentleman was on about after they'd met. Of course, the Luftwaffe struck that day, on September 15, with the worst daylight bombing raid of the entire war. And both her grandfather and her father were killed walking away from the Savoy Grill."

"How hard must that've been on Georgina?"

"It was terribly hard. Very definitely. That was part of the reason she didn't choose to live at Cairnwell until several years after the war. It brought back the loss of her family very forcefully. Of greater interest to you, perhaps, and why I didn't think of it earlier I don't know, is that the day before G. went to Oxford—"

"June 2?"

"I think that's right, yes. She called and told me she now knew what had upset her grandfather, and that when I came down to Oxford, which we'd planned for the first week in July, she'd have some interesting news."

"That's all she said?"

"Yes. I should've thought of it sooner."

"Who else would she have talked to, if something was bothering her, or she felt that she was in danger?"

"David Lindsay. Or her minister perhaps, whatever his name is. Those would be the only other two, as far as I know." Gwen leaned against the back of her mahogany chair, both elbows on the arms, watching a curl of smoke drift toward the ceiling. "There was one other thing she said that was a bit out of the ordinary when we had lunch in Aberdeen. It was the middle of May, and we talked about all sorts of things. Ross's business...Ah. That's a thought. You really ought to talk to Ross's nephew, Tommy Ogilvie. Or someone who's actually at

Fletcher. Arthur Shaw, I suppose. The acting general manager. Someone who could tell you about the business side of G.'s life.

"Anyway, I remember we talked about Devon House, and what I could do to drum up business. We were discussing how different people spend, or save, their money, and she asked if I understood collectors. The sort who'd sell their souls for a coin or a stamp or a piece of Sevres. We both agreed that we couldn't comprehend it. And then the conversation took another turn. It may have been nothing but a momentary thought, but I had the feeling, and I don't know why, that she asked in earnest. That she'd been thinking about collectors with serious purpose."

"Did she know any?"

"Not that I know of. David Lindsay has bought one or two old books over the years, but that's all I can think of. Though I seem to remember Georgina saying that Isabelle Hay is rather keen on buying antiques."

"What work did you do before you started the inn?"

"Why do you wish to know?" Gwen looked steadily at Ben and asked in a pleasant voice.

But Ben could see she expected a serious answer. "No real reason. Except that it could give me a greater degree of insight into the way you evaluate what's around you."

Gwen studied him silently for several seconds, then took another drag on her cigarette. "I was secretary to two generations of presidents in a family-owned manufacturing firm in Edinburgh. The gentleman I worked for the last several years was the grandson of the founder, and I was routinely expected to make decisions which should've been his to make. It was quite pitiable, and perhaps even inconceivable to anyone who hasn't observed such a situation. In what was, oddly enough, a very paternalistic sort of business. Employees were treated as children by son and grandson alike, though neither could cope with any but the mildest forms of unpleasantness. They were both blusterers in trivial matters, yet utterly unwilling to follow proper lines of command. I grew quite weary of working sixty hours a week, being paid not very much, and feeling myself condescended to as some sort of spinster aunt."

Ben had been staring at the ashtray, listening to the coldness that had taken control of her voice. And then he looked directly at her. "You never married?"

"No. Not that it's any of your business." She French inhaled again and smiled.

"I thought maybe your signet rings had once been used as wedding bands."

"Did you?" She twisted the larger one on her wedding ring finger before she said anything more. "These are Forbes rings. His. The ones we'd intended to use. Will was captain of a merchant vessel torpedoed in the North Atlantic."

"I'm sorry."

"I've only met two men in my life whom I thought worthy of the sacrifice of my own independence. One of them was Ross Fletcher." Gwen laughed and crushed her cigarette out in the small silver ashtray beside a potted white begonia. "Georgina used to tell me she'd write a codicil to her will asking Ross to marry me if she were to die first." Gwen's face turned very red very suddenly and tears gathered in her eyes and she got up and walked to the window. "She left me her clothes, you know. And most of her jewelry, and three or four very fine pieces of furniture I'd admired. She left me five thousand pounds outright, and all of Ross's fly rods. And all I want is Georgina to talk to on the telephone twice a week and meet once a month somewhere, the way we always did. I don't want to grow into an old woman, which I shall do in a very few years' time, with no one to talk to who understands in the slightest degree how I've lived my life."

"I know exactly what you mean. I feel that way myself."

Gwen shook her head very quickly, and then shoved her hands in the pockets of her khaki pants.

"But for me, the most important thing at the moment is that I need to understand Georgina. I've read some of her correspondence. I've read literary papers she's written. I've plowed through her checkbooks. But the woman herself, the kinds of things she would've talked about, with her husband, or with you. Her conception of herself, and what she wanted in life. The ways she would've puttered in her own house. I don't have a good sense of her, and I need one fast."

"She was always polite, but very forthright in her professional dealings. Extremely concerned with being rational and fair, yet also a bit naive. At least in my opinion. She was quite religious, you know, well past the age of reason. Very much different than I in that regard. Ross was the one who led her in that direction. Many years ago, of course. But she didn't suffer fools gladly in any circumstances, and she hated needlessly long discussions and any sort of beating about the bush."

"It sounds like I would've liked her."

"It-tisn't possible to sum someone up in a few words, is it? Not someone you've known well. It's much easier with a person you've just met. One quick caricature, and a smug sense of superiority."

"That's exactly right."

Neither of them spoke for a minute. They both just stared at the river.

"Well. I guess I ought to get going." Ben pushed his chair back and stood up.

"Would you care to see a lovely view on your way?"

"Sure."

"Then when you start back up the drive, don't go straight to the gate. Turn right, right away, into the side track. It takes you by the stables, which are leased out as flats, then past the kitchen garden. At the end of that, there's a wild bit of wood on your right. Get out and walk there. It leads to a lovely beech walk at the bottom of the wood by the water."

"I don't have time to walk far."

"At least trot into the small wood and look for Vaida's grave. For you see, an earlier owner of Devon House went on Scott's 1910 expedition to Antarctica. He was left at base camp, and later helped search for survivors. He brought home a sledge dog he admired very much, and buried her in the wood when she died years later. Very few people seem able to find her gravestone."

"Then I guess I'll have to give it a try."

"Good. I would. Then when you drive past a lone farm, after the wood, bear left at the turning, and you'll curve back around to the front drive."

Ben had walked the woods, and driven off, and was pulling out into the green tunnel just inside the front posts, ready to turn right toward the main road, when he saw Gwen running up the drive on his left with grim determination on her strong-boned face.

He was standing when she got to him, smiling to himself.

And she said, "Let me get my breath," before she put her hands on hips, and leaned forward, panting and staring at the ground.

"Did you think of something else?"

She nodded but didn't say anything for another few seconds. "Georgina's poems."

"I didn't know she wrote poems."

Gwen nodded and straightened halfway up. "*There* she said precisely what she thought."

"Did she publish them?"

"No, she never even talked about them with anyone but Ross. Of course she told me she wrote poems. And that she went through them at the end of every year and selected a handful to keep and add to her collected poems. She started writing poems at the age of ten. She was very determined then never to show them to her father."

"Did you ever read any?"

"She showed me four in all the years I knew her. She never thought them any good. She said she loved poetry far too much to take her own mediocrities seriously. No, they were more of a diary. Which helped her express what she felt, and analyze others, as nothing else could, with the added intellectual interest of working in poetic form."

"Do you know where she put them?"

"No, but I do know she kept them hidden. In earlier years, she packed the old portfolios in a cedar trunk. An antique marriage trunk of some kind, that was usually in her bedroom. Though what she's done with them recently I couldn't say. I do feel sure she would've had her current ones with her in Oxford. Though they would've been well hidden. Yes, well away from prying eyes."

"Then maybe I better go to Oxford."

"I would've thought you would've gone in any case."

"True, but the poems may make me go sooner."

"Did you find Vaida's grave?"

"Maybe. Why do you want to know?"

They both laughed. Then Ben said it was interesting, the wild woods and the grave, and he was glad he'd taken the time. Then he climbed back in his black Mini-Cooper. And waved as he pulled through the gate.

Jack Corelli stepped into the small wooden shed, which was so new it smelled of pine shavings, with a brown and black Harris hawk perched on his gloved hand. Her neck feathers were ruffled and her head was swiveling from side to side, while her black yellow-rimmed eyes fixed first on the window, then Jack's eyes, then the old-fashioned balance scale on the high bench.

"Okay, Jez, let's see how much you weigh." Jezebel hopped off his fist on to the bar balance and Jack dropped small brass weights into the balance dish. "One pound eleven ounces. That'll work, won't it? Let's put on your hood." He let her look at it first, and then she held her head still for Jack to slip it on.

She sat on his glove again, on his left fist, the tiny leather hood pulled tight by his teeth and his right hand, the bells jingling on the jesses (the thin leather thongs tied to her ankles) as he slid them in between his gloved fingers. "Let's go see what's out there."

They walked a quarter of a mile behind the shed to a wild grassy space where an evergreen wood turned into hardwoods on their left, and the ground gradually changed on the right from uneven grassland to heather and gorse.

As soon as he slipped off Jezebel's hood, her eyes flashed from side to side, seeing infinitely more than his—and then she flew, bells jingling, to perch on an oak branch fifteen yards away.

Her eyes flicked from left to right, from one tuft of grass to another, from branches beside and below, in trees nearby and far off, from scrub bushes back to grass, even before Jack began walking toward the gorse along the line of sycamores that curved away from the woods.

He pulled a dead day-old chick out of his canvas game bag and tore a leg off, slipping it between his left thumb and finger, walking and whistling for Jezebel, who flew to his fist and ate the piece of raw meat.

Jack watched the ground ahead, while Jezebel stared at a great deal more. And then, as he pulled his arm back and threw it forward, she flew up toward the band of sycamores, then turned and shot toward the gorse on the trail of a startled rabbit. She dove and missed and veered off toward the trees, perching where she could see what Jack might unearth, as well as the world beyond.

They hunted—Jack calling her back, making her stay close, feeding her pieces of chick—for almost an hour. And in that time there were four more misses, three more close strikes and one kill, when Jezebel swooped from a branch to pin a rabbit Jack flushed, her wings out as she sat on it, mantling it with her whole body, while ripping and swallowing tiny bits of flesh.

Jack let her eat for a minute, then told her to hop on his fist and fed her a piece of chick, while he slipped the rabbit in his bag. "You're a smart old girl, aren't you, Jez? I'll give you more rabbit when we get home."

She flew five more times on their way to the shed, snagging one more rabbit, who twisted away from her beak and claws down a convenient burrow. Then as Jack sent her off the last time, a low voice asked if they'd caught anything.

Jack turned to his right in time to see Ben step out from the edge of the fir woods. "Yeah. One rabbit."

"How often do you have to work with your birds?"

"Every day. You either train them or hunt them, if you want them to stay fit."

"Is she the kind of hawk that dives straight down?"

"No. Jezebel's a Harris hawk. Hawks are short-wings. They catch ground quarry like rabbits. Falcons are long-wings. They climb way up and stoop straight down, and can also catch birds in midair." Jack called Jezebel to his fist, gave her the last bit of baby chick, and slipped the hood over her eyes.

"You have other birds, right?"

"A male Harris and an American red-tail."

"So will they hunt if they aren't hungry?"

"Nope. You figure out what the right hunting weight is for each of them, and keep them right in that range. Hungry enough to hunt, but well fed and strong enough to fly well. You have to check their weight every day."

"She's beautiful."

Jack looked at Ben as though that was a ridiculous remark, and walked faster than before.

"I'd like to talk to you about Donald Murray."

"Why?"

"Because of Ellen."

Jack didn't stop walking, but he looked like he'd thought about it, before he considered Ben out the corners of his cold black eyes. "I don't know anything about Murray. I gotta put Jez away."

Jack opened the door to her wooden cage (six feet high by five feet wide) and she flew to her perch and worked on her feathers, while he pulled her water bowl out of a metal ring on the wall. "What does Donald Murray have to do with Ellen? And why talk to me, not her?"

"I'm her professor—"

"Yeah, I know." Jack looked studiously unimpressed as he closed the cage door.

"And she wants my help trying to decide what to do here. The quarry, the retreat, the idea of the falconry business. Whether to stay here full time, or part time, or try to sell."

"So where does Donald Murray come in?"

"He surprised her by the crypt last night, and she thought he was deliberately threatening. You've been around him. You may have seen him more than she has. Is he dangerous or nuts or the kind of guy who just plays games?"

"Did he touch her?" Jack was standing in front of the cages staring at Ben, not watching the hose as he filled the first of the metal bowls.

"No, he didn't. But I'm leaving tomorrow for a few days, and she'll be alone in the house. She's going to see if the cleaning lady can spend the night—"

"Her *name* is Grace MacNicol."

"Thanks. I haven't met her yet, so—"

"I never thought of Murray as dangerous, but I can move up to the house too."

"And you're trustworthy, are you?" Ben was smiling.

But Jack didn't look amused. "So who are you to act like you own her?" Jack had shut the hose off by holding it looped in his left hand, and he was staring hard at Ben.

"Nobody. Her aged mentor."

"Yeah, right." Jack fed and watered all three birds, as well as the ferret family, and he padlocked the doors to their cages without saying anything else. He straightened the shed then and put away the game bag, and locked the door behind him.

"Who would have a good sense of what Donald Murray's like?"

"Maybe Ramsay. Except he keeps to himself. Shaw too I guess. The sculptor. He's back. He's been hanging around a lot since Ellen got here."

"Because she'll decide about the quarry?"

Jack Corelli didn't say anything or look at Ben as they walked toward the woods behind the dower house.

Ben watched him surreptitiously out of the left edges of his eyes while gazing at the field across the road. "I think it worries Ellen that the coroner didn't know much about how Georgina died."

"I don't know anything about it." Jack was moving fast, taking long strides on long legs, swinging his arms and staring straight ahead.

Ben said, "I s'ppose it must've been food poisoning."

"No. Vomit got in her lungs and killed her."

"Yes, but Ellen's kind of wondering what made her that sick. Georgina had been eating in restaurants, and as far as they know, nobody else got sick or died."

"Yeah, but people react differently. There's gotta be varying susceptibility to food contamination."

"I don't know much about it. I'd like to watch you hunt sometime."

"Yeah?"

"I'd also like to know what kind of falconry business you have in mind."

"Okay. Some night when we both have time."

Donald Murray unlocked the outside door into the mud room, pushing against stacks of old newspapers that shifted just enough for him to slip inside. He locked it behind him and pulled the chain across, then threw his filthy woolen jacket on the newspapers.

He'd left Dog out, but the mud room still smelled of him. Dog and cat. Mostly cat. Seven of them at that moment, shut in the mud room: spoiled milk in a chipped bowl; old cat food crushed on the floor; chewed bones too old to attract flies; cat feces; cat urine; a blanket tossed down as a cat-and-dog bed in the corner; old rubber boots thrown along walls; clothes that had once belonged to dead parents and dead aunts hanging on pegs or crumpled on piles of yellowed magazines; rusted milk cans and bits of barn equipment; cobwebs hanging from the unpainted ceiling, holding once whitewashed walls together.

Donald didn't talk to the cats, as he wiped his forehead on his shirt sleeve and walked toward the kitchen, dried mud dropping off his boots; cats streaking away from his feet, sneezing, yellow matter in their eyes, shaking their heads like mites were chewing at their brains; slow, dull-coated, emaciated cats scrambling through as he opened the door to the kitchen.

He turned on the radio before he turned on the gas ring, and then he walked back around several open bags of garbage to the worn stone sink. His back was to the stove, and the door to the dining room beside it, and he was pouring water from the tap into an old battered kettle, when a voice behind him made him drop the kettle on the stone floor.

"What's the matter with you, Donald?" Ben was ten feet away from him and moving closer fast, his mouth tight and contemptuous and his voice cold and cutting. "You have to scare women and children to feel like a man?"

"How'd ye get in! Ye have no rright to be herre! Get out, do ye hearr me? Get out of my house now!"

"I watched you today, Donald." Ben twisted Donald around and shoved his chest against the outside wall, wrenching his right arm behind his back. "I've been watching you just like you spied on Georgina, and you're spying on Ellen now. I saw what you did to Dog today. And I heard what you said to your nephew's boy. You're a big man, aren't you, Donald? Yeah, a real tough guy."

"Ye have no right—"

"SHUT UP! Don't say another word till I tell you to! You got that?" Ben shoved Donald harder against the wall, and Donald nodded his head. "I knew a guy from New York when I was in Belgium during the war who was the same kind of coward you are. Are you listening to me, Donald?"

"Aye!"

"He'd find someone smaller and weaker, someone wounded already, a dog sometimes, even an orphan, some homeless kid begging for food on the street, and he'd push them any way he could. *You* know what I mean, don't you, Donald? He'd make them think their lives were in his hands. And then he'd play with them, and torture them slowly, like rats in a cage." Ben was right behind Donald Murray, looking down on the left side of Murray's face, staring at the red-rimmed eye, with the smell of filth in his nostrils as Donald cowered against the wall. "I'm not going to tell you what I did to him. I wasn't myself right then. I'd just found *hundreds* of dead American POWs that the Germans had machine-gunned at Malmedy, and I'd fought the four-day battle we took on because of them. I'd been up six days straight, and I was feeling really ragged, and I saw this little puny guy from New York kick a Belgian woman in the back."

"My hand!" Donald was shaking.

But Ben didn't let go of him. He leaned closer and whispered in his ear. "If you *ever* bother Ellen Winter in *any* way, *ever* again, I will make you wish you were *dead!* Listen to me now, Donald! I will teach you what suffering feels like. I will make you live with fear and pain till you will *never* be the same. Are you paying attention, Donald?"

"Aye!"

"So you understand what I'm saying?" Ben spun Donald around, put both hands on the front of his stinking shirt and picked him up and held him at his own eye level, keeping Donald's back against the cold stone wall.

Someone was knocking on the outside door. And Ben dropped Donald from where he was. Then walked into the mud room and unlocked the door for a worn looking woman holding a stack of folded clothes.

Dog was sitting beside her, thumping his tail, his long filthy matted brown coat shedding in uneven tufts, a festered cut across the top of his head, his timid eyes afraid to look at Ben.

"Ye've taken my breath away! I neverr expected to see a stranger in this house."

"I'm sorry. I didn't mean to startle you."

"Is my uncle at home a-tall?"

"He's in the kitchen."

"Well, I hardly know what to say to ye. Though this has been a month for surprises, and no mistake. Poor Georgina Witney, as she once was. That was a terrible blow. And Uncle, taking the train. None of us could believe our eyes. You're up at Cairnwell, are ye?"

"Yes. Where'd your uncle go?"

"I've no idea, and he won't say. He hasn't been away since I don't know when. I apologize for the state of things. Since Grandfather died, he lives as he pleases."

"Yes, I can see that."

"I wash his clothes, and I can make him change every otherr

week." She started to laugh, but there was something about Ben's face that cut the urge off in her throat.

"When did your uncle take the train?"

"Oh, a week or two ago. Right before Miss Georgina died. He was gone for two whole days."

"I see. Excuse me. I have to go." Ben stepped past her, out into a tangle of outside cats milling in the gravel by the door. He patted Dog's border collie–shaped head and looked at the cut, and then rubbed Dog's chin, when he was finally brave enough to let him.

Dog followed him all the way to the road after that. And Ben stopped and petted him, letting him lean against his legs, letting Dog sit and sigh and look up at him with hopeless eyes.

Ben told him to stay and started toward Cairnwell House.

Then he turned. And walked back to Murray's door.

The niece answered his knock, and the look on her face was alarmed this time, half frightened and half amazed.

"This is for your Uncle Donald." Ben handed her a twenty-pound note.

She took it, staring at it, with her mouth hanging open.

"Tell him I'm taking Dog."

"He—"

"Tell him too that I never want to hear he's got another dog. And it's time he started taking care of the cats."

"I beg your pardon?"

"Just tell him. He'll understand what I mean."

"Will he?" She smiled that time.

And Ben said, "Thanks," before he turned and walked toward Dog, who was sitting with his head hanging, watching Ben from the road.

CHAPTER FIVE

Sunday, June 18th

"I DON'T KNOW WHY, REALLY, but I haven't let this room since Georgina died. Of course, with you being a friend of Ellen Winter's, and knowing about the letter as you do…" The soft slow voice trailed away as Penelope Long walked into the bedroom, closed the door behind her, and handed Ben the key. "It was a terrible shock that last night, you know, actually hearing G. say she might soon die. Though nothing like the horror of watching her do so so very cruelly."

"It's a good thing you mailed the letter."

"I couldn't have lived with myself if I hadn't. It went against the grain, not mentioning it to the police, but I had promised G."

"Did Georgina seem upset that last night, or afraid?" Ben was standing with his back to the front windows watching Penelope Long, his mouth set and serious, his eyes dark and hidden, in the shadows made by the ceiling light.

"She was every bit as businesslike as usual. And that makes it sadder still." Penelope pulled her handkerchief from inside a brown tartan sleeve and wiped her eyes under her glasses. "She saw the danger, she faced it all alone, and then resigned herself to whatever came. She was a very strong person, Georgina. She didn't give way to displays of emotion, and she rarely allowed anyone to come to her aid in any way."

"Would you be able to find out what phone calls she got, and who her visitors were while she was here?"

"I can question the staff in the morning. I know there were telephone calls from students. And a colleague of hers called for her here two nights before she died. He's a Fellow at Magdalen, and he was escorting her to some sort of literary dinner. I've met him, but I can't recall his name. There was a young man too, who dropped by the morning she died and sat with her while she breakfasted on the terrace. Though I have no idea who he might have been."

"What did he look like?"

"I didn't see him. Sarah Smith did, while waiting table, and she said he was six feet tall, and quite thin, and had rather straight light brown hair. Rather like you, actually. There was nothing particularly eye-catching in his appearance. Though I don't mean to imply—"

"No, I understand. Georgina didn't say she was expecting anyone that morning?"

"She didn't, no, and I think she might've done if she had been."

"Can you give me the names and addresses of whatever guests ate breakfast on the terrace at the same time as Georgina? I'd also like to get in touch with the man who brought you the mushrooms."

"I shall have it all organized first thing tomorrow."

"Thank you. I appreciate it."

"I shouldn't think the mushrooms were in any way to blame. I ate an omelet precisely like Georgina's. The mushrooms had been sliced and sautéed together, and the cook simply spooned out a portion for each omelet from the fry pan."

"I understand, but I still may want to give him a call."

"Are you feeling peckish a-tall? I could make you up a bite of supper."

"No, I'm fine. I ate dinner on the train from Edinburgh to London."

"Well. I'll leave you to it then, shall I?"

"Thank you for all the help."

"Andrew Eastland! That's the name. The Fellow at Magdalen who escorted G. to the literary do at the Randolph."

"Good. That'll help a lot."

Penelope shut the door behind her.

And Ben turned and studied the room.

He began on the drawers in the desk. And then looked in all the other obvious places—the chest of drawers, the armoire, the bedside tables, beneath all the chair cushions and under the bed. He moved the area rugs in front of the fireplace and beside the bed, and then searched the bathroom.

When he came back, he walked to the bed. Then picked up the end of the mattress.

He found the portfolio in the middle, two or three feet from every edge.

He untied the ribbons in the chair by the fireplace and took out Georgina's poems.

The first page had her name on it, right in the center, followed, on another line, by "1961."

Ben looked to see if they were dated, or there was another way of determining whether they were arranged chronologically. Hoping he could figure out which ones she'd written last.

But there wasn't. And he started with the first one in the stack.

One fact
one sharp edge
one single-pointed piece of reality
and your life cracks.
Your past falls away
everything you thought was true
from the first moment you
opened your eyes
isn't.

Could he have known?
Could he have looked my mother in the eye?
Could he have raised me?
Or watched Elizabeth sigh?

Don't.
It's the eyes that say it.
Quiet.
above the lace ruff.
Hide it.
past the tea cups,
and over the withers of a nervous horse.
It's too late.
you know it-tis.
far too late already.
No.
No, it's not.
Don't listen.
Don't look at the eyes,
the slithering skin,
the flickering tongue,

the sideways slide.
Get out
of that part
of the garden.

The delicacy
the strength
the ability to see inside
past painted walls and fences
through smiles and shuttered flesh
and confusions of the soul.
To take that sight
to finger it and cut it and shape it till it lives
makes the rest look drab and pointless.
It seems fair
the obsession and the ruthlessness
for no one else sees and understands
and they have to be made to stand aside.
Except at night
alone
when the eyes blur
and the heart hurts
and the remembrances
look like pride
or madness.

innocent things—
an apple core
a walnut shell,
insides picked and eaten,
a torn satchel

dropped in the wood—
to tell me I'm being watched.
first, a face in the window,
a shadow in the trees,
the gate creaking open,
a footstep at night on a front slate—
bearable because of Ross.
worse in an empty shell
that creaks and sighs and shudders.
perhaps I should have left years ago.
fled.
decamped
given over.
given ground to madness
and let it breed
alone.

Ben laid the poems down and leaned his head against the upholstered chair.

There were fourteen poems, written in six months, that had to be taken seriously.

He sat for a while, making notes on a small leather-bound notepad. Then he read those four poems again and underlined a note he'd already written.

He looked at his watch and yawned, then picked up the next poem.

There's a bitterness there
that scorches the soul it touches.
The flesh that lies beside it
has withered away,

parched by the dry heat.
Yet goodness is always the reason given
for the curses and the condemnations
that flay far less than they exhaust.
Before I cover my head and seek sanctuary,
I pick through the embers
turning over this coal
and that charred stick
blowing away the ashes
and fanning the flames,
without intention,
as I search for the burning heart
consumed by envy and hurt pride
until I see,
finally,
where the hatred starts.

It's not blood,
or a deep seeded love of Ross
and his life's work.
I've known him since he was two
and there's nothing new in that direction.
the small blond head
looking toward his bed
and telling his mommy
he loved her too much to leave her,
one eye on a jam tart
one hand on his mother's heart
one mind working overtime
with an eye to the main chance.
Our little Tommy provides for Tommy

and when he tells you what he wants
there's another reason
deeper
darker
and more perverse.

Birds of prey
say something about the rest of us.
They won't hunt
if they're not hungry.
they watch
and arrange their feathers.
Though the slash of their claws
gives me pause.
the ripping beak
the cold eye,
like human eyes
with one desire.
They won't be mastered
these hawks and falcons.
they will hunt
with the one who helps,
who flushes the rabbits
and surprises the grouse
like a hunting dog
trained for their convenience.
And what about the one
who hunts with them?
the predator without wings
with a bigger brain?
Is it the chase,

or the blood,
or the wind in his face?
Or is it greed
for speed and power
that whips and drives
in spite of meat on the table
and a roof that won't leak.
Is it the land
in his hand
finally,
the urge to establish,
to govern,
to arrange and control
his fate and other's?
Would he kill
if the hate was hot enough
would he rip apart
with teeth and talon
to hold a heart
in his hand?

Ben stood up and walked to the front windows and stared at the empty terrace. He stretched his arms over his head while he listened to the sounds of students walking and laughing.

Then he sat down at the desk and called Alex to ask how Dog was.

Alex was in the sitting room at BalMacneil Farm when the call came through, he and Jane on the same deep sofa, backs against opposite ends, legs stretched out side by side, reading books and talking too, when something they read made them want to.

When the phone rang, Alex scrambled over the sofa back and grabbed it off the table, then lay back down, retrieving the book he'd dropped on Jane, before settling the phone on his thighs.

"Ben!...In Oxford, are you? Let me jot down the number." He found a scrap of paper in his shirt pocket and shoved it back when he'd finished. "You want to know about Dog, I presume? He's settling in rather well, actually. He attached himself to Jane straightaway and followed her all day. She's named him Joshua, as a means of encouragement, I expect, if that's acceptable to you...Really? He's rather a lovely golden color now, isn't he?... No, I think the trembling's better tonight, but he doesn't seem terribly fit. Though, of course, that may be a reaction to the shots Jennifer's given him. We'll be keeping him with us in our room tonight. And we will do, as long as he's here. He's lying here now, by the way, staring at Jane from beside the sofa...

"Not-a-tall. It is I, as you very well know, who am in your debt...Oh, I agree. You couldn't have left him where he was. You acted just as you should've done...Jennifer says the cut will heal all right in the end. It had been left like that for quite a while, though, and it had to be opened again and drained. You know, if you aren't able to take him to the States, we shall be more than happy to keep him with us...No, it's no imposition a-tall. He's a lovely chap, really...No, Jennifer's already left.

"What manuscripts?...Oh yes, of course! I have actually, just a quick glance...You know, do you, that the first line in Greek reads from left to right, while the second reads from right to left, and so on? Yes, and early Greek like this, from before the 1800s, is written without separation between words with the letters simply flowing together, so it can be a bit tedious, and I thought perhaps I'd start with the Witney manuscript instead. If, as you say, you'll be talking to the minister about the Greek memoir in the next few days, and can get the gist of it from him...You were right, of course. The Witney document does alternate between Medieval Church Latin and Medieval French. And I shall start on it first thing in the morning...Oh? Spoken by the man who saved Balnagard!... All right, yes...Jane sends her love...Best of luck on your end."

Monday, June 19th

The early morning sun, sliding over walls and around roofs, settled on Ben's face, warming his skin, making his muscles relax, as he sat in the southwest corner of The Parsonage terrace. He closed his eyes and let the peacefulness sink in. Till he remembered his oatmeal was getting cold, and his toast too, sitting in its metal rack.

He opened his briefcase and took out Georgina's poems, thinking how small the differences are that define cultures. Americans want their toast hot. Brits do everything they can think of to make the butter congeal on top.

Does time silence the senses?
Does it blind us to the secret self?
Do we see what we've been told to see
by long association,
by custom and courtesy,
by gentlemanly assumptions

by questions dropped
and absences explained away?

It happens in marriages.
the blind eye
the lapses overlooked
the glimpses into the abyss
that turn the insides cold with dread
that can't be remembered
and won't be named.
Couldn't friendship feel the same?
the longtime terror of being deceived
makes questions drop
like cries upon a coffin.

Am I ready yet?
Can I bear to care
for a living thing again?
Knowing I'll lose it
like Ross
and Bertie
and sweet Serene—
though heaven knows I shan't equate
the dogs and dear strong Ross.
He'd laugh though
to read this.
understanding all too well
how we loved too much
and took the blows to heart.
though when I am ready
I shall know where to look.

If Ross were here
I wouldn't have been such a coward.
we would've rescued.
we would've made a home.
Even today it's the nights I fear.
not knowing exactly what it is I hear.
wondering if I'm right
that he truly is a coward
and it's only neglect and not torture
reflected in those hopeless eyes.

Is it the outside?
the smooth skin
the tasteful decoration
the fine color mixed and laid
with an artist's hand
like lines drawn delicately around the mind's eye.
Is it the feel, the suppleness
of skin stretched upon the bones,
the spine
with silken cords that bind today
when tied and knotted by an artist
just as they were
before Shakespeare looked his neighbors in the eye
and drew their likeness true.

Yet what is the skin side
to the inside?
to the lines, the whorls, the curls
that make the meaning—
the pull and loosening

the prick and stick
the lightening and the tightening
of the signs that turn a mind
to times and sightings of worlds beyond the eye
the touch,
the hearing,
to truth and falsehood
beyond oneself
that calls to be discerned.

How could death be drawn by either—
by the pallid deadly call of coverings
or the living signs inside
that shame the shades of buried greed
lying silent
lying hidden
in the sinful soul of man.

"That's precisely where Georgina sat that last morning!" Penelope Long brushed her hand across her forehead and then pulled her rose-red sweater across her large bust as though the memory was too unsettling, or the breeze was too cold.

"That's what Sarah said." Ben had been drinking coffee, and he set his cup down and closed Georgina's portfolio, before he pushed his chair back and stood up. "Won't you sit down?"

"Thank you, I think perhaps I should." Penelope dropped rather suddenly into the cedar chair on Ben's left, while quietly telling him she'd "uncovered a bit of information."

"Would you like a cup of coffee?"

"No, thank you. I've drunk too much tea already. After we spoke last night, I remembered a telephone call Georgina received. I won't remember the chap's name, but I know where she was asked to return the call. She was to ring up Stephen Tucker's office. No, that's not right, his laboratory. I know Professor Tucker, you see, to recognize. He comes for dinner, he and his wife, five or six times a year."

"So a man called from his laboratory and asked Georgina to ring him back?"

"That's right, yes."

"Do you know where his lab is?"

"I think he's a Fellow of Balliol, but his laboratory would be in one of the science buildings. I can't think what sort of science it is. Physiology. Physics. Pathology perhaps? The university could tell you, I'm sure. Have you reached the English literature professor? Andrew Eastland?"

"Yes, I'm meeting him this morning at Magdalen College. Did you find the names and addresses of the other guests who ate breakfast on the terrace with Georgina?"

"I got onto it first thing. Here you are. A little list." She pulled it out of the pocket of her sweater, then twisted her handkerchief in her hand.

"Did Georgina talk to you in the last few months, or while she was here this time, about anything that was bothering her? Her work? Or Ross's business? Or anything at Cairnwell?"

"I suppose she did, yes. She and I often discussed The Parsonage. She understood, you see, because she'd known my husband, and she helped me through the early years after he died, when I was learning to run the hotel alone. We talked about her husband's business, Fletcher Tire and Rubber, much the same way. I don't think there was anyone else she could discuss it with, really. Professors don't have the first idea what it's like to train employees, and repair property, and spend the earth for new equipment, paying taxes all the while that make one feel one is being punished for attempting to manage a business."

"Did she talk about Fletcher Tire when she was here this time?"

"She told me the very first evening that it looked as though she might have to sell up. The manager at Fletcher, who'd stepped in when Ross became ill, doesn't have the full range of abilities the enterprise requires, and her attempts to bring in the managers Ross endorsed had so far ended in defeat. The death of one. The illness of another. The excessive demands of the third, which had all but halted negotiations. Yet, to whom ought she to sell? One must have an enthusiastic buyer, and searching for one can bring disaster."

"Did she have anyone in mind?"

"She had been approached by a competitor of Fletcher's here in England, which Ross and Georgina thought an unscrupulous firm, that had tried to buy Fletcher's in the past. Georgina had recently discovered that another very shady backdoor attempt was being made, using…I don't know if I should say anything more. I should hate to cast aspersions that might do harm."

"If Georgina was murdered though…" Ben sipped his coffee and watched Penelope over the rim of the cup.

"You're right of course. Yes. The ordinary rules of politeness can't be said to apply. It was Ross's nephew who made the latest approach, and G. felt sure there was an undisclosed reason that he was so insistent."

"A finder's fee? A payment of some kind for persuading her?"

"That's what Georgina believed. She hoped to sell Fletcher

to the employees, if that could be worked out. But if it couldn't, there is an American firm Ross respected and she thought she'd approach them. It's one they thought would treat the employees fairly, while running the business on a firm footing."

"Had she talked to her nephew about the American firm?"

"I have no idea. She told me she was going to tell him in no uncertain terms that the sale he was promoting would never go forward, but whether she had time to do so before she died I don't know. I do think she'd discussed the situation with Fletcher's interim manager, but I can't say that with absolute certainty."

"What's the name of the competitor?"

"British Tire." Penelope Long was playing with the pockets of her cardigan, looking very uncomfortable, as though she'd said things she wished she hadn't.

"You've been a real help and I appreciate it. Is there a place near here where I can get something photocopied?"

"We have a Xerox machine. I shall show you how to work it whenever you'd like. By the way, when you return to Cairnwell, would you please tell Ellen Winter that I very much regret the tone I took with her the morning Georgina died? I meant to mention it at the funeral and forgot. She rang here from the bus station, and I was in such a state, I simply told her Georgina couldn't come to the phone, and I'm afraid I was rather brusque."

"Ellen was in Oxford?"

"Yes, she'd taken the bus up from Heathrow, intending to see G. She caught the train up to Glasgow from here later."

"I see."

"Hasn't she mentioned it?"

"I suppose it must've slipped her mind."

rrrrr

Ben turned right into Banbury Road from The Parsonage, walked south past St. John's College, while looking across at The Eagle and Child where Tolkien and Lewis and their friends still sometimes met to discuss each other's books.

Ben passed Balliol College, turned left into Broad Street and looked at the books in Blackwell's windows, before turning right by the Sheldonian Theater. He walked along the front of the old Bodleian Library, passed the Radcliffe Camera, and turned left into High Street. He walked two more blocks alongside the honey-colored stone of All Souls and Queen's College, then on past a string of shops.

The sun was turning the pale gold sandstone in all the old buildings warm and buttery. The bits Ben could see behind the tourists who clogged the sidewalks and spilled out into the roads, stopping in front of him without warning, making him dodge to the side and decide to avoid as much of High Street as he could on his way back.

He walked the last block to Magdalen College at a snail's pace, then passed the pedimented gate to the grounds, ducking instead through a low doorway into a stone-floored entrance hall near the chapel.

Ben told the porter he was there to meet Andrew Eastland and walked through to the cloisters, the fifteenth-century stone quadrangle enclosed by pillared walkways with students' rooms overhead.

The cloister walks were cool in the bright sun, contemplative and peaceful, and Ben slowed his steps and gazed up stairways, looking too through the delicate tracery arches to the center square of fine green lawn.

He told himself that when he finished with Eastland, he

ought to sit on a bench in the cloister and ponder his own paths.

In England.

In Scotland.

At home.

Alone.

At Alderton College. Coming down on forty.

His wife dead. His best friend murdered.

A fight brewing at Alderton over the picking of another president.

Ben snorted quietly to himself as he considered the jockeying that had started that spring, the feinting and dodging, the name calling and covert whispering that had inflamed the ranks and erupted in faculty meetings. Making the same old questions stick in his throat.

Do I get involved directly this time? Do I sit on yet another useless committee and try to influence what I don't have the support to pull off? Or should I play the gadfly as usual? Biting underbellies. Pricking balloons. Tearing at tender spots. Trying to pick the critical moments for actually affecting the outcome.

Without Richard at Alderton it's harder. Though maybe it's easier too. The incomparable Professor West irritated the left more than I do. But there was some safety in numbers. And numbers are obviously dwindling in the fight to preserve a serious curriculum and maintain some standards of faculty behavior.

It's not easy trying to see what is, and not what you wish were true. While deciding what battles to fight.

Ben sighed audibly as he followed the corner of the cloister to the right, then walked through the arch in the center of the left wall out into an enormous stretch of lawn intersected by gravel paths. He was facing the wide Georgian expanse of New

Building, where Eastland had rooms on the left by the deer park. But Ben didn't take the path in that direction. He turned right instead toward the short stone bridge across the Cherwell River.

There were benches on either side of it, facing the grounds of the college, and he sat on the one on the right. And took out his copies of Georgina's poems.

Four hundred years.
And where do I go now?
No pity, no,
(shame, yes, revulsion at one's flesh)
when I, because of Ross,
will hardly be touched.
I won't be turned out on cold ground.
I shall find another spot to live with,
to paint and fix
to turn my mind from loneliness
and living in between
too old to pick it up again
    (and hold it with the old fire,
    to reach after new students and complicated work
    or new plans for planting,
    or the training of another dog,
    to listen to the fine wild ravings
    of an early morning wren
    the way I would with Ross
    when we would laugh and breathe again
    once the wrens were back in the crooked pine)
too young to want to close my eyes and go,
to turn my gaze away from this shore

to wait for it to end in settled silence.
Although I will go.
Twice.
I will walk through new rooms
and strange passages
through trees I haven't leaned against
past fields, I hope,
with stone walls set in grains and grasses.
I will lie too in the old bed
and read my books and think on long lost faces.
And when it pleases God
I will slip into that dateless light
and wait for Ross to find me.

(G.—Remember to do ending again. Need to imply that God, or Christ, will allow Ross to do so.)

✐   ✐   ✐

logic
cause and effect
the mind of the scientist
muddled by a grudge
fondled and talked to
and held against the heart
stroked and coddled and listened to in the dark
droning his own defense
blurred by drink and justified revenge
sanctified by the sound of beating wings
the smell of smoke
the floor blistering beneath his feet.

(G.—Should there be some physical description of CB?)

Ben looked around him—at the paths toward New Building, at the back of the cloisters on his left, along the walk behind them that led to High Street. Then he stood and looked over the low stone wall behind him to the other side of the Cherwell, at the paths and meadow beyond.

No one seemed to be looking for anyone. No one saw him and started in his direction. And he sat back down and wrote notes to himself in his small leather notebook.

He looked at his watch and stretched his shoulders.

And then read the last few of Georgina's poems.

After Shakespeare's XXX Sonnet

When I think of the regard that Ross had,
I wonder what response it drew in turn;
Was there the self-smitten laugh of a deceitful gad,
Or the self-deluded look that will not learn
To gaze upon the shades that all can see but us;
For all are guilty in this tangled life
Of turning from our selfish greed and lust
To blindly force the seeds of bitter strife
Instead of saying to the souls we love
That we are doubly wrong, that we have sinned,
That we beg pardon from our God above
For all that we have finished wrong within.
    No, this that I have found is different made;
    The cruel and twisted working of a miser's raid.

(G.—Is pirate's raid a better choice?)

It grew
the jealousy
and the resentment
when he became beholden
when a hand was opened
when a favor done.
He couldn't look at me
finally
without seeing the name
of what he called his own shame.
He thought he ought
to be grateful
and couldn't bear the obligation.
Rudeness and pique
made him feel better.
Better too for both
than hating Em,
when Em's was the mind
he saw in mine.
Why didn't I mind?
Why didn't I rage at the presumption
if not the irrationality?
Because I can still see Helen
her blond braids
her sea blue eyes
running from the words I'd hurled
in anger
in jealousy
to give it its real name
when I wanted desperately to be like her

to have her easy sureness
her warmth
her family
her selfless smile,
her way of winning
everyone because of the way she was
when I prickled
standing like a stick
on the side
afraid to hold out a hand.

What would he say
if he knew the new idea
is to help him?
would he break free
finally?
or would he hate me
more?

"Dr. Reese, I presume?" A small thin man in very rumpled tweeds was trotting toward Ben, carrying a small red book in his right hand and an old black pipe in the other.

"Dr. Eastland. Thanks for taking time to see me."

"You found your way all right, did you?"

"Yes. I've been to Magdalen before."

"And therefore you know to pronounce it 'maudlin.' Shall we take Addison's Walk? He studied here in the seventeenth century. Joseph Addison, the essayist. Hence the path's name. Yesterday's muddy spots are said to be drying up."

"Good, I'd like to."

"Excellent. It's too fine a day to spend indoors, with one's stale dust motes and academic ghosts. Shall we?" He'd dropped the book in an outside coat pocket, and was stretching his arm toward large trees and high shrubs on the other side of the river.

They crossed the Cherwell, making way on the bridge for a gaggle of German tourists, and turned left on the footpath that follows the river around the tree-ringed meadow in the center of the island.

"Now then, Dr. Reese, I wonder if I might ask you to explain more fully the reasons for your interest in Georgina Fletcher?"

Ben explained that his apprentice, Ellen Winter, had inherited Cairnwell from Georgina, and that Ellen was uncomfortable making the decisions her new situation demanded. Ben had been planning to be in Oxford doing his own work, and Ellen had asked him to find out what he could about Georgina's thinking shortly before she died, hoping it would help her decide what she should do with Cairnwell, in terms of the writers retreat, the falconry center, and the quarry. "Then when I talked to Penelope Long last night, she told me Georgina had given her the impression that she might not live long. I wonder if she said anything to you. Was she depressed, or did she know she was ill?"

Andrew Eastland had been listening with his hands clasped behind his back, his watery blue eyes fixed on the path in front of him, his shoulders hunched, his thin gray hair plastered across his brow. Then when Ben finished speaking, he popped his pipe in his mouth and lit it. "I don't know that I can be of much help. Georgina told me of the writers retreat. She mentioned it, in passing, but I wouldn't say there was any very full discussion. She said nothing a-tall about the other undertakings you mention."

"When was the last time you saw her?"

"When? I should think it was the evening of June 6. Yes, two days before she died. I called for her at The Parsonage and escorted her to a dinner meeting of an organization we'd both belonged to for many years. The Austen and Others Club. We're a disparate group of eighteenth-century literary enthusiasts, some academics, but several not. We play literary games, identify quotations, eat dishes referred to in tomes of the time, wear costumes, some of us, on various occasions, which pertain to authors and their works. That evening, Georgina seemed to especially enjoy herself, for a presentation was given to us by professional actors portraying Samuel Johnson, Joshua Reynolds, James Boswell, Mrs. Thrale, and Mrs. Johnson, declaiming excerpts from *The Life of Johnson.*"

"Georgina seemed perfectly normal? Not preoccupied, or distracted, or ill in any way?"

A cloud passed across the thin untroubled face and Andrew Eastland considered Ben silently before he spoke. "Well...there was one rather—how shall I put it?—disturbing moment, when a colleague of hers attacked her verbally in a thoroughly reprehensible manner. One wouldn't wish to mention names, of course, but he was clearly in his cups and the rest of the company was quite appalled. In the end, he was asked to leave."

"Was it a colleague of hers from Aberdeen?" Eastland nodded, while Ben stooped to look at a fern he'd never seen in the states. "Robbie MacAlpin perhaps?"

"Yes, as a matter of fact, it was. There seemed to be no provocation a-tall for the assault. Aside from the usual interdepartmental envy. He attacked her scholarship, and her literary taste, and suggested somewhat obliquely that it was time for her to retire. It was quite an appalling display, and that part of our august body near enough to hear the outburst arose and demanded an apology. He offered one, under pressure, and departed under his own steam."

"How did Georgina take it?"

"A matter of moments after he'd left, she seemed herself again. And then when I spoke to her on the phone the next afternoon, she told me he'd called and apologized that morning."

"Did she say anything about collectors of any kind?"

"Collectors? I can't say I see the connection."

"She talked about people who collect things to someone else, and Ellen wonders, for other reasons as well, if Georgina was thinking of adding to her own antiques and turning them into a serious collection. If Ellen can find out what Georgina wanted to do, she could display Georgina's antiques in a gallery, or a museum, or donate some somewhere in Georgina's memory."

"Ah. Yes." Eastland nodded as he relit his pipe, his forehead furrowed and his eyes preoccupied. "I suppose she did, now that you mention it. It was when we were walking home from The Others Club dinner. It was at the Randolph Hotel, you see, so it wasn't a long walk, and the night was lovely. She asked if I understood collectors. The sort who seem to lose all proportion. She said she knew someone who buys antiques in that way. Though how that might bear on what Miss Winter should do with Cairnwell, I couldn't say."

"It doesn't seem to help much, does it?"

"Georgina did mention too, a few days earlier, rather seriously, I thought, that she'd had a bit of a shock in the last few weeks. That one can think one knows one's family through and through only to be dumbfounded by what one discovers."

"I've seen that happen more than once."

"Yes."

"Did she say anything else about her family?"

"No. Not that I recall."

"Why would Georgina ask you about collectors?"

"I've a friend who's a seller of rare books here in Oxford, and G. and I have discussed his experiences over the years. Also, as a young man, I was interested, briefly, in rare books. I read a bit about bindings and first editions, but I quickly saw that such a path would lead to utter ruin. I have a great many books, of course, like most Oxford dons. Too many perhaps. Too many shelves groaning beneath them. Too many piles, alas, stacked on the bedroom floor. But they're generally of extremely undistinguished pedigree, and of very little value indeed. Except for the thought put forth in them. Which is, is it not, their most important attribute?"

"Exactly."

"Of course, all works of real antiquity and rarity have inexpressible intrinsic value. They contribute to our understanding of the development of the written word. Of illumination and printing, and their expressions of human art and knowledge. Though I, of course, possess no books or manuscripts of that sort. There have actually been collectors throughout history who've killed in order to possess fine books or manuscripts. Perhaps there still are today."

"The ex-monk intrigues me." Ben was squinting into the sun as he gazed at a punt on the river, a young girl lying in the bow, a young man poling the boat, talking with the intensity of someone his age discussing something he really cares about. "The Spaniard who'd run a monastery library that had its irreplaceable books stolen by 'unknown thieves.' Right before *he* disappeared and opened a rare book store in another city. He bought more books than he sold. And when someone else outbid him for the only known copy of some famous book at auction, the buyer and his house were burned a few days later, and the book was discovered in the ex-monk's shop."

"Don Vicente. He killed other men in Barcelona and stole their books as well." Eastland leaned against the trunk of a large maple and brushed leaves off the sides of his hard-soled shoes. "The book you refer to was *Edicts and Ordanances for Valencia* printed in the fifteenth century by Spain's first printer."

"Wasn't there someone else who'd sell rare books to put food on the table, then follow the buyers home and kill them later, stealing back the books he'd sold?"

"Yes. I can't recall the name, though. Look at the cow." She was black and white and leaning over a bush on their right, on the edge of the meadow pasture, staring fixedly at Ben and Andrew. "I have never understood the bovine intelligence."

"Georgina didn't collect books herself, did she?"

"No. No, I never had any sense of interest or knowledge on her part." Eastland clasped his hands behind his back and stared at the path in front of him. "She loved books, of course. The committing to memory, the savoring of what they said. But I never thought of her as the sort who'd collect anything. If she had—and this is pure speculation, of course—I would've thought it would've been antiques. She was very fond of architecture and landscape design."

"She restored Cairnwell really well."

"Yes. I do hate to cut short our chat, but I really must get back. I have a tutorial in a quarter of an hour."

"I'll walk back with you, if you don't mind, and then get on to my own work. When she asked about collectors, did you put her in touch with your book dealer friend?"

"I suggested she speak with him. Whether she did or not, I don't know."

"What's his name?"

"William Whitfield. Perhaps you should talk to him yourself. Do you have a piece of paper?"

Ben handed him a photocopy of one of Georgina's poems, after turning the paper over.

"Excellent. Now…" Andrew Eastland took out a fountain pen and drew Ben a map. "His store is in Jericho, so if you walk north on Walton Street, then turn left onto Cardigan Street…is it Cardigan? No, maybe Great Clarendon. Then right there onto…what is it?…King Street? I think so. The building is right back here." Andrew Eastland made an X on the map and handed the paper to Ben. "The shop is on the first floor. What you Americans call the second. And you'll have to ring the bell and wait for William to open the window above. He's a bit of an eccentric. He won't let just anyone in, but if he likes the look of you, he'll let you up. Tell him I sent you if he seems to hesitate."

"Thank you. I really appreciate it."

CHAPTER SIX

"EXCUSE ME. IS STEPHEN TUCKER HERE?" The long rectangular laboratory was packed with equipment (small, on countertops, large, standing on the floor), glassware sitting everywhere, tangles of tubing strung across the counters (around balances and ovens), centrifuges on either side of a lyophilizer, racks of test tubes, yards of petri dishes, ranks of bottles and refrigerators—making a maze that four men in stained white coats seemed part of, to Ben, when he watched them from just inside the door.

The youngest of them said, "He's in his office," and pointed toward the far end of the room.

Ben stuck his head through the door of what turned out to be a very small cubicle and introduced himself.

A tall man, about Ben's age (but with an abdomen that looked like a basketball was suspended below his belt), said, "Good morning." And turned away from a small dirty blackboard where lopsided circles and intertwining lines of squiggles leaned against long incomprehensible strings of letters, all drawn with pink and white chalk. He wiped chalk dust across the stains on his yellowed lab coat and gazed at Ben rather vaguely. "Let me see, we were meeting to discuss..."

"The call Georgina Fletcher received—"

"Of course, yes, I remember. What time has it gotten to be?" Stephen Tucker consulted the large clock behind his head, and then said, "Why don't we dash out for an early lunch and avoid the worst of the crowd?"

"Fine with me."

"Just let me finish this…" He was staring at the blackboard again, sitting in his chair now, its back crammed against his desk drawer, his right elbow in his left hand, the right hand, with the pink chalk, cradling the right side of his jaw.

Ben waited while Tucker erased half of what looked like a diagram of a cell, redrew the outline, and changed a nearby string of letters that seemed to consist mostly of K, L, T, G, and P. Tucker took out his handkerchief and blew his nose, smearing the pink chalk on his jaw, and then raked several strings of dark greasy hair across the top of an exposed scalp.

He swiveled the chair away from the blackboard, staring over Ben's head, then dropped the chalk in his lab coat pocket.

Ben didn't say anything.

And neither did Tucker. Until his gaze drifted to Ben's face and he looked slightly startled. "Ah."

"I'm Ben Reese." Ben laughed.

And Tucker smiled. "Of course you are, yes, I remember. We were on our way to lunch."

They were sitting under a grape arbor in a small enclosed garden that was part of The Turf, an old stone pub completely surrounded by a warren of buildings not too far from the Bodleian Library and the Bridge of Sighs.

"I'm sure you noticed that the path in through the buildings is nearly impossible to find, which is why there're no tourists here a-tall. Yet it's a very popular pub with the locals, and we were lucky to get in before the crowd."

"Yeah, I can imagine."

"I'll have the steak and kidney pie and a half-pint of bitter." The waiter was taking orders as though there were several things he'd rather do. And Stephen Tucker raised his eyebrows at Ben to encourage an early decision.

"A bowl of potato soup, whole grain bread with Cheshire cheese, a glass of water, and a cup of coffee, please."

"They do have an excellent bitter."

"It'll put me to sleep if I drink it at lunch."

"You Americans, it's a wonder you get anything done!"

Ben and Tucker both laughed, before Tucker leaned forward with his arms on the table and his forehead wrinkled up into what had once been his hairline. "So what is it you want to know?"

Ben gave Tucker the same explanation he'd given Eastland. That Ellen was interested in what Georgina was thinking at the end, hoping it would help her make decisions. "So I'm trying to find out who called Georgina Fletcher from your lab, and when the call was placed, so we can talk to whoever it was and find out if anything Georgina said applies to Ellen's situation."

"It was a friend of mine, actually. Jack Corelli. You must have met him at Cairnwell. He called Professor Fletcher the afternoon before she died."

"I watched Jack hunt with a hawk the day before yesterday."

"He wanted to have a word with Dr. Fletcher while she was here. I have no idea why, but I'm sure he'll be happy to discuss it with Miss Winter. I would've thought he might've mentioned it."

"He hasn't, but then he doesn't know Ellen wants to talk to whoever called her. How do you know him?" Ben was dragging his fork across his napkin, raking rows of parallel lines.

"Jack's a microbiologist. Though I suspect he may not be mentioning it at the moment. We met several years ago when I was in the States presenting a paper at the National Institutes of Health. Jack heard the talk while interviewing at the NIH for a postdoctoral position. He's a cell biologist, who worked at that time on cell transformation. Examining the ways in which chemicals of various sorts change normal cells into tumor cells."

"I wondered if he'd studied biology. He talked about food poisoning like he knew what he was doing."

"He would know a bit about pathogens, though that's not his area of specialization."

"Why is he working as a carpenter?"

"He's washed his hands of us. And I can't say I altogether blame him. He's had enough of the ambition and the territorialism. You know how it-tis, the bloodbaths that ensue in the pursuit of reputation and funding. He's decided to take his fate in his own hands. Literally in his own hands. Making his way with the sweat of his brow and confining his associates to his feathered friends." Stephen Tucker laughed, then swallowed a quarter of his glass of bitter. "He's quite an ideologue, our Jack, and I sympathize in a way. Though I think it is possible to maintain one's standards and still do work that's more significant than pounding nails. Not that pounding nails isn't significant, I hasten to add, for it-tis. But when one has the training and the abilities Jack has, well…you see what I mean I'm sure."

"What happened to make him want to get out of science?"

"He had terrifically bad luck. Two rotten eggs in a row

made him throw down the basket." Stephen Tucker looked pleased with the metaphor, while he chewed his first forkful of steak and kidney pie. "He had two less than exemplary lab directors. A Ph.D. advisor he abhorred who published papers on what was essentially Jack's work in a very prestigious journal without crediting Jack with the initial idea *or* the work itself. That's an oft-told tale, of course, as I'm sure you know. And that experience was followed by another unpleasant shock at a very well thought of university when he was working on his postdoc. He didn't go to the NIH, by the way. If they'd realized his had been the work published by his mentor, I think he would've been likely to.

"Jack was working on cell transformation, as I said, and his research was part of a grant that had been awarded by the NIH. Funds are doled out in stages, so if the first grant, which covers a very specific bit of research, is deemed successful, if it indicates that the track one is on is worth pursuing, then the researcher applies for a second allotment of grant money, which is generally larger and of longer duration. The work Jack was doing, under the professor who'd received the grant, was absolutely critical to the funding, but the results Jack was getting were—I don't know how to express this exactly without being technical—the results weren't such that it would've looked as though the path was worth pursuing. Therefore, the data his mentor submitted in order to get a renewal of the grant, very carefully avoided reporting Jack's results.

"He told Jack that once they had further funding, there would be no question of holding back the results in the long term, but that in order to get the money to study it further, a more positive picture had to be presented. He wouldn't allow Jack to publish the work anywhere else either, of course. And

Jack was outraged. He was really incensed, but he did agree to wait to publish. Then, after the second grant had been awarded, the mentor published a partial report in some journal, and again left out the negative results which very much looked to Jack like he was being deliberately misleading. Jack washed his hands of the whole business. He chucked his job, sold his car, moved his things into his parents' basement, and immediately took ship for England."

"I know exactly how that feels."

"Yes, and so do I. What I keep telling him is that he can be far more useful *in* a laboratory doing the work he does really well, and *fighting* the powers that be, than riding his motorbike up and down the country, flying his birds for his own amusement. I offered him a job here, when he was in Oxford this last time. And I hope he's considering it. He seems so wrapped up in this idea of the falconry center, I don't know if he'll come to his senses till he tries it and loses every penny he ever hopes to have."

"I suppose you both studied bacteriology?"

"Some, certainly. There are several bacteriologists at Oxford, as you'd expect, who are among the most learned in the world. Jack studied bacteriology and pathology quite a bit more than I before he settled into cell biology."

"May I ask something else? Even if it seems unrelated?"

"Certainly."

"Is there a germ, or a bacteria, or a pathogen of some kind that could kill someone really fast, and leave no trace, and be very easy to administer? Something that causes vomiting."

"You do know, don't you, that MI5 injected a Russian spy with Ricin in the leg with the point of an umbrella right in a London tube station?"

"No."

"Yes, and he died in a matter of seconds. But of course, what you're suggesting...no...no, it wouldn't be a fungus...a spore possibly, but I doubt it...not a parasite, certainly...timing wouldn't correspond...though I suppose it might be a bacterial toxin. One that could be...yes, and then introduced in food. It's possible, but quite rare..." He was chewing his steak and kidney pie, his eyes on the arbor overhead.

Ben didn't interrupt him. He ate his soup and his bread and cheese, while Stephen Tucker considered.

"Odd you should ask me that, actually. An acquaintance of mine called me after Dr. Fletcher died. A friend of the police pathologist, as it happens. And he wondered the same thing. But there's no easy answer, is there? Botulism would've been the first thing they'd look for. And of course, most bacterium would be killed in the process of cooking, so it would've had to be...except...No, I really haven't a clue. It's not my field, of course, but..." He swallowed another mouthful of bitter and looked directly at Ben. "Why do you want to know?"

"Curiosity more than anything else."

"But it is because of Georgina Fletcher's death?"

"In a way. You don't hear that much about food poisoning killing people, and when it does, it's not usually that fast."

"There're probably many more deaths because of food poisoning than we know. Though, as I understand it, Dr. Fletcher died of aspiration. She might well have recovered very nicely if vomit hadn't gotten into the airway. So it's a bit of a moot point."

"Maybe. That could certainly be true."

"I wonder what Jack made of it all? He left the day she died, you know, and I haven't heard from him since."

"Do you think he'll get back into microbiology?"

"I think he will do in the end. But I wouldn't be surprised if he went to a pharmaceutical company rather than a spot in academia. I suspect he'd like doing research with a more immediate application. Without all the forms of established professorial protocol."

"I can understand that, can't you?" Ben laid his spoon down and sipped his coffee.

"Yes, if the truth were known, I suppose I do. So how will you spend the rest of the afternoon?"

"I've got one more stop in Oxford, and then I think I'll take a bus out to Burford. Tonight I'll probably work at the Bodleian."

"The Cotswold Hills are lovely, aren't they, especially this time of year? Be sure to see the church."

"That's one of the things I intended to do."

"Ah, Dr. Tucker. A rather urgent call came through for you while you were at lunch." The young blond man leaned a pipette with a small rubber bulb on the top inside a large glass beaker, wiped his hands on a paper towel, and pulled a slip of paper out of the breast pocket of his lab coat. "It was your American friend, and he asked me to pass on a message."

Stephen Tucker took the note into his office, and then tried to decipher the nearly microscopic handwriting as he shrugged his arms into his lab coat.

If a man named Ben Reese asks you about me, don't tell him I was in Oxford, or that I'm a microbiologist. Will call you at home tonight.—Jack

ℭℭℭℭℭ

William Whitfield's shop had no sign above or beside the door. Only the number of the building in brass on brick.

Ben pushed the small brass button below the number and shaded his eyes as he looked at the upper window.

It opened, a minute or so later, and an almost hairless head stuck out at an odd angle, like a snapping turtle Ben had had as a kid. A ridge of yellowish skin, where eyebrows normally would have been, rose inquisitively and a pale tight mouth opened and closed, and then said, "Yes?" with a distracted edge.

"Andrew Eastland suggested I come see you."

Small colorless eyes behind thick black-framed glasses squinted suspiciously at Ben in silence. Then the thin-lipped mouth untucked itself slowly and a high, clipped, "Wait," ricocheted across the quiet of the narrow back street.

The black door opened in due time, held by the broad stubby fingers of the same elderly gentleman from upstairs who stood not much more than five feet tall in old-fashioned lace-up boots.

"Mr. Whitfield?"

"As you say, sir."

"I'm Ben Reese. I'm an archivist at a university in the States."

Mr. Whitfield said nothing more, but turned and began to climb the stairs. His back was twisted slightly to the right, and his right shoulder looked higher than the other, as he shifted sideways stiffly, in his ancient black suit, raising his short legs slowly, from one steep wooden stair to the next.

He stepped through another black door into a twenty-five-by-twenty-foot room completely filled with books. They stood crushed against each other on tightly packed rows of free-standing shelves, they climbed brick walls in jumbled stacks till they touched a high beamed ceiling, they totally blocked four large side windows, and leaned in piles on what looked like a wide-plank floor.

Ben closed his eyes and inhaled slowly, liking the musty scent of powdery leather and dry dust, of lemon oil and yellowed linen, of wood smoke, and pipe smoke, and a tentative whiff of cloves from a porcelain bowl of potpourri.

William Whitfield couldn't see Ben's face when Ben stopped in the doorway and smiled. Whitfield spoke to him over his shoulder as he brushed past a row of Victorian memoirs, his voice wavering along with the dust motes he stirred as he shuffled past. "Hesitate not to let me know, sir, should you require assistance in any particular. Prints, broadsides, maps, and all other manner of ephemera are presented in the east room. Science and mathematics are arranged in the alcove room on the south. Art and architecture are to be found through the opposite door."

Whitfield squeezed behind a high glass counter, then stood by an adjoining desk where he picked up a letter he'd apparently been reading when Ben had rung the bell.

Ben scanned three shelves of eighteenth-century leather-bound books in the English literature section—Johnson, Boswell, Oliver Goldsmith, Sterne, Sheridan, Swift. And wished there was time to browse and consider.

But there wasn't. And he walked to Whitfield's desk with a small navy blue Moroccan-bound copy of *Persuasion*. While Whitfield recorded the three pound purchase in a large ledger on the desk, Ben explained about Eastland and Georgina Fletcher, and asked if Georgina had come to see him.

"Would it be impertinent to ask, sir, how you yourself come to be concerned in the matter?" Whitfield still hadn't looked at Ben. He glanced behind him, and above him, and on either side, as well as at the plain brown wrapping paper he was folding around Ben's book, while Ben explained about Ellen Winter wanting to find out what Georgina would've done with Cairnwell.

Whitfield was silent for a moment, as he opened his desk drawer and closed it again for no apparent reason, his sallow oval face almost ageless, unusually smooth and nearly hairless, the face of a wise child trapped in an elderly cage. He cleared his throat once, softly, and then said, in his high dry voice, "We discussed the Elizabethans. Shakespeare. Spenser. Marlowe. The import of printers in that distant age. The provenance of particular folios. Methods used to falsify first editions. Lovers of books, sir, in a general way. And then she went the way she'd come," he motioned gravely toward the door, "never to return, as we now know. As fate has since arranged it."

Whitfield giggled then, for one split second, the smooth skinned head turned slightly to Ben's right, the small eyes closed completely behind his heavy lenses, one foot tapping in time to the Vivaldi wafting from a wireless at the end of his desk. "Forgive me, sir. I assure you I meant no disrespect. Your book."

"Thank you. Did she ask particular questions about lovers of books, or collectors?"

"One or two perhaps. Nothing of much moment." William Whitfield swiveled stiffly away from Ben and lowered himself carefully into a straight-backed wooden chair with a torn, crewel-covered cushion. "She did listen to my reminiscences with something more than patience. Or so I thought at the time."

"What kind of reminiscences?"

"Recollections. Hearsay." His voice was reedier and more breathless than it had been before as he pulled a pocket watch out of his threadbare vest and flipped open the lid. He clicked it shut and polished it with a papery thin linen handkerchief, before he said, "I told her of a rare book aficionado in the early years of this century."

"I'd like to hear about him too, if you have time. I work with collectors as an archivist, and I never cease to be amazed."

Whitfield closed his clothbound ledger and pushed it to the side of his desk, then covered his nose and mouth with both hands. It looked to Ben as though Whitfield almost glanced at him then. But no. He shut his eyes again and folded his hands on the edge of the desk. "I knew a gentleman, when I was a young man, whose uncle was Sir Alfred Dyson. They're both gone now, regrettably. Edward in the last war. Dyson years before at the country estate he'd inherited in Kent. He was one of the first of his generation to open his house as an hotel. I believe as early as 1930, when he found himself in financial straits during the Great Depression.

"Dyson was a man of settled character, and he was absolutely determined to keep his house as it was, a private house, a gentleman's home. Not merely a public hotel. He used the family silver and the old china, and he left his books on the library walls. Edward thought he oughtn't to. That it would be much too easy to purloin the rare books. That he should at least lock them away behind sturdy doors with a grill of some sort. But his Uncle Alfred declined to make a change."

Whitfield opened his eyes, cleared his throat, and gazed at the glass counter. "It was in early 1934 that Sir Alfred died suddenly, of stomach trouble in his own home. He'd just returned that afternoon from London, where he'd eaten a very hot curry at an Indian restaurant. He had a terribly tricky stomach, with a long history of gastrointestinal distress, and his doctor assumed it was that. The curry, you see, playing up his ulcer, or whatever the condition was. Though there was some conjecture that he'd eaten something questionable as well on the train home. He'd become ill an hour or so after dinner, and despite his doctor's best efforts, he died at one in the morning. There was no question of drugs or poison. That was looked into very thoroughly. His physician put it down to natural causes, and no one thought anything about it, including the coroner.

"My friend Edward inherited. And a few weeks later, when he looked through the library, he discovered that twelve volumes of rare books, mostly incunabula, were missing altogether. One book in particular, Nicholas Copernicus's 1543 *On the Revolutions of the Celestial Sphere,* one of five extant copies, which was thought to be nearly priceless, was a particularly sad loss indeed. Edward informed Interpol, as one did even in those days, when the international headquarters were still in Austria. But no information was ever uncovered. Edward thought it especially interesting that several manuscripts of similar worth had been left untouched. Among them some of the very oldest monastery gospels brought back from the Levant early in the eighteenth century by what may well have been the first western visitor. Yes, long before Stanhope or Curzon went out there. Two have since been donated by Edward's family to the British Museum."

"A Copernicus was taken, but the manuscripts were left?"

"Yes." William Whitfield was looking past Ben again, as though he were speaking to someone behind him. "A first edition of Sir Walter Raleigh's *History of the World* was found to be missing as well, and an early edition of Marco Polo. Latin or Italian, I don't recall which. There was also one volume at least from the Harley library."

"Weren't there two Harleys, a father and a son, who were both collectors?"

"In the late seventeenth and early eighteenth centuries. Yes, theirs was a wonderful library, now disbursed, alas, across the world. There may have been something by Hakluyt taken from Sir Alfred Dyson's collection as well, but I can't remember for certain."

"The Hakluyt who published accounts of early voyages?"

"Yes, the man himself. I do know Edward was very much unsettled by his uncle's death, and he made a point of questioning the butler who'd served dinner to Sir Alfred and his guest that last evening. That gentleman had noticed nothing untoward, and he and the rest of the staff had consumed the same food, with one exception. One course was eaten only by Sir Alfred. Something he'd brought back from Fortnum & Mason's. It may have been potted shrimps on toast, I can't be sure. Yet it was that that's led me to wonder if food poisoning might have played a part.

"Even so, the matter was further complicated by the fact that Sir Alfred had also discussed the possibility of selling several of the rare books, because of his straitened circumstances. And that well may have been what actually occurred. He could have sold the books privately to a collector who wished to conceal his identity, then hadn't had the opportunity to mention it to Edward. The books also could've been stolen at an entirely different time, before or after Sir Alfred died.

"Though Edward never believed that such was the case. For when he looked through the hotel guest book, after he'd discovered that the books were gone, he found that the appropriate page for the week of his uncle's death had been cut from the register. He questioned the butler, naturally, more than once, even though he'd retired after Sir Alfred's death. He was elderly and unwell and he died later that year without being able to remember the identity of the unknown guest, or any particulars that might have led to his discovery."

"That's interesting." Ben's jaw was off to the left and he was staring at Whitfield without seeing him. "Did Georgina ask any questions?"

"One that I recall, sir. The date the death occurred."

"Do you remember when it was?"

"February 11, 1934. The birthday of your humble servant. No, that was quite misleading. The day of my birth is February 11. The year was considerably earlier." He giggled, covered his lips with his hands, and stared at the brown paper parcel he'd tied with twine and already handed Ben.

"Does Andrew Eastland still collect books? He's seems very knowledgeable."

"He once did. He doesn't now, alas."

"Why? What happened?"

"He married his landlady's daughter, and she won't allow it." William Whitfield giggled again, with an index finger across his lips.

Tuesday, June 20th

Ben had taken a train from Oxford to London, caught the night coach from London to Edinburgh, breakfasted there, and caught another train to Perth, where he picked up his rental car and drove to the public library.

He talked to the local history librarian first, and then looked through back issues of *The Courier and Advertiser* till he found what he wanted. The librarian made a photocopy for him.

And then Ben glanced at the last week's papers. He started with the articles on the Eichmann trial in Israel. But nothing much had changed. Eichmann listened with obvious boredom in a bulletproof glass booth while the deaths of six million Jews were discussed in horrifying detail.

The situation in Germany was getting nasty too.

And Ben considered whether Kennedy had the ability or the guts to keep Khrushchev from cutting off Berlin.

It's interesting the way Khrushchev's part in the Soviet purges never gets mentioned in the press.

No, *The Courier,* like most papers, fills its space with more important things. Italian Ferraris taking the first four places in the Belgium Grand Prix. Lauren Bacall and Jason Robards not being able to marry in Vienna because they won't accept his Mexican divorce.

I might as well go find a phone book.

Ben dialed a local number, faked an English accent and asked if he might make an appointment to see Mr. Thomas Ogilvie Esq. at twelve o'clock noon.

Mr. Ogilvie had a luncheon appointment scheduled which wouldn't allow him to be back in the office until one thirty or a quarter to two.

Ben told himself not to sound pleased as he thanked her and hung up the receiver.

ɾɾɾɾ

He drove south down Tay Street, following the river, circling the block till he found a parking spot with a view of Ogilvie's building. Then he took out the photocopy and watched the door, thinking about Jack Corelli.

A microbiologist would know how to kill someone with something clever. And he was in Oxford when Georgina died.

As was Ellen Winter, of course. Who hasn't seen fit to mention a word to me about it.

The old guy who collects mushrooms knows what he's doing. Not that I thought it was mushrooms to begin with.

But what the machine tool salesman from Sheffield saw, eating breakfast across from G., *that* was actually interesting. A young woman with dark brown hair, drawn back like Ellen's, walking out the gate after giving G. a small cardboard box. Which was empty and on the table when G. got sick and went into the inn. But when Perkins, the salesman, pushed G.'s chair in, he saw a flake of what looked like chocolate inside the box. Only because he "loves espionage novels," and is "teaching himself to be observant."

I wonder if he's right that the unknown man with light brown hair who sat at the table with G. put some kind of powder in her coffee. Hers, or his, or both. Perkins couldn't see well enough to say for sure, but he says whoever it was had brought some kind of powder in a small container he took out of his coat pocket and put back while G. was away from the table.

I guess going to Burford may have been a waste of my time. But at least I confirmed dates for the Pryor family, and got the minister to say he'll study the parish records.

rrrrr

Tom Ogilvie was planning his afternoon as he brushed off the shoulders of his blue pinstripe suit and combed his light brown hair, using the small round mirror that hung inside a cupboard in his paneled office.

I think I shall tell Martin I ate a late breakfast and don't feel much like lunch. No more than tea and a scone perhaps. So that if I pay for his meal, as I can't avoid doing this time out, I shall have saved something approaching nine shillings and six pence. If I can then persuade him to rewrite his will, the expense of his lunch will be money well spent.

I shall nip into the bakery on my way back too, buy a day old loaf, hopefully brown, and have that for supper with an egg and a bit of cheese. I can then use what's left of the cheddar in a sandwich for tomorrow's lunch.

Perhaps I should retrieve my shirts at the laundry as well, and ask while I'm there if they can turn the cuffs on this suit, if I bring it in tomorrow when I wear the gray.

"Hazel…" Tom Ogilvie was in the outside office, holding his worn black briefcase and locking his office door, talking to his middle-aged secretary without looking in her direction. "If that woman phones from my rental property again this after-noon, tell her I have summoned a plumber, but she'll have to be a bit more patient. I haven't yet, but I shall do in the morn-ing. Help me remember before lunch."

"Yes, Mr. Ogilvie. Oh—"

He was out the door and down the hall, heading toward the front stairs, before she could finish her sentence.

If Uncle Ross had married someone with financial sense, there would've been a very different outcome. Georgina… well…I never did understand her, and yet giving the property to an acquaintance was an even more ridiculous act than I ever could've imagined. A schoolgirl from America with no legal claim of any sort who will undoubtedly sell the property in the blink of an eye to be back on her way to America. I told G. she should've sold Cairnwell years ago. It's just the sort of place that's fashionable with the nouveau riche. The sort who squander their capital to no purpose and are destitute in three generations. G. would've realized a considerable profit, *if* she'd been willing to wait for the right buyer. Which in turn could've been invested in property that would've paid.

What she's done with her stock in Fletcher makes me wish I'd throttled her when I had the chance. Aye, if I'd known how it stood, I would've managed things rather differently.

Yet, all may not be lost. Even considering the fact that the only way round it is to get to know this Ellen Winter and make her see sense. The two of us would then be able to do what we'd like with old Arthur Shaw.

Should I give dear Miss Winter Aunt G.'s translations? Would that help convince her of my good faith? Or would it simply put her back up to learn I'd carried them off?

Much good they did me, sad to say. There was nothing there a-tall to get me clear of the will.

I wonder if I should ask Hazel to bring her daily *Scotsman* into the office, before she uses it to wrap the fish? Thereby enabling me to cancel my own subscription.

When Thomas Ogilvie stepped out of the tall Georgian building and walked past Ben's car, Ben compared his face to the one in the photocopy lying on his left thigh.

Then he walked to the nearest phone box on the other side of South.

When Ogilvie's secretary answered, Ben used his own voice, but introduced himself as Alan Ferrell. "May I speak to Tom Ogilvie please?...Ah. It is lunchtime, isn't it? I hadn't noticed...The reason I'm calling is that I had an appointment with Mr. Ogilvie in Oxford on June 8. I waited at the Randolph Hotel from eight in the morning till almost ten, but he never showed up or bothered to call. I've only just returned from Italy, or I would've phoned sooner, but I'd like an explanation. We spoke in Oxford. I know he was there. Why didn't he keep his appointment or get in touch?...The eighth, yes. So you think he booked another appointment while he was in Oxford for the same time and forgot mine?...No, I'm sure it's not your fault...All right. Yes. I'll call another time. I have meetings the rest of the day and won't be easy to reach."

Ben stepped out of the round red telephone box, slid the paper in his coat pocket, and hummed a phrase from Beethoven's Sixth, as he walked toward his black Mini-Cooper.

CHAPTER SEVEN

TWO HOURS LATER, AFTER HAVING DRIVEN NORTH right past the front gate of Balnagard Castle, Ben was heading west following the northern shore of Loch Rannoch. The lake was on his left—the green-gray surface ruffling in a brisk wind, the sun slipping away and flitting out again, rain starting and stopping—as he looked for the driveway to David Lindsay's house.

He was driving slowly on a one-lane road where a dense evergreen forest, the Black Wood of Rannoch, covered the hills on the far side of the loch, and old hardwoods followed the road on Ben's side, their trunks almost touching the water in places, in narrow grassy strips on his left. He'd passed crags and sheer cliffs and outcroppings of rock close to the road on his right and sheep pasture climbing the stretches of long hill—but only a handful of houses.

Ben was looking for a rock with Dall Burn House carved on it, which David Lindsay had said wasn't easy to see. And that if he came to a stone bridge, he'd know he'd gone too far.

Ben had read David Lindsay's last book of poems on the train to Edinburgh the night before, and he was thinking about what to ask David Lindsay, and wondering what kind of a person he was. There was one poem of Lindsay's he couldn't get out of his mind. One weaving images of Icarus with the silken-threaded wings of paratroopers in the war shot on the way down, who hung, paralyzed or dead, like prey caught in the tentacles of poisonous jellyfish. It had made him think of the Poles at Arnhem. And the Eighty-second Airborne at Ste. Mère Église, hanging from trees by the church.

He'd been driving past pale lacy bracken under tall white birch, and he'd come to a clearing, on his right—a wide swath of field that swept up a long hill where a house sat almost at the top with evergreens gathered on both sides.

He could just see the beginning of a low humpback bridge, halfway around a curve. And he slowed almost to a stop till he found the overgrown driveway into the evergreen woods that bordered the long pasture. As he turned to the right, he saw Dall Burn House carved on a small rock that lay almost hidden by holly bushes beside the gravel drive.

There was a row of pine trees studded between the drive and the quick slipping stream on his left. And Ben opened his window in spite of the rain to listen to the sound of falling water and breathe the scent of wet pine.

He had to downshift into second to make it up the hill, then slow for the curve to the right at the top, into a clearing by a two-story white harled cottage, with its right end toward the loch.

He felt his pockets for his notebook, and put on his cor-duroy jacket, and then walked up the mossy flagstone path, overhung by ivy and dripping fern.

He knocked, and waited, and was just about to knock again, when a woman's face looked out the sidelight to the left of the wide oak door.

He said, "Hello. I'm Ben Reese," when the door opened.

And yet half a second later, she'd already finished saying, "I know," in an American accent. She looked straight at Ben and smiled with her eyes, at least as much as with her mouth, a skeptical sort of teasing grin, like she was waiting for him to catch up.

As soon as she'd smiled, he said, "Kate!" Then stood in the doorway and stared at her until she laughed.

"I know. Who would've believed it? But please, come in." She was wearing a V-necked cotton sweater, pale green over tan pants, and she was pushing the sleeves up as she moved away from the door.

"I never thought I'd see you again. What are you doing here?"

"David Lindsay is Graham's father."

"Is he? I had no idea." Ben had already decided Kate was more interesting looking than she'd been at nineteen, and he was trying to figure out why. The bones stood out better. More cheekbones. More jaw. And she seemed taller than Ben remembered too. Five-seven maybe. With shorter hair. Not quite shoulder length, but the same dark brown, parted on one side and tucked behind that ear. "I don't think Graham and I talked much about family. At least not that I remember."

"We spent a lot of time asking questions, you and Graham and I. During the war, at least. 'Where did the universe come from, and why? What's the future of civilization as we know it? And what are we supposed to be doing in it—if we survive the war?'" She'd shut the door, and was smiling at Ben as she edged back toward the stairs.

"Exactly."

"David just dozed off in the sitting room. He'll wake up in ten or fifteen minutes. Or we can get him up now if you're in a rush."

"No, that's okay. You and I can talk for a minute."

"Would you mind coming into the kitchen? I'm finishing up a batch of cookies."

"What'd you do after the war? You must've gone back to school."

"Oh, yeah. In English. I write semihistorical fiction, and even the occasional espionage novel. It's interesting. To me, at least. And it usually keeps food on the table. What about you?"

As they walked through the hall to the back of the house, Ben told her he'd become an archivist, which he hadn't even heard of as a possible occupation when they'd known each other before.

She arranged oatmeal cookies on a wire rack, as they talked about Wales in '43, when he was an American Ranger helping Graham Lindsay, the Scot she was about to marry, train a British commando unit.

"Remember how panicked Graham was the day we got married? How he looked at you from the front pew and said, 'I'd betterr take charrge of meself soon, or ye'll have to take my place in the cerremony'?" Kate and Ben both laughed. And then she asked if he'd married Jessie. "And where were you sent after Normandy?"

Ben told her all the things he rarely talked about. Nearly dying in Germany. Being flown to a railhead in France lashed under the undercarriage of a Piper Cub. Not marrying Jessie till he could count on being reasonably whole. Spending most of the first year and a half of their marriage lying in hospitals getting cut up and stitched back together.

"So the scar on your hand's from the war? And that's why you can't bend your finger?"

"Yes. I had to learn to write with my right hand."

"Does the scar go all the way up your arm?"

"It wraps up, and around, and goes over my shoulder." He was beginning to remember the way Kate asked questions he never would've asked. Calmly, impersonally, as though everything's worthy of being considered, and there's nothing she wouldn't answer herself.

"I won't ask if there're other scars." Her left eyebrow was set at an ironic angle, and she was smiling at Ben from the corners of her eyes.

Ben laughed as he took the oatmeal cookie she handed him, and said, "You're sure? You never avoided anything when I knew you before."

"I've gotten better. There may even be things I don't want to talk about too. Where'd you go back to school?"

"I finished in history at I.U., then got my master's in library science in rare books and special collections, and did my Ph.D. in American studies at the next two universities where Jessie taught.

"Does she teach English?"

"She did."

"Did that feel funny? You being a student and her being a professor?"

"No, we didn't care. We had twelve years before she died that were better than either one of us had any right to expect." He could see Kate was about to ask, so he told her. The premature baby. The two separate sets of complications that killed his wife and his son at the same time.

Ben was sitting on a wooden stool at the open end of the narrow U-shaped kitchen, watching Kate hold her hair out of her face as she leaned over the oven and examined the second sheet of cookies.

She stood up and stared at him, her eyebrows tight against her large blue eyes, her lips pulled in between her teeth against the matter-of-fact delivery. "I'm sorry, Ben."

"I know."

"How long ago did it happen?"

"Four years. Did you ever get my letter?"

"What letter?"

"I got your parents' address, once I remembered he taught at Northwestern, and I wrote and asked what had happened to you two. He wrote back and told me Graham had been killed, and that you were living in Chicago, but you were spending that summer in Scotland. He gave me an address over here, and I wrote but never heard back."

"I never got it. When was that?"

"I don't know exactly. Jessie and I were at Alderton by then. Maybe '53 or '4. How did Graham die?"

"Arnhem."

"I'm sorry, Kate."

"Yeah, one of Monty's brilliant ideas. The biggest parachute drop of the war behind German lines. You know, the Dutch underground told him there was a German Panzer Division there, and any idiot knows infantry doesn't do well against armor."

"Right, but Monty wouldn't call it off—"

"No. So Graham and the rest of them with British First Airborne got cut off and killed like sitting ducks, trying to take a bridge the rest of the Allies couldn't get to."

"I've heard that General Browning, Boy Browning, Daphne du Maurier's husband, told Monty when they were first planning the operation, 'I think we may be going one bridge too far.' And that wasn't the only screwup, by any means. But for you, thinking it was really botched must make it even worse."

"It used to. But grief is grief. Right? And you know what that's like." Kate Lindsay shrugged her shoulders and cocked her head to one side, then dropped a spoonful of batter onto another cookie sheet.

"I had years with Jessie, though, and you only had a few months. So you never went back to nursing?"

"I just did it to help during the war. I was only a practical nurse anyway, and I ended up doing mostly administrative stuff, even at the hospital in Wales. I was never any good at it. I got way too emotionally involved."

"You weren't at the hospital in Swansea when they sent me back after I went in at Omaha."

"No, I was transferred the day of the invasion. Were you one of the commandos attached to the Canadian Strike Force? The one that went into Omaha the night before D-Day?"

"Yep."

"I guessed that, but I didn't know. Were you badly hurt?"

"Not then. Just shrapnel in fairly safe places. Unlike 95 percent of the others who went in."

"Boy, were you lucky."

"Fortunate anyway, yes. So what are you doing here?"

"David's eighty-two and he needs somebody to live with him. His wife died six years ago. And he's got pretty bad glaucoma that's not going to do anything but get worse. He's in good shape physically. He walks all the time, and he doesn't have heart problems or anything life threatening, but his peripheral vision's terrible and he can fall over things without seeing them. He can stay alone for a few days. A neighbor can come in and make sure he's okay, but not permanently. Anyway, we get along well. He's an interesting person. He still writes poetry. And he understands why I have to have peace and quiet and be left alone to work. So I told him I'd stay here while he needs me. I built on a bedroom and bath for myself on the first floor. And I redid a shed as a studio in the woods."

"That sounds almost idyllic."

"Yes. David says that if he gets ill, he won't let me stay on. That he's already made other plans. But, we'll have to see what happens."

"You never remarried?" Ben was looking out the side window at the front edge of the fir forest, at the small harled house with wide front windows overlooking the loch.

"I never came close. How 'bout you?"

"Nope."

Neither one of them said anything else while she slipped the cookie sheet in the oven. Then she asked if he'd like a cup of coffee.

"Thanks."

"Black, right? So why do you want to talk to David?"

Ben told her all of it. About Georgina's letter and what he was trying to do.

And Kate said, "Why you?"

"Do you remember me talking about a professor I had as an undergraduate at I.U. named Richard West?"

Kate thought for a minute and nodded. "The tall guy who got you interested in literature?"

"Right. He was murdered in November, and I tracked down the killer. Then there was another case over here this summer that I helped solve for a friend."

"Ye know each otherr then, do ye?" David Lindsay was standing in the dining room ten feet behind Ben. He was as tall as Ben, but broader, with thick white hair curling around a massive head.

"We do, actually. This is the Ben Reese who was Graham's best man when we got married."

David Lindsay shook Ben's hand and then held it for a minute between both his own. "It's a vera great pleasurre to meet you. Graham wrote us about you from Wales. His mother and I tried to get to the wedding, but with trains full the way they were in the warr, it wasn't possible."

"Let me give you a plate of cookies to take wherever you decide to talk, and then I'll go back to work. You want coffee, David?" David nodded and Kate handed him a steaming mug. "Could I get one of you to take the cookies out of the oven when this goes off?" She handed Ben the timer after he said he'd be glad to, and then she asked if he wanted to stay for dinner.

"I can't. I wish I could. But I've got to drive back to Stonehaven. I'll come another time, if you'll invite me."

"Sure. Whenever you want."

"Shall we sit in the library?" David raised his eyebrows as he asked the question and they bristled like large white caterpillars. Which made Ben smile, as he followed David down the center hall to the library on the right by the front door.

"Sit yerself down, while I throw a log on the fire."

Ben sank into a low blue chair on the right of the red brick fireplace and watched sparrows squabble in a spruce tree on the edge of the back woods.

David poked three pine logs into place on smoldering coals, then eased himself into the chair that faced Ben. "Now, what can I do for you, young man?"

Ben told him everything. About the letter, and the postscript, and the investigation he was doing.

"I can't take it in! Who could have wanted to kill Georgina? It's vera disturbing indeed!"

"Did she say anything that seems related?"

"Nothing whatever. I knew she was more preoccupied than usual the last month or more. When we spoke on the telephone, and when we met our one last time in Aberdeen." He paused and blew his nose and then put the handkerchief back in his sweater vest. "As you've indicated yourself, one did hearr Robbie MacAlpin speak the occasional brash word to her, or one saw the irritated glance at a faculty meeting, but I wouldn't have thought it was anything vera significant."

"Georgina didn't refer to it?"

"No. She was vera much taken up with her writers retreat. Deciding how to select the candidates, and that sort of thing, and I didn't give a thought to the fact that she seemed preoccupied. Although, I do rememberr wondering, the last time we spoke, right before she went to Oxford, if she sounded somewhat unsettled concerning the future of the retreat. She didn't seem quite as cairtain as she had been that she'd be able to arrange it afterr all. I thought it might have been the expense of it, and I didn't like to inquire." David Lindsay waited for Ben to comment and sucked on an upper tooth.

"What was the animosity from MacAlpin about?"

"Personal ambition and jealousy, I should think. Insecurity too. And childish pique as well. Fed, no doubt, by the Allen Award."

"I don't know what that is."

"It's given by students and faculty to the most respected lecturer in the English department. Georgina won it four times. She was also awarded tenure at an early age. And Robbie has yet to receive either. Her book on Trollope was published by a vera fine publisher who rejected Rob's biography of Hardy. And then she was offered the summer post at Oxford, when I know he wanted it vera badly. He's working on a book on twentieth-century British novelists he hopes will be used in preparatory schools, and he felt the need of getting away from home and the distractions of his many offspring. Georgina was also a woman of independent means, and it's my opinion that he resented that above all. That she didn't need to work, but did. He seemed to think it was her presence and mine that kept him from fulfilling his promise. And he was vera pleased indeed when I retired."

"Is he a competent teacher?"

"Aye, I think he is. He's capable. He knows when a thing's proved and when it's not. Which is more than can be said for many professors and writerrs today."

"Exactly. And what do you do with people who hold mutually exclusive views without blinking an eye? I had a cab driver in London the other day tell me in one breath that his ex-wife is immoral for having had an affair, and then say in the next, when talking about a neighbor who'd robbed a store owner no one likes, that right and wrong are whatever we say they are for ourselves, and we don't have a right to evaluate anyone's behavior."

"If he were closely questioned, I suspect we'd find that he doesn't live that way a-tall. Every time he says 'this is fair' and 'that isn't,' he makes a liar of himself. I do think I should mention that Robbie MacAlpin's antipathy to G. may have to do with his wife, Emily, as well. She's a bacteriologist who already held a position at Aberdeen when he arrived to work on his doctorate, and he may be desperate to prove he can keep up."

"Why isn't he popular with his students?"

"He's too much a man of moods. Irascible one minute, fawning on his students the next. The former irritates. The latter breeds contempt. He's a seeker after attention too. You know the sort, I'm sure, and when he doesn't get it, others have been made to bear the brunt."

"Does he want what he wants enough to murder for it?"

"I wouldn't have thought so. Yet, how many murderers have I met? Aside from high-ranking officers. And the sort who roam the precincts of White Hall." David's face had set against itself and his eyes hardened on his last words.

And Ben changed the subject. "Did Georgina talk about anything surprising or unexpected in recent weeks?"

"Well, the last time we met, at luncheon in Aberdeen, she did say something about having to learn at her age that one can't rely on one's family."

"She didn't explain what she meant?"

"No. Though she did seem a bit worn those last weeks. Beaten down somehow, or disappointed. I thought she might be wearying of her many responsibilities."

"Do you think people took advantage of her?"

"No, she chose to be too kind. Which is rather a different matter."

"Have you read her poetry?"

"I have not! I had no idea she wrote poetry."

"Apparently she didn't talk to anyone about it except Ross and one childhood friend. She used her poems as a kind of diary, and she went out of her way not to take them seriously as literature."

"Aye. She would've done."

"She used them to analyze human nature too, as she saw it in people she knew."

"She was unusually careful not to discuss other people, and I always thought there must have been a definite reason. An indiscretion, perhaps, when she was a young girl. Committed by her, possibly. Or inflicted on her, either one."

"Who would she have referred to as C. B.?"

David Lindsay leaned his large white head against the back of his chair and settled his fingertips together beneath his chin. "I have no idea whatsoever."

The timer went off and Ben went to take out the cookies. And when he came back, he asked if Georgina had talked about collectors of any kind. Or of leaving her house to Ellen. Or there being some reason for giving it up.

"If she did refer to leaving Cairnwell, I didn't understand what she meant. Though I do remember one conversation that may be apropos. It was the last time we met in Aberdeen, two weeks before she went to Oxford. I was describing a book I'd bought titled Mont St. Michel and Chartres, which Henry Adams, the great-grandson of your President John Adams, wrote and privately published without putting his name on the title page. He gave copies to his friends and relations, and the one I bought was inscribed by him to his cousin Mabel. I paid a shilling for it, for it was on the 'cheap table' outside James Thin's in Edinburgh, but I knew it to be worth something more. I told Georgina I'd loan it to her when I'd finished, for the writing is quite fine. And I went on to describe a ratherr eccentric collector who was browsing in Thin's shop. It was then she asked what I thought of collectors."

"Did she steer the conversation to that specifically?"

"She did not. I brought it up myself."

"Are you a collector?"

"No. But I have learned something of the world of collecting from two friends, both long dead, who were dealers before the war. One in books. The other in antique furniture."

"How did you answer her?" Ben turned over another page in his notebook, then leaned forward with his elbows on his thighs.

"I told her of an event that took place many years ago."

"Was Georgina interested?"

"Moderately, I thought, yes."

"Would you be willing to tell me?"

"Yes, of course. You see, I learned of the incident from my late brotherr, who was then a solicitor in Inverness. It was years ago, in the twenties probably, that he drew up the wills of a book collector and his wife. The husband was a man of means, and though he collected later works as well, his primary interest was incunabula. By that I mean fifteenth-century books—"

"From the 'cradle period' of printing."

"Aye. Broadsides, scientific works, religious meditations. He wasn't a collector with a narrowly defined interest, but one who bought as his fancy took him. He died at his home near Grantown-on-Spey, and his wife, who was by then an invalid, decided to have his collection assessed in order to donate the most worthy books to a college library."

"When was this?"

"I should think it was 1930, but I can't say for certain. A young man was duly selected, a book dealer from Edinburgh, I believe, to evaluate the collection. He lived at the widow's country house while he sorted through the books, which was vera much the standard practice. During the weeks he was there, the invalid became quite attached to him and changed her will accordingly. She left him several of the most valuable works in her husband's collection, and then died quite soon thereafterr. She had a weak heart, and some sort of cancer, stomach cancer I think, or intestinal cancer, and she died terribly painfully."

"Was there vomiting involved, do you remember?"

"Possibly. I can't say absolutely. Though there were no signs whatever of any sort of drug or poison having been administered. Everyone involved with the case believed it to be vera much a matter of natural causes. My brother found it odd, however, that the young man who inherited the books should drop from sight so vera soon after receiving them. He moved rather quickly from the address he'd given. And it was my brother's considered opinion, after having ferreted out the partial inventory the husband had been compiling at his death, that one or two other volumes may have disappeared as well. It was a more innocent age perhaps, and no verra serious search was instituted, but my brother always suspected that those books had been stolen."

"Do you remember the man's name?"

"I never heard it. My brother took great pride in the discretion due his position. And, of course, the last time my brother and I discussed it was twenty-five years or more ago."

"When did the woman die?"

"The following winter. Early 1931, if the husband died in 1930. January perhaps. There was a terrible blizzard that delayed the arrival of the invalid's physician."

"Do you remember any of the books that were bequeathed, or ended up missing?"

"There were three by an early Venician printer."

"The Aldine Press? The anchor and dolphin pressmark?"

"Possibly. I don't recall. There was a first edition of Dante's Divine Comedy, I remember that. I can't quite—oh, and Seneca's Philosophies, if I'm not mistaken."

"I don't know why, but a lot of explorers and ships' captains, starting in the 1400s, at least from England, took Seneca's Philisophies to sea with them."

"Did they? Perhaps it suited such dangerous pursuits. There was another particularly fine book written in the English language. It may have had something to do with early science. There was another work as well, by an Elizabethan, but I shan't remember what."

Ben wrote something else in his notebook, and then leaned back in his chair. "How did Georgina react when you told her about the books, and the lady's death?"

"She discussed the urge to collect in broad terms. And referred in passing to her neighbor, Lady Hay, and her interest in collecting antiques." David Lindsay sighed and shook his head.

And Ben stared at the fire, for a minute, and sucked at the end of his pen. "Was there anything else that Georgina talked about that was unusual in any way? In the last months before her death?"

"Not that I remember."

The timer on the coffee table went off again.

And Ben thanked David for his help.

"Come on in, Ben. I'll just be a second." Kate was in her studio, the small rough-stuccoed stone cottage two hundred feet from the main house on the edge of the evergreen woods. She was sitting at a desk that had been built of pine planks, across the whole front wall of windows, typing on a large electric typewriter.

There were framed quotations standing on shelves between books, and Ben stood on Kate's left and read the one with the largest type that sat where she'd see it best.

IT'S EASIER TO PRAY FOR A BORE
THAN TO GO AND SEE HIM.

Ben smiled to himself and said, "C. S. Lewis," after the typing had stopped. "I know which I'd rather do. I fight it all the time."

"Me too. Small talk. Boredom. Petty exchanges. Talking to people who don't talk about anything else, even when you know they could. But then what I like isn't the only issue."

"No. Have you read a lot of Lewis?"

"That was reasonably discreet of you."

"Was it?"

"No, I'm not an agnostic anymore, in case you wanted to ask. I put up a very good fight, but I finally had to give in." They both laughed, before Kate stretched her arms over her head and ruffled the back of her hair. "Chesterton had a lot to do with it. And Lewis. And George MacDonald."

"I started thinking about it in Germany. I looked down on my own dead body, and knew someone was sending me back."

"I don't understand what you mean."

"I'd taken fifteen hits from a machine gun on a Tiger Tank and I was bleeding to death between the lines, right in the middle of a firefight. And then, suddenly, I was looking down, from somewhere above the ground, at me lying dead on a snowdrift. But then less than a second later, I knew, absolutely, that I'd live. That I was being sent back. And there was a mind with intentions that made that decision."

"How'd you react to that?"

"I studied all kinds of religious thought in the hospitals. And ended up where I'd started as a little kid, with the God I'd learned about from my parents and their church, but with a whole lot more depth and understanding."

"A lot of people never really study it again once they grow up, so they think the ten-year-old version they're still carrying around is all that it's about. You know, I've always wondered what Graham thought about just before he died. We never got to talk after he got shipped out."

"I know what you mean. I've wondered that about a lot of people. So, if I need some help with this investigation, would you be interested? I don't mean anything dangerous, but—"

"Sure. Let me know what I can do." She stood then, next to Ben, and put her hands in the back pockets of her linen pants.

"I'd like you to talk to someone named Robbie MacAlpin. David knows him."

"I met him once too, in Aberdeen."

"Good, that'll help. I'll call you about it later. I have to think about it more first."

"I'll be here, that's for sure."

"Thanks, Kate. I've got to go." Ben smiled and walked toward the door.

"Why don't you take some cookies for the road? I put a small paper bag to the left of the stove, and there's cheese on the counter, and strawberries too. Help yourself to whatever you want. I can come in and get it organized—"

"No, don't bother, you need to work."

"I'm glad you're alive, Dr. Benjamin Reese."

"You too. It makes the world feel friendlier." He smiled and started across the lawn toward the house, ignoring the rain, walking the way he always did. Till he looked back at Kate and waved.

Ian Cunningham was sitting on what was left of a cottage wall fifteen feet from the edge of a cliff, staring at the sea as it threw itself against high solitary rocks covered by crying birds. He'd started by considering the grass-covered ruins of the fishing village where he sat, but had then moved on to sermon illustrations. To how much he should quote from the Greek. And how much to talk of shepherds in ancient Palestine when discussing Jesus' description of himself as the Good Shepherd, who would "lay down his life for his sheep."

As "the door that leads to eternal life" too, I shall have to mention that. And that shepherds in Palestine, even today, lie down in the door of the sheepfold at night, becoming the door that protects their sheep from predators of every sort.

Rural Scots will appreciate that. They know sheep. And loss as well.

I wonder why Margaret asked me to send this particular sermon to the sculptor at Cairnwell? He's never darkened our door, and there's a very fine line indeed between friendly overtures and forcing one's beliefs upon an unsuspecting acquaintance.

I ought to wonder what time it-tis too, since... Oh, dear. Late again. Good thing it's my free day.

Ian Cunningham leapt off the wall, climbed to the top of the steep grass-covered headland and started down the left edge of the broccoli field toward the old church at Kinneff.

As he strode down the hill, Ian considered the seaward side of his church, sitting staunchly and peacefully parallel to the sea—a plain cream-colored harled stone church with an unassuming steeple. And he remembered the wonder he'd felt the first time he'd set eyes on it—the countryside tucked around it, the North Sea beside it, the view of a coast that was home to a plain and stalwart people he'd come to love with a fierceness that sometimes surprised him.

He thought about Alice Montgomery, lying ill in the hospital, as he took the path to the left at the bottom of the hill, then followed the curve of the drive to the right around the dressed stone wall, past the gate to his own front door, toward the church's car park—thinking what to do for her children, in addition to food and clothes.

No car in sight. Which seems rather odd. But no matter. I shall dash into the kirk, and make myself useful, while I wait for him to arrive.

Ian opened the black iron gate in the part of the stone wall that enclosed the church's earliest cemetery, and reminded himself to call round again to see how William Price was getting on since his wife's death.

I shall take him more of Margaret's scones. And lettuce and strawberries from the garden.

Ian could smell the old wood, the old hymnals, the mustiness of centuries spent on the edge of water, as soon as he opened the low wooden door to the vestry. He inhaled contentedly as he turned to his left, away from the stone stairs, and opened the door to the church itself.

He straightened papers on the guest table first, and then prayed for the young man driving up from St. Andrews. That as they discussed his research—the history of Kinneff Old Church, and the hiding of the Regalia from Cromwell's men—they would talk about the meaning behind church history. The Mind that created mind, as well as soul and spirit.

Ellen Winter listened to the scrape of someone else's shoes on cold stone as she opened the old wooden door to the sanctuary from the small wood-paneled vestry of Kinneff Old Church and called Ian Cunningham's name.

The tall thin sandy-haired man with his back to Ellen was pushing a mop at the end of the pews on the far side of the church by the long sea wall. He gazed out one of the windows at the fields rising up to the headlands, then leaned the mop on the high octagonal wooden pulpit, and began to straighten hymnals.

Ellen said Cunningham's name again, but the middle-aged man didn't turn, so she walked up the side aisle toward the stairs to the pulpit. But before she reached them, he looked up from a pew, and as soon as he saw her, he jumped.

"I'm sorry. I didn't mean to startle you, Mr. Cunningham."

"My dear, Ellen, it's not yourr fault a-tall. I'm becoming quite hard of hearing."

"You weren't before, when I lived here, were you?"

"I served in the artillery, you see, so it's worsening over time."

"Has the young man come up from St. Andrews yet?"

"No, he's terribly late. I was to meet him in the kirk, but if we walk to the manse and make ourselves a cup of tea, he'll stop there to find me I'm sure. No, I'll alter the note on the door."

"Why is he coming?"

"He's researching the kirk in the seventeenth century. The wife of the commander at Dunnottor Castle, and the wife of the ministerr here at Kinneff smuggled the Scepter and the Sword of State out of the besieged castle right through Cromwell's lines."

"Then they buried them under the kirk floor?"

"Yes, they did indeed. It was a time of bravery and a time of shame. Like every other, I suppose. I apologize, my dear. I forgot you'd have heard it all before." Ian Cunningham was walking toward the door, smiling at Ellen. His thin plain face saved from seeming cold or sharp by the kindness behind his eyes. "Yet what shall any of us do without Georgina? Margaret and I enjoyed her company so much. She was terribly wise, you know. And a wonderful influence in the kirk."

"I think you ought to read this." They were just inside the vestry door, and Ellen pulled Georgina's letter out of her purse and handed it to Ian.

"Bifocals. The bane of the middling and the aged. I was given my first pair yesterday, and I'm still utterly befuddled." He held the pages at arm's length, then moved them closer to his long narrow nose, and stood very still till he'd finished reading. "What a terribly sad business! Could she have been right, do you think? Murder seems so unlikely."

"But was she the kind of person who'd imagine it?"

"No. Not to have talked about murder with such conviction. And yet it seems so surprising. She never mentioned the first worrd." Ian rubbed the places where the dark plastic frames pressed on his large nose as he handed Ellen the letter. "What do you have in hand? Have you found an investigator?"

Ellen told him about Ben.

And he said, "That's a blessing anyway, having someone you know and trust. May I be of assistance in any way? I'd very much like to help Georgina see that justice is done. Let me just latch the gate behind us."

"Did Georgina bring you a sixteenth-century manuscript written in Greek and ask you to translate it for her?"

"She did. Yes. I finished it a very few days before she left for Oxford."

"The transcript wasn't in her desk, or in Oxford, or anywhere else in the house. At least not that we've found."

"How very odd. Though how the document could be connected with her death I don't know. I expect I threw out the first draft. The messy one I used to make the fair copy for her. Though I can't be altogether certain. Mind the door. It falls shut on one's back when one least expects it."

Ellen closed the manse's front door and followed Ian into the den on the right. She watched him drop into a torn leather chair barricaded behind papers and books piled neatly and carefully on an enormous mahogany desk, whose veneer was peeling off in chunks.

"If I kept it…" The long face peered across the stacks with an expression of patient contemplation. He shifted papers, and picked up books, and Ellen could see the hope die as he considered one spot, and then another. "It's no good I'm afraid."

"Can you remember the gist of what it said?"

"I should be able to sketch the most salient points." He stood and clasped his hands behind his narrow back, then stared at the floor as he walked from Ellen's side of the room to the other, where he turned to face her. "It was written by a woman named Alysoun Pryor Hume. Her father, John Pryor, had been murdered in the churchyard in Burford, England, in November 1546. His purse had been stolen, and the assumption was he'd been killed by a thief."

"Was Henry VIII still on the throne?" Ellen sat as she talked in a chair by the tall front window.

"He was, yes. And that's a very important point. For the widow Pryor, as well as her daughterr, Alysoun, had remained Roman Catholics. It was a very dangerous time for Catholics. Worship was prohibited. Their lands were being confiscated. They were being forced to the very periphery of the body politic. And John Pryor, unlike his wife, had converted to Henry's Church of England. Would you care for a cup of tea?"

"If you're going to have one yourself. What happened after his death?"

"Well, one Richard Witney, traderr, Pryor's neighbor to the west, suggested she take refuge in France until the English Crown became more tolerant. For at the death of John Pryor, she and her daughter lost all Protestant protection." Ian and Ellen had walked through the hall into the kitchen, and Ian was leaning over, trying to light the front burner of a tiny decrepit gas stove. "Witney had many times offered to buy a part of John Pryor's lands, and he now offered to buy the entire estate, at a fair but modest figure, with one significant proviso. Whenever she wished to return from France, he'd sell her her property at the very same figure for which he'd purchased it from her."

"That was nice of him."

"So Elinor thought. And she sold Richard Witney her lands without insisting that the proviso be put in the papers of sale. Then she moved her daughter and her elderly motherr to France, only weeks before Henry VIII died in early 1547. His Protestant son remained on the throne till his death in 1553, when he was succeeded by his older sisterr, Mary, a devout but humorless Roman Catholic."

"Then the Pryors come back from France?"

"They didn't, as a matter of fact. Elinor's mother had recently had a terrible stroke, apoplexy as it was called then. And of course, Mary's reign was fraught with intrigue and upheaval, since she set about persecuting Protestants as fanatically as Henry had the Roman Catholics. And though it was a very unusual sentiment at the time, Elinor Pryor was as opposed to persecution of Protestants as she had been that of Catholics."

"Elinor was an interesting woman."

"She was. She even read and wrote Latin, Greek, and French. And employed a cleric to tutor her daughter in all three languages. Then her motherr died, and Elinor Pryor started home across the channel with Alysoun. Yet a peaceful homecoming was not to be, for Elinor became gravely ill with feverr on the way and died in an English inn near the Dover coast. Alysoun, the writer of our memoir, made her way back to Burford with her motherr's remains, intent on repurchasing the Pryor estate. Cream?" Ian was bent over a tiny refrigerator, gazing across his shoulder at Ellen.

"Not for me, thanks."

"As fate would have it, of course, Bloody Mary had died only days before, and the Protestant Elizabeth was now on the throne, and Witney persuaded Alysoun to take the farmhouse that had previously been his for her own use until it could be determined whether Elizabeth would persecute Catholics as her half sister had persecuted Protestants."

"Alysoun must have been in shock by then."

"Indeed. Though Witney did treat her reasonably well, providing house servants and tenant farmers. But whenever she approached Witney asking to buy back the family home, there was always a reason why the transference of property had to be postponed. Yet, during that time, she taught the Witney daughter and son Latin and French. And the son became quite infatuated with her. The father, Richard Witney, packed young Robert off to Aberdeen, where he assumed the management of the fledgling family trading company. It wasn't long before Robert transformed it into a very prosperous concern, and married into the Leslie family, accepting Cairnwell House as the dowry. Have I introduced too many names and dates?"

"No, I think I'm following okay."

"Shortly thereafter, Alysoun Pryor converted to the Protestant faith and married Peter Hume, the bookish son of an Anglican minister. She asked Richard Witney again, with some considerable heat, to allow her to buy back what belonged to her, but he delayed and put her off. Then old Richard Witney died, and his son, Robert, inherited.

"Now, the father had agreed, unbeknownst to Alysoun, to sell the Pryor land to his own daughter's husband, and after he died, Robert fulfilled that agreement. His Scottish holdings were far more valuable by then, and he wished to invest the money from Burford in ships for his North Sea trade, despite a letter of appeal from Alysoun."

"That's awful! How could they treat her like that!" Ellen shook her head, then pushed a mug of tea to Ian across the table.

"So as Alysoun bore children, and the funds she'd once had to buy back her home diminished, the day came when she finally understood, once and for all, that she would never regain her ancestral lands. She had no choice but to live on sufferance on the Witney farm, even though she'd come to believe that Richard Witney had deliberately tricked her mother, and possibly murdered her father."

"That's disgusting!"

"He was quite an unhappy soul, of course. As was his son at Cairnwell. At least from what Georgina told me of the Witney manuscript she herself translated from the French."

"What happened to Alysoun?"

"Her fortunes declined, through bad crops, and the uninspired management of an impractical husband. Alysoun's three sons died very young, but her daughter, Mary, lived. Though she was no great intellect, unlike her parents, and grew up to be very fond of Robert Witney and his wife and children, when they came to Burford to visit.

"On the last page of the manuscript, Alysoun wrote that she intended to bequeath her memoir to Mary for safekeeping—even though Mary wouldn't be able to translate it or understand its significance—with very firm instructions that it was to be guarded with her own life, for it offered the key to an extremely important matter of Pryor family history. And thus the memoir ends."

"What happened to it after she gave it to Mary?"

"Georgina learned from Robert Witney's memoir—"

"That's the son?"

"Yes, that Mary's parents both died of a flux, Alysoun and Peter, when Mary was still quite young. It was then that Robert brought Mary to Cairnwell 'out of the goodness of his heart' to raise her with his own children...wait. That's a thought. Come with me, my dear, we may be in luck."

Ian Cunningham marched into the hall and stopped beside an old rickety telephone table behind the stairs. He took a pile of scrap paper out of a largish basket and began to shuffle through the pages.

"Did G. tell you anything else about the Witney manuscript?"

"No, she didn't."

"I'm a Pryor, so maybe I'm not being objective, but...a car just pulled up to the door."

"Did it?" He took the basket with him into his study and looked out the window beside his desk. "It's Margaret back from the shops." Ian opened the window and asked the short, pleasant-looking woman who'd waved to him when she'd heard the window, if she'd done anything with the rough draft of Georgina's manuscript.

"You threw it in the dust bin, and I fished it out—"

"I can't quite hear you."

"I PUT IT IN THE SCRAP BASKET BY THE TELEPHONE. It's close to the bottom, blank sides up, in amongst scraps of your old sermons."

"It's a good thing you're frugal! Of course you know that already, don't you, my dear? Ellen Winter's come to see us."

"I'm so glad! I shall be right in."

"Here it-tis! Now I feel much better."

"Ian, I PASSED A YOUNG MAN, THIS SIDE OF THE COAST ROAD, IN A VERY DELICATE-LOOKING CAR, SEARCHING FOR THE KIRK. I GAVE HIM DIRECTIONS AND HE OUGHT TO BE HERE ANY MOMENT."

"You were driving so speedily he couldn't keep up, is that it?" Ian squinted his eyes accusingly and laughed at the expression on Margaret's soft dimpled face.

"I DON'T WISH TO COMMIT MYSELF AT THE MOMENT. HAVE YOU ASKED ELLEN IF SHE'LL STAY TO TEA?"

"We've finished one pot and the kettle's on the boil. Come in and say hello. I shall dash out and bring in the groceries."

CHAPTER EIGHT

MICHAEL SHAW WAS SITTING on a dirt colored sofa in his shop staring at a limestone panel, a bas-relief, four feet high and eight feet wide, braced against a whitewashed wall.

Storm clouds rolled across the top, blown from left to right. A thin pointed cypress on the left edge behind a high stone wall was bent almost sideways by the rain and wind toward a second stone wall on the right, on the other side of a center opening. It was the only door to the sheepfold, and the shepherd lay across it on his left side, protecting the sheep with his own bent body hunched against the wind, long hair blowing across an unfinished face, arms stretched forward gathering lambs, sheep huddling against his legs, one small lamb standing on another tucking its head under the shepherd's coat. His crook leaned against the stone wall at the right edge of the panel, a crooked gnarled root hooked naturally at the top so that at second or third glance it looked like a twisted cross.

Almost everything about the sculpture could've been sentimental, but it wasn't. Because of the execution. The stark, elongated strength of the style. The cold impersonal power. The strange, elusive, painful sense of undisguised reality. Life, every day, without comfort or illusion. In real places. In real weather. Sheep and shepherds in all ages. Carved by a modernist who hates what's easy and predictable—who'd cut it out of Europe in the Middle Ages, and the East too, deliberately, Egypt and Samaria and Phoenicia.

There were still claw marks on the rock face. Parallel grooves from toothed chisels. Some of them he'd leave. Some he'd work out with flat chisels and files and the power grinder. Sandpaper too, on most of the surfaces. A matter of time and muscle. Nothing he couldn't do in his sleep.

"But why can't I see the face!" Michael Shaw had been staring at the shepherd for over an hour. Drawing pad across his knees. Crumpled paper on the concrete floor. Cigarette butts in a saucer on the sofa. A broken pencil snapped and thrown from where Michael leaned nearly horizontal—his head on loose stuffing in the back cushion, his long thin legs stretched out as far as they'd go. Agonizing, as usual, about his decisions.

I hope I've left enough stone to furrow the brow against the wind. At the jawline too, and across the lower face. Enough to open the mouth if I wish to and finish the beard as well. *If* and when I actually decide what it is I intend to do.

He'd locked his hands behind his head, and tightened his eyes into slits, and he was knotting the muscles of his jaws, and tapping his right foot on the floor to some hot interior beat. He was white with stone dust (blond beard and hair, bony face, mechanic's overalls, dust mask hanging around his neck), buried in a layer of powdery silt.

He stood up suddenly and shook himself like he itched all over, then picked up the carpenter's belt that held small and medium hammers and three or four favorite chisels. He turned his back on the panel and stalked to the long side wall to the bench by his big compressor. The noise was deafening, when he turned it on, and he switched it off again a minute or two later, still looking at the panel. Then he turned his back on it, fast and deliberately. And stared at a block of limestone on a high, heavy, three-foot square wooden table beside the long bench.

He picked up a medium hammer and a smooth chisel and walked around the block, considering the stone from every possible angle. It was two feet wide as well as deep, and not quite three feet tall, and he'd made chalk marks on most of its surfaces. A face and head had risen out of rock, a woman in middle-age, face turned to the side as though her attention had just been caught by someone on her left. By a question, perhaps, that mattered. That made her think and ponder and face the fact of decision.

The back of the head, the neck, the shoulders, none of that was out yet, but the face was alive. The intelligence, the intensity, the strength and loneliness and dedication. It was all there, concentrated in the eyes and mouth.

Michael pulled his dust mask into place, squinted from long practice, laid the end of the flat chisel against the woman's left temple and struck five quick chipping blows without feeling the jolt or the recoil or the weight of the hammer in his hands. He told himself to find his safety goggles, and he'd just turned to look on the bench, when a voice spoke behind him.

"You must've known Georgina really well."

Michael Shaw spun around to face a six-foot-tall, thin, broad-shouldered American with a quiet reserved skeptical expression in his large gray eyes.

"And who are you, may I ask?"

"Ben Reese. I knocked on the door when the compressor

was running and you couldn't hear me."

"What can I do for you?" Michael's eyes looked tired and edgy, and like the last thing he wanted was to talk to a live human being.

Ben stared at the bas-relief panel from behind the sofa, then walked closer and studied the surfaces of the stone. "Is this a commission?"

"Yes. A private chapel in Yorkshire. A Catholic family has recently purchased a grand house, and this is to go behind the altar to replace a Victorian hanging."

"Raised up? So you can see it above the altar?"

"It's to sit on a panel of limestone with an eight-inch border so that the bottom of this piece is four feet above the floor."

"It's an incredible gift, the talent you've been given."

"Is it? Then why have I *no* idea what to do with the shepherd's face?" Michael pulled his dust mask down, pinning his beard against his neck.

"You've obviously done research. You know about sheep pens in Palestine."

"The entire conception for a piece like this comes from the historical context. Are you an artist?"

"No. I do some restoration work on paintings. I do loose abstract oils once in a while, but I'm not what *I* mean by an artist."

"How would you approach the shepherd?"

"Very carefully. Have you read the Old Testament descriptions of us as sheep who need a shepherd, and the prophesies about the Shepherd who would one day come? Maybe you could compare those to what Jesus says about himself hundreds of years later?"

"I've read the passages the family wished me to depict."

Michael picked up a piece of pencil and leaned against the bench. "The crux of the difficulty comes from having to make art on a fixed schedule. You can't force yourself to produce an idea. They arrive on their own, in their own time."

"You're English?"

"My people are. We moved here twenty years ago when I was ten or eleven."

"Is it easier for you to carve people you know, or people you make up in your head?"

"There's no pattern a-tall. A face I've seen once can start something off, so I often sketch in restaurants and public places. Other times I begin with no idea in mind a-tall. Though I do think Ross's sculpture may have been the best work I've done, and I knew him nearly all my life."

"Could you get the delivery date for the panel postponed?" Ben was looking around the big stone barn at Michael's works in progress—the chimney surrounds leaning against walls, the niche and bowl of what looked like a wall-mounted fountain, broken bits of statuary being copied in full form—as well as uncut blocks and stacked slabs of stone.

"I shan't have a choice if I don't see my way soon. And that will push the next piece I'm scheduled to do later still. I'm not complaining, mind you. It wasn't very long ago that I had no commissions a-tall."

Ben was standing beside Shaw's Georgina, sliding his index finger down the bridge of her nose, following the flare of the nostril and the long delicate trough that ended in her upper lip. "I never met Georgina, but I've seen a lot of photographs. I can't imagine what it's like to be able to do what you do."

"It's all I *am* able to do, for better or worse. Look, I don't mean to be rude, I know you're Ellen's professor friend, but I'm not a-tall clear why you've come to see me."

"She's trying to decide what to do about the quarry, and she wanted me to talk to you and help her make a decision."

"Then I suppose now is as good a time as any." Michael Shaw jerked the dust mask over his head and tossed it on the bench. "I ought to fix myself a bite of supper too, while we talk. I never got round to lunch."

He walked over to the deep stone sink near the door to his apartment, tossed his overalls on a chair, and turned the water on full blast. He stuck his head straight under the faucet and washed his hair and beard with hand soap. Then toweled himself off, and opened the door to his flat.

"Would you care for soup?" Michael was standing by the two-burner stove in his big one-room living space opening a plastic bowl.

"Thanks, but Ellen's expecting me for dinner."

Michael poured what looked like vegetable soup into a dented pan and put it on the burner he'd already lit. "Then how can I help?"

"What reasons did Georgina give for wanting to close the quarry?"

"She couldn't afford to keep it going. Cutting stone without blasting is horrifically expensive. And she said an 'unexpected circumstance' had arisen which made it necessary for her to retrench. She said she'd forego the rent I pay now, that she'd let me stay in the studio without charge, but that the quarry cost more than she could justify. It was never a money-making proposition. Ross was largely doing me a kindness in opening it, though he was interested too, in the technology of it, the machinery primarily, and what he could learn about quarrying stone. And he did use the stone for repairs at Cairnwell."

"When did Georgina talk to you about the quarry?"

"About a week before she left for Oxford."

"How did you react?"

Michael Shaw's green-gray eyes were irritated, and he waited a minute before answering. "I don't see that my reaction is any of your concern."

"In a way it is. Ellen is a young woman a long way from home. I won't be here for more than a couple of weeks, and we've both seen what you did to Ross's statue. Ellen has a right to know what makes you that angry."

Michael lit a cigarette and opened a bottle of bitter. Then he sat in a metal café chair opposite Ben at the small rectangular wooden table and tipped his chair against the wall. "When Georgina told me, all I could think of was how it affected me. I'd had an especially beastly day. I thought I'd botched the shepherd panel beyond saving, and then, when the packers were crating up a chimney front, they badly chipped an end. I was terribly behind with my office work, and I was worrying about how I was to pay several large invoices, while waiting to receive the fees I'm owed. And it was then Georgina told me she was closing the quarry."

"Ah."

"I behaved like an infant. I exploded in a full-blown tantrum, and I've regretted it ever since." Michael Shaw rubbed one eye as though there were something in it, then walked to the stove and stirred the soup. "I told her I'd make her another statue of Ross, free of charge, of course, like the first, as soon as I found the right stone."

"Anger's a strange thing. The times I go over the brink and

won't admit it, not till a long time later, those are definitely the worst."

"It makes one look an even bigger fool."

"Yes. Did you like Georgina? I've found that there was quite a bit of conflict between her and those who knew her."

"Oh, no. No." Michael Shaw snorted and shook his head once very fast before he crushed his cigarette out in a stone ashtray. "No, I didn't like Georgina. Why should I? Because she and Ross took me all over Britain when I was a child, showing me castles and great houses and museums, when my own parents had no interest whatever in such things? Or because they gave me a start when I quit university, providing me with a private quarry, and a nearly perfect place to work, when my own parents were ready to commit hara-kari? No, I didn't like Georgina. Or feel any gratitude a-tall."

"I see."

"I owed them more than I could ever repay, and yet they tried terribly hard never to drive that home." Michael turned his back on Ben, poured soup in a bowl, grabbed a loaf of french bread and carried it back to the narrow table that was pushed up against the front window.

"Why were they so good to you?"

"No reason a-tall, except that that's the way they were, and they had no children of their own. I think they simply looked about them, and took an interest in friends' and relations' children who could use a bit of help or attention. I wasn't the only one by any means. They were very good to Tom Ogilvie, who was the cast-off son of Ross's lunatic sister. And there were local children too. And Jack, of course, in recent years. Perhaps Ellen, as well."

"Were your parents hurt by the Fletchers' involvement in

your life? I'm sorry, that's a personal question."

"Puzzled, I should think. Possibly a bit relieved."

"How soon did you wish you hadn't done what you did to the statue?" Ben's elbows were on the table and he was staring out the window at the thicket of trees between Michael's windows and the road.

"I walked home, poured myself a rather stiff drink, set the glass down without touching it, and dashed back to Cairnwell in the rain to tell Georgina what a fool I was and that I'd do another sculpture of Ross straightaway, as soon as I found the right stone."

"How did she react?"

"She let me in, handed me a towel, made me dinner, and talked to me about how to manage my financial affairs, once the quarry was closed. I shall finish both statues even though she's gone, you know. But this time I shall keep them myself."

"Ellen wants to publish some poems Georgina wrote, and one of them talks about someone called C. B. Ellen needs to check with whoever that is before she goes any further. Who would Georgina have referred to as C. B.?"

"Georgina wrote poetry?" Michael tore an end chunk off the long thin loaf of crusty bread, smeared butter on the broken side, and bit off a large hunk. "Help yourself. Do. Please."

Ben tore and buttered a piece for himself and ate most of it while he watched Michael.

"Was the poem complimentary?"

"Not particularly, no."

"I can't say for sure, of course. She knew many people, as you can imagine, whom I never met. But the name that comes to mind is Clive Baird. He worked in the chemistry lab at Fletcher's until Ross let him go eight or ten years ago. Clive had become a terrible drunk but would never admit it, and after he was fired, he nurtured a very nasty grudge against Ross. He used to ring him in the wee hours of the morning and rave till Ross rang off. Clive knew Tom Ogilvie rather well. I think they may have been at school together, though I don't know that for a fact."

"What sort of person is Tom Ogilvie? From what I've heard, he may think the house should've been his. And being a lawyer, he'd know how to make Ellen's life miserable if he wanted to."

"I assume you know what Georgina did with her stock in Fletcher Tire?"

"She gave Ellen 21 percent, to help care for Cairnwell, and left your father 30. Which means Tom has 49 percent, and can't sell without one of the others agreeing."

"He can't make *any* really serious decision alone, when he'd assumed he'd inherit it all. It's my father's belief that Georgina had no very high opinion of Tom's judgment where money and personal enrichment are concerned, and she decided to rein him in." Michael was leaning back in his chair, running his fingers through his thick curly beard.

"How did Tom take it?"

"Not terribly well. He drove to Fletcher's and accused my father of all sorts of underhanded practices, all in the most polite terms."

"Georgina was no fool. She must've had a good reason."

"Yet it was still a great surprise to all concerned."

"Someone told me Tom studied some kind of science before he took up the law. Biology maybe. Or bacteriology?"

"No, I'm sure he didn't. That was one of the long-standing debates Ross and Tom used to have. Ross thought Fletcher's should be run by someone who understood the science of it. It didn't have to be a chemist who'd been trained in the chemistry of rubber production, though that would've been preferred. He wanted the person in charge, the managing director, to have a scientific background that would enable him to learn the specifics well enough to make technically informed decisions. Tom always took issue, and Ross would laugh and say Tom couldn't be counted on to remember that the earth travels round the sun."

Ben considered the detached expression on Michael's face—the gaunt cheeks, the chiseled bone—trying to see the mind behind the deep-set hooded eyes. "You never considered following in your father's footsteps and going into chemistry yourself?"

"I have no scientific bent a-tall. I only just manage to grasp the rudiments one needs to carve stone. Neither is my father a scientist. No, that's one of the ironies of his present position, considering Ross's opinions. My father, at heart, will always remain a contented chartered accountant."

"So why do you need the quarry? Most sculptors don't work next to one."

"It's a tremendous convenience. Quarrymen cut what I need to order and set it in the shop straightaway without the cost of shipping. They crate and ship my pieces, and I can walk the quarry and find bits lying about that suggest something to me. I can discuss technical problems at any moment with experienced cutters, who also repair my compressors and pneumatic drills. That's not to say I can't stay here if the quarry's closed. I can order my stones elsewhere and have them shipped up. Though I do very much love the Cairnwell limestone, and I'm hoping to have quite a bit cut and laid aside, in case Ellen does decide to close it down."

"You were in Oxford when Georgina died?"

"Near there, at Abingdon, seeing to a commission. A design for a garden grotto whose centerpiece is to be a statue of a deceased dog." Michael smiled enigmatically, and drank the rest of his bitter. "I left Abingdon the day after Georgina died without having any idea she'd been taken ill."

"Did you see her while you were there?"

"I tried. I rang the day before she passed away and asked her to have dinner with me. I suggested I take a bus into Oxford, then call for her in a cab, and we'd run out to The Trout in Godstow. It's a wonderful spot right on the banks of the Thames. But she'd already made dinner plans and it couldn't be fitted in before I was to leave."

"Who was she having dinner with?"

"She didn't say. She was like that, you know. She kept her private business to herself." Michael Shaw hadn't finished his soup, but he pushed the bowl away and lit a cigarette. "I don't understand her death a-tall."

"I thought she choked while being sick."

"Yes, but what made her that ill? Flu? Food poisoning? No one else in the inn or the restaurants she'd eaten in became ill, from what I've heard. Why Georgina? It doesn't seem fair a-tall."

"A lot of things in life don't. What kind of person is Donald Murray?"

"He's a *very* odd bird who can also be a bit of a bully."

"And a coward?"

"Oh, yes. He used to sneak about here and pinch things from time to time, just to let me know he could do what he liked. But once I called his bluff, he took himself off with his tail between his legs."

"Good. He's been bothering Ellen."

"Has he? Then he needs to be sorted out."

"I hope I already have. Thank you for talking to me. I really appreciate it."

"Ellen mustn't feel awkward about the quarry. I like Ellen. Always have done. And she must do what's best for her own affairs."

"She'll be glad to hear you see it that way."

"It would go a long way to getting the crow off her back if she closed the quarry."

"The crow?"

"Our illustrious neighbor, Isabelle Hay. Tinkerbell, I sometimes call her, when I'm feeling especially charitable. It's the last name one would choose to describe her approach to life."

Ellen had left a note on Cairnwell's front door saying she'd put something Ben would enjoy reading in his bedroom, that his dinner was in the warming oven of the AGA stove, that she had a headache and had gone to bed.

Ben found Ian Cunningham's first draft translation of the Pryor memoir on the floor inside his bedroom door. And he read it in the dining room while he ate roast chicken and boiled potatoes.

He did his dishes and started up to his room, using the narrow turret stairs by the dining room door that curled past the sitting room (and Ellen's room and the great hall) on the second floor, to G.'s room on the third floor where he was staying.

He was thinking about the Pryor memoir, trying to imagine how Georgina felt when she first read it, as he stepped out into the third-floor hall not far from his door.

Directly across from him, on the wall of that long hall, was a portrait of a woman in a stiff white ruff—an Elizabethan portrait of an early Witney or Leslie. Ben stopped and stared at it for a second, then laughed and unlocked his door.

He tossed the memoir on the bed and walked back into the hall with one of Georgina's poems.

Don't.
It's the eyes that say it.
Quiet.
above the lace ruff.
Hide it.
past the teacups,
and over the withers of a nervous horse.
It's too late.
You know it-tis.
far too late already.
No.
No, it's not.
Don't listen.
Don't look at the eyes,
the slithering skin,
the flickering tongue,
the sideways slide.
Get out
of that part
of the garden.

They were all there. Lined up along the gallery by the guest rooms above the great hall. The woman in the lace ruff. The Georgian family in white wigs and watered gray silk behind a tea table thick with silver. A Stubbs painting of an emaciated horse, tail cut fashionably high, florid owner holding reins in front of his paunch on the far side of the horse's neck.

Think of the family name!

Think of Cairnwell!

Think how long we've had it, Georgina!

You can't just give it away now!

I wish I'd known her, Ben said to himself, as he closed his bedroom door. She had guts. She had human nature pegged. She looked at everything she'd been given, and tried to do it right.

There was a knock on the library door half an hour later. And Ben called to whoever it was to come in.

Jack Corelli closed the high white door behind him, then stood by the cinnamon wall as though he didn't know what to say. "I've been looking all over for you."

"Oh?"

"I need to talk to you."

"Sit down. Please. Has it started raining?"

"Yeah. Wind's blowing hard toward the coast."

Ben tossed two more logs on the fire, then sat back down in the wing chair on the left of the fireplace. He set a leather-bound book on a side table, just as Jack threw himself on the sofa that faced the fireplace.

"I'd like to ask a favor."

"What?"

"Don't tell anybody I'm a microbiologist." Jack had been carrying his leather motorcycle jacket and he dropped it then on the rug.

"I may have to tell Ellen."

"Why?"

"You live here. You work for her. I think she has a right to know. Why does it matter so much to you?"

"I don't like everybody knowing my business." Jack smoothed his Levi's and then stretched his legs out, setting one heavy motorcycle boot across the other.

Ben leaned back in his chair and locked his hands behind his head while he gazed noncommittally at Jack.

"I don't want to be treated a certain way because of what I do. I'm the same person whether I do science or hammer nails."

"Right. I agree."

"I want out of academia."

"I can understand that. I hate academic politicking, almost as much as I hate the arrogance, which means I want to run away a lot of the time too." Ben laughed.

But Jack didn't look amused. Especially his eyes, behind long black lashes. Hard. Dark. Very self-protective. "I'm not running away. I just don't want to be admired *or* ignored because of what I do." Jack said it fast and low with rising irritation.

"I know what you mean. I feel the same way."

"There's something I should tell you about Georgina."

"That you were with her the night before she died?"

"Yeah. So you found the plan for the falconry center?"

"It was in the purse she took with her the night before she died. Undated and unmailed, apparently. There was no envelope in her things, at least. Though that's obviously not conclusive. Mrs. Long identified the purse."

"We went out to dinner at a Chinese restaurant, and

stopped at The Bird and Baby for a drink."

"The Eagle and Child?"

"Yeah. Anyway, I had nothin' to do with her death."

"Why would I think you did?"

"Let's not beat around the bush, okay? I was with her. I'm a microbiologist. I could be said to know something about pathogens that attack the gut, even if that wasn't my area." Jack was leaning forward, his dark curly hair hanging across his forehead, his elbows on his knees, his eyes tired and frustrated.

"What reason would you have for wanting her dead?"

"No reason that makes any sense. Maybe I went berserk because she wouldn't let me do the falconry center."

"So what are you saying,—that you think Georgina was murdered?"

"I think it's a possibility. So do you. So does Ellen. She and I talked while you were gone."

"Did you."

"There're other things you should know too. I was the one who found Georgina's manuscripts. The one in Greek and the other one in French and Latin. I was taking the wall apart in Ross's study for the exterminators. They were treating the linen fold paneling for deathwatch beetle, and there was one loose panel. One that was left loose deliberately. I can show you what I mean if you're interested. Anyway, both manuscripts had been stashed inside."

"Can you show it to me tonight?"

"Yeah, whenever you want."

"Did Georgina tell you what they said after she'd translated them?"

"No, but I knew it was important. That it had something to do with her family, and that she was shaken by whatever it was. She began to talk about her family as though she wasn't sure what kind of people they were. She didn't say that right out. Just a word here and there that I pieced together. I saw her more than anyone, probably. We ate dinner together a lot. She and Colin and I sometimes. And I could see there was a big change."

"Did you know Ellen would inherit?"

"No." Jack looked away toward the fire and pulled a pack of Luckies out of his shirt pocket.

"What do you think of Tom Ogilvie?"

"He's a money-grubbing weasel." Jack inhaled and threw the match in the fire. "He was up here last night, you know. He's real interested in Ellen all of a sudden, or he was acting like he was at least. If he had Ellen, he'd have Cairnwell. He could sell it, put the money in his mattress, and count it late at night."

"You mean he seemed romantically interested?"

"I don't know. Maybe not exactly."

"You're not too fond of Tom."

"No, I'm not too fond of Tom." Jack scratched the stubble on his jaw, then took another drag on his cigarette.

"Has Donald Murray put in an appearance?"

"Nope. Not another peep out of him."

"Did anything else happen the last few weeks before Georgina died that struck you as being unusual?"

"Nothing obvious. Except that she was worried about something."

"Did Georgina talk about collectors of any kind?"

"Not that I remember. She said it looked to her like Isabelle Hay must be starting an antique shop, that there was furniture being delivered all the time. But nothing else."

"How could you murder someone and produce the symptoms that killed Georgina?"

"I don't know. I've been thinking about it since we talked the other day. I discussed it with Tucker yesterday too. It's not my field *or* his, so I could miss a lot. I worked with cell transformation. Trying to understand the way normal cells change into cancer cells. I haven't dealt with foodborne pathogens for a long time."

"The police didn't find anything unusual. No botulism or suspicious bacteria. I don't know anything about it, that goes without saying, but could you take a bacterium that causes vomiting, maybe something that's normally found in the human intestinal tract, and kill someone with it? Could you put bacteria that would usually make you sick into food or drink in such a large quantity it could kill you?"

"You can grow pathogens in volume, sure. You could concentrate certain pathogens too, using conventional separations, or simple fractionation, and then you could introduce them in various ways. Whether death would be caused or not would obviously depend on the organism, and a lot of other variables. What pathogens would make sense, I don't know."

"If a bacterium occurred normally in the body, the autopsy report wouldn't find anything unusual. Right?"

"There are cases where that would be true, but evaluating organisms in fecal flora isn't easy anyway."

"So conceivably you could concentrate the right bug, and feed it to somebody, and have it kill the person fast enough that they don't have time to say what they've eaten, or what they know, or that they believe they're being killed?"

"That kind of speed would be extremely unusual. There must be organisms that could be used that way, but I don't know what they'd be. It wouldn't be fungi or parasites. It's highly unlikely anyhow, not if death occurred in such a short period of time. By that I mean the time period from when she first became ill to the time she died. *If* she would've died that fast, *if* she hadn't choked. There're an awful lot of factors to consider." Jack had already tossed his first cigarette in the fire, and he took out another Lucky and lit it with an old metal Zippo. "If I had to guess, I'd say it's a bacterium that produces spores, and that the spores produce toxin. So it'd be a case of intoxication rather than infection. I also suspect that the spores had already produced the toxin—that the toxin was ingested in food or drink."

"I don't understand the last statement."

"It's the time factor. It would've happened a lot faster if the food was contaminated with the toxin, instead of spores being eaten and then sometime later producing toxin in the GI tract."

"I see." Ben smiled to himself at the interest and the concentration on Jack's face, as Jack turned and looked directly at him.

"I say something funny?"

"No, not at all. The bug—or should I say the toxin?—would have to be in some form you could carry around with you safely. That wouldn't affect you, or contaminate the rest of the world. And it would probably help too if it could be stored for long periods of time."

"That could be done. The toxin could be concentrated and then lyophilized. Or even just concentrated and air dried."

"What's lyophilized?"

"Freeze dried. A powder you could keep in a jar."

"But it could be air dried? Without equipment?"

"Probably. It'd take longer and be stickier. But what's the point? Georgina died because vomit got into the airway."

"Something caused the illness. An illness that was swift and terrible, that maybe would've killed her anyway."

"Maybe. But you don't know that." Jack was lying back against the couch, looking at Ben through half-shut eyes blowing smoke rings at the ceiling.

"True. But would you be willing to look at the possibilities?"

"Yeah. I could go up to Aberdeen tomorrow and see what I can find in the university library. *Bergey's Unabridged Manual of Systematic Bacteriology* might be the place to start, although..." Jack was staring at the fire and he didn't say anything for several seconds.

"Do you know anyone in the department there? Dr. Emily MacAlpin maybe?"

"I know who she is. She works with James Shewan. I met him at a lecture of his in the States three or four years ago. They're supposed to be naming a genus after him."

"Could you find out what MacAlpin does? Whether she works with the kinds of bacteria that could kill someone?"

"She doesn't. They don't do any medical bacteriology at Aberdeen. Shewan and the rest of the department look at bacteria that interact with organisms in the environment. The kind of bug that reduces trivalent iron to divalent iron. Organisms in Arctic sediments. Sulfate-reducing bacteria. It's all nonmedical. Nobody there would fit."

"But they are microbiologists. They could come up with a bacterium and make it work, right?"

"I s'ppose. Given the right library, and the right colleagues to consult. *And* a source for the right bacterial toxin. But the researchers at Aberdeen are less likely candidates than any microbiologist or bacteriologist who deals with human or animal pathology."

"Could a chemist pull it off? A chemist who works with something unrelated, like rubber chemistry? Or cutting fluids?"

"A chemist would know how to do the concentration techniques, and the lyophilization. If that's what was used. But understanding the toxins, or picking the right bacterium? If he worked at a university where there was a medical bacteriology lab, maybe. Where there're people to consult and a way of classifying bugs and then buying them."

"I don't know anything about it, unfortunately."

"Why would you? How many people do?"

"Do you have time to show me the place where you found the memoirs?"

"Sure. They were back here in Ross's study." Jack walked through the door on the left side of the fireplace by the long wall of outside windows into a small dark-paneled room that looked out on both the front drive and the inside courtyard by the gate.

The paneling was old, sixteenth century probably—the walls covered with rows of linen fold panels that were three feet high and a foot and a half wide, the wood carved so that it looked as though fabric had been folded at the top and bottom, inside a raised three-inch border.

Jack walked to a panel four or five feet to the right of the fireplace, the bottom of it three and a half feet or so from the floor, and pushed up on the carved panel. It wasn't fastened and it slid up, so that the bottom could be raised and pulled out above the lower edge of the "picture frame" border. When it was in place, the panel slid into a slot made from L-shaped molding, inside the bottom border and the lower six inches of the sides. A horizontal board (one inch by four inches by almost a foot and a half wide) sat just below, inside the frame border. And Jack grabbed a tiny wooden peg at its left end and pulled the board up and out of the wall—exposing an empty space, twelve or fourteen inches deep, with another horizontal board at the bottom.

"That's where the manuscripts were hidden."

"Something any joiner could have made any time since the Celts invaded." Ben was sliding his hands along the carving of the linen fold panel he held, while he studied the inside of the cache.

"The workmanship everywhere in the room is amazing, especially when you think about the kind of tools joiners had in the sixteenth century. The panel hadn't been moved in a lotta years. There was dust and cobwebs everywhere."

"Who was interested in navigation and exploration?" Ben was pointing at the carved freestanding bookcase behind Ross's desk.

"Ross. But the old books belonged to the Witneys and the Leslies."

"I've been reading a navigational log I found in here from one of the Witney trading ships. The captain's log of the *Unicorn* on a voyage for salt cod. They went to Newfoundland and the Grand Banks, and it's really well illustrated."

"What do you mean by 'illustrated'?"

"All British traders and Royal Navy ships were required to sketch every landfall they made. So they drew or did watercolors of the landscape and the vegetation, and the animals and any people they saw, in as much detail as they could. Anyway, there are several logs here from the Witney ships."

"Yeah, but I remember Georgina telling us one night at dinner, a few weeks before she went to Oxford, that two of the

Witney logs were missing. She hardly ever looked at them, after Ross died. But she'd wanted to check on something, I don't know what, and they weren't in here where they should've been. Then a couple of days after that, she found them in the library, under a stack of other books on the table beside the sofa."

"How did she react?"

"You could see it bothered her to think she could've over-looked them. Like maybe she was losing her grip."

"Who was here when she mentioned it at dinner?"

"A lot of people that night. It was kind of a dinner party for Georgina's birthday. Ogilvie, me, Ian Cunningham and his wife, Colin Ramsay from the dower house, and Michael Shaw. The poet also, from Loch Rannoch. Georgina had met him in Aberdeen and driven him down. Anna Morrison was here, the retired housekeeper who raised G. And the Hays were invited too. They stopped in to say a lukewarm hello and have a drink, but they didn't stay to dinner."

"Did Georgina talk about the logs over drinks too? While the Hays were here?"

"I think that's when she brought it up. She used it as an example of losing your memory as you get old."

"Then the books appeared in the next few days? Or had they already turned up before that, and she just told the story?" Ben laid a leather-bound book back on the shelf. And turned around toward Jack.

"No, they showed up later."

"So you'll go to Aberdeen tomorrow?"

"If it's okay with Ellen. If she doesn't need me to do some-thing else."

CHAPTER NINE

Wednesday, June 21st

"JOHN?" ISABELLE HAY STOOD IN THE DOOR to her kitchen watching her husband at his desk in the study writing laboriously in his small cramped hand, notes and papers stacked on the desk, piles weighted down by resource books—one hand resting on a letter to an anxious mother from a battle-hardened private killed in Sicily.

Gillie, John's bolster-shaped chocolate Lab, white around the mouth and stiff with age, thumped her tail as she looked up at Isabelle.

But John hadn't heard her. He rarely had the last year, not the first time she spoke. And she decided not to call to him again, but to wrestle with the table herself. It wouldn't be good for his heart anyway, not as weak as he'd been.

It's so hard. Kind sweet John. The financial strain. The hearing and the heart. No one to talk with who truly shares his longing to honor those who fought in the last war.

Though why *I* should expect justice, I can't imagine.

Not when men like Ross Fletcher and his father before him profit from those they exploit. Aniline dye, turning lips blue and killing later. Carbon black sweated out the skin. Horrible burns too, too numerous to count. Ether and benzene, both debilitating. Unsafe machines *ripping* away arms and legs. And for what? *Tires!* Made from the blood of good men.

Well, I won't play the hypocrite and pretend I'm not glad all the Fletchers are dead!

Dear Papa. Sweet sad Papa. Gone too soon, but not forgotten. Mama killed by the loneliness as surely as a bullet to the brain.

Yet one must soldier on, as John would say.

And it looks as though I shall need a hat.

Isabelle Hay stood staring at the scullery shelves, till she shook herself awake, and gathered the newspapers, steel wool, rubber gloves, and varnish remover—arranging the small items in a wooden trog—worrying over the money.

I shall never know how much John lost, of course. In investments he never should've made. Trusting that ne'er-do-well he was at school with half a lifetime ago. Julia's cancer was a terrible blow. The only one of his daughters who ever gave him the time of day. Though considering the way they treated me after we married, why would one be surprised? Still, John *has* coped with her death better than I feared he would.

But why he thinks the only way to provide for me is to finish his book on the Black Watch I shall never know! Battalion histories never pay! And yet how can I tell him that? How can I look him in the eye and say it's pointless, and take away the one work left to him?

Then why do I dwell upon it day after day? Is what I do any different? Can I actually hope to make a way for us by buying bits and pieces of old junk, brightening them up and selling them again at other people's shops? Not unless a miracle occurs, and I've seen precious few of those. No, we shall still have to sell up and take a wee flat somewhere in a dark and dingy street.

It will kill John. I know it will.

And yet how am I to prevent it?

Isabelle closed her eyes and rubbed her forehead with her left hand, before she tied an apron over her gardening dress and walked out the back through the scullery door.

She set everything down at the end of the old barn by the garden shed, and pulled open the wide double doors. A pine hutch stood between her and the walnut dining table and she considered what she should move first. The chairs and the small kitchen table on the left of the table? Or the Victorian sideboard on the right?

The Georgian chairs were easier, and she carried them and the small pine table outside to the cobbled courtyard. Then she tugged at the inlaid hexagonal walnut table. Its pedestal was made of four Gothic style legs, connected by bottom braces and carved arches, with lion heads at the ends of the legs. And the screech of them fighting the stone floor made Isabelle wince, before she stopped to consider the unevenness of the stones and what might happen to the legs if she dragged it further.

She moved clockwise and tried to slide the table that way, but one of the legs stuck stubbornly on a stone. She bent down to examine the feet, and caught movement, or some sort of change in the light, outside the barn on her right.

"Do you need some help? I was running past Colin's house when I looked up and saw you struggling. I'm Ben Reese, by the way. I'm staying up at Cairnwell."

"Running?" She stared at his sweatpants and sweatshirt as

though they were the first she'd seen.

"I usually make myself shuffle a couple of miles a day." Ben smiled at her long pinched face, while he swung his arms to loosen up his back.

"One only has a cairtain amount of cartilage, you know, in ones joints. And once it's worn away, well...bone will rub on bone. I was a nurrse, once upon a time, and I saw many sad cases of joint disintegration. My name is Isabelle Hay. Lady Isabelle Hay. And yes, I am having a bit of difficulty shifting the pedestal table."

"It's a great piece." Ben was standing over it examining the wood grain and the inlay. "It actually looks a lot like one of Pugin's."

"Pugin?"

"He was an early nineteenth-century architect. There's a table of his quite a bit like this in the Victoria and Albert Museum."

"Is there indeed?" She was rubbing the small of her long back, staring at the table intently.

"Where do you want it?"

"Here on the cobbles." Isabelle took off her straw hat, dropped it on a chair and rubbed the red line on her forehead.

Ben picked up one side, repositioned the feet, pulled the table out the double doors, and studied the surface with his head to one side. "Are you a collector?"

"No."

"You've got quite a few pieces here."

"Yes. Thank you vera much for your help." She spread newspapers on the stones and arranged the supplies from the trog.

"This must be a good time to restore and resell antiques. So many old houses are being sold or abandoned or given to the National Trust, that there must be things on the market that need work, but are valuable pieces. How are you going to refinish it?" Ben was eyeing the gallon of stripper and trying not to look appalled.

"I shall strip away the old finish, then varnish it once again."

"With a brush?"

"Yes, why wouldn't I?" She stared impatiently at Ben while she pulled steel wool out of an old paper bag.

Ben slid his fingers across the inlay work and then looked straight at Isabelle. "Would you like a suggestion, or would you rather I minded my own business?"

"Are you qualified? Are you an expert of some kind?"

"I'm an archivist at a university, and I've had to do work like this myself."

"I see. Then what would you suggest?"

Ben told her how to clean it with number three rubbing compound on a soft cloth and not go through the finish. How to French polish it using four layers of trace cloth wrapped on a large ball of cotton with a few drops of shellac mixed with paraffin (or linseed or mineral) oil, and work in very small circles on a quarter of the table at a time, always moving, even as she picked her hand up or laid it down, and then end with long pendulumlike swings to take off all the circle marks. He told her how to clean the carving, and French polish that too. Before he said, "It's a museum quality table, and it'd be a shame to lower the value. If it were me, I think I'd leave it the way it is and call in an appraiser."

"I see." Isabelle stood quietly for a moment and almost smiled at Ben. "I suppose one might strip the pine hutch?"

"I would."

"And wax it with a bit of paste wax?"

"Yes, exactly."

"Then may I trouble you to put the table back where it was in the barn?"

"It's no trouble at all."

"Thank you." She arranged the newspaper around the hutch, then pulled on her rubber gloves and grabbed the stripper, the brush, and an empty paint can.

"I'm actually glad we met, because I wanted to talk to you about something else. Ellen Winter is trying to decide what to do with Cairnwell. The pony trekking, and the footpath, and the quarry. And she asked me to stop by and get your reactions."

"Did she! She gave me to understand when we last spoke that she had no interest whatever in what I thought."

"She's under a lot of pressure. She's got big decisions to make, and she's young. She never expected to be in this position."

"Aye." Isabelle Hay poured stripper into the empty can and began brushing it on the high pine hutch. "What would you say is the value of the inlaid table on the open market today?"

"I don't know the market here very well, but if it's a Pugin, I'd sell it through a really good dealer, or one of the London auction houses. Assuming, of course, that you want to sell it. If you don't, and if you decide to refinish it, I think I might hire a professional. French polishing's hard to do because it dries so fast. Where'd you find the table?"

"A house sale nearr Bath."

"Is that where you were when Georgina died?"

"About that time, yes."

"So what's your objection to the footpath? It doesn't come down your side of Chapelton Road at all."

"The wee animals in the fields and woods will sufferr with walkers traipsing across the country."

"Aren't people allowed to cross private land everywhere in Scotland?"

"Aye, but it's not the same as a footpath. There'll be many more on the paths as time goes on. And think of the wee songbirds as well. Now that Georgina's brash young American has brought in his predatory hawks."

"He's just hunting rabbits and mice now. He doesn't have the kind of falcons and hawks that catch birds in midair."

Isabelle had taken off one glove and was rubbing the head of a large orange-and-white tabby cat who stood arched against her legs. "This is Abby. She and her brotherrs were born in the barn last year."

"Does she catch birds?"

"Only vera infrequently. I see what you're thinking, young man. I'm not a fool. She's kept quite busy with mice."

"Your objection to the quarry is the noise and bustle of the truck?"

"Aye, and the arrogance of the Witneys and the Fletchers. Acting as though they own the entire countryside and have no need to be concerned with the wishes of anyone but themselves."

"You've known them a long time?"

"Oh, aye."

"But you've only lived here since after the war?"

"My husband's people have been here almost a hundred years. Though their principal residence is in Yorkshire."

"You feel the same way about the pony trekking?"

"Why should we have to endure the noise and confusion of a pack of wee brats who could easily ride their ponies elsewhere?"

"Yes, I see. Well, I'll tell Ellen what you've said. What kind of nursing did you do before you married? My aunt's a nurse, and I just wondered." Ben looked as young and well meaning as he could and rubbed the back of his neck.

"I supervised wards in several hospitals before *and* during the war."

"That must've been demanding work. Well. Thanks. I hope I see you again before I leave."

So what do I know for sure?

Not much. Unfortunately.

Not even enough to hit hard in one direction.

Except that G.'s vitamins and aspirin, the ones left in the bottles, at least, were perfectly normal. According to the lab in Perth. Which wasn't much of a surprise.

The librarian in Perth didn't find much either. Name and date of the death in Kent. Not even the name in Grantown-on-Spey. And that was predictable too.

Ben stopped running, picked up a large chunk of rock from Cairnwell's back drive and threw it to the edge of the evergreens.

So where do I go from there?

Donald Murray, the farmer? Highly unlikely. For a lot of reasons. Including no known link to microbiology. Tom Ogilvie? He could be working with Clive Baird, the ex-chemist from Fletcher's. And Tom *may* have put some kind of powder in Georgina's coffee. Except that Perkins the salesman thought he might've added it to his own too, and that doesn't make much sense. There's what's his name too. Robbie MacAlpin. Unlikely also, according to Jack, who should know something about it. If, in fact, *he's* telling the truth. And why he wouldn't I don't know.

Still, Robbie, with his wife the microbiologist and his long-time attitude to Georgina, makes more sense than Michael Shaw the sculptor.

But any of them could have a friend or a relative who's a microbiologist, or a hospital technician, who could supply the bacteria or the toxin.

If it actually was bacteria or toxin that killed G.

So how can I track down unknown relatives and discon-nected acquaintances with no real leads to go on?

There's still Jack Corelli. Ability. Opportunity.

Yes, but motive? Because Georgina wouldn't let him do his center? How does killing her help?

Maybe he saw the will, and thought Ellen would be easier to control than G.?

That's quite a leap, but maybe. Maybe he's a lot crazier than he looks.

Where would he have done the work? At Stephen Tucker's lab in Oxford? Not with all the technicians watching him. No, but he could've done it at night. There *or* here.

Of course, Tucker hadn't seen Jack for months before G. died. If *he's* telling the truth. *And* if timing matters. Freeze-dried toxin would keep almost indefinitely.

And what about the package the salesman saw on Georgina's table? Was it chocolate? Left by a woman with dark brown hair pulled back in a ponytail?

And why hasn't Ellen told me she was in Oxford?

Cairnwell and a lot of stock in Fletcher's could tempt a certain kind of person.

Isabelle Hay has to be considered. Even though I know next to nothing about her. The fact that she collects...

Rats. The Triumph's back in the shed.

But. That doesn't mean he's home.

Ben wiped the sweat off his forehead with the sleeve of his sweatshirt. Then knocked on Jack's door and waited.

He knocked again and waited longer.

Then let himself in without too much difficulty, and examined the inside of the cottage before searching the shed in back.

Ben and Ellen were sitting at Anna Morrison's lace-covered dining room table, waiting for her to come back from the kitchen, when Ellen looked at Ben as though she'd just remembered something important. "I meant to tell you this morning that Tom Ogilvie drove up day before yesterday while you were gone, and tried to talk me into selling Fletcher's to one of their competitors. He was trying hard to be charming, but he really gave me the creeps."

"What competitor?"

"Not Dunlop, the other one. British Tire. Also, Alex called for you this morning. You're supposed to call him tonight, to get all the details, but he and I talked for a long time, and the general gist of the Witney memoir—"

"Which was written by the son?"

"Yeah, Robert, the one who moved up here and got Cairnwell by marrying a Leslie. He actually wrote, right there in black and white, that his father had murdered John Pryor in a fit of temper when Pryor wouldn't sell him his woods, and that he'd pretty much stolen the whole Pryor estate, and that his father had asked him to make it right. To give the land back to my family and make 'additional recompense.' But that he, the son, hadn't had the guts either. He'd built more ships and warehouses up here, and he needed the money from the estate in Burford. So he did what his father had arranged to do, and sold the Pryor estate to his sister's husband and used the money here. Which we knew from what G. told Ian Cunningham."

"What a guy!"

"Yeah. Robert *claimed* it haunted him the rest of his life, but it couldn't have bothered him too much since he didn't do anything about it. He was really sick when he was finishing the memoir, and he was afraid for his immortal soul, he said. So he secreted the manuscript away in the wall, along with Alysoun Pryor's memoir, but told his son where to find them in the last letter he wrote to him. He told him the bare bones of what he and the grandfather had done, and he asked his son, the grandson, to do what was right in that same letter. Robert still hadn't told his wife, the Leslie that brought him Cairnwell, because he said he was too ashamed. But *I* think he wanted to keep what he had and not have to repay my family. Alex said Robert had begun to think he was on his deathbed by the last page of the memoir, and his son had been sent for and was apparently riding home from England."

"Pretty pathetic."

"That's one way of putting it!" Ellen looked disgusted, her blue eyes icy and her mouth clamped tight against her teeth.

"Maybe that was the paper Georgina's grandfather found in the attic. The one he was taking to London to show her dad. It could've been a letter written later than Richard's generation too, by some other family member, that said the same thing. Because both could explain Georgina's grandfather's reaction."

"I'd like to know how many generations *didn't* do what they knew they should do for my family!"

"Scary thought, isn't it? Human nature being what it is."

"My grandmother worked for them as a cook! A family that murdered one of her ancestors and kept his land! And yet they must've stood by, generation after generation, and watched the Pryors, who'd educated *them,* for heaven's sake, become their servants."

"Although, how many generations read the letter and knew about the memoir we don't know. They both could've stayed hidden since the sixteen hundreds. But I do know that's a question that tormented Georgina. You can see it in the poems."

"Why wouldn't it? It makes me want to spit!"

"How'd the Pryor memoir end up at Cairnwell?"

"Alysoun's daughter, Mary, the one who wasn't super bright, was taken to live with Robert's family at Cairnwell after her parents died. She didn't understand Greek and the importance of what her mother had written and she gave Robert the memoir for safekeeping. So I guess, in his defense, he could've destroyed it and didn't. So maybe that's something. Alex says he talked about that decision a lot in his journal."

Ben looked at the irritation beginning to cool on Ellen's face, and he asked if she'd told Anna before he got there, about Georgina's letter and why they needed to talk to her.

"Yes." Ellen took a long slow breath and rolled up the sleeves of her dark blue blouse. "She's very intelligent, and she knows the background of a lot of people around here, so we need to find out what she knows. I couldn't see how else to get her to talk. She won't say anything to anybody else, I'm sure of that. Oh, and here's the list of answers to the questions you asked before you left."

Ben took the folded legal pad pages that Ellen pulled from her purse and slipped them into the breast pocket of his corduroy jacket. "What did Alex say about Joshua the dog?"

"He's fine. He's stopped shaking around the family, but he was chased by a cow, and he still looks fairly embarrassed." Ellen had closed her eyes and was rubbing both temples with two fingers.

"I was chased by the whole herd the first time I went to Balnagard."

"Were you?"

"I was walking through the pasture by the river, before they'd put up a fence they have now that makes a path outside it, and a couple of cows started following me. The whole herd came to see what they were doing, and then they all started running at me. I finally had to jump the fence. And of course the whole family, and what seemed like most of the employees, just happened to have been watching from the back windows, so I still hear about it today."

"I'll bet."

The kitchen door opened and Anna Morrison came in, a platter of cold smoked salmon in one hand, a large plate of carefully trimmed toast in the other. She set them both between Ellen and Ben in the center of a ring of bowls filled with onion, lemon, lettuce, and capers, and asked if they'd care for butter. They both told her not to bother. So she perched on a straight-backed chair and poured tea. She was tiny, no more than five feet tall, and very neatly dressed in a plain black skirt and cream-colored blouse with a cameo pin at the throat.

Ellen said, "The lunch looks wonderful, and you're very

kind to go to this much trouble. I was just telling Ben that you were the housekeeper at Cairnwell for many years, and that I've known you since I was little, when we came over a lot to visit G."

"I knew both Ellen's grandparents *vera* well, and her mother when she was a child, but I *never* thought I'd get to know Ellen as well. America's so vera far away. Would you care for cream or sugar?"

They chatted for a minute while they ate, Anna keeping the conversation afloat in a quiet dignified manner, entertaining visitors much the way she had at Cairnwell, the small wrinkled face calm and intelligent, the gray eyes questioning and evaluating, the mouth controlled but pleasant, the soft gray hair pulled back in a chignon.

"Somebody said you helped raise Georgina." Ben sprinkled capers on his salmon, before he looked across at Anna.

"Aye, I did. I loved Georgina vera much. We never had children of our own, Mac and I, and though I was given a great many duties at Cairnwell over the years, many of them vera broadening and vera interesting, it was raising Miss Georgina that's meant the most by far. I was just a wee slip of a girl then, in 1901, and Ellen's grandmother taught me how to care for her." Anna looked at Ellen and patted the hand that was closest to her. "Little did I think then that I'd come to love Georgina like the daughter I was never given." Anna stopped speaking for a moment. She looked out the window to her right, and blotted the corners of her eyes with her napkin. "If Georgina *was* murdered, I'd vera much like to help you find her killer."

"What do you think of Donald Murray?"

"Not a great deal. My younger brother and sister went to grammar school with him. He was intelligent, but quite peculiar even then. He kept to himself a great deal, but he was also the sort who torments the younger and weaker. He's gotten stranger as time has gone by. More vicious, in my opinion. Though he was always the sort who could be made to cry and run home. I hate to think what he would've turned into if he hadn't been. He won't throw a thing away, ye know. Or care for what he's inherited. And he can't abide alteration of any sort. Ye can't live that way, in my experience. Whether ye like it or no. Georgina's grandmotherr had no use for him a-tall. Even when he was a child, she could hardly abide the sight of him. Of course, she had vera little sympathy for children at the best of times."

"What do you know about Isabelle Hay?"

"Ah, well, I've known Isabelle more years than I care to rememberr. I'm eighty this year, and I expect I'm ten years older than she. I was raised in Stonehaven as a wee child, and her father had a tobacconist shop there, though he lost it early on and went to work at Fletcher Tire. He moved his family to Millgowan, the village Ross's father built for his workers west of Aberdeen, for the factory was well out in the countryside and houses had to be provided. It was a model village, unlike some. Clean and vera neatly done."

"How old would Isabelle have been then?"

"Fourteen or fifteen I should think, for I'd been at Cairnwell four or five years, when her father was hurt in the plant. He was feeding raw rubber into one of the machines that made rubberized cloth, and he caught his arm in the rollers. There was a great red Stop button on the side of the machine, and his brotherr was standing right next to it, but he froze on his feet and didn't push it. Isabelle's father lost his arm, and spent months in hospital, before he went back to Fletcher's as an elevator operator. He'd taken to drink much earlierr. I believe it played a part in why he couldn't make a go of the tobacconists, but it got far worse after the accident. It was a vera sad thing, his injury. I wouldn't wish to brush it aside."

"It's horrible." Ellen's face was squeezed shut and she shuddered slightly as though she couldn't keep from imagining it in detail.

"Ye see, his brother was the sort who fainted at the sight of blood, and of course he felt terrible. But relations were strained in the family ever after. And then, sad to say, years later, when Isabelle's father was in his fifties, he was so inebriated one night in Aberdeen he stepped in front of a lorry and was killed. Isabelle has always been vera bitter. She blamed the Fletchers, Ross and his father before him. And even though she rarely talks about her family now, I know she dwells on it still. She made quite a spectacle of herself over the quarry, for all the world to see. Turning up at the village meeting in the company of the local poacher, making herself look a proper fool."

"Was Fletcher's a dangerous place to work?"

"Ah, well, no tire company was vera safe in the early years of the century. None of them knew the best way to do things. Not even in the 1920s. They were only just learning about making rubber, and building tires as well. There were firms I know that seemed to care vera little how their men were treated, British Tire in particular, but the Fletchers made the factory as clean and safe as they knew how, when working with molds and hot rubber. They dumped carbon black down closed shoots before anyone else. They set enormous fans where the ether and benzene were being used, and then stopped using both as soon as they could. But it certainly wasn't nearly as safe as it is today, when they can mechanize the worst bits. Two of my cousins were at Fletchers, and I know it was rough dirty work."

"So how is Tom Ogilvie related to Georgina?"

"His mother was Ross Fletcher's sister. She was nothing a-tall like Ross *or* their parents. She was a willful, difficult to please, not terribly intelligent woman who threw one husband overr afterr another and drank far more than was good for her, or anyone else who was standing nearby. That's not a-tall kind of me to say, and I wouldn't in the normal way, but I'm trying to help as best I can."

"No, I understand. So is Tom like her? Does he want what he wants enough to do whatever it takes to get it?"

"I suppose it might depend on what he wanted. Tom's motherr was a frightful spendthrift. Tom, I'm equally sorry to say, has gone the other way. He wears shabby clothes. He lives in a wee, damp, crumbling house and he begrudges even the most modest sum to have it cleaned. He apparently lives on little besides porridge, potatoes, and toasted cheese sandwiches, and yet all the while, you'll remember, he's a solicitor who does rather well for himself."

"How do you know how he lives?" Ben was sprinkling chopped onion on a thin slice of salmon.

"My niece used to clean for him, fourr or five times a year. Though I can say, from my own experience, that he'll drop a word from time to time that would lead one to believe he has a great deal tucked away in banks and bonds and various investments. One can clearly see his self-satisfaction, *and* his disdain too for those who haven't put by as many pounds sterling as he. I've known his sort before, and it rarely ends well."

"Would Tom be capable of killing Georgina?" Ben had been making notes in his notebook, but he put down his pen and speared the last of his lettuce.

"I wouldn't wish to venture a guess. I can't see why he

would wish to. Unless he expected to inherit Cairnwell. Or was desperate to get his hands on her stock in Fletcher's. Colin Ramsay might be able to tell you more. He's lived in the dowerr house since 1955 when I retired, and I know Georgina and Ross often had him to dinner."

"Anna, I hate to do this, but I have to run." Ellen touched Anna on the shoulder as she pushed her chair back and stood up. "I'm meeting an electrician at Cairnwell, and I didn't realize it was this late. It was a wonderful lunch. Thank you. I'll bring you G.'s photo albums this week."

"I shall look forward to it vera much indeed."

"I'll see you later, Ben."

"Thanks, Ellen." He watched Ellen smile, as she closed the door. And then asked Anna how Colin and Georgina had met.

Anna took a sip of tea and carefully blotted the corner of her lips. "Ross and Colin were at school together as boys, though Colin was several years older. They weren't friends at that time, but they met again years later at a meeting of some sort in Edinburgh. Ross hired Colin, I think in the thirties, to help with his purchasing agreements. Colin had been raised in the East. Singapore, perhaps, I can't be sure. And he worked well with Ross's rubber suppliers. They were vera good friends, the last years especially, after Colin retired. Once Ross and Georgina sold their house in Aberdeen and moved here year round. Colin never married, but I remember Georgina saying years ago that she very much admired the way he sent letters and postcards from wherever he went, while working for Fletcher's, to the child of a family friend. Apparently it was quite a sad case. A young girl, I believe, terribly afflicted by infantile paralysis."

"What was Ross like?"

"He was a vera fine man. Vera principled. Vera intelligent. He met several of this century's most important figures, during the war, you know, as well as through his business, and he was planning to write a memoir. Not about himself. He never would've wished to do that. But describing those he'd met."

"I haven't found anything about it in his papers."

"You should do. He made a scrapbook of ideas to be used in the book, and I know Georgina would've kept it. Pictures and notes and remembrances of his, of where and how he met the people he found most fascinating and how he planned to write about them. They weren't all educated, or important, mind. One of them was a tire builder from Aberdeen who worked for Ross for years. He loved opera, and art, and he'd educated himself to a remarkable degree. He made beautiful beeswax candles, and studied astronomy as well. Ross admired him tremendously."

"Where would I find the scrapbook?"

"I couldn't possibly say. I've only been to Cairnwell to visit Georgina in recent years. And to help organize one or two dinner parties. But I should look in their bedroom if I were you. There used to be a blanket trunk there where she kept her poems, and she might have put his scrapbook there too. You know about her poems, do you?"

Ben nodded, and asked if most of the people at Cairnwell knew about them too. "The ones who cleaned, or worked on the estate?"

"I wouldn't have thought so." Anna folded her napkin and pushed a hairpin back in her chignon. "I'd be vera much surprised if they did. Georgina was vera careful to shut her poems away. I knew when she first started writing them. And she mentioned them to me once in a vera great while, but neverr in any detail."

"In one of her poems, she referred to someone she called C. B. Do you know who that could be?"

"No. Not to say straightaway. She knew so many people. Up at the university, and at Fletcher's too."

"What about Clive Baird?"

"Him! I suppose it could be, yes. He really was a bit of a thorn in Ross's side. He went to work for a competitor they had no respect for a-tall, and he violated his agreement in doing so. Ross enforced it in some way. Made him work in anotherr part of the competitor's lab, or threatened to prosecute if he handed on privileged information. But it only held for a matter of a few years. Now Clive Baird can do what he'd like."

Anna finished the last of her tea, then fingered the cameo at her neck. "Odd you should mention Clive Baird today. He's here, ye see. Visiting his aunt, right here in Newtonhill. I saw her in the green grocer's this morning. He works in England, you know, Egham I think, near London."

"Where does she live?"

"Forty-seven Queen's Lane. One block east toward the sea, then one block north on the east side of the street. I've heard, but I don't know that there's any truth to it, that Clive and Tom Ogilvie have invested in real estate togetherr in the poorest part of Perth. It may not have turned out vera well, though I don't know that for a fact. For Clive's aunt, who worries about him as ye might expect, told me this morning that he's gone to the bank for anotherr loan, and he wanted her to sign as well. She wouldn't. She's quite good with finances, and she doesn't make hasty decisions."

"I don't know much about Clive, and hearing that helps. Does Isabelle Hay have any doctor friends? Anyone she kept up with after she married and moved here?"

"She does, yes. I met him myself by her front door when I was staying at Cairnwell. A chap at the hospital, The Royal Infirmary in Aberdeen. I believe he's in charge of the laboratory. They served together somewhere during the war. She and John Hay both knew him. Though I couldn't possibly rememberr his name."

"One other question. Is anyone at Cairnwell, or any friend of Georgina's and Ross's, a collector of anything? Books, or antiques, or something like that?"

"Not that I know of. Not that I've ever heard." Anna poured milk in a fresh cup of tea and sipped it while watching Ben. "Ellen's mother collects books, of course. I expect you know that. Has done since she was a child. Long before she took up the antique trade."

"Do you know what kind of books?"

"Something particular. But I won't recall what after all these years."

Ben left his car in front of Anna Morrison's black-shuttered cottage and went to look for Clive Baird. Clive's aunt said he was meeting a friend in a tea shop down the street. And Ben walked those two blocks through Newtonhill (a small, white, slate-roofed, heavily shuttered village on top of a high headland), fighting the wind off the sea, while trying to glance at the notes Ellen had given him at lunch.

He was told at the tea shop that Clive had come in with his aunt, had waited a few minutes after she'd left, but had then paid up and gone out. The tea shop owner and the waitress conferred in quiet tones and then suggested he try the public house across the street.

ʕʕʕʕ

Ben didn't know what Clive looked like, but there were no likely possibilities in the first small public room of The Dog and Duck, a quiet dignified family pub—old, beamed, white-washed, and comfortable with a fire burning in the raised hearth at the right end of the old carved bar. The only customer was a short, squat elderly man with enormous ears sprouting tufts of white hair from their darkened interiors, who wore a black worsted suit (that had weathered a pea-soup green) with a very yellowed white shirt and a worn tartan tie. He was ordering lunch from the proprietor when Ben came in, and he glared at Ben behind his thick black-framed glasses as though he resented the interruption.

"Shepherds pie, boiled potatoes as well, none of that parrs-ley muck on the plate anywhere a-tall, a half-pint of bitterr, and one or two of your potato rolls. Fresh, mind. None of your left-overs from yesterday!"

The proprietor, who was a few years older than Ben and spoke as though he'd been to an English university, assured the elderly gentleman that nothing could've induced him to foist the first sprig of parsley upon him. He turned away, smiling quietly to himself, after nodding in Ben's direction.

Then he withdrew to the kitchen, the fragrance of roasting meat and oniony soup wafting pleasantly out the door before it closed behind him.

Ben walked around the room looking at old framed photographs of fish from rivers and bays, at fishermen smiling self-consciously, at boat owners in rain gear standing by wooden dinghies, at dogs and guns beside hunters in waxed canvas coats holding strings of game birds and rabbits.

The proprietor returned and set a place for the elderly gentleman at a small square table by the fire. He handed him his glass of bitter and wiped his own hands on a bar rag.

"May I help you a-tall, sir?"

Ben turned from a signed black-and-white photo dated 1912 of a Witney with a string of salmon, and smiled at the neat trim dark-haired man in tweeds. "I'm looking for someone named Clive Baird, and I wonder if he might be here."

"Aye, he's here. In the room through the arch just there, sitting by himself in the corner. I shan't serve him any more drink. And it might be well if you could persuade him to eat a bite of something."

"I'll see what I can do. I'll have a cup of coffee myself. And could you bring me some crackers and fruit? Grapes or strawberries or whatever you have?"

"Aye, with the greatest of pleasure."

Ben thanked him and walked past the elderly man (who was eating his shepherds pie with a fixed and sour stare), and stepped through a low arch into a larger beamed room warm with the scent of wood smoke and the crackle of dry logs.

There were three businessmen having lunch, salesmen by the sound of them, discussing an order, and four middle-aged women eating soup and chatting.

In the right back corner sat a narrow-shouldered man with a pint of lager half drunk in front of him next to a glass of Scotch whiskey with a half inch left in the bottom. His hands were cupped around the whiskey glass, and his eyes were fixed on the table.

His face was frozen and sagging, dulled and red and empty looking, his hands and arms an unhealthy color, yellowish and possibly swollen. His hair was thin and a faded sort of reddish blond. His nose was large and long, his eyes brownish and small, his mouth lax and loose. A cigarette lay burning in an ashtray in front of him, a long ash almost to the filter.

Ben watched for a minute, and then walked over and introduced himself. "Ellen Winter, the young woman who inherited Cairnwell, is my student in the States, and since I was here, she's asked me to help her evaluate some of her decisions."

Clive Baird didn't say anything. He looked up at Ben without any perceptible change of expression.

"May I sit down?"

"Why would you wish to speak to me?" It was a gravelly voice, a smoker's voice, flat and almost atonal.

"One of the questions Ellen has to decide is what to do about Fletcher Tire and Rubber. She was given stock, but she has no direct experience with the business. I understand you used to work for Fletcher and still work in the field, and it occurred to me, when I happened to learn that you were here for the day in Newtonhill, that your perspective might be substantially different from the one she's gotten from Arthur Shaw. Do you know Shaw? He's been managing the firm since Ross became ill."

Clive said something obscene and lit another cigarette. "The professional flatterer? The 'agreeable supporter'? If Ross had stopped while walking down the hall, Arthur's tiny wee nose would've broken, or suffered a worse fate still." Clive laughed and took another sip of whiskey.

Ben's food arrived, and he pushed the plate between them. "Help yourself to the fruit and crackers. Would you like a cup of coffee?"

"No, I bloody well wouldn't!"

"What kind of work do you do?"

"Research chemistry. Twenty years in synthetic rubber. Hadn't been for me, Fletcher would've been done for after the last war. I'm not the only one who would tell ye that. There're many at Fletcher who saw what happened." Clive's words weren't exactly slurred, but he was swallowing the ends, and his eyes didn't look completely focused.

"How would you evaluate Fletcher Tire's position in the market today?"

"A dead and distant third behind Dunlop and British Tire. Aye, if *I* owned stock, and someone approached me, I'd leap at the opportunity."

"I was told you live in Egham, England." Clive didn't say anything or show any sign of disagreement. "That's not too far from Oxford is it?"

"Why do you care?" He finished the Scotch and reached for the cigarettes by his left hand.

"How do you know Tom Ogilvie?"

"I met him through our illustrious and deceased Mr. Fletcher. Used him as a solicitor when my fatherr passed away."

"And then you bought property together in Perth?"

"Who told ye that?"

"You and Tom want to sell Fletcher to British Tire, and Tom needs Ellen to go along. What's in it for you, aside from revenge on Ross? A finder's fee if British Tire buys?"

Clive Baird's face flushed more than it had already. His small agate brown eyes focused on Ben as he bumped his lager and slopped it on the table. "I'll thank you to leave now, ye bloody sod. I have nothing more to say to you a-tall!"

When Ben walked into his bedroom at Cairnwell, he found that Ellen had pushed a note under his door saying she was at the gardener's house with the electrician, and that Ian

Cunningham had called. That he remembered a conversation he and Georgina had two or three weeks before she went to Oxford, and he thought perhaps he should tell Ben. Ian could drive up to Cairnwell the following day, or Ben could come see him in Kinneff that afternoon, whichever was more convenient.

An hour later, Ben had already woven his way through the town of Stonehaven—a very old fishing port on a large bay, four or five miles south of Cairnwell—and he'd taken the coast road south again past the ruins of Dunnottar Castle. He drove half an hour more through rolling grain fields, shaken out like soft down quilts on the high cliffs, until he turned left onto a slightly angled one-lane road running obliquely toward the ocean through barley, broccoli, and beets. He passed a small car on the berm, a young man and young woman unable to look at each other, both faces strained and silent, right where the road took a quick twist left around a farmhouse, then right again down a high hill toward a thick green woods. The woods were on Ben's right, when he got to them, maples and other hardwoods, the ground deep in English ivy, a barley field blowing down the hill on his left straight to the old church at Kinneff nestled at the bottom of that long steep hill.

He pulled in and parked by the wrought iron gate in the high curving wall, and was opening his door as a tall sandy-haired man stood up on the other side, a wide stripe of dirt on his cheek and a hoe in his gloved hands.

"Mr. Reese?"

"Ben would make me feel better."

"Yes, of course. Thank you so much for coming. I took a

funeral this morning, and I've a wedding tonight, and I promised my wife I'd weed the front beds while polishing my Sunday sermon. If I'd driven to Cairnwell I would have gotten very little accomplished indeed. Come in whichever way you'd like, in by the front gate, or round through the cemetery to the back walk."

They sat in the shade in the front garden on wicker chairs facing the boxwood ring around an ancient stone sundial in the center of the circle drive. Ben sipped lemonade and listened to Ian, while gazing at the beds along the wall.

"You asked when did we meet? Well, I would've thought it was two weeks or more before Georgina left for Oxford. She came for dinnerr, and we found ourselves discussing Wales. It was a rambling sort of conversation that began with my wife's Welsh family, and then turned to an article G. had read about a wonderful old castle being sold quite close to a village that's becoming known for its used books. I can't think of the name, but I know it's on a river."

"Hay-on-Wye maybe?"

"That's it, yes. The very one. I was reminded of an incident that took place there, as we spoke, and I mentioned it to Georgina. I'd heard about it years ago from my older brother's father-in-law. He's passed away now, but he was a physician in Wales for many years. Georgina seemed quite interested, and I thought perhaps I should mention it to you as well. Especially after you and I spoke, when you rang the other night."

"Good. I'm glad you remembered."

"It seems that one of the very first bookdealers in Hay-on-Wye was a woman, which was quite unusual years ago, and when she was selling up and retiring, something occurred that struck our physician friend as odd and a bit unsettling. Her stock of books was generally rather undistinguished, but she was known to have a really wonderful volume of hand-painted watercolor illustrations of your first Roanoke Colony. The Indians, the settlers, the flora and fauna, all painted by a man named John White—"

"Who became Roanoke's governor, they think, as well as the grandfather of Virginia Dare. I've actually handled the original presentation copy in the British Museum that he painted for Queen Elizabeth. I was staggered by it, and one of the curators had a full set of slides made for me, which was very out of the ordinary, and extremely kind. Anyway, I think there were four or five copies made during White's life, engraved and hand colored by a London printer, copied from the Queen's original."

"The woman in Wales had one of those early copies. And another book of real value as well, though I won't think of the name. I believe it was the first European description of a voyage to the new world to mention tobacco."

"Then I think it's by a Franciscan friar named André Thevet."

"Is it? How very remarkable." Ian sipped his lemonade and crossed one leg over the other. "Certainly, book fanciers of all sorts traipsed in and out of the Welsh woman's shop, picking up bits and pieces. And yet the finest books weren't sold. Either she was asking an exorbitant price, or she wasn't offering them for sale, and I don't remember which. Then came the day when she was seen eating lunch with a stranger in a tea shop and they had a disagreement. Nothing terribly uncivilized apparently, but an obvious difference of opinion. The gentleman left her at the table to visit the loo, then came back and talked to her again very amiably, before excusing himself, saying he was late for an appointment. She took out a book and read while she finished her lunch and ordered a pot of tea. She asked the waitress if she'd mind if she stayed on a bit. That she was expecting a business associate from somewhere in England to arrive at any time.

"An hour or so later, before this business associate arrived, she was suddenly taken ill. She became violently sick, was taken to hospital, and there she died later that same afternoon. She was always very careful to lock her shop, and yet it was discovered that the door had been left unlocked, and the John White book and the early history were subsequently found to be missing."

"Were the missing books reported to Interpol?"

"That I don't know. But there was another point of interest, as well. It seems the saltshaker on the table where the bookstore ownerr had eaten was nowhere to be found at the end of the day. It might never have been put on the table, of course, but the waitress claimed in very fierce terms that it had been, first thing that morning, along with all the rest."

"I see." Ben stared at the wall behind Ian Cunningham, while Ian wiped his glasses on the bottom of his shirt. But Ben didn't say anything for several seconds, after he finished his lemonade. "What was the cause of death?"

"I don't think they had the first idea, to tell you the truth. Though I believe the coroner's report said 'food poisoning of unknown origin.' There was some question of wild mushrooms she'd collected herself the day before, but nothing conclusive was ever discovered."

"When did this shop owner die?"

"Late forties I should think. Not too long after the war."

"Do you remember her name?"

"No, I'm afraid I don't."

"How did Georgina react when you told her?"

"She seemed interested. She asked the same sorts of questions you've asked, and we touched briefly upon collectors as well."

"What did she say about collectors?"

"Nothing very substantive. We wondered why some become obsessed and others don't." Ian drank the last of his lemonade and drummed his fingers on the arms of his chair while he watched Ben write a note in his notebook. "By the way, were there young people in a car at the top of the hill, when you drove down?"

"Yes."

"They were here for a chat before you arrived. I thought I saw them pulling over toward the edge, but the farmhouse blocks the view. I wouldn't be that age again for anything on God's green earth."

"I know. Neither would I."

CHAPTER TEN

THE WINDOWS AND DOORS WERE ALL SHUT at Colin's house, even though the sun was out and the air was still and it must've been almost eighty degrees.

He was sitting in his kitchen, a kettle on the small stove almost to the boil, a teapot on the pine table.

He pulled his old brown sweater around him as he stared out the front window at Cairnwell's back drive, thinking how odd it seemed to shiver during the day and sweat at night.

Last night was much the worst it's been. Previous night was little more than an inconvenience. Can't understand the variation.

Lucky Winifred came to do the wash, or I'd have no clean pajamas or dressing gowns left.

Heart's definitely stronger. Five or six days without medication. Though that's not to say the reprieve will last.

May have to give up the house too, if this young person of G's. decides to sell up. Can't believe she won't. Can't expect her to become an expatriate. Far too much work that needs doing on the estate to organize it properly from the other side of the world, even if she rented it out.

Where would I go if she does sell up? Lease another house

in Aberdeen? *Much* easier said than done, with my architectural requirements. Particularly in the old part, near the university, where I should feel at home.

One could move south to England. Climate's gentler in winter. No friends to speak of now, though, anywhere in Britain. Not with Ross and Georgina gone.

It would be good to see Malaya again. Lush jungle. Hot spicy smells of the villages. Dark smiles of the women. Wonderful dialects. All the Malays, Indians, Chinese. Though one does perspire there day and night. Even when one isn't plagued by the maddening sort of bone marrow botch up I suffer from now.

It was a nearly idyllic childhood, running wild across the plantation. Even with Mother pining over little Edgar. Unlike Father. Only prepared to teach me mathematics with a raised voice and a leather strap. No, Mother took time to read me Dickens till the day she died in Glasgow. Wonder why I can see her so clearly, painting under the spreading trees, cooling her forehead with lavender cologne, when she's been dead for fifty-five years?

Like to see Malaya again. Whether I'm well enough for the journey's another matter. Ship wouldn't be difficult. Medical men on board. Once there, however…heat, humidity, lack of sanitation, lamentable state of their medical services. No, it's civilization for me, I'm afraid. At least in the near future.

Even so, looking at it straight on, how much will sophisticated care help?

Precious little, if the medical Johnnies are right. With their carefully evasive replies to my infrequent nervous queries.

How much time can I have? A few months? A year? Two, if I'm very lucky? And saying it-tisn't so will *not* help me use the time well.

All the old fellows from Fletcher's are passing away. Retirement, then death. With little of interest in between. MacArthur. Carter. Allan. Williams is off being pampered near Bath. He and his incoherent wife.

Never gave a thought to any of them while Ross was alive. Excellent company, Ross and Georgina both. Discuss any subject, having lived such varied lives.

Terrible shame Georgina had to die so young. Much she wanted to accomplish that's now been left undone.

No one left here whom I can talk to in any serious way. Or feel the sort of sympathy she and I shared.

Perhaps we *are* prisoners of our time and generation. As much as temperament and interest.

At least I *have* compelling interests. Many my age don't.

Wonder if I should tell this young person, this Ellen Winter, that I'm not quite easy in my mind about Georgina's death? It may, in fact, be my duty to ask if it doesn't seem unexpected that Georgina should be taken so very ill as to die of the illness's effects. Wouldn't want to alarm her, but it might be a good idea to raise the issue.

Who is *this,* I wonder, walking toward the door? Can't see the face because of the…ah, the American friend of hers. The archivist. Perhaps I can persuade him to use the side door.

Ben heard the knock on the front window and saw Colin smile a gentle self-deprecating embarrassed smile and wave him around toward the left of the house.

Colin met him there by the scullery door, then invited him in, and offered him a cup of tea.

"I just drank two glasses of lemonade, but thank you anyway. I wonder if I could ask you a couple of questions? I'm trying to help Ellen make some decisions."

"Yes, of course. Would you mind if we sat in the kitchen?"

Colin's face was a yellowish gray and it looked almost waxy to Ben. He wondered if it was tiring for Colin to stand for very long, as he followed him to the kitchen table and watched Colin sink slowly into a Windsor chair. Colin poured himself a cup of tea, and pushed a plate of biscuits across the table toward Ben.

Ben thanked him, and shook his head. "Before I talk about what affects Ellen, may I ask you something that's of interest to me? I know you worked for Fletcher Tire for many years, and I wonder if you happen to know whether there are bacteria associated with rubber?"

"There are, yes. Bacteria grow on rubber. Even the synthetic rubber generally used today."

"So Fletcher's does bacteriology in their lab?"

"I don't know how extensive the work is, but some is certainly undertaken."

"Do you know what kind of bacteria they work with?"

"No, I never had reason to learn. Fletcher's has always had a first-class laboratory, but other than that I couldn't say."

"I met a microbiologist in Oxford, and we talked about all sorts of things, and he was telling me all the places bugs grow, and mentioned rubber, and I just got to wondering whether that's something tire companies would have to work around."

"I see."

"I can't imagine bugs growing on rocks and metal and synthetic rubber. I guess I never thought about it before, and it's interesting to me. Anyway, what I need to talk to you about is that Ellen's having to think about the writers retreat Georgina was planning, and I got to wondering if you know Robbie MacAlpin, and if you do, was he helping Georgina plan the retreat?"

"The English professor from G.'s department? I've met him. I know who he is. But other than that, I couldn't say."

"Did he come to the house this winter, or spring?"

"Certainly in the last two or three months. To a dinner, I think. Can't recall exactly when. I was in hospital having my blood rearranged more than once in the last few months, and he could've been here other times and I might not have known. I go in every two to four weeks. Four weeks, if I'm very lucky. And I haven't been just recently."

"That can't be easy."

"No. But complaining won't help a-tall."

"I guess we'll have to call MacAlpin and ask. Were any of Ross's and Georgina's friends collectors of any kind? Antiques? Paintings? Jewelry? Books?"

"Not to my knowledge. I know David Lindsay, the retired professor, he used to buy the occasional print. Or maybe it was old books, I can't remember. But he didn't do so often, or invest much money in the enterprise. Not from what I remember G. saying. Of course, Isabelle Hay has been seen to be acquiring quite a few pieces of furniture in the last year. But what the significance might be, I couldn't say."

"Someone told Ellen that Georgina wanted to donate her antiques to some museum, and that she'd had a friend who was a collector, and we got to thinking that whoever it was could help Ellen figure out how to do what Georgina would've done, in her honor."

"I can't think who that would be. You're sure you won't take tea?"

"No, thank you, I have to run." Ben looked around the kitchen as he stood up, at the old mullioned windows in the thick plastered stone walls, at the smooth flagstone floor and the heavy oak door. "This must be a comfortable house to live in."

"It's a wonderful house. Very much a tiny version of Cairnwell. Many fewer rooms, but much the same arrangement. Built later, of course. No one seems to know when."

"I appreciate the help, Colin. Please sit still. I can let myself out." Ben was on his way to the scullery by the time he'd finished the last sentence.

"Perhaps we'll meet tonight. Ellen has invited me for dinner. She's unusually kind, for a young person. Of course, she would be. Georgina was an excellent judge of character. Ross often asked her to help with personnel matters at Fletcher's."

"How was the relationship between employees and management at Fletcher's?"

"I can't say recently, in the last five or six years. But when I was there, even when I first arrived, long after Ross had assumed control, I thought relations were unusually good. When Ross Fletcher died, the funeral cortege was two miles long. And a surprising number of workers were actually in tears."

"It's too bad more businesses aren't like that. I'll see you tonight, Colin."

"Ellen has asked me to write her a letter describing what my future plans would be, as to leasing the house here at Cairnwell. I'm not quite sure what to say."

"She just wants to know what you would like to have happen about the house if you had your way. If you had a choice, would you stay here always? Or are your long-term plans to move to a warmer climate, like a lot of people today? Tell her anything that will help her decide how to make her own plans."

"I see. Yes. Thank you. That does clarify the situation. It's very kind of her to be concerned."

Ben stood at the end of his bed, in what had been Ross and Georgina's room, and looked through the contents of the camphor wood trunk for the second time. There were blankets on top, with old lace and linen. There were letters Ross had written Georgina before they were married. There was a portfolio of all the poems G. had kept during her life except for the current year. There was a pair of ivory satin shoes with rhinestone covered heels (very small, very beautiful, wrapped in a silk scarf and stored in a plastic bag) with a note in a hand Ben hadn't seen before that said, "Your Mother's Evening slippers, circa 1898."

But Ross's scrapbook wasn't there.

Ben had been through the desk in Ross's study, and he'd been on the phone to Arthur Shaw at Fletcher's asking what (among several other things) he might know about the scrapbook, and could it be at Fletcher's? Ben had looked through the bookcases in the study too, and the drawers and files in Georgina's office behind the kitchen. He'd looked superficially through the handwritten notes Ross had taken at various Royal Scottish Geographical Society lectures, and glanced too at some of their newsletters (organized in boxes on shelves near the laird's lug).

Ben sat, finally, in a Queen Anne chair in the bedroom's corner turret, one step up from the rest of the floor, staring out the back window at a copse of Scotch pine, thinking about where to look next.

The kitchen, the seven other bedrooms, the closets, the cloak room, the sitting room, the great hall?

The number of possibilities was mildly depressing.

And he decided to read the notes Ellen had given him and think about the scrapbook later.

ANSWERS TO YOUR QUESTIONS:

Georgina's Will

Lawyers say G. discussed her will with them Monday, May 29. Asked for rush job. G. signed will and took home copy on May 30. Will witnessed by two employees in solicitors' office.

Grace MacNicol, cleaning lady, doing laundry and cleaning in kitchen and scullery same day, May 30, by G.'s office saw that G. had come home from being out and laid briefcase on desk, then was disturbed by plumber needing to talk about trouble in upstairs bath. Grace saw Jack Corelli reading some sort of papers on G.'s desk a few minutes later. Could have been will. Tom Ogilvie came to visit later same day. Was alone in office waiting for G. to come back, possibly from a walk with Jack. Therefore possible he saw will.

Tom and Georgina were thought by Jack at dinner to be extremely irritated with each other.

Locations at time of G.'s death

Donald Murray at Edinburgh at lawyers making his own will. (Bill from lawyer came in niece's mail. Husband opened it without noticing. Donald indignant. Niece told me when walking across fields from Muchalls Village.) Colin in

*Royal Infirmary hospital in Aberdeen. There twelve days
(in on June 2, out on 13). Pneumonia as well as blood trouble.
Don't know where Jack was for sure. Asked him. Said
Oxford and acted insulted. Don't know if he was serious.
Found out by subterfuge with English dept. secretary that
Robbie MacAlpin was in Oxford. Michael Shaw in
Abingdon near Oxford. Isabelle Hay in Bath, not far from
Oxford, according to her cleaning lady. Ian Cunningham
away visiting daughter in Gullane south of Edinburgh.*

Ben folded the pages from Ellen's legal pad, laid a length of
thread on top and between them, and locked them in his briefcase. Then he stared at the four-poster bed, and thought about
calling Kate.

No, she'll call me as soon as she knows anything. But I
need to remember to ask if I can buy her books in Aberdeen.

More important, at the moment, is whether Jack's right.
Because if it *was* a bacterial toxin, concentrated enough to kill,
it could've been put in anything. A cup of coffee. A spoonful of
sugar. A saltshaker even. I assume. Which could explain the
woman in Wales.

Powdered toxin could've been put in a vitamin too. By
anyone who knew Georgina took them. Dump the vitamins
out of one capsule, substitute the toxin, fit the capsule back
together, put it in the bottle, and wait for Georgina to swallow
it at random.

If you were smart, you'd wait till just before she left for
Oxford and stay several hundred miles away.

If that's what happened—and I don't know that it did, of
course—it wouldn't matter that Jack or Tom Ogilvie or Robbie
MacAlpin were in Oxford. Or that Isabelle Hay and Michael

Shaw were close by in Bath and Abingdon.

If it was in a vitamin and not her food.

And if it was murder and not natural causes.

Ben reached into the box of Royal Scottish Geographical Society newsletters he'd been glancing through, took out the January issue from 1931, and then sat at Georgina's desk. He'd gotten to the section listing lecturers for the year, when a name in that list caught his eye. He said, "I wonder if that's the same family?"

Right before there was a no-nonsense knock on his door.

Ben told whoever it was to come in.

And Jack stuck his head around the corner, while Ben put the lid on the newsletters. Jack dropped into the chair by the fireplace, leaned against the back, and said, "I went up to Aberdeen this morning," while he lit a cigarette and threw the match in the fireplace.

"What'd you find out about Dr. MacAlpin?"

"She knows a lot about the bacteria that eat iron, and another type of bacteria that eat a very specific mineral from under the North Sea, but that's about it. I looked at her lab. I glanced at her publications. I talked to people who work with her, and then met with Shewan. It doesn't look like it's her to me. It could be. She could find out who to talk to at what university, and how to get her hands on the right bacterial toxin, but I see no reason to think she has."

"Thanks. I appreciate the help."

"Yeah." Jack didn't say anything else for a minute. He sat and stared at the cold grate, while he French inhaled his Lucky Strike. "Can I ask you a question?"

"Sure."

"Are you involved with Ellen?"

"What? You mean personally? No. Why would you ask that?"

"You don't know?" Jack was looking right at Ben and his whole face looked defensive.

"She's my student. My apprentice. I couldn't ethically consider it. She's young enough to be my daughter anyway."

"She's almost twenty-five. What's that make her, twelve or thirteen years younger? That's not too young for you to be interested."

"There's too big a divide between her generation and mine."

"What's that mean?"

"The war. The Depression." Ben had his eyes half closed and his jaw off to the side, as he gazed at Jack and told himself not to smile. "So are you interested in Ellen?"

"No, I didn't say that. I just wondered, that's all."

"I think she's a good kid, and plenty smart, and I hope she gets to grow up to be what's she's supposed to be—"

"But—"

The phone rang on Georgina's desk and they both waited for Ellen to pick it up wherever she was in the house. When she hadn't picked it up after the fourth ring, Ben reached for the receiver.

Jack said, "I'm still working on the toxin." And shut the door behind him.

"Ben? This is Kate." She was sitting in her office looking down across the front sweep of pasture to Loch Rannoch, watching sheep nibble and switch their tails in patches of sun and shadow. "No, I'm fine...I went to see MacAlpin yesterday. He and David worked together, of course, and I took him a book that David had said he could borrow...Yeah, I did that too. But I didn't see any sign of rare or valuable books. I talked my way into his office in the English department, and looked around there. And then met him at his house later. That's not to say he couldn't have books hidden somewhere, but I guess I'd be surprised. I showed him David's first edition of *Paradise Lost*. It's a beautiful book, and it's got to be worth something, but Robbie didn't seem to have any interest in it at all. Not the fire-behind-the-eyes you'd expect with collectors. Even if you assume he would've been trying to hide it...

"No, you're right, he's *not* the best actor to begin with. He's sort of a hothead type who can't hide much of anything...No, I don't....He was baby-sitting with the kids while his wife was at the university, and they were screaming, and he was trying to cope and work on a book too, and I helped him smooth things out a little. And that made it easy to see most of the house while I was at it...Right. And after that he seemed more willing to talk...Why? Because I'm a woman?...Yeah, maybe. You're probably right. Anyhow, I think he's beginning to ask himself if he hated Georgina without much reason. He told me about shouting at her in Oxford. He brought it up himself. And I think the longer he talked, the more he saw how petty it was. I can't say that for sure. It may just be the fact that she's dead...Yeah, funny how death can make us look at the way we've behaved with a lot more objectivity than we did when whoever it is was alive...Unless we start idealizing the person instead, and glossing over reality, which I find even more irritating...

"No, it's largely a subjective reaction. I just didn't see any evidence that he's a collector. He could be hiding his rare books somewhere, but so could anybody." Kate leaned back in her chair, smoothing her thick dark hair behind her right ear, while she smiled to herself as Ben talked.

"Sure...Whenever you think...So how are you doing yourself?...Did you?...So it looks to you like books, doesn't it? I mean that seems to be the recurring theme...Right...So how will you find out?...*That's* clever!...There's somewhere you can stand and watch without being seen?...But you'll be careful? Whatever this person uses is really lethal and it's got to hit way too fast. I'm telling *you*, right? Like you'd never think of it yourself...What? Do I get homesick? Is that what you said?...Yes, there's a small distant voice that keeps saying, 'This is a foreign country.' I guess if I had more of a life for myself there, it'd be worse. But yeah, America's still home, and this is just kind of a long-term temporary stay. Anyway, I better get going...That's okay. I was glad to help...You too. Let me know, okay?...Bye, Ben."

Kate dropped the heavy black receiver into its cradle and rolled another sheet of paper into her IBM. She turned on the power and stared at the page, once she'd read the handwritten revisions on a wooden stand to the right.

She gazed at the paper for two or three minutes. And then took her fingers off the keys. She stood up and stretched her shoulders and then set her hands on her hips. She was staring at Loch Rannoch—at the wind, ruffling the green and black mosaic of small jagged reflections from rock and trees, pushing the ridges of short choppy waves from the far side of the loch across on an angle to the left. The sun tucked itself behind a heavy dark cloud with mist hanging below it, shrouding the tops of the pointed firs on either side of the pasture, hiding her view of the highlands.

Kate stood still and watched, mesmerized by the wildness,

and the delicacy of it too. Till she said, "Okay, fine, so why are you doing this when you've still got chapter nine to finish?"

It's not like it's any big deal. Just dialogue you've already thought about.

Why am I standing here thinking about Ben instead of my own work?

He makes me think of Graham, I know that. He makes 1943 and '4 seem real again. The smile in his voice, behind the seriousness. Bringing Graham back. The way they used to needle each other and then laugh, when we took those walks on the beach.

But Ben isn't Graham.

He's a friend. An acquaintance, really.

Someone I once knew well, but don't now.

I've thought about him since the war. He was kind, and interesting, and I liked him.

Graham liked him even more. Maybe because they trained rangers together in tricky situations. Where what he did made the difference between life and death.

Why wouldn't I wonder what happened to him, and how well they patched him up after he was hurt?

But I'm thirty-six years old. And I've got a life of my own. A life I've built. Minute by minute. Choice by choice.

Ever since Graham died.

Ben and I could never have what I had with Graham. Or he had with Jessie either. The telepathic thread that gives. And goes everywhere. And has no end.

Fine.

You've got a book due in September and you've got to rework fourteen chapters too many more times.

I wonder why I keep waiting for Ben to call me Kit?

❧❧❧❧

Ben and Ellen stood at the fireplace end of Cairnwell's dining room and considered the long trestle table stretching away to the French doors. Candles were lit, places were set, water was already poured, when Ellen said, "Does it matter where everyone sits?"

"No. But they'll all be here, except for Donald Murray? What did he say when you asked him?"

"Nothing. He wouldn't answer me. He shook his head the whole time I talked and then just walked away."

"We'll figure out some way to approach him later. If it ends up being necessary. And I guess I don't think it will be. It's a good thing you can cook."

Ellen smiled, and then looked embarrassed, as she pushed two wooden candlesticks farther apart on the high sideboard that had once been a clerk's desk. "It won't be fancy. Roast beef and potatoes, then strawberries and cream for dessert."

"You know, you couldn't get beef in Britain for years after the war. Probably till '51 or '2. Just whale meat and horse meat. And powdered everything else."

"Ooooh." Ellen's whole face looked repulsed.

And Ben laughed. "I don't think most Americans understand how hard the war was over here. Where would I find copies of *Who's Who*? Old ones from the twenties or thirties. Did I see some in Georgina's office?"

"I think so. I think there's a set in a cabinet, with boxes from the university stacked in front of it."

"Why didn't you tell me you were in Oxford the day Georgina died?"

"Didn't I?" Ellen turned her back to Ben, straightening a place mat and adjusting a fork. "I thought I told you the day you got here."

Ben didn't say anything. He just stared at her thin back, at the braided ponytail hanging across the tan silk collar, listening to the sound of her breathing.

"I landed at Heathrow really early in the morning and took a bus to Oxford. I thought I'd spend some time with Aunt Georgina, if she was free, and then take a train up to Glasgow, and over to Edinburgh and up north from there. I called the inn from the bus station, and Mrs. Long told me G. wasn't there and they didn't know when she'd be back. They must've just taken her to the hospital, and I guess my name didn't mean anything to Mrs. Long right then, so she didn't tell me any more. I just grabbed a cab to the train station and took the first train to Glasgow."

"It would've been a lot faster to go from Heathrow into London and up to Edinburgh from there."

"Yeah, but I hate London traffic, and G. didn't have morning classes, and I thought I'd get to Oxford early enough that I'd catch her before she left."

"I see."

"I thought I told you." Ellen's thin fingers were fidgeting, smoothing her black skirt, playing with one pearl earring.

"There's something else I need to ask you too. Sometime during dinner will you mention something about rare books in whatever context seems to fit the conversation? About me working with them or something?"

"Before they give me their letters explaining what they want me to do about Cairnwell?"

"It doesn't matter when to me, except that it has to be done before anyone gets up to leave. Would you mention, too, that you're leaving after dinner to take the photo albums to Anna?"

"Sure. I can do that. Oh, I know what I meant to tell you.

Ian Cunningham called right after you left his house, and said he'd remembered a conversation he thinks might be important. The night before G. left for Oxford, he called her to talk about some kind of parish business, something she'd been doing for him. He hadn't spoken to her in three or four days, and as they were talking, he thought she sounded preoccupied, and he asked her if she was worried about going to Oxford. What she said was, 'I've seen a book where it doesn't belong.' He asked what she meant, and she answered with something like, 'It's nothing to worry about, and I shouldn't have bothered you.'"

"That's interesting."

"She said she was in Aberdeen that day too."

"You must know a lot about book collecting. With your mother being a collector."

"Not really. I never thought about it." Ellen looked away again and rearranged one of the peonies in the cream-colored pitcher on the table. "I don't like the writers she collects. She started with a Victorian named Sabine Baring-Gould when she was a little kid. Then moved on to Disraeli, and the Brontës, and the du Maurier family. And I never paid much attention."

"Baring-Gould was a Renaissance man."

"Oh, I almost forgot. This came for me this afternoon, and I think you ought to read it."

"Thanks." Ben took the envelope and put it in the inside pocket of his jacket. "I'll read it after dinner."

"So you're an archivist, Mr. Reese?" Tom Ogilvie—his long face closed and noncommittal, his shoulders tight against his chair, his back toward the French doors—played with the fork on his dessert plate, as he watched Ben on his left, in the center of the long side of the table, pour himself a cup of coffee.

"I work with ancient coins and documents, and restore paintings, and classify all sorts of unexpected stuff that donors have given the university."

"Doesn't Alderton have quite a collection of rare books?" Ellen was sitting at the other end of the table opposite Tom, handing whipped cream to Isabelle, who was sitting on her right next to Ben.

"That's one of the reasons I'm over here, actually. We've been given quite a few important books and manuscripts, including incunabula and ephemera, and I'm—"

"What, pray tell, is ephemera?" Isabelle Hay asked in her low clipped voice.

Ellen said, "Pamphlets and tracts and broadsheets. Like Samuel Johnson's 'Rambler.' Pieces that usually get thrown away, but have a lot to say about their time." Ben's eyes met Ellen's and she dropped hers before he did. "That's what my mother says anyway. Is that right, Dr. Reese?"

Ben nodded and sipped his coffee. "I work with colleagues here in Britain, in libraries and museums, who help me date or authenticate what we've got, and also ask me to bring artifacts too, for them to study and photograph for their collections."

"What sorts of things?" Robbie MacAlpin, short and square-faced, red-headed and fidgety, his elbows on the table on Ben's right, was swirling his brandy in his glass.

"Well, we have a forty-two-line German manuscript Bible that predates Gutenberg. It was hand-illuminated in a monastery near Mainz, and there's some evidence it may have been the Bible Gutenberg used as the model for his printed text."

"How very interesting." Isabelle Hay had just eaten her last strawberry and was setting her spoon on her plate. "I wish John had been well enough to come to dinner. He's a student of military history, and he'd enjoy discussing the artifacts he's inherited from the family estate."

Jack Corelli snorted fairly quietly, then lit a cigarette, staring hotly across the table at the wall behind Isabelle and Ben.

Colin took two small white pills out of a pillbox and slipped them under his tongue.

Michael Shaw pushed his plate away, lit a cigarette too, and asked what else Alderton had that Ben thought was especially interesting.

"We have a Spanish antiphonal from 1250."

"What's an antiphonal?" Ellen looked at Ben while stirring whipped cream in her coffee.

"It's a church hymnal from a monastery. It's hand-illuminated with really spectacular capital letters in gold and lapis lazuli. There's a resurrection scene that's amazing. But there're caricatures too, in some of the letters. Tiny animals and small impish human faces with beards and pointy hats. I'm still amazed that a small school in the middle of Ohio would own anything like it. We've got other really fine artifacts too. A lot more than I would've expected."

"What size is it?"

"The university?"

Michael Shaw said, "No, the hymnbook."

"It's vellum, and maybe two and a half feet high by two feet wide, with oak boards covered in dark brown cowhide."

Isabelle Hay touched her lips with her napkin before asking how his university had acquired it.

"Nobody seems to know. It was there when I arrived in '52."

"What other rare books are there?" Ellen sipped her coffee, then passed the brandy to Colin.

"Well…we have two first editions of Dante's *Divine Comedy*. And several American collections that are quite exceptional. Including the handwritten journal of a Private Flohr, a German-speaking mercenary from Strasbourg who wrote about his experiences in the American Revolution. One donor gave us a very valuable collection of materials from European explorers with a concentration on those who discovered the New World."

"What sorts of books would that include?" Tom Ogilvie was pulling his shirt cuffs out from under his faded gray suit and his voice sounded more polite than interested.

"As far back as Columbus and Cabot, the sponsors of the voyages of exploration expected the captains to illustrate every landfall with sketches of some sort, or watercolor paintings, and describe or draw the animal life and the plants. All British Royal Navy captains, certainly starting with Drake, were required to do the same. There're supposed to be thousands of ships' logs today in the naval archives in Greenwich that nobody's ever studied. Which makes me want to do it myself. Anyway, this American donor I was talking about amassed an amazing number of very important examples of ships' logs and landfall manuscripts and illustrations, and I found them not too long after I started at Alderton. Nothing was really cataloged before I came. Boxes and trunks were in attics and basements in all the old university buildings, so a large part of my work has been to find what's lying hidden, evaluate whatever artifacts there are, restore them if needed, and catalog them properly. Do any of you know what happened to John Cabot's papers?"

Ben looked at the faces gathered around the table and waited for someone to speak.

Isabelle Hay sat straight as a stick with her hands in her lap and her lips pressed together. Ellen spooned another strawberry onto her plate. Colin mopped his brow with his napkin as though he were feeling warm, as though he were tired and uncomfortable and probably preferred to go home. Jack Corelli rolled a match back and forth on his place mat. Michael Shaw had taken out a pencil and was sketching a face on an envelope. Tom Ogilvie pulled a small cardboard box from his pocket, took out a pinch of powder and dropped it in his coffee. Robbie MacAlpin poured himself a second brandy and pushed the decanter toward Ben.

"Would anyone care for shortbread?" Ellen had gotten a plate from the sideboard and was handing it to Isabelle Hay. "I don't remember anything about Cabot."

"He was Italian, but he settled in England. And he made landfall in 1497 in the New World in what he called Cabot's Bay, either on Newfoundland or Cape Breton Island, but nobody knows which. In 1498, he led a much larger expedition, but the expedition was lost, either before *or* after he made it to the New World. There were reports of crew members getting safely back to England saying they'd been to the New World, but there aren't any accepted explanations of what happened to that expedition. And none of Cabot's papers are thought to have survived. None. Not just his papers pertaining to that expedition. May I ask you not to tell anyone else what I'm going to say next?" Ben looked around the table and everyone duly nodded or murmured some sort of agreement. "The American collector I mention believed he'd uncovered papers belonging to John Cabot, as well as his son, Sebastian, *including* illustrations of that first landfall in Cabot's Bay."

"They must be worth plenty." Jack Corelli glanced at Ellen, then undid his tie and opened his collar.

"If they *are* Cabot's papers, yes. Even if they're fifteenth-century forgeries they'd be valuable. But just the thought of them having been written by Cabot, in his own hand, the description of his own first reaction to finding land after all that time at sea—that keeps me awake at night. Any person's papers from that age would be fascinating, but John Cabot changed our conception of the world. Of course, realistically speaking, this kind of thing usually turns out to be something else. But it is fifteenth-century stuff. At least *I* think so. And I'm taking it down to the British Museum tomorrow and staying for a couple days. I've got three or four things they want to see."

"Does your university have anything that relates to Scotland?" Tom Ogilvie looked at his wristwatch as he asked. And then cleared his throat.

"Several things, actually, and I've brought two of them with me. Samuel Johnson wrote a journal of his only trip to, and across, Scotland called *Journey to the Western Islands*. James Boswell, his friend and biographer, went with him and wrote a journal too. But before they left Boswell's house in Edinburgh to start on their tour, Johnson had been working on an autobiography, and he put it in an unlocked drawer in Mrs. Boswell's charge. His autobiography was never published, or discovered later, and no one has any idea what happened to it. We do know that Johnson lost his notes on his tour of the Hebrides before he got home to London, and that he assumed it was on one of the coaches traveling south from Edinburgh. They were never found in Boswell's home, and they're still thought to have been lost en route.

"Well, a young man who was a student at Alderton in the 1850s left a leather trunk of family papers to the university when he died in the 1890s. His family had originally come from Scotland, the grandfather in the late 1780s, as a tutor to a wealthy English family. I started sorting through the papers last fall, and right at the bottom I found a manuscript tied with ribbon. The title page reads, 'A Short Life of Johnson, by Samuel Johnson.' I think all the internal evidence is consistent with the language, expression, and thought we'd have reason to expect from Johnson at that time. It's the right kind of linen paper, and the watermarks from London are all appropriate, but it's not written in his hand. What *is* in his hand, in my opinion, is the writing in a six inch by four inch calf-bound volume, *Notes on a Tour to the Hebrides,* which was under the autobiography in the trunk."

"What are the chances of that being real?" Jack was finishing his brandy, and the dark brown eyes above the rim of the glass were cool and clearly skeptical. "I can't believe a discovery like that still happens today."

Ben laughed and said, "Not often, maybe. But it happens. Boswell's actual handwritten journal, taken with him all across Scotland on that trip with Johnson, which was later published as *Journal of a Tour to the Hebrides,* was discovered sometime right around 1930 in Malahide Castle near Dublin in a croquet box, in a cupboard, along with a hundred pages of Boswell's manuscript of his famous *Life of Johnson.*"

Robbie MacAlpin said, "Do you think the autobiography was a copy? Someone had read the original and copied it out?"

"I do, yes."

"That is fascinating, isn't it?" Tom Ogilvie folded his napkin and pushed his chair away from the table. "Even so, I shall have to toddle along. It's nearly ten. It's a two-hour drive home, and I ought to make a start. Thank you for a lovely dinner, Ellen. And thank you very much indeed for being interested in my views on the future of both Fletcher's and Cairnwell. I shall wait to hear from you at your earliest convenience."

"I didn't realize it was that late. I'm supposed to take Georgina's photo albums over to Anna Morrison tonight so she can put captions under the pictures, and I guess I better go. I'm sorry. I apologize for rushing off."

The dinner party broke up as Ben watched, searching faces. Trying to see behind eyes. "I think I'll walk over to that little village across the coast road. I haven't seen it, and I'd like to get some exercise. I can't remember what it's called."

Colin said, "Muchalls," as he stepped out of the dining room into the front hall.

"How long would it take to walk over there and back?"

"An hour I should think." Colin was buttoning his jacket, and wrapping a scarf around his neck. "At your pace, of course, not mine."

"That should get my blood moving."

"Do you feel like company?" Michael Shaw asked as he stooped through the door into the hall, his long legs and arms relaxed and swinging, looking like a Gaciometti drawing.

"I think Ellen said she wanted to talk to you about something."

Ellen turned when she heard her name and looked at Ben for a second as though she had no idea what he was talking about. But then she recovered and said, "Yes, there's something I want to show you in Georgina's sitting room. Good night, Jack. Good night, Lady Hay. I'll see you tomorrow, Colin. I'll come down and we'll talk about the dower house."

Ben told everyone good night, saying he had to run upstairs and change his shoes.

Then Robbie MacAlpin thanked Ellen "for a lovely dinner."

"You're very welcome."

"I feel quite at a loss, really, having learned from you of Georgina's plans for her writers retreat. Perhaps..." Robbie looked around—at Colin walking pathetically slowly across the gravel court, at Jack's head charging away from the other side of the curtain wall gate, at Tom Ogilvie's old gray Morris Minor as it sputtered toward the front drive, at Michael Shaw standing back by the turret stairs just outside the dining room door, at Ben's back, as it disappeared up the whitewashed stairs. Robbie MacAlpin brushed his hand across his stiff red hair and spoke even more quietly to Ellen. "You see, I had no idea she intended to offer me a place at her retreat. A real chance to stay here and work without interruption. It's quite unsettling, you see, for I've...well, I was never very willing to see her point of view. Perhaps I was even—"

"Jealous of her? Her reputation, and her tenure, and her money?"

Robbie MacAlpin's head spun toward Ellen, and he shook it quickly back and forth. "No, that isn't it a-tall. I simply..." His mouth was open, but he didn't say anything else.

Ellen looked at him, her eyes cold and critical, her wide mouth pinched and pulled to one side, ready to resist any rationalization. "Maybe I shouldn't have been so blunt."

"I don't know...I...well...anyway, you have my letter. If you do see your way clear to go on with the writers retreat, I would be very grateful if you would consider me too. Just as you would anyone else."

ꞃ ꞃ ꞃ ꞃ

Ben whistled "Greensleeves" across the front courtyard, past the edge of the stone well, out through the gate in the curtain wall, then right toward the front drive. He turned right again by the griffin gate, toward the sea coast road and the village of Muchalls.

It was almost dark, that teal blue–navy blue ink-stained sky painters almost never get right, cut by cold stars—and he whistled his way as he watched it, toward the first left turning in the farm track up past a roundel of beech. He passed the circle of beech trees, covering a low very round hill, walking between it on his left behind a stone wall and a hedgerow and wall on his right—whistling more quietly the farther he went. He followed the track ten yards past the woods, then jumped the wall and ducked back into the trees and listened.

An inland wind was blowing from the other side of Cairnwell, and the beeches were rustling around him, one high slender trunk creaking as it bent above him.

Nothing else, though. No footsteps. No signs of anyone following him from the house.

He slipped behind a hundred-year-old tree and waited, under high willowy branches bending gently in the wind, where he could see the track between the woods and Cairnwell.

Small animals scurried in the gorse in the hedgerows. An owl hunted between Ben and the sea.

Michael Shaw walked out the griffin gate and turned away toward the quarry.

Ellen drove out a minute or two later.

And Ben looked at his watch and decided on fifteen minutes.

And he spent them listening, watching. Deciding on the scullery door, where he wouldn't be easy to see.

CHAPTER ELEVEN

ON CAIRNWELL'S THIRD FLOOR, on the other side of the hall from the opening of the turret stairs into the portrait gallery, was another archway to another turret stair that went nowhere. It had been abandoned as the house had been changed and added to, and all that was left were eight or ten stone stairs curving between a stone floor and a stone ceiling. There Georgina had set a sculpture by Michael Shaw, just inside the archway to the sealed stairs, a cloaked medieval-looking woman, four feet high and two and a half feet wide, a woman who's stooping down, just beginning to pull the hem of her gown above the toe of her shoe.

Guests at Cairnwell always stopped short and stared twice at the white marble woman, who looked transparent at first glance in front of the whitewashed stairs even though she was so real when you studied her it was almost eerie. They asked themselves why it had been put there too, usually, wondering what it said about Georgina's sense of humor.

Ben could've reached out and touched the woman's left arm, from where he waited behind the sealed stairs, with his back to the gallery and the door to his room on his left, on the other side of the archway into the abandoned stairs.

He'd been waiting for almost half an hour, and he was

telling himself it had to be soon.

If our friend the book collector actually comes tonight.

He may think it's too risky, and wait till I get back from London.

If that happens, and the books and the museum trip I made up don't work, I'll have to think of something else to make him make a move fast.

Yeah, but if this guy's as obsessed as I think he is, I'd be surprised if he can restrain himself.

What is it with human nature that we hate to wait as much as we do? Is it just wanting what we want when we want it?

Ah. Ellen's letter. I should've thought of it sooner.

He took it out of his pocket, out of the envelope postmarked Oxford, four days before.

18 June 1961

Dear Miss Winter,

I returned from Italy only yesterday and learned to my dismay and astonishment that Dr. Fletcher has died. After discovering that you are her heir, and are now at Cairnwell, I thought it only fitting to offer my condolences.

I was an undergraduate student of Dr. Fletcher's at Aberdeen, and would not now be beginning graduate work at Oxford if I had not had her help and guidance. Her influence on my life and work cannot be overemphasized, and my admiration for her will always remain both deep and heartfelt.

It is with gratitude that I think back on my last day in Oxford before I left on holiday. Dr. Fletcher and I ate lunch the day before I left, and I learned then of her affection for

coffee-and-cream-filled chocolates from a certain confec-
tioner's in Cornmarket Street. I bought her one that after-
noon and took it to her early the next morning before I
boarded the bus for Heathrow.

We had a wonderful chat at lunch and a very pleasant
few minutes that last morning for which I shall always be
grateful. It seems truly inconceivable that she should have
died not long thereafter.

You have my deepest sympathy.
Sincerely,
Amanda Grace

Ben smiled at the woman beside him, while quietly tapping his canine teeth on the left side of his jaw.

Then he waited again, thinking about Ellen. Time, hanging
on him hard. Making him shift from one foot to the other and
fight a cough at the back of his throat.

He told himself not to notice, to concentrate on how to
prove everything he suspected. When there wasn't any proof at
all, that he could see. That four murders had been committed
in thirty years for the same reason, with the same method, by a
twisted soul. Four lives for linen and calfskin. For ink and fin-
gerprints and printed words.

Although it could've been more than one murderer too,
instead of someone who's old enough to have been around that
long. A father could've committed the first two murders. Then
his son or daughter could've murdered the others. *Or* a mother
and daughter, either one.

Ben was thinking about Georgina's poem, the one he'd
been keeping in his pocket. And he pulled it out and read it
again in the half-light from the hall.

Is it the outside?
the smooth skin
the tasteful decoration
the fine color mixed and laid
with an artist's hand
like lines drawn delicately around the mind's eye.
Is it the feel, the suppleness
of skin stretched upon the bones,
the spine
with silken cords that bind today
when tied and knotted by an artist
just as they were
before Shakespeare looked his neighbors in the eye
and drew their likeness true.

Yet what is the skin side
to the inside?
to the lines, the whorls, the curls
that make the meaning—
the pull and loosening
the prick and stick
the lightening and the tightening
of the signs that turn a mind
to times and sightings of worlds beyond the eye
the touch
the hearing,
to truth and falsehood
beyond oneself
that calls to be discerned.

How could death be drawn by either—
by the pallid deadly call of coverings
or the living signs inside
that shame the shades of buried greed
lying silent
lying hidden
in the sinful soul of men.

Ben knew it wasn't a memorable poem, but he smiled at the way her mind worked, pinning thought to image. For it was that poem, the sense he'd had in it of Georgina's presence—the depth of her concern and craft and concentration—that had helped keep him going in one direction rather than any other, almost from the start.

So assuming I'm right, and it is a book collector, and Jack's right too, and he did use a toxin—what do I do next?

I'll have to search his house sometime. Even if he wouldn't be stupid enough to make the toxin easy to find.

Where would you put it? In the spice rack next to the salt? As a secret sinister joke? Maybe. A certain sort of murderer might.

But not this guy. Too cautious. Too humorless. Too dangerous too. If someone else came in and cooked a meal.

He'd never leave the books where anyone could find them. And there must be a lot of them, if he's been doing this for thirty years. No, he'd make a very safe place and keep them hidden. But I bet he's got them close to him. Where he can hold them in his hands and think about who wrote them or illuminated them or copied the words with a quill pen. Or printed those letters in a certain city at a certain time. It may be the person who owned the books too that appeals to him. The one who underlined the words, or wrote the notes in the margin.

Or kissed the gold leaf in the leather before he did. But it's the ones who sailed to unknown coasts that he's obsessed with.

Nuts. It's almost eleven-fifteen.

He knows when to expect me back, so it's got to be soon. Or some other day or night, when he knows I'm gone.

Ben swallowed a yawn, and was just raising his hand to the back of his neck when he heard a shoe scratch across the stone stair where he'd sprinkled a line of fine gravel.

He held his breath for a second, as he turned the left side of his head against the cold wall behind him so he could stare sideways through the archway of the sealed stairs to the spot in the gallery where anyone would have to stand to open his bed-room door.

It sounded like a man's shoes. Moving slowly. One quiet cautious step at a time. One stair, and another. Then the brush of shoe across sisal on the hall floor.

Whoever it was stood there on the woven rush. Waiting. Listening. Watching, undoubtedly, both sides of the portrait hall. Letting his breath come slower and deeper. *If*, in fact, it was a man.

Whoever it was was moving. Pausing between steps.

And then he was standing by Ben's bedroom door, reaching quickly, turning the handle softly, slipping into Ben's room, closing the door behind him.

Ben almost bit his lower lip in disgust.

Because he'd been right. And seeing Colin's face with his own eyes made him hopping mad.

He told himself to knock it off. That emotion gets in the way more times than it helps.

And then he crouched down on his heels, so he'd be harder to see when Colin walked toward him.

He won't come out right away. It'll take him time to look everywhere and find nothing.

So what do I do first? Go through the old *Who's Who*s and see if I can find the Ramsay who spoke to the Royal Scottish Geographical Society, in case he's related to this jerk. Even if it's not very likely, it's still got to be done.

I've got to find Ross's scrapbook too, of people he planned to write about. He loved the RSGS, and maybe this Dr. Richard Ramsay, who talked to them about medicine in Malaya, is one of those. If a minor miracle's occurred.

Colin *was* raised in the east somewhere. So there's got to be some kind of possibility that they're related.

Of course, if any of that's true, Georgina would've seen the importance of the scrapbook. At least once she'd found "the book where it didn't belong." So before she went to Oxford, she might have put the scrapbook where nobody would find it.

Ah. That's what I would've done.

Why did it take me this long?

Ben's door opened and shut fast. And Colin scuttled past Ben into the turret stairs, then down to the first floor.

Less than five minutes later, Ben was in Ross's study. He'd closed the heavy crewel drapes, and turned on a small lamp, and he was pushing up on the linen fold panel where the Witney manuscripts had been hidden.

Once it was up far enough that its bottom had cleared the lower frame, he pulled it forward and down and laid it on the sheepskin rug.

He took out the board that had formed the top of the box-like space where the manuscripts had been hidden. And then he used his flashlight on the inside, trying to see the surface of the four-by-sixteen inch board at the bottom.

It had been cut to fit without pegs or nails, to sit on some sort of support moldings, probably around the perimeter, making a frame underneath.

On the left side, on one of the short end walls of the wooden box, Ben could just see the marks he'd thought he remembered. There were similar scratches on the left half of the front and back too, but none anywhere on the right.

The marks could've been made when the linen fold was being taken apart to treat the wood for deathwatch beetle.

But they also could've been made later.

He'd brought a hammer from the scullery, and he held the metal head in his right hand, and hit the left side of the bottom board with the flat end of the handle.

The left side dropped down, the right end snapped up—and Ben pulled the board out from inside the linen fold framing.

The support moldings on the left end, and the left halves of the front and back frames, had been chiseled out and replaced with a thick band of putty, though the support moldings on the right side were still the original wood.

There, in the space below, was a loose-leaf scrapbook standing on end. And Ben congratulated Georgina silently for seeing how to do what she knew had to be done.

He sat on the floor and turned pages, till he found the section he was hoping for.

It started with *The Times* obituary, December 17, 1934, of Richard Weldon Ramsay, "a well-respected bacteriologist on the Faculty of the Institute of Bacteriology and Immunology,

University of Glasgow, and the Faculty of the Western Infirmary…survived by his son, Colin Archibald Ramsay."

On the next page, Ben found the first of Ross Fletcher's notes on Richard Ramsay's lecture in May 1931 at The Royal Scottish Geographical Society. And he read that Ramsay, after making "several cogent remarks on the geographical and cultural features observed during his years in Singapore and Malaya," described the high points of the medical work he'd done in Malaya with rural populations largely associated with the rubber plantations he was then employed by.

Ramsay had trained in London at The Institute of Tropical Medicine and Hygiene, spent several years in Singapore, moved his family to Malaya in 1896, used opportunities there (through 1902 when he returned with his family to Scotland) to conduct field research on tropical diseases in the indigenous population. Parasites were of particular interest to him, and he'd set up a laboratory in his rubber company offices to conduct basic research while performing his work as a physician.

Then, on the fifth page of notes on Ramsay's remarks, Ross recorded an event that took place in 1901 when Ramsay was called in to a neighboring plantation:

Three Chinese workers seriously ill with vomiting of unexplained origin. Elderly woman, elderly man, two-year-old grandson died. Others in family ill, but recovered.

Treated subjects. Onset of vomiting one to two hours after food consumption. Gathered remains of last meal for analysis—large amount cooked rice remained, small portion uncooked vegetables and fruit left from last food preparation. Woman died six hours after onset of "emetic episodes." Boy seven hours after onset. Man eight hours after.

Collected fecal and other body samples from deceased and survivors for analysis.

Analyzed rice and vegetables for presence of harmful or unexpected organisms.

No suspicious organism could be cultured from food or body samples.

Interesting research opportunity.

Fed cooked vegetables to mice. No result. Fed cooked rice to laboratory mice. Mice died with comparable symptoms to Ramsay's patients.

R. hypothesized that a harmful organism in rice was killed by cooking preparation, but that a harmful toxin remains in rice after cooking. Perhaps cooking, or storing procedures after cooking, optimized growth of toxin in already cooked rice.

Therefore began to suspect lethal toxin is HEAT STABLE.

Used primitive methods (chemical fractionation? etc.) of concentrating whatever toxins (originally produced by microorganism) might be present in macerated rice. Tested several concentrated isolated fractions on mice. After introduction of one specific fraction, mice died in much shorter time.

Collected this highly concentrated product (which he strongly suspects is a toxin produced by a microorganism, which had lived and grown in rice prior to cooking). Wonders if toxin may have grown rapidly in unrefrigerated storing conditions after cooking.

R. concentrated toxin still further. Repeated experiment. Mice died sooner. Lyophilized the deadly toxin (which apparently means reduced to a stable concentrated powder under very low temperatures, though he didn't explain *fully), and brought toxin with him to Scotland when he took position at Univ. of Glasgow in 1902.*

Doesn't know what this toxin is. Nothing in literature appears to apply.

Maintains laboratories at Glasgow Univ. and country home near Edinburgh. Has not yet completed work on toxin. Pressure of teaching work at University and affiliated Western Infirmary, as well as pressing research for his work there, have forced him to postpone his study of lethal toxin. Hopes to proceed once retired, if not before.

Used as example of interesting opportunity for medical research in foreign lands.

Described incidents of other more common and important diseases resulting from other dietary and food preparation procedures among Malays, emphasizing importance of parasites in tropical settings...

Ben read the rest of Ross's notes on Richard Ramsay's lecture, then took paper out of Ross's desk, and copied the notes on the toxin word for word.

He put his copy in his pocket, then slipped Ross's scrapbook back in the linen fold wall. He pounded a small nail in the left end of the back wall of the cavity and carefully balanced the bottom board on that nail and the right hand molding.

He replaced the linen fold panel.

And went to call Anna Morrison.

Thursday, June 22th

Ben was driving almost straight west, on his way to Port Appin, thinking it was a very good thing that Colin's cleaning lady was up at six and still home.

I don't know how I would've found out who Colin writes his postcards to, or where she lives, without Winifred, since nobody else, even Anna, knew the girl's name.

Why did Ellen look so irritated when I left? Because I wouldn't tell her who it is, and where I'm going? I told her I'm doing it to protect her, and I explained as well as I could.

She'll treat Colin the way she always has, if she doesn't know not to. Which will keep him from seeing a reason to put toxin in her coffee while I'm gone—or disappear, either one.

It was one of Ben's favorite drives, around the eastern half of Loch Creran. East and then back around that long narrow loch.

It was too late for the bluebells, for the roadsides and fields to be purple with them, but it was still spectacular. Evergreen forests covering high steep hills on either side of a narrow valley. A handful of isolated whitewashed cottages. One lonely castle. A couple of white harled houses, large and rambling, tucked into ridges above the banks. A single white sailboat pulled up on the beach, just where the road doubled back west around the east end of the lake toward the coast. Three white gulls there studying the shallows, before they turned back to sea.

Ben watched, and tried not to think about anything else, until he'd gotten to the northwest end of Loch Creran, and cut up to the right into a smaller valley, the Strath of Appin (heath and hills and evergreens on either side), and then edged away to the left on an even narrower one-lane road toward the empty spot on the map called Port Appin.

In the middle of a slow left curve, a stretch of water appeared on Ben's right, and there on an island, hardly bigger than it was, sat Castle Stalker—narrow, gray, a pepper pot castle in the middle of Loch Laiche that made Ben want to find a row boat and spend the afternoon.

It can't be more than a mile and a half to Port Appin. Maybe there'll be time to walk back and see it tonight.

It was less than a mile to Druimneil House (the long, low, white gabled coaching inn where Ben was staying)—through lush trees and leafy shrubs, wild rose and iris, rhododendron and fern, wildflowers and waterbirds—along the length of Loch Linnhe, which lay like a wide, green ribbon of water on his right, larger than any of the lochs he'd passed, and no more than a hundred yards down a gentle slope from the inn. From Druimneil House. Where Harriet Hamilton lived and worked and got letters from Colin Ramsay.

"May I help a-tall?" A red-haired teenager with wide freckles and pink cheeks smiled at Ben as she pulled off a large blue apron. "I was away in the back and didna hear ye come in. I hope ye haven't waited long, sirr."

"No, I just got here. I'm Ben Reese. I booked a room this morning."

"Shall I have a wee peek at the book?" Her shoulder-length dark red hair fell on either side of her face as she leaned over the ledger on the desk. "Aye, here it-tis. I'm sorry to say we've nay got a rooom with a view o' the loch. Though we do have a lovely wee room in the back."

"That's fine." Ben filled in a registration card while asking if it was convenient to speak to Harriet Hamilton.

"Ah, well, ye see, Harriet Hamilton that was, is Mrs. Harriet Barclay now, and she's away for the day staying with friends across the loch on Lismore."

"I called this morning and a man told me she'd be here all day."

"Ye must've phoned quite early. I don't think it was half-eight when the captain's wife radioed over, Captain Ferguson, ye see, and asked them to luncheon, and the Barclays decided to take a wee holiday. It's been ever so long since they've had a day to themselves. And they were away on the next ferry."

"Is there another ferry?"

"In three or four minutes' time. You can't take a car, though—"

"Is there a ferry back later?"

"Aye, at five-fifteen."

"Where!"

"Out the front and to your left, it's nay but a half a mile or so, but—"

Ben ran through the first bend to the right, and back around another to the left, then straight toward a long stone jetty.

A small, green, wooden-hulled ferry, rubber tires strung around the outside edge of the deck, was just beginning to back away from the wharf.

Ben ran at it, skipping a considerable number of stairs that led down to the jetty, sprinted the length of the wharf, and leapt over cold dark water onto the bow of the boat, landing at the last second, sticking to the deck with his desert boots, catching himself with his good hand.

The ferry captain gazed at Ben through the windscreen, his thick jet-black brows pulled low under a grimy brown cap, his lower lip rolled way down over his beard, out of habit apparently, and concentration, as he backed and turned the ferry toward Lismore.

The water was rough, with the wind whipping down the loch from the open ocean at its western end, hitting the boat's left side, once it had turned to face the Isle of Lismore. The shallow ferry pitched and rolled across three-quarters of a mile of fast water, as Ben sat on a wooden bench inside the cabin watching the handful of passengers (the retired people and small farmers, by the look of them) trying not to watch him. The smell of the sea—the seaweed, the fish, the wet wood and rope—was as much a part of the ferry as it was the open air. And Ben inhaled it slowly, taking the same kind of pleasure in it he'd felt the first time he'd smelled it at age twelve, on an island off the coast of Georgia.

When they docked, Ben paid the captain, then climbed the old stone stairs to look for a ferry office, only to find there wasn't one. Most of the other passengers were heading toward the bicycles by an open shed—only two or three toward two small rusted trucks.

Ben walked toward a stout-legged sixtyish woman in heavy gray sweaters and knitted cap, who was preparing to climb on an aged bicycle, and asked directions to Captain Ferguson's house.

"It's a bit of a walk, I'm afraid. Three miles to Clachan village, which is quite easy to miss, for it's only a string of three or four houses past a tiny kirk. Well worth seeing, though, the kirk. Built on the remains of St. Moulag's Cathedral. Still, if you walk on a hundred yards or so past the kirk, you'll come to a gray stone house on the right, back a bit from the road inside a stone wall. The front garden's the first really lovely one you'll have come to, and you'll see a wide path leading away up the hill just on the other side. That's the Fergusons there. The stone house with the garden under high trees."

"I stay on this road?"

"Yes, you turn to neither left nor right."

"Thanks. I appreciate the help."

The Englishwoman waved and was gone, sweaters flapping, heavy black brogues pedaling hard against the wind.

It looked like it was windy most of the time on Lismore, for the trees and bushes on the hill on Ben's right, as he walked southwest into the wind, were bent way over to the right away from the sea and the strip of low grassy land on his left, where the ground dropped down to a sand and pebble beach, fifty feet or so from the road.

There were rocks strewn through the grass on that side, and a handful of sheep wandered around them, cropping the vegetation close, bolting occasionally through the sand and shale, then back again to the thin strip of green.

But the land changed quickly, on the Isle of Lismore. And as he ran and walked, it opened out from the hill on his right to a flatter stretch closer to the center of the island, where he could see across Lismore to the Morvern coast on his right, and the tip of the Isle of Mull on his left, when he looked southwest toward Oban.

The wind was ferocious in the open, cold and cutting when the sun was covered. But when he would come to a left-hand hill, it would block the wind and warm him, in the sun, and he'd have to take his windbreaker off and tie it around his waist.

There were a few small cottages and run-down barns. And he did pass a solitary red cow grazing in the road, turning from one grassy side to the other, utterly unperturbed by him or the postman, in a tiny red truck, who waved at both Ben and the cow.

Half a mile later, a nervous-looking mud-covered mare

stood huddled over her blackish bay colt and stared at Ben with wild-eyed distrust from the other side of a wire fence.

Ben walked before he got to them, and talked to them quietly as he passed, and only started jogging again fifty feet past.

It was pushing four and he had to hurry. He had to have time to talk to Harriet and catch the ferry back.

Because if Colin did send Harriet Hamilton postcards from the places the book owners died, they'd be some kind of corroboration. The woman in Grantown-on-Spey. Alfred Dyson in Biddenden, Kent. The bookstore owner in Hay-on-Wye.

It's too much to expect that she'd save them. But she might remember something and agree to testify.

That still may be a lot to ask. She was only a kid in the thirties. Why would she remember when he went where?

At least Interpol's got records from back then. And if all goes well, their list of stolen books should be waiting for me at Cairnwell when I get back tomorrow.

The fact that Colin searched my room is no kind of evidence. And neither is who his father was, or what kind of toxin he had in his lab thirty years ago.

I have to tie Colin to the toxin directly. And to one of the murders. Which probably means through the stolen books.

If Georgina had known for sure, when she saw that "book where it didn't belong," that whatever it was was stolen, I think she would've done something more direct right then. Although I bet that's when she hid Ross's scrapbook. Maybe she only really realized what she'd seen after she talked to the book dealer in Oxford.

Here's the church. Finally.

Why does St. Moulag sound familiar?

Was he the Irish monk who was racing another monk, in

small boats, on their way to convert Scotland? The ones who agreed that whoever touched land first would start the mission. And when the other guy got ahead of him, on the way to some island, the one behind cut his finger off and threw it on shore so he'd win? Was that Moulag?

Why don't I pay attention to names the way I used to?

As he came around the left-hand turn under tall old trees, Ben saw the house with the garden on his right. He opened the iron gate, walked through the perennial beds on the gravel path, heading for the side door on the left, when a fiftyish woman wearing a straw hat and gardening gloves, stepped out to meet him.

"May I help a-tall?"

"Mrs. Ferguson?"

"Yes."

"I'm looking for Harriet Barclay."

"You've missed her, I'm sorry to say. She and Owen have gone off to Castle Coeffin."

"Where's that?"

Ben must have looked noticeably put out, because Mrs. Ferguson laughed and said, "Not to worry, you can catch them up I'm sure. Take the farm track here, just past the garden, and start up the hill across the pasture. When the path angles off to the right and disappears, you should just see the outline of a footpath in the grass on your left. Go over the hill on that path, and down the other side toward Morvern, then look down below the cliff you'll be standing upon, and you should see the ruins of a castle on a point of land below."

"How far is it?"

"It's a mile I should think to the castle, if you don't lose your way on the headlands. But Harriet won't have gone that far. Unless Owen carried her down the cliff."

"Thanks!"

Ben ran up the gravel-and-mud track, then across springy close-cropped grass cut in places by a muddy path, climbing north up a gradual hill scattered with buttercups and tiny white daisies.

He walked and ran across unmarked land that had been trampled by countless sheep, and then tried to work his way around a running spring and a wide band of turf it had turned into squelching muck.

But finally he looked down, past a lower ledge of land, to the northwestern half of Loch Linnhe, and the grass and vine-covered ruined stones of the turrets of Castle Coeffin.

He could see a blond man climbing the steep ground around those ruins. But between him and Ben, on the wide lower ledge of land, was a woman on a camp stool painting, metal crutches lying beside her, easel set up in front of her as she faced the ruins.

Ben yelled, "Mrs. Barclay!"

And she turned around and waved him down.

He thought about what he'd decided to say, as he walked down the grass incline. But the more he rehearsed it silently to himself, the more ridiculous it sounded.

"Do I understand you correctly? This young American woman, Mrs. Fletcher's heir, is giving a birthday party for Uncle Colin, especially now because he's ill, and she, being American, has decided to organize the party games after a television program that's popular in the United States?"

"Right. *This Is Your Life.* The host describes earlier events in a person's life, or people the person has known, and shows pictures of places the person has been—a vacation spot or a house he once lived in—and then the person identifies the people or the places in the photos. Then some of those people he knows, whom he hasn't seen in years, walk out on stage to surprise him."

"I see." Harriet Hamilton Barclay was wiping her brushes and considering her finished canvas—a clean, competent watercolor of Castle Coeffin. "It's a lovely spot, isn't it? A Norse castle, of course. Many, many hundreds of years old."

"I suppose it must sound sort of ludicrous to you. Never having seen the program." Ben was trying not to sound as self-conscious as he felt, scrambling for a reason to pry into Colin's past.

"No...well...I can't quite imagine it." Harriet Barclay was watching Ben, her blue eyes squinting against the sun, as she held her light brown hair back to keep it from blowing in her face.

"Georgina told Ellen that Colin Ramsay used to send you postcards from wherever it was he traveled, and Ellen thought that perhaps you'd remember where he was at particular times, and we could put that in the script. Remind him of where he'd been, and who he'd met, and that sort of thing. And we'd read a few postcards, if you have any, and then perhaps you, if the date's convenient for you, would be willing to come visit as a surprise."

"It's not very easy for me to get away, I'm sorry to say, but we shall try to make the effort for Uncle Colin. He traveled all over the world, you know, as well as the length and breadth of Scotland and England, right up to the time he retired."

"Wales too? And Ireland?"

"Oh, yes. Wales more than once, I remember. Quite a long time ago."

"He's not really your uncle though, is he?"

"Oh, no. No, he was at school in Glasgow with my mother's brother, and she and Colin met when they were quite young. He stayed in touch with her, over the years, and after I contracted infantile paralysis, he took to sending me postcards to cheer me up. I have them all, actually."

"You do?" Ben swallowed and looked at Loch Linnhe.

"It was Mother's idea, initially. That we would put them in a scrapbook, and look up each spot in the encyclopedia, then read about the history, and the principal features, and make a study of all his stops. She thought it would take me away from a rather...confined world, and teach me to enjoy learning, while broadening my horizons." Harriet Barclay laughed as she faced the wind and tied a red silk scarf under her chin.

"And you still have the book?" Ben squatted down and sat on his heels.

"I do, yes. Three, in fact. You're welcome to borrow them if you'd like. If you promise me faithfully to take very good care of them. Mother still looks at them, and I'd hate to lose them at this late date. Do you have the time? My watch seems to have stopped."

"Twenty after four."

"We shall have to start if we're to catch the last ferry." She set both hands around her mouth and shouted, *"Owen!"* The blond man below them turned toward her, and she pointed to her wristwatch and waved for him to come up.

"We may not be able to walk back in time."

"*I* won't, I don't know about you." Harriet laughed, but Ben didn't, till he saw the easiness and the humor in her eyes.

"We'll start back, and Owen will catch us up. Polly Ferguson is driving us to the dock."

Harriet had folded the easel, shoved it in a large canvas carryall, put the box of watercolors in another section, and propped the block of watercolor paper with the painting beside it. Then she reached for her crutches, fitted the metal and leather cuffs around her upper arms and swung herself up. She leaned down and locked the mechanisms on her leg braces, and began pushing and pulling and twisting her way toward the gentlest incline on the hill.

"I can get the bag and the stool for you."

"You needn't, you know. Owen will retrieve them when he comes up."

"I don't mind. He's got farther to walk. So you're English not Scottish?"

"Yes, I was born in the Lakes District."

Ben and Harriet were sitting next to each other on a comfortable sofa in the sitting room at Druimneil House—a claret red room with white woodwork and a blazing fire, old oil paintings and books on the walls, oriental rugs on wood floors around overstuffed sofas and deep chairs.

They were drinking coffee after dinner, the scrapbooks on the big leather ottoman in front of the fire, looking at postcards of Jakarta and Singapore and an exotic hotel in Bangkok.

There were photos of places closer to home too, with dated messages to Harriet written in Colin's hand. Somerset. Kent. Edinburgh. Grantown-on-Spey. Wales. London. Cawdor. The Isle of Skye. Along with letters on hotel stationery.

"Does Colin write other people as faithfully as he does you?"

"I shouldn't think so. I'm his one emotional tie, unless I'm very much mistaken. You see, once my father abandoned us, a year or so after I became ill, my mother brought us up here to live and work in her uncle's inn. Colin seemed to think we'd be terribly cut off, and he began writing and sending me post-cards. My father left us without so much as a good-bye, and here we at least had a place to live and food on the table, even though my mother wasn't paid in wages in the early years. It was the Depression, you'll remember. Very few people traveled. So it was the ferry that kept us going."

"So were you the family Colin never had?"

"Yes, I think we were. It's my opinion that Mother was the only woman he ever cared about for himself, and that was a very long time ago, when he was eighteen or twenty, I should think. He never could bring himself to marry. He much prefers to be on his own. And yet corresponding with me gave him a certain sense of emotional experience without any sort of embarrassing entanglement. He could enjoy the consolations of feeling helpful, and live just as he pleased."

"Sounds like you understand him pretty well."

"Perhaps. I have given him a fair amount of thought."

"What did he do before he went to Fletcher's?"

"I don't know all of it by any means, but I do know he couldn't serve in the First War. A punctured eardrum, I think. Mother said he worked in a hospital, to help the war effort, with all the men at the front. It might have been the laboratory. Or the dispensing pharmacy. I don't recall which. His father was a bacteriologist, you know, and very well thought of indeed. One of the early frustrations of Colin's life was that his father expected him to become a physician, and Colin's inter-ests never lay in that direction."

"What about after the First War?"

"He traveled through Europe for a year or so, and then taught a while. History, I think, in a boys' prep school. And then he went to work in Edinburgh in an antiquarian shop. It must've been around 1920, when he would've been thirty or so. Used books and periodicals, that sort of thing. He worked there for seven or eight years. He'd inherited a bit of money from his mother, and he eventually set up on his own. Then the Depression struck, and times became terribly difficult. And when he met Ross again in the early thirties, he went off to Malaya to sort out problems Ross was having in the rubber trade. I believe he closed his business, sold his books, and went to Ross on a permanent basis within the year. He traveled for Ross, of course, and he took holidays on his own in later years, and sent me postcards wherever he went."

"The scrapbooks are really going to help us. His birthday is next week, the twenty-ninth, and this gives us time to go through the information and work up an interesting evening. Do you think you'll be able to come?"

"I hope so, but I shall have to talk to Owen and look at the work schedule for everyone else. How is Uncle Colin, by the way? He wasn't a-tall well when he came to us at Christmas. Owen's brother drove Colin over, and the trip tired him terribly."

"I think he's still weak, and his color isn't good, but he seems to get around all right and be in fairly good spirits. You won't tell him about the party, or us borrowing the scrapbooks, I hope? It *has* to be a surprise. If he knows, it'll ruin the whole thing. He probably wouldn't even come. He's not the bon vivant type."

"No, he certainly isn't. I promise not to say a word."

"Has he kept up his interest in used and rare books?"

"No, he gave it up years ago. Though he does read a great deal of history, but...Owen, my dear! Dinner was lovely."

"It was excellent." Ben picked up a scrapbook to make room on the ottoman for Owen's cup of tea.

"That's very kind." Owen stood with his back to the fire and smiled at Harriet before he looked at Ben. "It's all in the ingredients, really. Local lamb, homegrown fruits and vegetables. We have a wonderful butcher, the freshest of fish, and a very large garden here at the inn, so it would be difficult to go too far wrong."

"When I use the same ingredients, it does not come out nearly as well, I assure you!" Harriet laughed and smiled at her husband, and her wide plain face softened in the glow from the fire.

Owen looked pleased, before he glanced away as though the attention embarrassed him, and began rolling down the sleeves of his dark green shirt. "You're not too tired, Harriet?"

"No, I'm fine. We're expecting our first child in December, and Owen has become protective."

Owen laughed and said, "Someone has to take you in hand! She works too hard, Mr. Reese. Showing her paintings in Glasgow. Overseeing the running of the inn. Coaching girls' soccer at the local school."

"Soccer?"

"I never expected to, I can assure you. I used to watch the boys play when I was a child, and I discussed it a great deal with my Uncle Albert. He's passed away now, but he was a coach, and an excellent player. And I find I enjoy the challenge."

"Yes, and when she tells them not to mind the buffetings and the rain and the aches and pains and get on with it, they jolly well do, as well they might." Owen had sat on the arm of the sofa, and he laid his hand on the back of her head.

"I wonder if I could ask you to do me a favor, Mr. Reese?" Harriet had taken Owen's hand before she turned toward Ben.

"Call me Ben, please. Yes, of course."

"Would you come to meet Mother? She's not well, and it doesn't do to let her mix with the usual guests, but she does love a bit of excitement, and I thought perhaps I might take you back."

"I'd be happy to meet her."

"This is her photograph here, by the way, in the front of the first scrapbook. She must've been about my age, thirty-four or five, I should think, when that was taken, up by Stalker Castle."

It was the picture of a very beautiful woman, light hair pulled back from a classical oval face, large eyes, flawless teeth, a gentle sad expression that made her look more interesting than she might have looked if she'd smiled.

"Her appearance has changed a great deal, of course. She's just cut her hair herself, and it's a bit pathetic looking. She's hard of hearing too, so you may have to shout."

Elsie Hamilton was sitting in a tan chair in a blue flowered dress, a light yellow sweater around her shoulders, her pure white hair sticking straight out from her face as though it had been cut short in patches with pinking shears.

A television blared in a corner of her sitting room, in the neat white cottage behind the inn. A middle-aged woman knitted in an overstuffed chair, as Mrs. Hamilton played with her skirt. She didn't seem to be watching the forties movie on the screen, but her head was bobbing to the dance band.

"Mother, I'd like you to meet Mr. Reese. He's an American friend of Uncle Colin's."

"What!" The sound was an assault like the squawk of a blue jay, frustrated and sharp with ill will.

Harriet repeated what she'd said in a louder voice.

And her mother managed, "Oh, yes?" as her watery blue eyes glanced almost aimlessly in Ben's direction.

"He's come from seeing Uncle Colin. He says Colin hasn't been well."

"Why should he be? I'm not!" She was plucking at her skirt, picking it up in small experimental swishes, raising it two inches, then three, and four, waving the skirt to the right and left above surprisingly good-looking knees.

"I thought perhaps you'd want to say hello."

"Why? Why should I want to?" She was picking her skirt up higher this time, smiling like a naughty child.

"You don't get many visitors, and I thought—"

"All he ever cared about were his bloody old books! Whatever good they may do him!" She said it loudly and viciously and pulled her skirt over her head.

"That's enough now, dearie, it doesn't do to be naughty, does it?" The small middle-aged woman calmly laid down her knitting, and smiled a commiserating sort of smile at Harriet as she walked toward Mrs. Hamilton. "It's time for a wee biscuit and a nice glass of juice. Would you like your apricot again, or the orange this time? You do say you love the orange..."

"I'm sorry." Harriet's crutches crunched on the gravel court as she shifted her weight and pulled herself across toward the inn's back door.

"Don't be."

"I can't do anything with her when she's like that, and I can't predict. She was quite pleasant this morning. Very much herself, actually. She was always a very dignified, quiet, proper sort of person, and I know she would be terribly upset if she could see how she behaves now. I only hoped that a visit might cheer her up."

"We may be worse when we're her age; you never know."

"Perhaps that's what I find so appalling."

"Me too. I know exactly what you mean."

"Will you start in the morning?"

"Early. Before five probably."

"Then we shall pack you a breakfast to take along. We'll give you a thermos of coffee, and then retrieve it next week at Cairnwell. If we aren't able to get away, you shall simply have to come back and spend more time."

"I'd like that very much. Here, let me get the door."

Friday, June 23rd

It was just after Dundee, on the A92, an hour or so from Cairnwell, that Ben began to feel sick.

He ate an oatcake from the basket Owen had packed for him, thinking he might have drunk too much coffee on too empty a stomach.

But it didn't get better. It got worse. The nausea and the cold sweats and the ache in the middle of his abdomen.

He told himself not to think about it. To concentrate on how to get Colin out of his house long enough to look for the books and the toxin.

And he reminded himself to ask Colin's cleaning lady, and maybe even Anna too, if Colin had a house in Aberdeen still, or rented a garage, or some kind of storage space somewhere near Cairnwell, where he could hide what he didn't want found if he didn't keep it at Cairnwell.

Ben pulled the car over before Arbroath, and a few miles later after Montrose, and threw up in the bushes facing the North Sea.

He had a fever that was going up fast. He felt dry and

thirsty and his mouth was papery and hot. But it was the cramps and the ache in his gut that worried him and made the blood beat fast at his throat.

After Montrose, he drove with his window down to get the wind on his face, and he slid his hand under his belt and examined the hard hot surface of his stomach, while he thought about which made the most sense. Food poisoning. Or flu. Or Colin's toxin.

But who could've given it to me? I haven't taken any kind of capsule, even vitamins, since I found Georgina's in her stuff from Oxford. I haven't eaten anything weird. I fixed what I brought from Cairnwell myself, and the timing would've been off then anyway. I haven't bought anything on the road, and the food at Druimneil is excellent. Unless—

No. Not Harriet. Why would she help Colin kill me?

She might've called him, if she'd thought what I was doing with the birthday was too weird to take seriously. That wouldn't be a big surprise, having known him all those years.

And I guess Colin could've told her I'm persecuting him. That I'm trying to connect him with murders he didn't commit, and she believed him.

He could've given her a capsule some other time. Something to give her mother if the misery got to be too much. Although I can't see Harriet murdering her, even if she told herself it was mercy killing.

Maybe she emptied the capsule into my coffee without thinking it would kill me. Colin could've said it would just calm her mother down, and she thought—

Why? Why am I doing this?

It could be the fever. Maybe. But I've got no evidence at all, and I'm blowing everything out of proportion. When what I need to do is concentrate on getting myself to the hospital.

Ben pulled the car over and vomited violently by the parking area above Dunnottar Castle. At Hillside too. And Charlestown. And just as he came into Aberdeen.

He was limp and ashen and covered with sweat. And he unbuckled his belt and unzipped his corduroy pants, because any kind of pressure on his abdomen was excruciating.

He'd put the map of Aberdeen across the space between his seat and the passenger seat on his left, but he was having trouble reading it. He couldn't focus on street signs either. Not well. Not like normal.

And when he came to the next stop sign he leaned his head back against the seat and closed his eyes.

Then he was sick in the paper bag that held his egg salad sandwich.

He was praying off and on, and telling himself to relax, to breathe as deeply as he could without making the throbbing worse.

Then finally, after stopping to ask directions from a woman pushing a pram, he was in the parking lot of the Royal Infirmary in Aberdeen, shutting off the engine and staring at the front of a huge gray granite building.

He didn't see a door to the emergency room anywhere, and no sign either, pointing in the right direction. So he staggered through the carved stone pillars under the granite portico in the center of that long front wall.

Walking took his breath away. He had to bend over and shuffle and his legs were trembling. But at least he couldn't hurt anyone else, the way he could've with his car.

He was leaning on the front desk, pulling a wheelchair toward himself from the right-hand end.

And then he was in the emergency ward, in a wheelchair, struggling to pull himself up, swaying in front of another desk (even though he couldn't have said how he got there), hearing himself, from somewhere very far away, say, "It may be appendicitis, but I may've been poisoned by an emetic toxin. If it's appendicitis, it's come on extremely fast, and the pain is really intense."

The middle-aged receptionist asked him a string of asinine questions with a pompous look on her face and pushed a pile of forms in front of him with a bored sigh, and he closed his eyes and told himself not to grab her by the throat.

Her final instruction was to wait right where he was. And then she marched off with an empty mug.

Ben walked into the ward, found an empty bed, opened a drawer in the bedside table, pulled out an enamel bedpan, lay down on his left side with it under his mouth, and closed his eyes.

He was shivering. And he was crouching. Running low across a field toward a hedgerow, carrying the Springfield he took across Europe, a bolt-action Olympic competition rifle with a ten-power scope.

He didn't make it before the American strafing started, and he dove headfirst into a foxhole and landed on a body covered by a sheet of snow. He couldn't move till the formation had flown over. So he lay on top of a bloated body, his left arm protecting his face, while mosquitoes from the hedgerows swarmed all over him.

He was wondering why mosquitoes and snow seemed odd, when the strafing stopped and he slid off the dead body, and found that the fingers of his right hand had been wrapped around the vertebrae of the corpse's open backbone. He lurched away and looked down and realized unexpectedly that the face belonged to his grandfather and there were bugs crawling out his neck. They were slithering out of his ears too, and they looked like sea creatures—tiny lobsters and small squid, black and purple and brown, pinching off flesh with pincers, ripping it away with serrated beaks. Ben tried to pick them off, or squash them as they crawled out, but they bit and flew away.

His grandfather's eyes were open, above the gaping rip in his throat, and as Ben watched, the stiff brittle deadness of his face began to thaw. The cold glassy look melted, as life edged across the eyes. And then they jerked toward him, and the lips moved under a quivering white mustache, starting, and straining, until finally, very slowly, they said, "Send...the boy...to me."

Ben was home then. His mother's face was gazing down at him as he read a book on the living room floor. Her soft blue eyes studying him, as she put papers away in the desk, smiling at him the way she always did, while she hummed something he couldn't place.

Then he was in the big orchard, carrying his own Springfield, the one he'd been raised on as a kid, heading out after rabbit and squirrel, telling himself he had to bring down a buck soon, because his dad was sick again and couldn't work. Bronchitis in tattered lungs, gassed in the First War. Ready to turn into pneumonia the next time he coughed.

There were apples on all the trees, and he was hungry, and he reached for one, but it squished in his hand, and he couldn't figure out why he hadn't seen that it was rotten.

He was thinking about his mom, holding herself together,

pregnant again, and tired, and worried about his dad.

It was all there in the lines around her eyes when Ben looked back at her watching him from the kitchen door, as he trotted from the orchard toward his grandfather's woods.

His sister Abby ran around his mother's skirts, rushing after him, heading toward the pond between them. She fell through the ice while Ben shouted and tried to get to her.

But he couldn't.

He was caught in a slick of quicksand. Struggling and sinking, snow on top of it and falling fast, cold and wet and so heavy, so thick, so smothering it was impossible to pull his head up, even though a voice in his ear said, "Are ye able to hearr me, Mr. Reese? You're in recoverry now. The operation went vera well indeed. Can ye hearr me a-tall? Can ye say yourr name for me?"

Ben opened an eye, an hour or two later, and saw a woman in white, her face down close to his, repeating his name over and over and over.

He nodded and said it too and drifted off again into a sunny day, somewhere where there were thick green trees and bright colored birds and the sound of the ocean in the distance, the rhythmic rumble of surf, the hiss of shingle sliding, voices talking about tea time, and someone who was bleeding where he shouldn't be after an appendectomy, and a broken leg that still had to be set.

Ben shivered, and tried to open his eyes, but he couldn't seem to make himself move anything. He said blanket under his breath, three or four times, as though he'd fallen into the rhythm of it and couldn't get out. But no one was close to him anyway. And maybe the sunshine would warm him up.

He was watching Journey, watching him run wild in a huge

field, taking a corner with his body leaning one way and his head the other. He heard Journey call to a horse in the barn, his ribs pumping in and out as he forced the wild whinny, then he wheeled and ran straight at Ben as the wind rushed through the trees behind him. Ben heard the scatter of leaves, and he heard Journey talking to him, telling him to come home.

Jessie stepped out from behind Journey, in Levi's and muddy boots, talking to Ben and smiling, but he couldn't hear the words.

Then he was lying in a pool of blood in three feet of snow, in the woods near Trier, pine trees shattering and splintering above him from the big German guns, two Tiger tanks firing across him, American's firing everything they had behind him. He'd picked white splinters of bone out of his left arm and leg, and packed snow into all the holes as well as he could, but there was blood pumping out in sticky streams, and he watched it pulse in time to the 88s.

"Will ye open your eyes now, Mr. Reese? You're in the recovery ward. The operation went vera well, but you must stop pulling at your left arm. We have you attached to an intravenous drip…Aye, that's better. Lie still and try to open your eyes…Aye, ye're doing fine…Can ye tell me your name?… Good, ye got it in one."

She was gone again and he hadn't asked for a blanket. And it was cold where he was, shivering in the woods, in the high drifts, wet, cold, snow down his coat collar, water in his boots, toes freezing, hands numb, anti-aircraft guns in front of him, maybe a mile away, pitch dark everywhere, a new kid behind him. No rifle now, of his own. Not behind the lines, no. Just his British commando knife, and his hatchet, and the wire inside his belt.

He'd stopped running, and was leaning against a tree, holding his breath. Listening. Because someone had come up next to him. He could feel hot breath on his forehead.

Why was she standing there looking at him?

Why wasn't she talking?

He thought he said "Nurse?" but she didn't answer, and whether he said it out loud he couldn't tell. He told himself to open his eyes, but he couldn't make them move.

He could feel the pain starting, in his stomach. Just beginning to raise its head again, like a sleeping wolf stirring in his gut.

And he could feel someone fooling with the tubes on the stand. There was a tug on the line to the soft side of his elbow, but no explanation of any kind, and Ben told himself to open his eyes.

Now.

Come on.

OPEN YOUR EYES NOW!

A man wearing a white cap and mask was standing by his drip bag. A tall man in a surgical gown.

It wasn't his surgeon. Who was smaller and younger.

No, this one had white hair at the edge of the cap and large curling eyebrows that were almost black.

Ben had seen them before, and he began to wonder where, while he watched, telling himself over and over not to close his eyes.

Whoever he was, he wasn't looking at Ben. He was holding the plastic tube in one hand, sliding his fingers toward a yellowish rubber connector between the clear tubes.

In his right hand was a hypodermic.

And Ben said "NO!"

But nothing came out.

No one moved.

The man didn't look at his face.

He just raised the hypodermic as Ben stared at the short rubber tube.

"NOOOOOO!"

It sounded like a scalded dog.

And the man jumped.

As Ben wrenched his own hand away from the metal stand with the bag and the tubes.

He heard someone shout, "Hey! What're ye doin'!" from somewhere far away. And he heard the metal stand crash on the floor.

He felt the rip in his left arm as the needles and tubes tore away from his flesh.

And he saw Colin Ramsay turn and run.

Help me.

Please!

DON'T LEAVE ME ALONE!

Ben couldn't tell if he'd said it.

But someone else went out in the hall.

And another person, an older woman, was standing by his bed repeating things that didn't matter. "That was *very* naughty of you, wasn't it? Very naughty indeed. You mustn't tamper with the drip tube, and you must lie *very* still, or you'll injure yourself terribly. I shall have to go off and get another drip, and I want you to behave yourself. Promise me now, for if you don't, I shall have to strap you down, and we neither of us wants that, now do we?"

Ben wanted to tell her not to leave him. That someone was trying to kill him. And he tried, but nothing came out.

He couldn't let himself sleep. He knew that.

No. It wasn't safe.

He'd fallen into a round well. A well with high stone walls. He was fifty feet down, treading water, trying to make himself float. Legs weighted down with something heavy. Cold. Tired. Too tired to keep moving his feet. In a space too narrow to stretch out.

He was trying to keep his mouth up above the surface. Dying of cold. And heat. Trying to open his eyes. But he couldn't.

He heard someone, deep inside the well, say the word "Kit!" very quietly.

"Ben?" Ellen Winter was standing at the side of Ben's bed holding a hardcover book and a green bottle dwarfed by a blue hydrangea.

Ben forced himself to open his eyes, and then took a minute to focus before he said, "Ellen."

"Sorry to interrupt, but I shall have to ask you to leave while I examine Mr. Reese." A short very blond man in his early forties with tortoiseshell half-glasses on the end of his nose and a stethoscope around his neck had stepped between Ellen and Ben's bed. "I'm Dr. Roberts. I performed his appendectomy."

"I understand. I'll wait outside in the hall." Ellen put the bottle and the book on the bedside table and closed the curtain behind her.

Roberts read Ben's chart, while scratching the back of his head. Then he laid the clipboard on the bedside table and dropped his glasses in the breast pocket of his white coat. "It was a very near thing, Mr. Reese, very near indeed. Your appendix had ruptured before we got in, and there are complications now from peritonitis. We're pumping antibiotics into you, as you might expect, and we have every hope of a successful outcome, but you are not out of the woods yet, not by a long chalk. We shall be keeping you here for some days, on a course of penicillin and sulfa drugs."

"Are the nurses watching my door?"

"You mustn't worry in any way. We've—"

"Can they see my door from their desk?"

"We've an excellent staff, and they'll take very good care indeed."

"They have to watch my room!"

"Why is that, Mr. Reese?"

"An old man's trying to kill me. Tall. White hair. Black eyebrows. He tried to inject bacterial toxin into my drip in recovery."

"Did he, indeed? Yes. Well, we shall certainly take care that no one is allowed to poison you." The doctor smiled condescendingly as he listened to Ben's heart, and Ben had to overcome an almost overpowering urge to kick him where it would do the most good.

"I shall leave you to get some rest now, Mr. Reese. And I shall drop by again in the morning."

"Send Ellen back in please."

"All right. But only for a moment."

Ben's eyes were closed when she sat down in the chair beside his bed, and when he opened them and worked at focusing on her face, he thought she looked like she was debating whether she should leave and let him sleep. He made himself say, "Ellen. Good. I have to talk to you…I'm sorry…hand me the bedpan, would you?"

Ben was sick again.

Then he set the bedpan on the table on the far side of his bed.

Ellen said, "I'm glad you had the hospital call before you went into surgery," as though she knew he must be embarrassed and was trying to make it easier. "Everyone felt terrible. Colin was there and Jack. They both asked me to say hello. And then later we had an emergency at Cairnwell too. Colin drove home late this afternoon after having been out, and I was walking by his house right after he got back, and I saw him slumped at the wheel like he'd passed out. He'd had one of his spells with his heart I guess, just as he got home, and his blood is all messed up again, very anemic and I don't know what else, and we put him to bed in the old housekeeper's room by the dining room in the big house. The doctor's been to see him twice already, and he's sending a nurse several times a day, and Winifred's staying round the clock. I guess he has to stay in bed for five or six days at least."

"Keep him there till after I get out."

"Why? I don't understand."

"He killed Georgina."

"No."

"He tried to kill me in recovery."

"Really? You don't think you could've been delirious."

"Yeah, but he still tried to kill me. He was about to inject toxin in the rubber connectors in my IV." Ben was talking very quietly, very slowly, with obvious effort. And Ellen leaned over closer to hear him better. "I've got more proof than I did have, but not enough. You have to keep him at Cairnwell."

"Okay. Whatever you say."

"Tell Jack. Get him to move into the house to help and don't leave Colin alone. Act like normal, so he won't know you know, but don't give him a chance to put anything in your food."

"He's sedated now, and the doctor says he's keeping him that way for several days."

Ben tried to say, "Thank God," but it was getting harder to talk.

A large blond nurse pulled the curtain open at the foot of the bed and said, "I shall have to ask you to leave, Miss. Visiting hours are nearly over, and Mr. Reese is due for an injection. He also needs his rest, as you can see."

"What time is it?"

"It's eight-thirty at night."

"The same day I got here?"

"Yes. I put a letter for you in the book." Ellen leaned down and whispered "From Interpol" in his ear.

"Good."

"Good-bye Ben."

"Thank you."

"I'm glad you're okay." Ellen turned and waved to him from the door. Just as the nurse stuck a thermometer in Ben's mouth and wrapped a blood pressure cuff around his arm.

He was delirious all the next day. His temperature was almost a hundred and five, and he couldn't tell who was real and who he was dreaming.

He was turned and washed and rolled over. He was fed juice and water and crushed ice. He was given injections, and blood was sucked out of him, and one of his nurses made such a flap about his scars, he wanted to tell her to leave.

The following day, he wasn't any better. There were whispered conferences on whether to change the antibiotics, and what to change them to if they did. He seemed more restless, and more worried. And shortly before dinnertime, he made such an issue of calling Ellen Winter even though there wasn't a phone in his room, that a nurse agreed to place the call for him and relay messages.

"Ask if Colin is still at Cairnwell."

She did, and came back to say that the gentleman he referred to was at Cairnwell and still sedated.

Ben said, "Thank you," pushed himself painfully to his left side, pulled a pillow a few inches from his stomach, curled his right arm around it and went to sleep.

When Ellen and Jack came to see him that night, he couldn't wake up.

And they went home worried, even though the nurses told them he'd begun to sleep more soundly and his fever was down a degree.

Ben woke up the next morning scratching the stubble on his chin. He listened to the two other men in his room, the heavy-set one on his right snoring loudly enough to rattle the windows, the other muttering to himself as though he were hopelessly deranged.

Ben ate what they brought for breakfast—porridge, juice, milk. Then he reached for the book Ellen had brought him and pulled out the letter from Interpol, with the attached list of stolen books, organized by date and location.

After dinner when Ellen came to see him, she said Colin was better, that he was still in bed and being kept quiet, but his last dose of sedative would be given later that night.

Ben asked if Jack was still staying at the big house.

And Ellen said, "He'll be there till you get back."

"Ask him to stick around tonight, okay? I'll go down to the lobby and use the pay phone so I can ask him a couple of questions."

"He ought to be back from training the hawks by eight."

"Do you have a key to Colin's house?"

"Yes."

"With you?"

"I think so. Why?"

"I want to stop at the dower house first, when they finally let me out of here, so why don't you give me the key now while we're thinking about it."

"I guess I can use his if I have to. Winifred has one too." Ellen looked at Ben consideringly, but she gave it to him without asking anything else.

They talked for another few minutes, fighting the noises on either side of the curtain around Ben's bed. And then he told her he was tired and thought maybe he'd try to read. "Thanks for the *Brideshead Revisited.*"

"You're welcome. It's the best thing I've read by Waugh. Anyway, I'll see you tomorrow."

"Thanks, Ellen."

"Oh, Kate called. She's driving over to see you tomorrow. Good night." Ellen watched him for a minute, her ponytail across her left shoulder, her dark straight eyebrows pulled low over steady inscrutable eyes. And then she turned and left.

Ben stood up slowly and carefully. And took his clothes out of the cupboard beside his bed.

ГГГГГ

It was eight-thirty when he parked his car by the building where Jack kept his birds. He hadn't passed anyone on his way from the coast road. Jack had already fed the hawks and gone. And Ben walked very slowly, very carefully, taking the straightest fastest way to the back of the dower house through the evergreen woods, without anyone having seen him.

He let himself in by the scullery door, and took out the flashlight he'd picked up from his car. He wiped his forehead with his handkerchief, too, and the cold sweat on the back of his neck, before he made himself take a breath.

He glanced through the kitchen, and at the laundry area and storage in the scullery, and walked into the dining room behind the kitchen, which was a smaller version of the dining room at Cairnwell—an old kitchen with a groin-vaulted ceiling, converted by Georgina in the fifties.

Ben considered the possibilities, and then started with the sideboard and found nothing. He went out through the front hall and opened the door to the sitting room.

There were French doors facing the back, and bookshelves on the end wall, and a half-bath behind the square stairs at that end of the hall.

But there was nothing anywhere downstairs that struck Ben.

So very carefully, very slowly, holding one hand against his abdomen, Ben started up the turret stairs that were just like Cairnwell's, at the end of the hall by the dining room.

They were the first steps he'd climbed since surgery, and he found out immediately why they told you not to for several weeks, because it felt as though his insides were about to fall out on the floor.

But he made it, one step at a time, pulling himself up with his left hand on the thick rope banister.

There were two bedrooms upstairs and a library. And Ben started with the library above the kitchen. It wasn't a large room, and every inch of wall space was lined with books. There was a wall of literary classics, a wall of biography, another of British and early American history, and a handful of books on explorers in inexpensive editions.

Ben took books off every shelf, looking for false backs, or shelves that swiveled, and didn't find the first sign of anything that looked suspicious. He went through the desk, the filing cabinet, the walls where the old shutters folded back into the side walls of the windows, and found nothing that shouldn't have been there, or connected Colin to rare books.

He pulled back the area rugs and studied the floors. And then started on Colin's bedroom behind the study and above the dining room.

Double bed. Large fireplace (above the much bigger one in the dining room). Chest of drawers. Armoire. No built-in closet. Adjoining bathroom. Second bedroom beyond.

He found nothing to raise an eyebrow. No caches in the walls or floor. Nothing in the square stairs, at the guest room end of the hall. Nothing in the downstairs hall, as he made his way back to the dining room, after having eased himself down the stairs.

He hadn't looked through the scullery or the kitchen as carefully as he could have.

But he leaned against the cool plaster wall before he opened the dining room door.

He was dizzy. His fever was on the way up.

And the pain in his gut was getting worse.

The kitchen took him longer than any other room—cupboards, drawers, checking the flagstones in the floor, looking in canisters and tins, and at the herbs and spices in the rack on the wall.

He worked through the scullery again. All the storage places that held tape, glue, silver polish, buckets, mops, cleaning solutions, household paints and brushes, laundry baskets and gardening tools.

And he still didn't find anything that looked suspicious.

Ben got a small glass of water and drank it all. And then he walked back into the dining room.

He had to sit down for a minute, to rest and catch his breath, before he started on the flagstone floor. And he sat with his back to the French doors, facing the high wide fireplace.

It had been copied from Cairnwell's, but it wasn't as large. Eight feet wide instead of twelve. Six feet high, not eight. The same kind of woodburner sitting right in the center.

It hit him like a blow to the brain, when it came to him. And he said something incomprehensible as he walked toward the fireplace, looking at the width of the right wall, remembering that side of the kitchen, staring at the bottom where there was a small wooden door at Cairnwell, propped open with a stone.

There was no wooden door in Colin's fireplace. It was a regular wall of rounded irregular stones cemented close together, exactly like the rest of the fireplace.

Ben got down on his knees, cradling his abdomen with one hand to keep it from falling out from under him as he bent over, and studied four or five flagstones in the raised floor on the right of the wood-burning stove.

It almost looked as though there was a wide curve—not

lighter than the surrounding stones but duller, maybe even a slight groove on the surface—arcing out from the bottom of the right-hand wall.

He laid the side of his face close to the floor, and smiled to himself as he straightened up.

He studied the right-hand wall then, with the magnifying glass from his key ring, searching for a crack between stones and cement.

They were all natural irregularly shaped rocks of unequal sizes and different thicknesses fitted closely together. And he couldn't see anything that seemed unusual. There were several stones that stuck out from the surface enough that you could clamp your fingers around them. And when he started examining one of them, one that was six or seven inches in diameter, he saw one section around the edge that looked like a hairline crack.

Ben pulled on the rock with his right hand and was stunned to find out how weak he was.

His fever had gotten worse, just in the last hour, and he shivered before he could stop himself.

Then he clamped both hands on the rock and pulled. And the stone slid out of the wall.

It had been carved like a stopper in a bottle, wide at the surface and tapered toward the inside end, and underneath it was a metal bar, six inches wide and an inch high, that had been pushed from left to right under two metal bands. A surface bolt. On a stone door. A two-inch thick, poured concrete door, maybe three feet high and two and a half feet wide, covered with shallow slices of stone on the outside—slices that had been pushed onto the surface of wet concrete so they extended across the edges of the door.

Ben sat back on his heels and smiled as he slid the bar to the left and pulled the door out away from the opening. It swung out smoothly on two very large SOSS hinges completely invisible from the outside, exposing the small wheel behind the sliced stone, on the outside corner of the bottom of the door, that allowed the heavy door to slide open and closed without scraping the floor any more noticeably than it had.

He used his flashlight to look inside at the old abandoned turret stair, almost exactly like the one at Cairnwell.

Except that these stairs were covered with books. Hundreds of them probably—the smallest at the inner left-hand edge of each step, where the two-and-a-half-foot pie-shaped stairs were narrowest.

Ben crawled through the doorway then looked till he found a light switch inside on the left. The wires to it were strung around the round wall from the kitchen (probably near the telephone table) through a hole drilled in the stone.

When Ben looked back at the doorway, and realized how much the floor sloped, he put his flashlight across the left-hand corner of the threshold to keep the door from rolling shut and jarring the bolt closed.

He stood up again as painlessly as he could, and looked around at the round walls of the turret stair, circled on the outside edge by a plenum—an air space—a foot or so wide, that had originally moved warm air up from the fireplace to heat the bedroom above.

Ben turned toward the section of the turret room on his left, that had been widened away from the start of the stairs hundreds of years before, and studied the wooden bookcase standing there on the floor. Colin's largest books and manuscripts were stacked there, along with a handful of smaller books and a carefully tied portfolio. A small metal table sat beside it, and lying on top were bookmen's tools—an ivory spatula for turning fragile pages, a heavy carved wooden book stand, two big foam triangles for holding and opening large delicate books, and two pairs of white cotton gloves.

There was a wooden box on the table too, a little larger than a cigar box, in which bottles of ink and glue, three small paintbrushes, and a short stack of bookplates were neatly arranged around four Vicks inhalers, a small pair of scissors, two packages of different size needles and a large spool of heavy thread.

When Ben saw the Vicks inhalers, he laughed, briefly—and then doubled over because of the pain. He sat down tentatively on the metal chair and picked up one of the inhalers.

He unscrewed the lid that looked like a short plastic test tube, and examined the inhaler itself—the cream-colored plastic tube with holes in its rounded top.

It looked normal. And it smelled like Vicks.

But Ben slid the blade of his pocketknife between the cylinder and the bottom rim, and snapped it away from the tube.

He pulled out a tuft of cotton and a piece of Vicks-impregnated cord. Then he smiled and turned the tube over.

A small glass bottle, an inch and a half long and maybe three-eights of an inch in diameter, with a black screw-top lid—filled with white powder—slid into the palm of his hand.

Ben hummed something he couldn't have named, as he put the inhaler back together and slipped it in one of the buttoned back pockets of his brown corduroy pants.

He was still smiling when he turned to the bookcase and opened the first folio volume of the two volume first edition of

Johnson's dictionary. He read the title page of Swift's own copy of *Gulliver's Travels,* and glanced through the portfolio of eighteenth-century French political tracts. He looked at two beautifully made editions from the Aldine press in Vienna—a 1502 Dante *Divine Comedy* and a 1501 Horace, the first Aldine "pocket book" ever printed. Ben read the spines of the ten or so nineteenth- and twentieth-century titles on travel, exploration, and diplomacy in Central Asia, China, the Caucasus, India, and Eastern Turkey—many of them related to the Great Game between British India and Czarist Russia.

Then he picked up five books decorated with fore-edge painting (English, from the early 1800s, two of them carved as well), and bent the edges of the pages to see the paintings of ships, and horse races, and drawing room scenes hidden by gold leaf.

They were all books various bibliomaniacs might give their eyeteeth for. But they weren't the ones on the list from Interpol that could tie Colin to the murders.

Where was Lord Dyson's *On the Revolutions of the Celestial Spheres* by Copernicus? Or his Raleigh? Or his *A Brief and Trve Report of the New Fovnd Land of Virginia* by Hariot? Where were his two Hakluyt books of voyages? And *A Trve Reporte of the Laste Voyage into the West and Northwest Regions, &c. Worthily Atchieved by Capteine Frobisher,* written by Dionysius Settle?

The Welsh woman book dealer's book of illustrations by John White wasn't there. Or the Thevet *Les Singvlaritez De La France Antarctiqve, Avtrement Nommée Ameriqve,* with the first description of tobacco.

Any of those could've been on the stairs. But there were gaps there and on the bookcase shelves, as though books had been grabbed fast.

Colin must be ready to run.

He knew I'd set him up as soon as he searched my room and didn't find anything. That's why he came after me in the hospital, even if he didn't talk to Harriet.

He'll take the books he cares about most, along with the ones he stole. Assuming there's any difference.

Even if he'd killed me in the hospital, he'd have to go someplace safe. I've found out too much, and he knows it, without knowing who I've told.

So where would he have hidden them? In his car maybe? Or his garage? Somewhere he could get to them fast.

Ben had been climbing the right side edge of the steps, the strip eight or ten inches wide that wasn't covered with books. Slowly, carefully, balancing by the open edge, glancing at titles and bindings, on his way to wherever the stairs led.

He was starting into the third turn, when he thought he heard something below him. He stood perfectly still and listened.

Not breathing. Not blinking.

Listening to something muffled and indistinct.

A soft quick shuffle. A careful intake of breath.

Then the lights went out.

And Ben was left blinking in the dark. A long drop to a stone floor an inch from his right foot.

"I must commend your perseverance, Dr. Reese. Even though it's been extremely tiresome. You and I could've had wonderful conversations, with our love of the written word. Yes, the highest and noblest of human achievements."

"One of them at least. Depending. Capable of great good, as well as evil. I'd like to talk to you about your Columbus letters, and the Latin Marco Polo too, and it'd be easier if you turned on the light so we could look at them."

"We could have broadened each other's perspectives. And discussed the excitement of the chase. Though now, regrettably, in your unenviable position, all such considerations have become a luxury. If you should decide you don't fancy the thought of starving to death in the dark, at least another less 'unhappy alternative is before you.' Ah. That's a thought. One rarely finds a worthy opponent, and perhaps I should offer you a reprieve. Yes, why not? If you identify the origin of that quote, I shall reward you with an unlocked door."

"No, you won't. You can't afford to."

"How sad. You don't know it, do you? Of course, American institutions of higher learning are not as sound as ours."

"Generally, I think that's true. Except in science and mathematics. *Pride and Prejudice* by Jane Austen."

"I congratulate you, of course. You're quite right in both your assertions. Though it gives me no pleasure, I can assure you. Nothing like the grief of losing dear Georgina, of course. And I hope you'll do me the courtesy of believing that to be true, for if there had been a way round her death, I would've taken it gladly. Even so, as I was saying earlier, if you wish to avoid a long and lingering death, you could do worse than to swallow the contents of the vial you took from the box. I've retrieved the others, but you may keep that with my compliments. Good-bye, Dr. Reese."

"Wait! What kind of toxin is it?"

"I can't say unequivocally, but my father came to believe, in the last months of his life, that it was probably *Bacillus cereus*. The bacteria was identified in the 1800s, yet the properties of its toxin, its heat stability, and the deadliness of its concentrated form, hadn't then been recognized by anyone but my father.

They haven't yet, as far as I know. *If*, in fact, he was right. And he wasn't always, as any son knows too well. Good night, Dr. Reese."

"Before you—"

Ben could hear the door rolling shut, the grate of the weight of it, the squeak of the wheel.

NO! DON'T!

He didn't say it out loud.

He wouldn't have given Colin the satisfaction.

And then he could hear, as he strained in the dark, not the bolt, he didn't think, but the stone plug grinding back hard into place.

God, I don't want to die in the dark!

He'd been all right during the war. Hiding in tight places. In holes and crevices. In cisterns and rubble. In trees and on roofs. In blackness, as much as anything.

But in the last two years, he'd dreamt that he was buried alive, in mud or sand or body parts, more times than he could think about. And a year ago, in Chicago, when he went through a German sub in the science museum, he wanted to shove everyone in front of him out of the way, so he could break his way out to the exit.

Logic had kept him from giving in, from becoming a prisoner to an irrational urge. But it was there on the stairs, gnawing at him in the dark. In a narrow round-walled shaft with a long hard fall to a stone floor inches to the right of his right shoe—rare books packed around his feet, and on every other stair, above and below.

He was sweating and his jaws had clenched. His mouth was dry with adrenaline and fever. And he told himself to make a move and get himself out.

Colin'll block the stairs, if they're open above. Or lock the opening so it can't be forced. But it still could be a better shot than the concrete door to the fireplace.

Ben had already leaned to his left till his hand touched the stone turnstile in the center. And he stepped up on the empty space on the next tread.

Suffocating wouldn't be fun.

No. But the stairway can't be completely airtight.

It's what are the chances of being heard, that's the real question.

Inside solid stone.

Ben climbed to the next step with his right arm above his head, feeling for the ceiling, wondering how soon Jack would find the car and come looking.

Tomorrow probably. Unless Colin hot-wires it, and leaves it where it won't be found.

On the third step, Ben hit books that fell on the step below, setting up a chain reaction on a lot of other stairs, knocking far too many off the edge to the floor.

When he got to the fourth step, he raised his right hand again and touched stone.

Cold. Hard. Solid. No cracks. No seams.

No way out up above.

Ben leaned away from the edge till he could touch the stone turnstile with his right hand. He swiveled his body to the left and shifted his feet on the narrow stairs, till he heard more books that couldn't be replaced crack against a stone floor. More landed on others on the stairs below, and they fell. Rare, old, fragile, a few unique—the kind of books Ben had spent years identifying, cataloging, and restoring.

The risers for every step had been built high under narrow

treads, which meant he had to turn his feet nearly sideways, in his size twelve shoes, to be able to step down. And every time he did, he'd damage what he'd spent a lot of his life saving.

He reached down with the toe of his right shoe, steadying himself in the dark with his left hand on the turnstile, feeling for the empty space on the outside edge of the stair.

Books slithered out from under his shoe, sliding down onto more stairs below him, hitting too many other books that ripped and tore on the floor.

He felt like a blind rat, suffocating in a live trap. Until he told himself to stop being ridiculous, and remember what crossing a minefield's like—as he slid his right foot down toward the next step.

There were books everywhere. And he couldn't find a place to set his foot.

Fine, then light a match.

Just stop making the same mistakes!

There were only four left, in a match box from a restaurant in Perth. Short. Thin. Wooden. Cheap. Too many that hadn't lit. Matches he'd need to open the concrete door.

But he struck one, and it caught. And he saw four books in his way on the next step.

He looked over the edge into the plenum, but the light from the match didn't make it far enough for him to tell how high he was.

And then he was in the dark again, saying sit on the step above. Use your hands to clear the step below, then slide down and sit there.

It wasn't easy, standing sideways in total darkness, one foot in front of the other on the narrow stair, trying to squat down and rearrange the books on the step above him, then sit on a narrow strip on the outside edge of a stair and keep from falling. Especially with his incision throbbing, and the pain behind it getting worse. With fever licking at logic, making him hallucinate strange shapes in the dark.

But finally he was sitting, his left hip hanging above the stone floor, his stomach burning against his legs, as he leaned over to feel the step below his feet.

It took longer than he wanted it to, to sit and move the books beneath, then ease himself down on whatever slice of backside fit on the narrow stair, before he started on the next.

But he'd made it down six or seven stairs, when he thought he heard a phone ring, faintly, coming from the right. Behind him about five o'clock.

It rang three or four times, then stopped, the sound filtering through the hole drilled for the wires to the light switch.

He heard one short sound, like a single word, and told himself to hurry.

He dropped a book off the open edge, and tried to figure the length of the fall, at twelve feet per second. But he couldn't count less than a second, and it had to be too far to ease himself down. Not without ripping his insides. He couldn't catch himself anyway, or roll the way he normally would, when he hit the stone floor, in a space not much more than a foot wide.

He stood up, grabbed the turnstile with his right hand and stepped from stair to stair, letting books fall the way they'd fall.

He stumbled off the next to the last step, sideways and down against the desk. And the pain in his gut when he landed made him grab the desk and gasp. But he was on the floor, half standing, and mobile.

He heard another sound, and turned to his right, feeling his way to the circular wall, following the wires strung from the light switch to the two-inch hole drilled into the kitchen. Into a cabinet, apparently, since there was no light coming through at all.

He laid his ear against the hole and listened, but there was nothing. No breathing. No movement. No sound of any kind.

He was turning away in disgust when he finally heard a voice.

Colin, saying, "The bay south of Dunnottar then...forty-five minutes or an hour."

Then there was nothing but the dark.

Ben groped toward the concrete door, his left hand straight in front of him, his right hand working its way along the book-case sitting out from the wall on his right, then on across the table, till he took a corner of the metal chair in his knee.

He tried the light switch, without expecting it to work, knowing Colin would've cut the wires, or pulled the fuse.

He felt his way down toward the low door on his left and found the upper hinge on the right side. He slid his fingers along the top edge of the door to the left, till he'd found the joint between the door and the left-hand wall, where he knew the bolt crossed a few inches down on the outside.

Ben's eyes were closed as he concentrated in the dark, sliding his hands up the side crack, trying to picture how the joint was made. Finding one small space above that upper left-hand corner where the rock above the door had been carved on the outside so the stone plug could stick up above the door and conceal the bolt and the corner.

The space was irregularly shaped—an inch and a half high maybe, and maybe two inches wide, and the depth of the concrete door. Too high, and not big enough, for him to reach down and slide the bolt.

He'd have to hammer the plug out.

And he tried to remember what he'd seen on the table.

Paint brushes that weren't beefy enough. An ivory spatula that would break fast. Scissors, maybe, from the wooden box, probably way too flimsy.

Ben stood up, holding his stomach again against the feel of it flopping out, and turned around to the right.

The wooden box was gone, when he felt the top of the table.

But there was a metal chair.

And Ben backed up, dragging it after him, till he stood in front of the door.

He knelt down, carefully, pulled the chair over on its side and fitted one thin leg into the small space above the corner of the door. He tried to push it in on an angle, so the other three legs wouldn't hit the wall at the same time, but it was hard to get it right in the dark.

Holding the chair strained his incision, and he had to figure out a way to hit it hard enough to dislodge the stone plug without injuring himself.

He shoved it once. And again harder.

And he actually yelled something inflammatory that time, because it felt like it was tearing his insides apart.

Then he grabbed the leg tighter in his left hand, with the opposite side of the chair back in his right, and knocked it against the stone as hard as he could.

The stone plug clattered across the fireplace hearth, just as Ben dropped the chair and doubled over on his side on the floor.

He moaned once, briefly. And then wiped the sweat from his eyes on his sleeve.

As soon as he could move again, he knelt in front of the door and felt for the bolt.

He still couldn't get to it with his fingers.

And he reached down and unbuckled his belt.

It wasn't stitched along the top, and he opened the length of it and pulled out the fine stiff wire he kept doubled along the inside. Then he took out a three-foot string impregnated with industrial diamond dust, and laid both of them across his thighs.

He'd been carrying them since 1943. Even though he couldn't have explained why, except that it came from scouting with the Nighttime Special, and watching the ones who went out with him die.

The odds got better with the string and the wire, in an imperfect world like his.

And he hadn't seen any reason to make himself stop since.

He felt for the space above the corner joint and snaked half the string through so it dropped down and hung across the bolt.

With his eyes open this time, straining again in the dark, he bent one end of the wire into a small hook.

Then he pulled out the match box and lit a match.

The head flared fast and burned out.

And Ben wiped the sweat off his forehead with his sleeve again before he felt for the next to the last match.

He held it, burning, in his left hand, as he slid the wire hook through the vertical slit between the door and the wall on the left, trying to grab the dangling string and pull it toward him under the bolt.

He couldn't get it through. Not that time.

And not the next.

He'd touched it with the hook, and he'd almost hooked it. But then it had slipped away from the slit.

He was trying again, holding the very end of the match, when it burned out between the tips of his left middle finger and thumb.

Ben felt his pockets for a scrap of paper, so he wouldn't have to rip a page out of a book, and found a sheet of note-book paper in the breast pocket of his jacket. He rolled it into a long tube, then twisted it several times, and lit the last match.

The match burned steadily and the paper caught. Which was more than he had a right to expect.

His forehead was pressed against the stone above the door, as he strained to see how to hook the string, pulling and losing it, sweat rolling in his eyes, the paper burning way too fast, flames running at his fingers, as he worked the string toward the crack.

He had to turn the hook vertically to fit it through the slit, while keeping the string pinned inside it between the stone and concrete, as he pulled.

He lost it again.

And again.

And again.

And then he had to drop the paper before it burned him.

It sputtered for a second, as it went out.

So only the ash was glowing when Ben grabbed the string with his left hand.

He took a breath again, finally, in the dark, with one end of the string in each hand. And started sawing the metal bolt.

CHAPTER THIRTEEN

"No, I'm fine, Ellen. Is Jack there?...But the Triumph's still there?...Good! Find him and tell him to get to Dunnottar...I know it's closed. Just tell him to climb the fence and get down the stairs and go through the hole in the cliff...No, on the right. Under the castle on the south and out to that little bay. As fast as he can get there, okay? Tell him not to run through the arch though. Get him to stand where he can listen to me talk to Colin. If there's a way he can do that...Right, I'm on my way now and I need help."

Ben hung up, and then forced himself to trot to the car.

He was exhausted. His fever was up. The pain in his abdomen was constant. And as he put his hands in his pockets for his car keys, he could feel blood on the front of his pants. Wet, sticky, soaked through the bandage. Through boxer shorts. Through corduroy pants. A patch ten inches by six or eight, from what he could see when he opened his car door and looked at the damage.

He wasn't gushing. It wasn't a fatal hemorrhage. But he'd have to get stitched up again and he'd have to keep it clean.

He reached into the backseat, grabbed an old flannel shirt he'd thrown there when he left Port Appin, and folded it three or four times from top to bottom so that the sleeves stuck out on either side. He wrapped it around his hips and abdomen, pulling it tight and knotting it on his left hip.

Then he eased himself into the car, and started south toward Stonehaven.

He kept backtracking—working at how long he'd taken to get out of the stair room, and how long Colin had been gone, and whether there was still time to get there (assuming he could make it down the stairs at Dunnottar before morning), before Colin got away.

So where would he go by boat?

Norway? Denmark?

Norway's closer. And the coast is rougher and less populated. So it's got to be easier to slip into in a small boat and not be seen.

The arrogance is breathtaking.

Four people, and for what!

He can't be allowed to get away with it.

It was after eleven when Ben pulled into the parking lot on the hill in front of the ruins of Dunnottar.

Colin's car wasn't there. But then it wouldn't be. He wouldn't want the police to see it when they patrolled the coast road, and he'd probably hidden it behind one of the outbuildings on the farm across from the entrance.

It was still surprisingly light, because it was so far north. And the moon was up, above the sea, lighting the cliffs that rushed up and out in irregular shards and hollows.

Ben tightened the shirt across his abdomen, then gritted his teeth as he dragged his legs over the wooden gate in the wire fence across the path.

The hill-cliff he was on was like a high flat spit of land that dropped off on the right into a narrow gorge, and he watched a white waterfall shatter toward him in the dark blue night from the other side of that gorge, as he walked and then trotted as many steps as he could, toward the ocean side of the hill.

There, a hundred and forty steps led down toward the sea, to a narrow band of land at the bottom, where the climb started again, on the other side, to the high rock hill where the broken walls of Dunnottar stood silhouetted on a sharp rocky summit. That spit of land that held the castle was like the next stone bead on the string he was standing on, and the wind rushed through the crack between them, whipping Ben's hair in his face and his coat around him, till he buttoned it as he started down the stairs.

He pressed the shirt-bandage against his stomach, trying not to think about the stairs, as he strained to see the bottom land, the low narrow strip between the jutting cliff he was on and the hill that held Dunnottar. There, on the right side of Dunnottar, away from the high main gate to the castle (hidden from where he was by a vertical rib of rock), was a flying buttress of sandstone that jutted down from the edge of the ruins to a grass-covered mound that rolled to meet the bottom land.

In the middle of that rocky buttress was a low rock arch into a short cavelike tunnel that led out to the small bay at the foot of the castle's postern gate. There, a narrow half-moon beach curved around a protected cove where the sea lay quiet, without the tangle of high jagged rocks that stretched up and down the coast.

Ben told himself not to think about whether Colin was still there—to concentrate on each awkward three-foot-deep step, and ignore the sharp hot slice through the center of his gut when he stepped from one to the next.

There was more blood on his pants. He could feel the sticky cold clamminess of it on his right thigh whenever he raised that leg. And the effort it took to move his legs got nastier each time he tried.

He did what he always did in circumstances like those. He told himself he'd lived through worse. Flying through treetops in a German January strapped under a Piper Cub.

All he could do was do what he could do. And ask that the rest would happen the way it should.

He stepped off the last step and tried to trot to the right around the curve of grass, toward the black-arched hole in the shadow of the rock wall.

He waited when he got to it, feeling his pants pockets for his pocketknife and the roll of wire from his belt. Then he braced his chest against the rock on the right of the arched entrance, and slid his head to the left around the edge.

He studied the darkness, and the light through the arch at the end, listening before he stepped in.

He felt his way along the uneven ground, over loose stones and jagged rocks, toward the patch of light from the cove.

Colin was there. Thank God.

He was standing on the beach near the edge of the water, mopping his brow between two suitcases, watching a forty-foot fishing boat, a quarter of a mile away, ride the waves into the cove.

A small man wearing rain gear cut the engine and threw an anchor off the far side of the stern, before he turned and started toward the bow.

Then, while Colin watched the second anchor drop, Ben tackled him from behind.

He twisted Colin's right arm behind his back, jerking his thumb toward his forearm, dragging him over to the left toward the castle, behind a vertical ridge of rock wall where they couldn't be seen from the sea. He shoved him against the soft sandstone cliff, shaking loose pebbles down on both of them, and then pulled Colin's left arm behind him and bound both hands with wire.

Colin screamed as Ben pulled his arms up higher.

Till Ben hissed, *"Shut up!"* in his right ear, tightening the wire, talking in a quiet bloodless voice. "No noise! No sign to your friend in the boat. When he gets close enough to talk to, *I'll* give him a reason why you've changed your mind and you'll agree. You're also going to tell me the truth *right now,* the first time. You got that? You understand me, Colin? Do I make myself perfectly clear?"

"Yes!" He'd lowered his voice.

But Ben didn't relax the pressure on his arms.

"Why'd you kill Georgina? Because she found you with a book that wasn't yours?"

"She came through the woods! She walked right in through the French windows and saw Raleigh's *History of the World* on the dining room table. She'd never rushed in before without phoning!"

"Did she know it was stolen, or did it just start her thinking?"

"The ships' logs set her off earlier. She knew I'd been a collector, and one could see her pondering then."

"You killed her with one of her vitamins?" Colin didn't say anything, and Ben shoved him harder against the cliff.

"Yes!"

"And Lord Alfred Dyson caught you taking something."

"The Copernicus. The Marco Polo. He was such a *perfect* gentleman. Said he'd ring the police later 'once we'd discussed the matter over a civilized meal.' I told him I'd only borrowed the books, but it made no impression. If I weren't 'brought to justice,' I'd 'perpetrate another crime in another home' and he 'would be responsible.' You must see what it meant. Incarceration. Separation from my entire collection, when *I* truly *appreciate* the history of human discovery! I've assembled an impressive and important collection. I'm *not* the sort who collects for the covers, or the cachet."

"I assume you took the other eight books while he was dying." Colin nodded, and Ben had to fight the urge to strangle him while he had the chance. "So you've carried the toxin ever since you killed the woman who left you her books?"

"I was taking a vial to Father in Glasgow from the lab at home, when I saw how ill Mrs. Rathbone was and performed an act of charity."

"Did you? No one's got a right to decide that."

"There are some who would disagree."

"So? There's always someone who'll disagree with every moral tenet of civilized society. The toxin in the saltshaker in Wales was clever."

"Can you imagine? John White's account with illustrations, which is nearly unique, as well as the André Thevet, in a secondhand shop in Hay-on-Wye? I couldn't afford to buy them. Neither could I let them go to an ignorant biscuit tycoon who couldn't have read the first word!"

"Tonight you were going to Norway?" Ben was looking at the cove, leaning around the high rib of rock, watching the inflatable dinghy being dragged down from the wheelhouse.

"I shall speak frankly, Dr. Reese. For *you*, of all people, should understand. I have little more than a few months to live. Why shouldn't I spend what time I have making arrangements to donate my collection to those individuals and institutions that will truly appreciate the collection I've carefully accumulated and cataloged? I've always admired Pepys's method of disbursing his books, and I'm formulating a plan of my own."

Colin was shaking slightly, leaning limply against the rock, when his knees began to give way. Ben told him to stand up, and pulled him up by the elbow, gritting his own teeth against the strain.

"We have to get my cases away from the incoming tide!"

"Who's in the fishing boat?"

"Alan MacLeish. The books in my valise—"

"What did you tell him?"

"I'm taking a holiday in Norway while writing a paper for an antiquarian journal, and I wanted to see what it was like to cross in a small craft the way the early Scots did as smugglers and traders."

"He's a friend?"

"One of Georgina's. From the kirk in Kinneff."

The dinghy was heading straight toward shore, when Ben put his arm through Colin's and began walking him toward the tunnel as naturally as he could.

"You must save the suitcases! I promise on my word of honor to stand right here."

"That doesn't mean a whole lot with you, does it?"

"You of all people!" Colin's face was already gray and glistening in the moonlight, before it twisted against a wave of pain. "Pills! In my jacket!"

Ben listened to Colin wheeze, and thought of Richard West, his best friend, dying on his desk in Ohio because his murderer wouldn't give him his nitroglycerin.

Ben dropped the end of the wire and searched Colin's pockets with both hands. He opened a small cardboard box, saw a handful of pills on a bed of cotton, and asked how many.

Colin whispered, "Three!"

And Ben dropped them on his tongue—a second before Colin jerked his knee up and smashed Ben in the stomach.

A ripping grinding stab of pain rocked him, and he doubled over against it, while Colin shuffled toward the suitcases across egg-shaped stones that slid and clattered under his hard-soled shoes.

Ben shouted, "JACK!" as loudly as he could.

But nothing happened.

Half a minute crawled by, with Ben hugging his stomach, trying to get himself to go after Colin. He was making himself straighten, trying to move above the pain, while Colin watched for the dinghy that had disappeared behind the one cluster of high rocks between the beach and the fishing boat.

It was right then that Jack Corelli stepped out of the tunnel and sauntered toward Colin. He took him by one elbow, turned him away from the beach, and waved to the dinghy as he grabbed the soft-sided valise. He kept Colin moving, pulling him up the path toward the archway in the rock, talking to Ben over his shoulder. "Can you get rid of the guy in the boat and meet me at the stairs?"

"Yeah, and boy am I glad to see you." Ben was taking off his jacket so he could hold it in front of the blood stains when he turned toward Alan MacLeish.

He waited till MacLeish was close enough to talk to, and then he shouted, "Mr. MacLeish! Can you hear me?"

"Aye!"

"Colin's been taken ill. I'm Ben Reese. I'm staying at Cairnwell. A friend and I are driving him to the hospital. Can he settle with you later? For your time and effort?"

MacLeish shook his head and yelled, "Nay, tell Mr. Ramsay not to think of it! I'll call in the morning to ask how he's getting on."

"Thanks! I'll tell him."

Alan MacLeish waved from sixty feet away, then turned the dinghy back toward the boat, taking the waves straight on.

"I'd rip something if I carried a case full of books." Ben was holding his hand against his incision, talking to Jack, looking at the stairs up the side of the cliff.

Colin was sitting at the bottom, staring at the ground, sweat standing on his forehead, his chin trembling as though he were cold, his face working against anger as much as despair.

Or so it looked to Ben, who was retying the shirt that was soaked through, seeing then for the first time how much he'd bled since Colin had kneed him in the stomach.

"I'll get the suitcase if you'll watch him."

"Thanks, Jack. What would I do without you?"

Ben and Colin licked their wounds in silence.

And then Jack was back, setting the suitcase on the grass. "I'll grab one, and get Colin up the stairs, and then come back for the other. Get up." Jack started pulling Colin to his feet, his left hand under his right arm.

"I ought to be more help."

"Yeah, it's all your fault your appendix ruptured. Are *you* sorry old man?" Jack was hauling Colin, stepping him up to each new stair. "Do you wish you hadn't murdered her? Or are you just ticked you didn't get away with it?"

Colin didn't answer. He let himself be dragged up one step at a time. Slowly. Mechanically. Like a windup toy running down.

The wind was relentless in that crack between the cliffs, battering them in the face, blowing them backwards as they leaned into it and tried not to lose their balance.

Ben was in too much pain already. And it was worse climbing than it had been coming down. He was so exhausted he had to force himself not to sit and stay there in spite of the wind. Even the thought of lying in a hospital bed was beginning to sound good. Cool sheets. Dark room. A chance to do nothing but sleep and heal.

He told himself to knock it off and think about what to do next. To get Jack to take Colin and the suitcases to the police, and then drop him at the hospital.

They could interview him there, after he'd been stitched up again. And he'd give them the toxin then that he'd taken from Colin. He ought to get Jack to tell them about the Vicks inhalers Colin had on him—or in the suitcases. And that the scrapbooks with the cards and letters tying Colin to the other crimes were in the trunk of Ben's car. The memo from Interpol too, with the list of what books had been stolen when.

He had to stop and rest, just for a second. And he looked up into the wind and saw Colin and Jack twenty long steps above him. He was squinting up at them when Colin stopped walking.

He crumpled. In slow motion. Doubling over toward the next step.

Ben stood helpless, watching, too many feet away, as Jack

lunged to grab Colin, to keep him from falling off the cliff.

Ben screamed, "PILLS! IN HIS COAT POCKET!"

But Jack didn't understand what he'd said. The wind blew Ben's words the other way, between Dunnottar and the cliff they were climbing toward the north bay.

Jack still held Colin with one hand, and cupped his hand around his ear with his other.

"PILLS IN HIS COAT POCKET!"

Jack nodded his head and leaned down to Colin. Then he shook him, slowly, and slapped his face, one side and the other, trying to bring him back.

Ben was climbing faster, one foot, pant, and then the next, holding his gut with his left hand and leaning on the cliff with his right.

Colin was dead when he got there.

Lying on his back, one leg straight, one bent, hands wired neatly behind his back.

Monday, July 10th

It was two weeks after that, that Ben stood on the cliff again and looked down at those stairs, while he buttoned his coat collar against the wind.

He took them slowly and stiffly, but not like he expected his guts to fall on the ground the way he had the last time.

And then he stood in the south cove and gazed at the rising sea, at hundreds of seabirds, mostly gulls, white against the green patches on red sandstone cliffs, wheeling and screaming, battling the wind and the spray from ragged waves.

Ben looked up at the postern gate in the castle wall on his left, the small, arched, studded wooden door cut high in the rock wall, where the scepter of Scotland had been smuggled out under Cromwell's nose.

He looked at his watch, then walked to the right a few steps nearer the stream that trickled toward the sea. It ran from the waterfall in the cleft close to the road, on the parcel of pastureland owned by a friend of Georgina's.

Ben was supposed to meet Ellen and Jack there, where Jack was bringing a hawk to hunt rabbits for the farmer.

But no one was anywhere to be seen—till he stepped around a tall curve of rock, in between gorse bushes and brambles, nearer the fence that separated the park from the farm.

Jack and Ellen were on the other side with their backs to Ben, thirty yards farther up the rubble-stone ravine. Jack was standing behind Ellen, a Harris hawk on her left fist, both his arms wrapped around hers, guiding her as she got ready to pull the bird's hood off and let Jezebel fly.

Jack was looking down at Ellen, not Jezebel. And he kissed the side of Ellen's forehead, and her left cheek, and her mouth as she turned her head.

Ben watched for not much more than a second. And backed around the rock.

He walked through the stone arch, out to the low ground and the grass, and turned this time to his right, up the path to the castle.

It was a long climb on a dirt track to a cobblestone lane of long shallow stairs cut toward the heart of the cliff between high stone walls, just wide enough for a horse.

Ben could almost hear the beat of hooves, ringing on the stones, sparks shooting from metal shoes, horses clattering up to the first arched door, men in armor, in kilts and cloaks, leading horses through, then left fast in front of four cannon ports facing the low door, inside the outside arch.

Ben walked slowly, wondering how much had changed since then in the minds of soldiers and shepherds, and what it had been like for the chatelaine and the shepherd's wife under siege on the edge of the earth.

The walls got narrower and the turns sharper before he came to the ticket booth where he paid and bought a guide book. And then he climbed steeper steps, slowly, through another arched tunnel, up into the broad flat lawn where sheep and cattle and horses had grazed when the castle was a city protecting itself.

He walked straight ahead toward the ruins of the chapel, past the remains of the first castle keep and the stables on the right behind it. Then he stood in front of the chapel's arched door frame looking at the low stone water well on his left, twenty feet wide and full, inside the U-shaped ruins of Dunnottar's primary living quarters.

There was a tall thin man with wild blond hair and a thick beard sitting on the grass with his back to Ben, facing the castle's public apartments. And Ben watched him for a minute before he walked up behind him and said, "I thought it was you."

"Ben!" Michael Shaw started to stand up.

But Ben put his hand on his shoulder and sat down on the grass beside him.

Michael had a drawing pad on his lap, and he pulled the cover across the drawing he'd been working on before he laid the pad on the grass. "It's still a shock, you know. Colin! Murdering four people for nothing but books!"

"I'm glad I *don't* understand it, myself. But maybe if I didn't get to play with the stuff that belongs to Alderton, I would."

"Possibly. It's a bit of a moot point."

"Of course, in my worst moments, I wish I'd told Colin he didn't focus enough as a collector, just to irritate him. Would you do me a favor? Would you tell Ellen that when I saw that she and Jack were busy, I didn't want to bother her, and I'll talk to her later from the States?"

"Of course. Has she decided about the writers retreat?"

"No. Her mother's on her way over to help. How's your sculpture of Ross coming?"

"Reasonably well, I think."

"Would you send me pictures of it? And the bust of Georgina too?"

"Of course."

"I thought the shepherd came out well."

"You helped, you know, you and the Cunninghams. I read what you suggested first, and then Ian sent a sermon. Mrs. Cunningham had already copied his files and posted them to me weeks before. I did use Ross's mouth and Georgina's eyes. I thought perhaps you might've noticed."

"No. I wish I had. If you ever do something small a college professor could afford, send me pictures of that too, and give me a chance before you sell it."

"I will, yes."

"It's haunting, isn't it? Dunnottar. It makes me feel like I could see other people from other ages, if I could just get around the corners fast enough."

"Yes, that's exactly it. How are you feeling, by the way? You look a bit ragged, if you don't mind my saying so."

"I'm not back to normal, but I'll be fine. Take care, Michael. I hope I see you again."

Monday, July 17th

"Which ones interest you the most?" Ben had just walked up behind Kate and was looking down at her smooth dark hair, where she sat at the long refectory table in the middle of Balnagard's big library with thirty or forty old leather books spread across black oak boards.

"They're all spectacular. But I guess the Copernicus. Even though it's depressing too. It was Jesus who said, 'the truth will set you free,' and yet it was his church that persecuted Copernicus!"

"I know, it's pathetic. But it's made up of imperfect people. And when it wielded almost unlimited power, a *lot* of people went into it for all the wrong reasons. Every age has its blind spots too, and ridiculous prejudices, obviously, just like ours. But it's really infuriating."

Kate slid one long white-gloved finger across the pale cover of the huge four-hundred-page Copernicus. And then picked up a five-by-seven-inch book bound in red morocco. "I love the engravings in the Marco Polo. This one from 1483."

"Or 1484. Nobody seems to know which. Columbus took an earlier edition on his voyage to the New World. And some people say it was reading Marco Polo years before that first made him think about sailing west to reach the east."

"John White's illustrations are breathtaking, the hand-painted flowers and the faces of the Indians. Actually, everything lying here is amazing."

"I know."

"What's the Latin Francis Drake about?"

"It's the original account from 1588 of his expedition in '85 and '86 when he burned St. Augustine, and then rescued Raleigh's first settlers on Roanoke Island off North Carolina."

"It would've been called Virginia then, right?"

"Right."

"What's the big gold stamp on the Drake?"

"The seal of the Earl of Walsingham."

"So this was his own personal copy. That's amazing. He would've known Drake too. He funded his expeditions as secretary of state for Queen Elizabeth."

Ben laughed and said, "Very good. For a fiction writer."

"Don't sound so surprised! So it's Scotland Yard that's letting you and Alex examine the books Colin stole?"

"We can photograph whatever we want too, which I've been doing for Alderton's library, while collating them, in my own strange way, before I hand them over. Then the Yard will track down the rightful owners, working with Interpol. The books that legally belonged to Colin will go to Harriet, with the rest of his estate. You still want to walk to the river?"

Kate nodded and stood up, pulling her hair away from the collar of her black linen shirt.

They went out the low studded oak door into the courtyard opposite Balnagard's front door, and walked through the archway into the forecourt on their left, under a huge rack of stag's antlers, and turned left again toward the drawbridge across the dry moat.

"Look at Alex." Ben had stepped off the drawbridge and turned right, and he was looking past the vegetable garden on the left, opposite the stables, at Alex, walking toward them, carrying a satchel and pointing at the garden wall with his other hand. "Do you think Alex is talking to himself?"

"Looks like it to me. *I* do if I'm working on dialogue. The boxer's cute, isn't he, leaping along beside him? The big black lab looks so gentle."

"Yeah, if you don't try to cut his nails. Here comes Jane. With Joshua sticking to her like glue."

Jane Chisholm, having appeared from behind the gardener's office, was trotting up behind Alex. And he stopped and swung round and wrapped his left arm around her shoulders. They were talking and smiling at each other, while walking in a swarm of dogs.

"So when are you coming back to the States, Kit?"

"Early December." Kate didn't look at Ben. She stared at a row of espaliered fruit trees against a high stone wall. "Nobody's called me that since Graham was killed."

"I'm sorry. I just—"

"No, it's fine."

Neither one of them said anything else.

Ben stared at the stables.

And Kate put her hands in the pockets of her black cords. "I thought what you said about Alderton's collections last night at dinner was interesting. I wouldn't have expected a college that small to own the works it owns."

"The donors have been really good to us." Ben didn't say anything else for a moment, while he waved at Alex and Jane. "I don't know for sure that I'll be at Alderton in December, but maybe, if you had a couple of extra days at Christmas, I could show you some of the pieces in the collection. Good morning, Jane. Hi, Alex. Stay down, Jake. Good to see you, Jeremiah."

Joshua had walked up shyly and was standing by Ben's left leg. "Hello, Joshua. You're a very good boy." Ben rubbed his ears and patted his left shoulder, and Joshua stood quietly, trembling slightly when Jake the boxer bumped into him. "I love you too, Jake. Stand still and I'll pet you."

"Joshua is a sweet boy, isn't he?" Alex was gazing fondly at Joshua's uneasy expression. Until his own eyes clouded over and his mouth tightened. "I've come to a rather disturbing realization." He was looking at Ben, waiting for him to answer.

"Why? What do you mean exactly?"

"I may be guilty of an obsession similar to Colin's."

"You didn't even know what you'd inherited when I started sorting through your things."

"I knew the books. I knew what we had and what they

meant, even if I didn't know what they were worth. You see, years ago in Edinburgh, the summer after my first year at Oxford when I was researching sixth-century Celts at the university library, I happened into a used bookshop and found the entire library of one of the local gentry who'd recently passed away. The basement and the back room of the shop were filled with his books, and I saw straightaway that a great number of them pertained to the early Welsh, and the Celts, and the sixth and seventh century all across Britain. I bought the library en bloc for a very fair sum, wrote a check on the spot, and shifted the books all that day to my parents' house in town."

"What's wrong with that?" Ben was still patting Joshua and Jake, without looking up at Alex.

"Ah, well, the next day, when I returned to collect the last few boxes, the bookstore owner told me in some agitation that a dreadful mistake had been made. The widow of the library's owner had not intended that all the books go to him, only a very small number. The rest were to have been donated to Cambridge, and he asked that I return them. A better person might've done. But I knew my area of research even then, and I felt absolutely convinced that I would never find another affordable collection that would suit my work as well. Even today, I couldn't stay here at Balnagard and work as I do if it weren't for that library. Yet, I'm beginning to think I acted wrongly." Alex was staring at Ben, looking subdued and ill at ease.

"You're the only one who should have an opinion."

"Wasn't it a selfish act? Aren't we to do better than that? Wouldn't the books I needed have been provided another time? If I'd 'given away my coat,' or 'gone the extra mile'?"

"You might donate books Cambridge particularly has need

of now, Alex. Or pay to help refurbish some part of their collections."

"Thank you, Jane, yes. Perhaps I could."

"I shall see you all at lunch, shall I?" Jane was looking at Ben and Kate, smiling and shading her eyes with her hand. "I must rush to make certain the tea shop is in order before the first visitors arrive. Although Ben, now that I think of it, would you come with me for just a moment?"

"Sure."

"I shall stay and talk to Kate." Alex had set his satchel down and was polishing his reading glasses on his handkerchief. "Tell me more of these novels you've written. I generally write unadulterated history, though I've recently begun a second historical novel, much to my own surprise."

He and Kate were talking about plotting when Ben and Jane walked into the forecourt and zagged left through a cobbled courtyard toward the newly converted storage area Jane had just turned into a tea shop.

She took her keys out of her pocket as she stooped toward the lock, and talked to Ben over her shoulder. "It's nothing important really, but I've wanted you to know how much Alex and I both like Kate. After you go home, if you want us to invite her down occasionally, and David Lindsay as well, just to give them a bit of a change and so forth, Alex and I would be happy to."

"I'm sure she'd like that. But don't feel you have to because of me. I don't know her that well myself. We hadn't talked since the war, until three or four weeks ago." Ben was pulling a weed at the base of an evergreen shrub in a stone tub with no expression on his face at all.

"Ah. I see. Yes. Well, it's none of my affair, of course. And I expect you like being alone. With your work and your travel.

And your horse, of course. I mustn't forget your horse. He must be quite a bit of company. Yes, I'm sure you must be quite content, after all your years alone."

"Very funny." Ben laughed and looked at Jane.

But she gazed at him coolly for minute, before she opened the small paned door. "I don't know that it-tis funny, actually. But to each his own. I shall see you both at lunch. Joshua, you stay with Ben, there's a good boy."

The door shut behind Jane.

And then opened a second later. "I'm sorry I snapped at you. It's none of my business and I had no right a-tall."

"That's okay."

"I had a very unpleasant discussion with the elder two boys at breakfast, and I haven't sorted it out. They were quite accustomed to having no money a-tall, and having other people think they did, and not being bothered by either. But now that the guns are being sold at Sothebys they're beginning to think spending it might be delightful indeed. 'I want this. And I want that. And why can't we have thus and so?' You know the sort of thing I mean. And yet I do the same myself. Wondering if I could put in a dishwasher, of all things, and refurbish the upstairs bath."

"Would that be so horrible? You're setting up the charity in Jonathan MacLean's memory, and you do all kinds of things for the people on the estate."

"Yes, but that's our responsibility. I do *not* want to look back on our days of very straitened circumstances as the best time of our lives, because we've been ruined by a blessing we've been given."

"You know what? I think you and Alex will figure it out just fine."

"I hope so. I do sincerely hope so."

❧❧❧❧❧

Five minutes later, Ben and Kate and Joshua had just started toward the stables, when a small red postal van rattled up to the drawbridge.

"Good morning. I've a telegram for Benjamin Reese."

"I'm Ben Reese."

"Here ye are then, sirr. And will there be a reply, or no?" He was a small man, ruddy, alert, looking out his rolled-down window with a sharp appraising eye. "It's a lovely grand place, Balnagard. One can only hope the tea shop can set it to rights."

Ben studied him for a minute. Then opened the telegram without answering.

It's not Jack (stop) I tried to call (stop) Alex's phone out of order (stop) Please call before you leave for Ohio (stop) Ellen

"I would like to send an answer, yes."

The delivery man handed Ben a pad of forms and a ball-point pen.

Maybe it should be Jack. I'm old. I'm your teacher. I'll call from Ohio. Hope all goes well with Cairnwell.
Your doddering archivist-instructor.

"Still want to walk?" Kate was rubbing Joshua's ears as she glanced at the back of the delivery van, slipping through the arch in the wall to the road.

"Let me run in first and tell Jane the phone's out of order. That's why Ellen sent a telegram, in case you were thinking of asking."

"Me? Certainly not. I'm actually getting better." Kate smiled, and then waited, talking to Joshua mostly, till Ben came back across the drawbridge. "You're sure you're not too tired?"

"No, I need to walk. Come on, Josh. You come with us."

"Do you think he'll be okay with Jake and Jeremiah, or is three a crowd with dogs too?"

"I don't know. He might do better if he was somewhere on his own."

They talked about Colin past the stables and the walled garden and up around the outbuildings to the path that led down through the evergreen woods to the bottomland.

The cows hadn't been turned out yet, and Ben and Kate walked along the fence beside their pasture toward the paddock where Malamaze and Matthew were watching their progress between mouthfuls of grass.

Joshua walked right behind Ben, his ears down and his tail tucked.

"You said Colin wanted to donate his books the way Pepys left his to Cambridge, but I don't know how he did it."

"The books were offered to Magdalene College, with first right of refusal, and then to Trinity College, both of them at Cambridge, with one stipulation. That whichever college accepted them was to keep them absolutely intact and unaltered in perpetuity, and the other college was to check on the books annually and take them as their own if any changes were found. So all his books are housed in the same order Pepys arranged them, on the same shelves he had built about 1700."

"So it's a perfectly preserved picture of the world from two hundred and fifty years ago?"

"Right. Which could be what he intended."

"I think I'd like to write about Georgina." Kate was walking fast, her arms loose and her chin up, studying the smooth broad valley and checkered hills on the other side of the River Tay. "As soon as she found out what her family had done to Ellen's, she decided right then to give her the house. That took guts. And then she had to deal with Colin, knowing he could kill her. How hard must that have been? Both at the same time? And look at Colin too. His one emotional attachment, the one thing that helped make him human, was precisely what led you to him. How's that for irony?"

"We still could've found the room with the books, but Harriet certainly helped. You want to write it as fiction?"

"I think so. The murder investigation mostly. Changing the names, of course. I'd have to study rare books and microbiology. And microbiology won't be easy for me."

"You'd manage. I read two of your books in the hospital, and I didn't think they were half bad."

"Thank you. I think." Kate smiled, but didn't say anything else for a minute, as she stared at the moor climbing toward the highlands on the left across the Tay. Then she watched a string of ducks fly south above the river. "What about Ellen?"

"What about Ellen?"

"You know what I mean. Is she in love with you? I talked to her three times on the phone, and I came away with a definite impression."

"I think she has ideas about me."

"Ah. A romanticized view."

"From the war, and the work I do, and the murder stuff I've been involved with. If she really saw how boring my life is day to day she'd run in the opposite direction. And I *am* too old for her. You know what I mean. I'm more serious. More quiet. More self-contained than I would've been without the war."

Kate smiled cryptically. And then she looked sideways at Ben. "I don't think either one of us could turn our backs on the lives we've made."

"I'm not sure I know what you mean."

"We make it hard for anyone to get to us. Neither one of us even has a dog. You have a horse, so I guess that counts. But I'm not sure people like you and me, who found what we wanted and had it taken away, can stand to do it again."

"I don't want to marry someone and wish I was alone again, that's for sure."

"I know. I don't either." Kate's eyes were hidden and her voice sounded cool and detached. "Do you like doing the murder investigations?"

"Yes and no. I think the ones that fall into my lap have to be picked up. But I don't like the lying you have to do to get people to talk. Look at Matthew. He's such a good boy."

The big chestnut gelding was swishing his tail and flicking his ears against the flies on his way over to see Ben and Kate.

"You stay here, Joshua. Stay outside the fence."

Ben and Kate climbed the wooden cross rails that were lined with wire fencing, as Joshua stood and looked lost.

"So you think you'll take Joshua home with you, Ben?"

"I don't know what to do. I hate the thought of putting him in a cage and flying him back in the baggage compartment. He's so traumatized already, and he's happy here. He loves Jane, at least. If not the other dogs. So I don't know. I don't suppose you'd want to take him, would you?"

"Would it be hard for him to adjust to another place?"

"He seems more attached to people than dogs, oddly enough. Considering his background. And with you he'd be the center of attention."

"I'd have to ask David too. He likes dogs, but it might be hard for him to take care of him when I travel."

"Too much commitment too?"

"Don't look so smug! Why's Matthew licking your shirt?"

"Horses don't, usually. But I think he's telling me he likes me. I hope so, anyway."

"Ah." Kate reached out tentatively and stroked the smooth coppery neck, and then patted him on the withers. "Okay, I'll take the dog."

"Maybe you better think about it."

"No, maybe I better not. Maybe I should do what I want to do without looking at it too carefully."

"Maybe." Ben eyes crinkled at the corners as he grinned at Joshua, who whined from the other side of the fence.

"So you've finished your testimony in the other case? The murder of Jonathan MacLean?"

"Yep. This week. Now I'm free to go home."

"I ought to too, as a matter of fact, and not stay to lunch. I ought to make myself go back and work."

Joshua whined again, and Ben said, "It's okay, we'll be there in just a minute. You do know how to discipline a dog, don't you? You wouldn't spoil him and let him be a jerk?"

"I have trained dogs before." Kate was watching Ben while tapping a stick against her knee. "Although whether my approach comes up to your standards I don't know."

"That's true. That's a question that has to be asked."

They both laughed, and Kate threw the stick in Ben's direction as they started to climb the fence. It landed a few feet from Joshua. And he cringed and rolled on his back.

"It's okay, Joshua, Kate was just kidding."

Ben and Kate both knelt beside him and talked to him and

rubbed his ears, till he looked at them again and wagged his tail.

"I'll make you copies of Georgina's poems. They'll help give you a sense of what she was really like."

"Thanks, that'd be great."

"So will you let me know when you'll be in Chicago?"

"Sure. I don't know if I'll have time to come to Alderton, but—"

"I don't know if I'll be there either—"

"Yeah, you said that before."

"But even if we can't meet in Ohio, we could at least talk on the phone, and you could tell me how Joshua's doing."

"I'll give you a call either way. I'd like to know what Georgina's last words were too. You don't know, by any chance, do you?"

Ben looked hard at Joshua, and sat back on his heels. Then he shook his head and smiled at Kate. "I do, as a matter of fact. And I probably should've thought about them more than I have."

Acknowledgments

I HARDLY KNOW WHERE TO START—except, of course, with John Reed, Ph.D., who helps prune my plot ideas, and *still* puts up with questions about life as an archivist and World War II scout. David Munro, Ph.D., director of The Royal Scottish Geographical Society, helped me in Scotland, finding the perfect locations (Muchalls Castle is Cairnwell House; Eden House became Devon House)—while answering a string of questions about Scotland few people could. Mr. and Mrs. Anthony Sharp told me stories about Eden House that started me thinking. (And Vaida the sled dog is buried in their wood.) The staff at Kinnaird (the inn that's the real location for Balnagard Castle) was extremely helpful as usual, especially Bob Grant, who taught me as much about fly-fishing on the Tay as I was able to learn. Walter Yellowlees, M.D., kindly helped with the history of medical practice in Britain. And the architect, Michael Beattie, discussed the church at Old Kinneff. I hunted with a Harris hawk at the Perthshire Falconry Services at Braco Castle, and learned too from the staff of the Northeast Falconry Center. Liz Asbitt of Swindon, England helped with Oxford in the early sixties, especially microbiology at Oxford University.

In the States, Michael Bauman, Ph.D., Hillsdale College, answered different questions about Oxford. And Steve Love, chief editorial writer, The Akron *Beacon Journal,* sent me his "Wheels of Fortune" series (David Giffels and Steve Love) on the history of rubber in Akron. I was helped by several physicians and microbiologists, among them Garry T. Cole, Ph.D., and Michael D. P. Boyle, Ph.D., who were both *extremely* helpful. Harold Rossmore, Ph.D., helped as he always does, even with microbiology at Aberdeen University. I was given much needed assistance by several book collectors and dealers, all of whom were patient and generous—Robert Mulon-Miller, Michael Zinman, Robert and Ruth Iglehart, Donald Shelby, Steven Farber, M.D., and James Ravin, M.D. My agent, Pam Strickler, and my editors—Rod Morris at Multnomah and Joe Blades at Ballantine—put up with me as I bumbled along, and offered good advice throughout.

A large part of the pleasure of writing is learning from people you wouldn't meet otherwise while studying things you normally couldn't. All these people gave me great memories, while teaching me what I needed to know.